STEPHEN PAUL THOMAS

CLUSTER

Novel

Stephen Paul Thomas: Cluster
2014
Originally published in Hungarian:
Stephen Paul Thomas: Gócpont (2012)

Cover and inner design, graphics:
Istvan Tomasovszki

English Translation copyright © István Tomasovszki
Translated by: **Ákos Nicolas Roth and Katarina Peters**
English Copy Editor:
Paige Duke
www.thepaigeduke.com

Printed edition ISBN 978-963-89985-0-7
Publishing
Hungarian Version
© 2012, Articity Publishing and Media Ltd. Hungary
English Version
©2014, Articity Publishing and Media Ltd. Hungary
All text in this book © Tomasovszki István

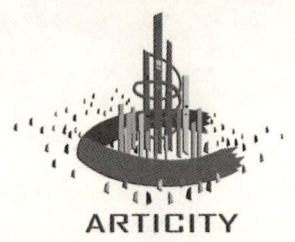

This book is the intellectual property of the Author, Istvan Tomasovszki (writing under the alias of Stephen Paul Thomas). Any copying, digitalizing, republishing, quotes, internet publishing of any part or the whole text is prohibited without the permission of the Author.
www.articity.com
www.stephenpaulthomas.com
Printing:
Reálszisztéma Dabasi Nyomda Zrt. Hungary
General Manager:
Magdolna Vágó

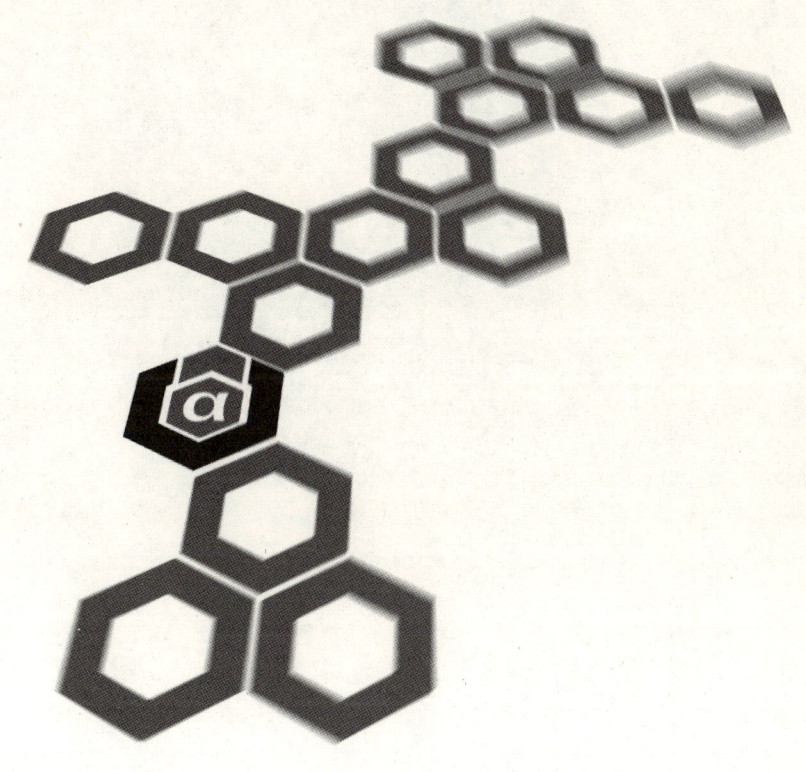

All of the people in this book, living or dead, or possibly alive in the future are purely fictional. Any similarity with real names is a subject of science-fictional incident.

Therefore, it is clear that this novel is fictional, and this book is not a guidebook. Any matching with future similar events is the subject of the strange SF conjunction.

To my son:

*I give what I have, as best I can,
Not the fleeting gold of fools,
It's no cat let out of the bag,
It's where your dream will turn to truth,
Hold onto faith, it's all you'll get...*

(Istvan Tomasovszki: Advise for the road, to the son)

Part I

Unmei
(Fate)
運命

1.

The skybus raced haplessly towards its inevitable fate in the evening traffic. It forged ahead on one of the rush-hour-choked roads of the Mars New Home Colony, with floating cars bouncing off it like popcorn jumping out of a frying pan. The roof of the bus burst open, like a flowering rose, leaving behind a shower of sparkling particles of plastic and metal. This particular airway offered a wide berth around the Shield Tower, before descending in a gentle slope towards the terminal, where the bus was supposed to land, on the second floor platform of the Central Station. At least that was what the schedule said.

But it seemed that, today, the schedule had been overturned.

It certainly had not been part of Chris McAllister's plans that morning to jump from the butterfly-winged door of a speeding police pursuit vehicle onto a runaway skybus with a burst-open top. He switched the patrol car to automatic and silenced the collision signal's incessant beeping. All he needed now was for the autopilot to divert the vehicle because of some dangerous object or wreckage, just at the very moment of his jump!

He was not prepared for this particular contingency. If he'd known about it this morning, he'd have packed a parachute.

Although, truth be told, it was precisely for such moments of excitement that he'd applied to the corporation at the age of eighteen. Even in detective stories, he used to love chase scenes, but over the course of the passing years he had come to realise that real-life events didn't unfold as they do in action movies. Just the same, he lived for the service, the life of a cop. That was why his wife had divorced him. She never understood how he could be so attached to his profession. 'You don't know the meaning of the word "calling,"' Chris used to tell her. A *calling* is something else, something special; people are capable of doing anything for a calling.

Even climbing onto the top of a speeding patrol car.

In fact, it wasn't until he was clinging to the roof that he fully appreciated just what a tall order he was attempting to undertake. The wind whipped at his side, adding to an already precarious situation—not to mention the flying debris breaking loose from the bus. His hat had vanished into the distance, and tiny metal fragments pelted his already balding scalp.

He set the patrol car to close pursuit, so that it would tail the bus and hopefully keep the skimmers that were slamming against its side from sweeping away his car.

'Well, OK, here goes. If this is where I have to croak, so be it,' he said, and kicked off from the hood of the vehicle.

'No, no, no!' he slammed painfully onto the top of the bus as he landed. His knee collapsed under him, just like the last time. He'd been chasing that spooked guy in one of the botanical garden greenhouses, and the window frame caved in under him. At the last moment, he'd managed to clutch onto one of the pillars, but the iron struts pulverised his right knee. Since then, he'd been forced to wear a knee brace to work, though it didn't help much. At fifty-five, he couldn't handle pain in the same way he used to. But he struggled on; he would keep working, even if it killed him.

What was it that made him carry on? Maybe just those two sets of eyes that watched him with such respect, looked up to him like some kind of superhero. Those starry eyes were unforgettable. He was spending less and less time with his boys, though. Things with his wife had deteriorated so badly that she had left the Colony with the children and moved back to Earth. And so, he could only spend three months every year on Earth with the kids—he couldn't see them any more frequently than that. No superior would dispense with his best man for longer than that. Best man—who was getting older and whose knee happened to be falling to pieces!

As he crawled forward, dragging himself along the wastewater pipes, his face a picture of torment, he saw his colleagues arrive: two patrol floaters flew in front of the bus as guardians, so as to clear a way through the traffic.

'It won't be enough, guys, not nearly enough,' he growled between his teeth, thinking that if he couldn't reach the cabin, nothing could save the seven-ton vehicle and its passengers from the impact. Not to mention the passengers waiting for the skybus, although his colleagues had already started the evacuation.

With a great deal of pain, he managed to reach the first emergency exit. Thank heavens, it opened easily. A stepladder was folded up like an accordion; he swung it open and extended it towards the passenger compartment. Inside, terrified screaming proved just how serious the situation was, in case anyone hadn't yet realized it. He started his descent. One or two men tried to help by holding the stepladder.

A sudden jolt shook the bus: they had just hit the Shield Tower. Luckily, they only skimmed one side, but the bus had lost its right-side stabilizer. Without it, the runaway monster spun wildly out of control. Chris and those passengers who weren't strapped in rolled about, trying to find equilibrium on their seats and on the remaining walls, like hamsters in a rotating wheel. The other passengers hung upside down from the ceiling. It was a surreal sight to see the shower of cards, keys, data-chips, watches, and communicators, as the objects fell from their pockets.

The spinning slowly subsided, the bus now flying on an even keel once again, although not exactly in an ideal position. The worst of it was that Chris now had to battle his way forward along the roof, which had a sizeable chunk missing, where the wind came roaring in like mad.

'Give me your hand!' shouted a heavy-set man, hanging above the gap. 'I'll swing you over, if you can hang onto me!'

It seemed like a good idea, *as long as the seatbelt holds*, Chris thought. The man rolled up his jacket to his elbows and extended both hands. Chris took two steps backwards, hoping it would give him enough momentum. He gathered all his strength and jumped.

It all resembled a badly choreographed aerial trapeze show. In lieu of a sequined outfit, a slightly paunchy artist appeared, dressed in a cop jacket, without a safety rope. They were a fledgling troupe with an untrained catcher, performing some 150 metres above the stage. The enthusiastic, buzzing audience was the only redeeming quality, the motivating force for the sensational performance.

The rookie catcher swung him with such verve that Chris nearly ended up spread-eagled against the windshield. Notwithstanding, the pair almost looked like a well-trained team—they might've even repeated the act again, on safer ground!

The driver's seat was empty. The pilot must have been sucked out by the wind or pushed out through the gaping hole behind his seat by an earlier collision. His seatbelt had not been buckled, so it dangled loosely in the wind, undamaged.

Chris had never driven a floater as big as this bus before but he felt that, on this particular occasion, he couldn't very well say no, even if he wanted to.

'Computer!' he shouted over the driving wind, trying to pull himself up by the pilot's unclaimed seatbelt. He had no idea what to expect from the driving console, shattered to pieces by the explosion. Perhaps a bit of aid wouldn't go amiss. They didn't have much time left for teamwork, only five minutes left before they reached the terminal.

Although the controls weren't responding, they were at least keeping the vehicle on a perfect descending course, Chris thought. But he quickly realized the gentle descent was pure coincidence when they flew at full speed right through a billboard the size of a football field; luckily it was made of a much softer material than the bus.

Chris climbed up and tapped the navigation orb on the console. Nothing happened. He'd been almost certain this would happen. The 'almost' part had, however, contained a slight ray of hope, which now flew out the window into the whirling wind.

'This is Chris McAllister. You don't have much time left to come up with something! At this speed, we have three, maybe four minutes, max before impact. Hurry up, because when I'm in trouble, time somehow speeds up!'

'One minute and help will be there; hold the wheel until then! Keep up the good work!' came the voice of Central Control. The request was farcical, since he wasn't doing anything at all, apart from standing and balancing himself on the rooftop of a downward speeding bus.

There was no more shouting or screaming in the back, as if everyone had become resigned to their lot. Of course, there were those who chose to faint instead, which, under the circumstances, was not too hard a feat.

'And here we are,' a voice announced on Chris's radio. 'Rob Breitner, special towing service.'

A colossal piece of junk, equipped with chains and hoists, crept up in front of them. Whatever it was, its proportions were reassuring.

'Great!' said Chris, and he really meant it. 'What's the plan?'

'Oh, the plan is remarkably simple,' said his newly appointed rescuer. 'If you're anywhere near the cockpit, then you'd better move. Get out of there, quick!'

'Terrific!' replied Chris, but he no longer felt that he meant it.

'I'll slow down the bus, switch over, and stop the driving mechanism.'

'A breath-taking plan.' Which it was, indeed. 'Go ahead, there isn't much time left.'

He stood up and signalled to his tried-and-tested partner. Thank God, his catcher had not fainted. In fact, he had been following events fairly well, with a certain sense of rhythm, extending his hand at just the right moment.

There wasn't much room in the front for a quick push-off. He leaned his foot against the windshield and kicked himself off.

Just in time, because Rob applied the brakes rather forcefully in front of the bus, trying to slow down the vehicle. Thus, Chris's well-built handler had to swing even wider so that his rookie aerial partner could land beyond the hole.

After this, everything went as if it were just part of a daily routine: the robotic arms of the towing equipment grabbed hold of the front of the wreckage, Rob switched the machine into automatic mode, then in a hair-raising stunt, balanced himself on one arm and jumped on top of the bus. He clipped the karabiner on his belt onto one of the ladders, then, hanging down on one side, reached for the control panel. There, he took out a small tool and quickly removed one of the components. In spite of this, the uncontrollable vehicle continued to rush along at the same top speed, beginning to twist the towing vehicle out of alignment.

It was possible that Rob actually knew a lot about flying vehicles: he must've been shown how to remove the panel of a towing engine properly in one of his classes, in case of a failure. Though he probably hadn't learned the subsequent solution during his exam. But maybe he'd seen it in some action movie: pushing himself off the side of the bus, he used the heel of his iron-shod boots, to kick between the panels with overwhelming force. At this point, the driving gears of the bus ground to a halt, enabling the towing vehicle to safely guide its load down into an empty back-street. The robot-pilot deposited the bus at street level with a light thud.

Upside down, of course...

None of this fazed the passengers. They applauded and cheered like travellers at the successful landing of a cheap flight... although, these passengers really did have reason to rejoice.

A few minutes later, the ambulance arrived, as did the firemen. They attended to the injured passengers, taking over from Chris, who shook hands with his robust aerial artist partner. The men wished each other all the best—until the next show—before parting.

Chris walked over to his patrol car, hovering a few metres away, opened up a cold drink, and called in over the radio:

'Patrol twenty-six to base.'

'Go ahead, twenty-six!'

'I've ended up not far from base. There are some slightly injured passengers, with bruises. The pilot, however, is missing, probably sucked out of the vehicle when the ceiling burst open.'

'Understood, Chris. I'll send out some small units to track back along the bus's trail, although the traffic people and the cleaners are already working at the site. It caused quite a mess. So far, there have been no reports of any unclaimed corpses.'

'All right. So, now I'll go and get myself together, drop in on the doctor since my knee is trying hard to explode. This solo duty isn't easy. If Pete were here, at least he'd have invited me for a beer after work.'

'You did well! Dog bones heal! So, see you here in a while, Chris. . . .'

'Thanks, Wanda. Believe it or not, I was very lucky and had a great partner!'

'Come and tell us all about it, we'll be waiting for you!'

*

9 hours earlier

Noah thought he was going to puke right there, in the middle of the terminal, but he managed to make it to the men's room just in time. The sign saying 'premises being cleaned' had been outside for a long time but, finally, it was taken away. He, on the other hand, had made enough mess to keep the sign out for a whole week!

A tormented face looked back at him from the mirror. Sunken eyes, red nose, sweat dripping off his forehead. There was no doubt, he would not be allowed onto the flight to the Moon.

For months he'd had this feeling, that something was not right with his metabolism. At first, he had been overcome by nausea, usually at night. The clamminess of his body had become routine and he kept gulping water all the time. Next had come the dizziness, but not the common kind: it attacked him out of nowhere, with such force that it made collapse sometimes. Then, once the vertigo had subsided, a tornado-like vomiting fit followed. Anywhere, anytime, unstoppable.

When fitting the implant, they'd told him that would age after a while, but nobody had warned him that it would happen so soon. Barely one hundred and twenty-five days had passed since the implant. He'd called the emergency line—the one he was supposed to call if he had any problems—at least forty times, but all he got was a friendly voice telling him that all the operators were busy and he would have to wait. He was put on hold for two hours before his communicator went flat.

He was well aware that he only had himself to blame for his present indisposition. He should not have drunk so much over the past few hours. The information guide said repeatedly that the consumption of alcohol and drugs was not recommended, to say the least.

On previous occasions, he'd gotten responses on the emergency line and then they'd sent out their duty doctor in an emergency vehicle. The doctor had given him an extra-strong shot with the same active ingredient as in the tablets he had to take every second day. The doc said it would help stop leakage from the implant.

'In certain cases,' followed by a lengthy list in the information guide (alcohol, drugs, virus contamination, high fever, used in conjunction with certain genetic treatments and some other unknown expressions) 'the implant could cause an oozing infection of the brain stem. In the course of clinical trials, this oozing only occurred to a limited degree, the infection in all cases being equivalent to a mild viral infection.' Although he'd had mild viral infections before, this rather resembled a severe bacterial infection.

Perhaps this was the peak point and from here on in, the mild phase would begin. It simply had to be left alone, so that the system would have a chance to prevail. And, of course, no more guzzling.

He stepped out into the wide transit corridor and leaned up against the wall. He thought he was going to throw up again, but the gobbet remained stuck in his throat. Gathering his strength, he took a deep breath and proceeded to Gate 22. He stepped onto the middle of the moving walkway but got off after only a few metres, as the movement brought on his nausea again. He would rather lug his bag along with solid ground under his feet. Perhaps it would not be quite as awful on the flight to the Moon, since the speed stabilisers had put an end to all types of uncomfortable, stomach-churning space sicknesses. That is, if he were allowed on the plane at all.

He looked up at the indicator to check if there was any delay to his flight but, with this move, the ground started to shake. The gobbet in his throat broke free...

'Good Lord, man!' said the man facing him. The stream of sick spewing out of Noah's throat completely covered him. The man's uniform looked dreadful, splashed with this dubious-coloured liquid. Some drops of it had landed on his face and his glasses but, in his consternation, the man had not yet had a chance to wipe them off. He seemed to be some kind of pilot because he was wearing a Mars Metro-Trans employee's uniform. He might have been the driver of a skybus or a floating rail motor vehicle.

'Ahh, I beg your pardon, I didn't mean to...' Noah said and started to wipe the ruby-red jacket with a cleaning cloth. 'I'm terribly sorry. I don't know what to do about this, my stomach churns over in the most unexpected circumstances.'

'Then you must really hate flying, if you get sick even before take-off,' said the tall, greying pilot, who meanwhile accepted another handkerchief and started to wipe his neck and face. 'It looks like you're heading towards one of the ferries.'

'That's right. I'm heading to the Moon. My name is Noah Simpson,' he said, clumsily extending his hand, 'Concession Matters Specialist, long-term Land-Lease on any of the colonies. When I get back from the Moon, I'd like to invite you for a drink, to make up for what's just happened?'

'No problem. Don't worry about it, though I'll need to change my jacket before boarding my vehicle. But I can stop off at headquarters, where I keep an older one, and I'll send this one to be cleaned,' smiled the man. 'I'm Jim Kingston, bus driver, officially Floating Bus Pilot.

Pleasure to meet you! We could, perhaps, have met under more pleasant circumstances.'

'Right you are. I'm glad you are so understanding and kind. Here's my card. Please call me in about two weeks; I'll probably be back by then.'

'OK,' said the pilot, carefully assessing the man with worried eyes. 'You should see the doctor on duty at the terminal, though, because they won't let you on board in that condition.'

'I'll do that,' lied Noah. It was obvious that he couldn't miss out on a 2.5 million New Dollar deal by being late for the trip. Even if he died on the spot after signing the contract, let him be a millionaire—at least for half a minute. 'You're right. I could use some rest in this mad rat-race. Thank you for the advice, see you later! And, once again, please forgive me!'

'No problem,' said the driver, turning back as he walked away. 'Thank God it didn't touch the cake. It's my daughter's birthday tonight; I'm sending it to her to welcome her home from school!' he raised a cake box into the air and waved good-bye.

As the two of them set off on their separate ways, Noah saw in his peripheral vision that the driver was still watching him, so he proceeded toward the 'First Aid Post' sign. He stopped around the corner and watched his departing victim folding his jacket away from his body, so that his trousers, at least, would not be stained, before setting off in the opposite direction.

That was just what Noah was waiting for and, coming out from around the corner, he walked back towards the departure gate. He was definitely feeling better. All he needed was for everything to come out so he could get over this sickness. The beads of sweat on his face had dried up and, as he looked at his reflection in a store window, the normal colour of his skin had started to come back. This way, he might succeed in boarding the ferry.

'Sir, could you place your wrist on the machine, please, so that we may record your biometric information? Thank you.' said the female attendant sitting at the counter, reciting the standard, memorized text.

She barely glanced at him and said nothing more. She stared at the monitor as her fingers danced across the keyboard.

'Sir,' she had nailed it, for sure; she had nailed it, *the biometrics don't lie*, thought Noah, 'According to our data, you are running a temperature, the cytotoxic killer cells, the T-lymphocytes, are highly active, you have a possible mild infection. . . ' After a short pause, she took out a scanner, 'But the way I see it, the temperature is not so high as to prevent you from boarding.'

Yes! Noah wanted to shout out for joy over his narrow escape.

'In fact, it has reduced considerably. I welcome you on behalf of the crew, and I wish you a pleasant journey!' By now, her smile was broad and conforming to regulations, whereas Noah's was serene.

He wouldn't miss the negotiations, and he wouldn't lose the 2.5 million ND bonus.

And so, he would become a leading contract negotiator for the company, after one hundred and twenty-five days of continuous work without sleep. And just think—before, he had been a small, two-bit crook, a nobody. That's what you call a career!

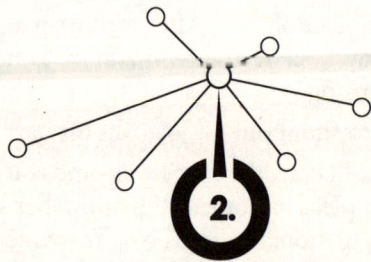

The clattering twin turbines of the military helicopter stirred up an artificial gale in the void left by the low-pressure cyclone that had earlier swept over the Indian Ocean. Racing along, just skimming the surface of the quiet water, the "bumble bee" (as they referred to the copter amongst themselves) was making its way towards the navigation route southeast off the coast, with four soldiers from the Indian Coast Guard on board. They had been en route for twenty minutes when the captain of a freighter called them. He had spotted a Malaysian pirate ship being tossed about on the ocean swell, seemingly rudderless and derelict. In all probability, the full force of the cyclone had taken its toll on ship and crew, although there were no visible signs of damage to its hull.

At first, the captain of the freighter thought this might be the usual trap and had raised the energy shield of his hovercraft and fired two warning shots, aiming just next to the speedboat. Just to let anyone on board know that stalking such a small vessel was not worth their while. There was no reaction to the shots. So, mustering up sufficient courage, the captain drew closer, threw out a buoy to mark the ship's position, and immediately notified the Coast Guard. He informed them by radio that he had to continue on his way and couldn't wait for the unit to arrive but promised to be within reach, anyway, should they wish to question him about the incident. He also said that, as soon as he arrived, he would report in to the harbour patrol in East Africa to get updates about the investigation.

It was Rusti Kadam, already considered a seasoned veteran, who spoke to the captain of the freighter. He had served fourteen years in the marines, fought in the second Asian conflict, and had disembarked in Australia on the side of the allied forces against the New China Army. He was well-educated and battle-hardened but had left the forces simply because he'd had enough of the war.

After returning to civvy street, he spent some time loafing aimlessly around Delhi, the megalopolis of the Eternal Light: he felt lost, unable to fit in anywhere. His friends had perished or had been demobbed; many had even gone off-planet, and there were those who had flipped and gone bonkers.... He also suffered from post-traumatic 'escapades,' as he called them, likening these events to 'total blackouts.' These moments often turned into nightly brawls, he was just too caught up in the memories of battle trauma. Of course, on such occasions, he ended up in a cell on the outskirts, or in bed with some strange woman who beat the hell out of him because he couldn't pay her.

That was when he stumbled upon Barto, who was now his best friend and pilot of this super copter who, at one low point in his private life, had also sunk down into the 'subculture of insignificance.' This was what Barto cynically called the company of self-important gangster nobodies, fallen streetwalkers, and sickly noodle-cooks. After two days of sinking into the morass together, they'd started the long climb upward, out of it, and became buddies. Later on, Barto had taken him to his unit, where he was accepted for what he was. He found himself amongst his peers once again, without feeling any obligation to explain to anyone about his past. The Coast Guard needed seasoned veterans who could handle a gun properly because the gangs and guerrilla organizations were regaining their strength in the void left by the Asian conflict. Some of them had gained a foothold not only in the Mother-colony, on Earth, but also on the Moon. They financed their operations by running nefarious activities on Earth and laundering the money through other colonies.

One of these activities was privateering, a pastime practiced for centuries. Late descendants of infamous buccaneer captains, these pirates, marauding over the waters, didn't leave any wounded behind. When they launched a surprise attack, they slaughtered the entire crew of the targeted freighter or amphibious craft. For this reason, navigation routes between Europe, Asia, and Africa were being continually pushed southwards, farther from shore, in order to render surprise attacks more difficult. Companies providing ships with arms had also increased their business, thanks to orders for state-of-the-art shields or on-board ordnance. But the pirates couldn't be stopped, only slowed down, as they too dipped into the arms market and made their own purchases. There were months when medium-sized freighters, of several tens of thousands of tons, were swallowed up in the dark reaches of the ocean. According to the images from reconnaissance satellites, they resurfaced again in some far-Eastern harbour. Attempting to recover them was hopeless, as the territories were under the control of well-armed gangs, and no one was prepared to risk retrieving them in the unknown warzone. So, the ocean liner companies switched to even larger amphibians. Any attempted assault on them demanded bigger organization and firepower, but a few such incidents occurred anyway.

'There, at heading one-four-two, half a kilometre away,' spoke the navigator and copilot, who was sitting beside Barto.

'Rusti, get ready, we'll be descending soon, provided the field is clear.'

Rusti merely nodded acknowledgement; he was ready, the karabiner already attached to his belt. He was sitting by the door, waiting for the action to start. At moments like this, he was overcome by the same feeling he'd had in the war. He wasn't sure whether he still needed this feeling. At first, it resembled euphoria, and he wouldn't resist that too much, but, afterwards, the post-traumatic stress returned and he'd have to face it later, in due course.

'Well then, here goes!' said Barto, giving a thumbs-up. The chopper suddenly decelerated and flew slowly and gracefully around the ship three times, whipping up the still waters. On the deck, nothing moved; but inside, a light was flickering. The pilot pulled on the cyclic stick, the motors roared, and the door opened.

'Go! All clear! According to the scanners, there's no life on board the ship,' shouted the navigator over the rumble. 'I don't register any communication jammer or force field that may be hiding anyone.'

'Just be careful, pal,' Barto reminded him but he was already on the rope, halfway down to the ship. For action such as this, the driving mechanisms were angled away from the fuselage, to prevent their descending mate being blown away. It only lasted three seconds, and Rusti had already unfastened his karabiner. The rope retracted and the chopper elegantly repositioned itself in an approximately fifteen metres-high parking hover.

Rusti stood on the enlarged side of the stern, where one-man minicopters were able to land. The boat was a recently built, modern ship. There were no weapon-like objects on it that he could see, but that didn't mean there wasn't something hidden under the ship's steel plating, like a downward-opening crenel. The two colossal cowlings proved that this was not just any old light craft: it was capable of being pushed up to about four hundred kilometres per hour above the waves, on the plasma-generated layer.

Cat-like, with his weapon ready to fire, he approached the downward companionway. Light glimmered up from below, flickering as the boat rocked in the copter-induced waves. Had it not been for his military history, he would probably be calling for reinforcements on the radio by now, given how eerie the scene was. He had good reason to worry, he'd seen it before—the alluring glimmer of light in the dark desert nights, heard desperate cries for help in the distance. He'd seen dozens of well-constructed booby traps. The soldiers of the New China Army had not been deterred by anything back then. Admittedly, the allies had not always played fair either. That had been a bloody and dirty war.

At the top of the stairs, he crouched down and dispatched a dragonfly-drone. The drone was no bigger than the insect that was its namesake. With its diaphanous wings, it made its way soundlessly, eschewing all obstacles and conveying the images to his helmet display.

Inside, Rusti saw a battery-operated lamp hanging from the ceiling—the source of the swinging play of light. The dragonfly bypassed it and headed towards the depths of the cabin. The floor was covered with water, drenched by the waves of the passing cyclone. Abandoned weapons, boxes of ammunition, spent and empty magazines and cartridge cases, lay scattered about everywhere. On the walls were traces of energy beams and bullets, in the foreground the remains of the ripped-up furnishings. It looked like some sort of battle had raged with an invisible enemy.

The drone returned. Rusti placed it back in its box and lowered himself down the companionway. He remained cautious because it was usually overconfidence that sent a person stumbling into a trap or falling down a mineshaft. He waded mid-calf through the seawater, using the barrel of his gun to carefully push aside any object floating towards him, in case it was a bomb in disguise. He had just crossed over to the area used as a kitchen, when he heard the noise. It was as if someone was banging on the hull of the ship, or as if something was being continuously slammed up against its side by the rolling swell.

'Barto, the right side of the ship—have a look at the right side of the ship, there's something there,' he called up to the copter through the radio, 'Something keeps hitting the side all the time with the swell.'

'Right!' the pilot acknowledged. 'I'll take a look.'

The ship rocked about more vigorously, in the roar of the chopper's drive propulsion. The racket receded and then drew closer again, as Barto flew the chopper around in small circles to see what was in the water.

'Get outside immediately, man overboard, I repeat, man overboard!! At the bow, starboard side!' His voice snapped through the headphones.

Taking the stairs two at a time, Rusti was soon up on deck. He switched on his helmet-lamp and began inspecting the side of the ship. He spotted the corpse of a dead man floating on his back, or at least it looked like a corpse, because it wasn't moving and was white as chalk. He bent over the rail, grabbed the sleeve of a camouflage-coloured jacket, and started pulling him up onto the deck by the straps of his jerkin.

'Damn it, you sure are heavy,' muttered Rusti. He was exhausted by the time he had wrestled the body full of water on board.

'He's dead,' he panted into the communicator. 'At least . . . there's no heartbeat, the scanner doesn't show anything. He could be one of the pirates . . . he's wearing a bulletproof vest.'

'OK,' acknowledged the copilot, 'bring him closer, away from the edge, untie him, then anchor the ship. The tug is on its way, they'll be here within an hour. When you're finished, we'll haul you back up and return to base.'

'Roger . . . got it,' replied Rusti, pointing his thumb upwards to confirm that he had understood everything and that, as soon as he got his breath back, he would start the entrusted tasks. Despite his stamina, he'd soon be fifty-two; maybe he should be thinking about retiring.

Rusti grabbed the heavy-set Malaysian man by his armpits but kept losing his grip. So, he caught hold of the fastening strap on his bulletproof vest and dragged him along the gondola drive mechanism to the ventilation shaft, sitting him upright by pulling up his knees. All that remained to do was to take the fastening tape out of his backpack and he could go to the chopper. Turning up the visor on his helmet, he pulled off his gloves and took off his backpack.

As he was reaching for the plastic clamps, he heard a whisper.

A whisper from the very same man, the man with no heartbeat, the man he had just fished out of the ocean.

The man who was as bloated as a days-old sea-corpse.

Now he was whispering something in Malay, staring glassy-eyed, straight in front of him.

Rusti recoiled, thinking that he was dreaming, or that he was having another post-traumatic hallucination.

'Can you hear that?' he asked, in consternation, placing the communicator on his wrist close to the man's mouth. 'This man is talking but he has no heartbeat, or didn't have any, he was deader than a doornail just a few minutes ago.'

'Yes, we can hear. Wait a minute while I unearth all my non-existent Malaysian knowledge' said Barto, listening closely on the other end of the line. Meanwhile, the man continued to whisper something, barely audible.

'He says that the Devil himself visited them,' said Bart, shouting over the chopper's rumbling, 'that the Devil was their guest. Something like that. Try to get some more out of him!'

'Try to get some more?' Rusti shook his head in disbelief and watched as the man mumbled, staring straight in front of him, words that were incomprehensible to Rusti. Surely, he couldn't be alive, or he had to be unconscious. He tried to feel for the man's pulse but either it wasn't there or he couldn't feel it through the skin softened to a pulp. The scanner didn't show any blood circulation or heart function either.

'This is a zombie' he said into the radio but, in a fit of despair, he stripped off the man's vest and jacket so that he could at least see if he was breathing. He had to be, had to be sucking in air or he wouldn't be able to use his voice. To his great astonishment, the man's ribcage was rising and falling rhythmically. Rusti bent closer to listen for cardiac sounds; he no longer trusted the scanner.

At this point, a rattle broke out of the man's mouth and a salt-water discharge spewed out onto Rusti's neck and face. Some of it even got into his mouth.

'Arrrggghhh . . .' he groaned and sprang to his feet. Snorting, he tried to get rid of the foul-smelling substance. Meanwhile, the Malaysian regained full consciousness, his head turned scarlet, and he gesticulated violently in the air. His eyes rolled dementedly in their sockets. He was trying to stand up, when Rusti braced himself and pointed the gun at him.

'Don't move, sit back down where you were,' he pointed the gun towards the ventilators. 'You're not going to do anything stupid. You'll do exactly as I say!'

The same discharge continued to run from the man's nose. It was hideous, especially since Rusti's face, hair, and neck were covered in it. Why on earth had he turned up his visor? Though it was pointless to fret about that now.

But the Malaysian pirate was coming closer and closer, repeating the same sentence, ever more loudly. He ignored Rusti's order, maybe he hadn't even heard it.

With a powerful, perfectly measured kick to the back of the knee, Rusti brought the man down. With his free hand, he pulled out the wrist cuffs—*Well, well! How fast it all happened under stress*—and handcuffed him to the pipe. In the meantime, the man kept shouting, with boundless energy and ever-increasing lung power in Rusti's face and, to the latter's great amazement, switching to Hindi:

'The Devil came to visit us and soon he will be eating at your table!'

Rusti couldn't shake the image of those lunatic eyes from his mind. Later, when he was sitting in the chopper, still wiping his face, they continued to dance around in his brain, with a deep purple glow.

14 hours earlier

He hadn't counted on this when he'd arrived at the camp. He'd known they would be a hard sell, but hadn't expected this much resistance. That his offer, which was a pretty grandiose business gesture, wouldn't interest them at all.

Yet, during the preliminary negotiations, everything had been gliding along as smoothly as a fully-fledged ballet-troupe falling flat on their faces on polished ice. The leader, Okan something or other—that's all he had said about himself—had, in fact, shown keen interest in his weapons. He was also very interested in the shield generator and the energy-jammer, called the *electrostop*, that was capable of blocking the entire power supply of any ship for several hours. They were remarkably simple but still extremely effective weapons, having carried off first prize at weapon-exhibitions in several countries, because of their user-friendly functionality. The price was also deemed acceptable by the Malaysian; in fact, they had agreed on virtually everything—even on the fact that he wouldn't have to travel halfway around the world in order to sign the deal. Just the same, he was here with them, on the other side of the globe without really knowing why. Why was this half-a-million old credit deal so important to him . . . ?

The rotten queasiness had started when he stepped off the plane. The New Chinese were examining everything in the area, they had superb scanners and they had almost thrown him out of the arrival terminal. Of course, this was not Australia, a law-abiding country, where he would have had the right to protest. Outside of New Zealand

and India, the only free state left was the land of the kangaroos. All the others had been swallowed up by the New China Empire following the two nuclear wars that had been confined to Asia. He could only reach the old Malaysian territories through these parts, where petty, feuding warlords controlled all commerce. Including the arms trade, of course.

'Mr. Alexei Sverlov, I am delighted that you found time to spare for us, although I must say we're not interested in your arms at that price.' Okan wore his long braided black hair twisted into a floral-patterned kerchief. A tall, emaciated figure, resembling a scarecrow, he did not look like a chief. At least, not compared to the other man, who was introduced as his bodyguard. That one looked like a corpulent, overweight ass, parading about pompously in his camouflage jacket and bulletproof vest. Yes, he looked more like the sort of person that could make his men pluck the moon out of the sky and lay it at his feet, just by banging on the table.

'But, Mr. Okan . . .' Alex started for about the fifth time into the same sentence. He was curious as to when the chief would stop bargaining. If he failed, then he himself would get up and bow out because at this price it simply wasn't worth his while to sell the weapons. And then they would both go their separate ways peacefully. That is, if they let him leave here alive. . . .

'Please be understanding and kind to me; I have a wife and four children too, a family to support,' he lied, adding on two additional children, to heighten the effect. Those two were born from an illegal relationship, and he was no longer with their mother.

Alexei knew well how to conduct a strategic negotiation, having been brought up on it. His father had been one of the biggest legitimate arms dealers in the Russian Federation. That, however, had only lasted until New China occupied Russia's Asian territories and his father's clientele was taken over by one of the biggest Chinese arms dealers, Chu Jun. It was then that the family fled to Moscow, in the European part of the Independent Russian Federation. Out of sheer defiance, his father continued the business and started dealing with China's biggest rivals, India and the Malaysian dissidents. This, of course, was not looked upon very favourably by the leaders of the New China arms trade business: hired assassins ended his life in front of his Moscow store.

Not long after that, they approached Alexei with the implant proposal. The future looked bright again with this resourceful device. With the help of the implant, he was able to work, travel, sell, expand, and prosper, for unlimited periods, without sleep... to make up for all that had been destroyed by those shots fired in front of their store. He was, of course, able to spend just as much time playing cards and roulette, gambling on horses, making love... and that was no mean feat either. All that, in exchange for the slight nausea that he had to endure every morning, after a couple of beers the night before. Although he did once have a brief fainting episode, lasting maybe five minutes. But he'd had quite a lot to drink beforehand, even though it was strictly forbidden by the suppliers of the implant.

Oh yes, and then there was that number, to be called in case of trouble. He had tried it a few times over the past two hours because he felt something he had never felt before: his stomach kept trying to tear loose from its natural position, he kept sweating, and he was maybe even running a fever. They had told him to read the full contract, with all of its protocols, but on one of the self-indulgent nights he'd lit up a cigar with it, so now he no longer had a chance to read it. He did, however, have the emergency number tattooed onto the back of his hand, in case he ever fell unconscious, when all of this got out of control.

Now it appeared that it would get out of control, with a vengeance. He could have thrown up onto each and every plate laid out in the neat row in front of him. But luckily, the lump stopped in his throat.

'Mr. Sverlov, please maintain some respect for honesty as the most important basis of negotiations. We are well aware that you have two children from a previous relationship.'

Drop dead, thought Alex.

'We have been watching you and your house for days. We have men in Russia, and you are not the only potential arms dealer we're considering.'

'Please forgive me for my slip of the tongue,' Alex tried to make up for his error. 'You're right, let's stay on the side of integrity.' *How far that is from the truth!* he thought to himself.

'To conclude matters, we'd be interested in your weapons if we could get a better discount on the seven containers.'

'Alright,' replied Alex, but he felt far from alright. He felt nauscous again, and dizzy. 'We can discuss it but, first, may I step out for a breath of fresh air? Perhaps it's the food or its unfamiliar taste. . . .'

He had barely emerged from the shack, modelled after last century's bamboo huts, when he immediately started coughing up something horribly bitter. He managed to get rid of it: there it was, stinking, among the stones. A big, brown, mongrel dog arrived and licked the disgusting substance. This upset his stomach even more, so he deemed it advisable to return to the meeting. The dog followed him through the bulrush door and settled down in his owner, Okan's, lap. Sniffing the man for a long time, the dog started to lick his mouth. Okan ignored it for a while, then pushed the dog away. The dog sniffed at, and bit into, a big part of the food piled up in front of them, until the bodyguard finally managed to chase it out of the room.

Great! An appetizing lunch awaited him.

'Alexei, my dear friend. We knew your father, he was a good man, until the day of his unfortunate death. In his memory, I beg you to lower the prices.' Okan started to nibble at the rice and chicken from one of the many little plates arranged in front of him. Sweet chili sauce dripped from his hand, the sight of which made Alex's stomach start churning again.

'Since you drew my father's memory into our conversation,' Alex started, swallowing another big lump trying to surface, 'I cannot say no. We can stop at 420,000, if it suits you. Plus the extras that are being installed onto the ship: the *electrostop*, and the smaller energy cannon. These are entirely free of charge, my personal gift as a token of my esteem.'

It felt good to actually state the final amount, which made him relax with a slight tingle coursing through his legs.

Okan shouted something in Malaysian, the door opened, and seven men came in and sat themselves down around the food. They all started in on it at the same time, the oily sauce running down the men's necks. Broken teeth in terrible condition, with bits of putrid meat caught between them, grinned at Alex. They were slapping him on the back, urging him to eat and then to drink from the foul-smelling fruit brew. As if it had been distilled from yak-droppings . . .

... It reminded him of the stable smells from his childhood, high up somewhere in the East, at his grandmother's place ...
... And then he fainted.

Okan had planned to hold a demonstration for his men, of course, but it was too late to run out to sea, so they shot an old fishing boat in the port to pieces. He couldn't care less if the Russian was knocked out. He had probably drunk too much or had a stomach infection. By morning, he was still unconscious, but that didn't bother Okan very much either.

On the other hand, he was already preparing to immobilize a medium-sized freighter, or even a hovercraft, with the electrostop. After that, he would use the smaller energy cannon to blast a hole in the stern and then board the ship.

He tried to round up the men by blowing on the horn. Four of them were lying in their own filth; he somehow managed to pull three of them to their feet, though he himself started to retch, barely able to stand. But a tough old freebooter couldn't stop now, when he had been given the very best equipment available on the market. They took the Russian on board; the fresh sea breeze would bring him around, but they had barely got him halfway when they noticed that he was dead. He had no heartbeat and wasn't breathing. Not long after they had dropped anchor near the navigation route, Daeng, the bodyguard, threw him overboard.

They'd already been waiting quite a while for a suitable victim, when Okan suddenly fell very ill. Everything turned black before him. Then he started hearing voices and he imagined seeing men of the Indian Coastguard swarming all over the boat. He emptied an entire magazine into the moving shapes, but they just kept streaming down the stairs. Later, when the magazines ran out, he switched to the energy weapon. He continued firing at the phantom figures. A few minutes later, he blacked out. The seawater, which he had seen as surging military units, continued to flow into the cabin in the wake of the two-hundred-kilometre-per-hour wind stirred up by the cyclone.

Daeng was still holding on somehow, although he was feeling worse and worse. He had fled the cabin when the chief started shooting everything in sight. He tied a rope around his waist so that the wind wouldn't sweep him overboard. He was unable to restart the engines because Okan had shattered the navigation console. He'd been holding on for about an hour on the right side of the ship, clutching the rail. That was when he saw the Russian, as he hoisted himself up, holding on to the severed anchor rope.

Floating on his back, Alex was being tossed about on the ocean in the midst of a tropical storm, when he came to. His foot was entangled in a rope, which was pulling him back and forth across the waves towards a ship glistening whitely in the distance.

Much to his surprise, despite the frightening circumstances, he felt completely alright. The nausea had stopped; perhaps he felt a little cold but his energy had returned once again. Clutching the rope, he began pulling himself towards the unknown ship. It must be Okan's motor torpedo-boat, he recognized the two huge gondola drive mechanisms. They had thrown him overboard when he fainted, trying to get rid of him.

These fainting spells were happening quite frequently now, and the bastards at the other end of the emergency line had not been answering the phone. They sold the implants but their after-sales customer service was atrocious.

That fat character whom he had seen in the bamboo house was standing in front of him when he pulled himself on board. The man mumbled something in Malaysian, backing up whilst holding his two hands out in front of him, then scrabbling at his side, probably looking for his weapon. At that point, Alex launched himself at the fatso's belly with renewed strength—driven by his survival instinct. The man staggered and fell over the railing.

The storm was still raging with enormous fury, which prompted Alex to peek carefully down into the cabin. Okan was the only one there, his obviously lifeless body leaning against the wall, an energy weapon trained rigidly at the stairs. Alex cautiously removed Okan's finger from the trigger and stuck the weapon into his belt. Making sure that the pirate chief was definitely dead, he dragged his body up onto the deck and committed it to the waves.

On returning to the cabin, he realized that the boat was immobile. The electronics, on which these modern machines were nowadays entirely dependent, were in piece; though, in all probability, they had duplicated the navigator as well as the steering control. However, he had no idea how to set up the auxiliary standby systems, or even how to find where they were located. Instead, he looked for some sauce-free food and examined the radios. But he neither found any food, nor was able to get the radios to work.

He had no idea how much time had passed—possibly two, or three, hours. He tried to get some rest, even though he didn't feel the least bit tired. He did something that he hadn't done for two hundred days: he closed his eyes and tried to sleep. Just to make time pass. But he didn't succeed. The implant wouldn't let him.

Now, for the first time ever, he would have liked to free himself from it for a short while. Maybe just for an hour.

The time would have been ideal for resting, as the storm outside had abated.

Just then, two explosions rocked the boat, a couple of seconds apart. The shock wave hurled the boat with considerable force, first to the left and then to the right, as the projectiles hit the water. As the sound resembled the impact of bullets from small-calibre weapons, he understood that they were only meant as a warning. There was no muzzle-blast, so presumably it was some kind of energy weapon. So this, he hoped, was either the Coast Guard or a giant amphibian. Crouching under one of the tables, he waited for silence again.

He felt a larger body grating against the left side of the sea-rover. He then ventured out of the cabin, into the glare of blinding lights, with his hands held high, naturally.

'My name is Alexei Sverlov! I was a hostage but I escaped! Please, help me!'

'*Idite syuda!* (Come here!)' shouted the person directing the light, to someone else, a few decks above his head.

Thank heavens, a Russian ship! Alex thought, calming instantly, and he waited for them to lower a rope ladder down to him.

'*Davaj, davaj!* (Move, move!),' they urged him from above. Alex grabbed the ladder and started to climb.

Now, he blessed the implant again. In spite of his weakened state, waking from unconsciousness, without food or water, he climbed upwards like an athlete. He jumped onto the deck with ease, where they spread a blanket over his shoulders. One of the sailors climbed down and tied a GPS buoy to the ship.

The captain was very kind, welcoming him as if they were old friends. A great big, genuine Russian bear. After all, when someone rescues a fellow countryman in the middle of the Indian Ocean, he should also be a perfect host. It wasn't hard to convince him not to say a word about Alex to the local Coast Guard. His generous offer of a newly developed defence weapon (which gave protection against the effects of the *electrostop*) helped considerably in effacing certain memories!

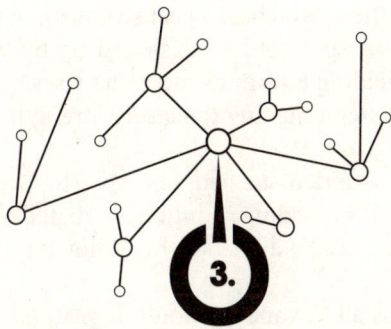

'He was still alive when they found him,' said Suzanne Blanchart, a slight French accent tinging her English. She was new at the corporation, a court anatomist. She had completed her degree at the Sorbonne in Paris a few years before but, unable to find a job on Earth, she had come to the New Home Colony on Mars. She was a short, fragile woman, and the laser-cutter with which she was approaching the corpse's skull looked oddly out of place in her hand.

'No . . .' Steve Cavanaugh looked with inquiring scepticism at the man's covered body—a huge metal antenna was protruding from just below the left shoulder, straight through his chest. 'He was skewered on this and yet he lived?'

'Yes, he lived and talked,' she said, 'asking for his wife to be informed and for her to be told that he loved her, and his daughter too, very much. And he also said something about a man at the terminal and that no one should eat any of the birthday cake. But he couldn't finish what he was saying, as he died at that exact moment. It was a miracle that he lived that long anyway, considering the antenna went straight through the left ventricle of his heart and out through his breastbone. 'Voila!' she said, lifting the blanket off the naked corpse.

'A horrible death,' said Steve, recoiling, with a grimace. 'I've seen many deaths, but never one like this.'

'Neither have I,' said the woman, holding up her hand. 'If you don't want to get soiled, then stand back because I'm about to wield the knife.'

And, in fact, tiny spots of blood, boiled up by the laser, speckled the glass mask shielding Suzanne's face. The laser should have caused less bleeding. But after adjusting the laser's strength, even more blood burst forth.

'Oh-là-là!' she sounded startled, and she stopped cutting. 'This is very, very strange. The bleeding should have abated by now, as it is now nearly three hours since he died, but this is flowing as if his heart were still pumping.'

'No . . .' this was all Cavanaugh could repeat, his vocabulary being rather restricted whenever he was flummoxed. 'There's no such thing.'

'Apparently, there is,' said Suzanne, trying to find a pulse on the neck of the man presumed dead. 'There is no pulse,' she smiled, perhaps for her own reassurance. 'Now he is dead for sure. But the blood continues to spurt as if a hundred watermills were at work. This is a curious case, with a curious corpse.'

She reached for the laser lance again, slicing the skin along his forehead and folding it back onto his face. This was not particularly to Cavanaugh's liking; maybe he would be better off leaving, since he wasn't too interested in the rest of it. He had only dropped in to see if the guy had truly had an accident with the bus or if he'd been thrown out of there as a result of aggression or assault. Because the doc hadn't found any signs pointing to a felony (except perhaps for that 80 cm-long antenna sticking out of his chest), maybe he could close the matter and leave the rest to Suzanne.

'Well then, I'll be on my way,' his last words came at precisely the same moment as the woman started sawing through the skull with a small cutting disk. 'You can manage on your own, right?'

'You're running away, Steve,' she smiled at him archly, 'but I need someone to help me pull this pole out of him. A strong man's hand.'

Cavanaugh said nothing, just held his nose, signalling he'd had enough of this.

'OK,' she nodded. 'I'll find someone next door in the dissecting room, you coward!' She signalled to the departing man with her hand to confirm that she would call him with the results. Or just call him. She found him attractive; perhaps there could be something more than just a formal working relationship.

Cavanaugh set off for the swing-door but halted for a moment and listened to the whine of the circular saw. He positively hated that sound—but he fancied the tiny doctor. He could imagine them spending a romantic dinner together in the revolving restaurant of the Lookout Tower, or in some small eatery in Mars Soho. Or in a sushi bar in the Old Colony, just a few hours' hoverflight away from the New Colony. Perhaps she, too, hoped he would stay longer, but he couldn't stand all that disembowelling. In fact, he couldn't even imagine ever being attracted to someone who chopped up dead bodies, day after day.

The door was already flapping shut behind him when he heard the hissing sound. It was as if a cylinder of compressed air had burst open and gas was steadily escaping from it. Then he heard the scream and a metallic clatter.

As he rushed into the dissecting room, he was faced with an insane sight: the corpse that had been lying on the table earlier was tearing at the compressed-air circular saw tube, even though the top of his skull was already missing. He stumbled forward on his broken right leg, whilst the antenna protruding from his chest trailed along the floor. That was the metallic sound. Suzanne was hiding behind the other dissecting table, panting heavily, but visibly recovering from her consternation. Not so Cavanaugh. . . .

'No. . . .' All he could utter was the same word as before, but all the same he found his handgun and was ready to empty the entire magazine at the zombie.

'Don't!' Suzanne signalled with her open palm that there was no immediate need for help—he was saying something!

In fact, the man was indeed mumbling something. It was simultaneously a disgusting and crazy sight to watch a barely audible whisper emerging from the man's purple lips, just visible under the skin folded back onto his face. Both of them had to concentrate hard to understand what he could be saying, because the compressed air pipe was snaking around on the floor. Suzanne managed to turn it off, so they were finally able to hear what the man was whispering.

'That man at the terminal, it's from him.' None of his body parts were moving now, only his mouth. Collapsed on his knees, propped up by the antenna, with blood pulsating from his head, he murmured: 'The man at the terminal. . . .'

At that point, his exposed brain exploded into pieces, covering everything around him, including Cavanaugh. Suzanne was only saved by her protective clothing. Steve picked at the shreds clinging to his hair and clothes, when the woman admonished him:

'Don't touch it!' she enunciated the words slowly, articulating them as if to emphasise that this was a very dangerous situation. 'This whole thing is much more serious than I thought. Don't touch anything—not your clothing, nor your face. I'll go outside and take off these clothes and change into another protective suit; don't move a muscle in the meantime!'

Cavanaugh slowly put his weapon away. He didn't quite understand what had happened during these past few minutes, but he did as he was told. He had become used to following orders over the years.

Suzanne had already been gone for two minutes, when the corpse fell over with a dull thump. From the cavity where his brain had been, a greenish liquid trickled out toward the central drain-hole. He felt he had to break his promise to Suzanne and prevent it from reaching the drain. He was there in two strides and caught the strange substance in a medical tray.

The substance gathered in the bottom of the tray but didn't stop in its recessed part, continuing to move about. This was not normal for a liquid substance, even an amateur could see that! He carefully drew his fingers further back, so as not to touch it.

When he looked up, Suzanne was standing beside him. She wore a kind of hermetically sealed spacesuit, equipped with an independent breathing system. She cautiously removed the tray from his hand and locked it into one of the incubators standing in the corner. She covered the drain-hole in the floor with thick adhesive tape. When she was done, she walked over to the switch by the door and turned it off. In front of the swing-door, a thick metallic gate slid out from recesses in the wall. In the dissecting room and the corridors, red lights started to glow.

'Everything seems to indicate that we're not going to be leaving here anytime soon,' said Cavanaugh jokingly, turning to the woman, with a half-smile in the corner of his mouth.

'That's right, and now I am going to undress you,' she said, without the slightest hint of jest in her voice. 'Then we're going to burn your clothes in that furnace. And you're going into that disinfecting cabin and taking a shower. Inside you'll find a nightshirt, which you will put on. There is only one door through which you can exit, it will lead you to an isolation chamber. Unfortunately, you'll have to stay there until we can conduct more thorough tests on you. I'll undergo these tests as well; I'll be in the isolation chamber next to yours.

'No. . . .' said Steve with his usual dumbfounded face.

Suzanne loved this trait in him too.

'Yes. And . . .' she paused for breath, 'I'm very sorry!' A compassionate teardrop glistened in the corner of her eye

The doctor started to undress him carefully, taking care to ensure that the fabric remnants didn't touch the man's skin. She placed his clothes in a bag marked 'Contagious.'

Steve Cavanaugh just wished this was all happening in a different place, under different circumstances.

*

3 hours earlier

The corpse of the bus pilot was found stuck on a radio antenna. The police skycar was hovering right next to the antenna, waiting for the technicians, because they had been unable to extricate the man, skewered through the middle of his body. All they could do was to wrap black foil around him, with great difficulty at that, so that the appalling sight of his dead body would not be so conspicuous. Many of the inhabitants from the neighbouring houses were taking videos and photos; the evening tabloid would certainly carry enough pictures of the event and from different angles as well. The traffic police had also made an appearance because the event had caused a bottleneck in the late-night traffic. Although this second, late-night peak was not as big, the gaping and picture-snapping rubberneckers were boosting the flood with their vehicles, floating erratically one atop the other.

As soon as the technicians arrived, the location was cordoned off with floating buoys and screens, closing off further views from the curious crowds. After a brief deliberation, they decided to saw off the antenna. Salvaging the antenna or removing the body was impossible: the rod was too deeply embedded between the ribs and underneath the shoulder-blade.

A crane unit had also been sent out; they didn't want to take any chances. If the antenna broke off at its lower part, where it was as thick as a man's thigh, gradually thinning towards its upper part, it could crash down to the ground or even onto the roof terraces.

Two of the servicemen hooked themselves onto the rigging platform of the antenna and proceeded to climb up the service ladder, towards the body.

'I'll immobilise the lower part,' said Peter Köpke. Thanks to his German ancestry, he always set about any task with precise, almost rigorous, planning. 'Go up another ten metres and attach the second strap to that karabiner.' He pointed to the contraption above his head. 'Make it snappy, lad, because at this pace we won't be finished even by midnight! After that, the nightly frost will set in and we shan't be able to do a thing.'

Suarez Pereira was the 'lad,' or the 'dork.' They called him all kinds of names, as he was the youngest member of the heavy machinery unit. He happened to be as sprightly as a lizard, with his slight body shape. Precisely for this reason, he was found suitable right away, at the first tests. At pole climbing and over the obstacle course, he was always the first to reach the finish line. Agility and resilience were great pluses for wreckers and crane operators. When an expressway in the sky was bottlenecked, they crept and crawled along, rescuing distressed floaters. They'd seen sports cars flown through and wedged in billboards because the driver was too wrapped up admiring the firm breasts of the beauty in the advertisement. There were even drunk drivers crashing into apartment buildings in the outlying districts, where tall buildings were not protected from collisions.

Now here was this bus, scorching along above the city, without a driver. And when should the automatic engine cut-out fail—Peter fumed—if not in the midst of the biggest disaster, when the driver gets to fall sick, as well. The rest of the unit was also hard at work, cleaning the shield tower, or picking up the wreckage along the route pathway.

They ended up with the dirty job, removing the driver off the high-rise antenna.

'He looks like shit!' yelled down Suarez, but the strong wind carried away his voice.

'Use the radio,' Peter yelled back, taking out the communicator and pressing the button once. The radio crackled in the lad's pocked.

'Oh yeah, I always forget, sorry. I'm still wet behind the ears, you know!'

'I know, Dork! Are you ready?'

'Yes. You can come on up!' the lad signalled an OK, giving the thumbs-up.

Peter knew they couldn't climb together for long; he would probably have to stop about three metres below the corpse. He was far heavier than the lad, and the bus pilot had to weigh about a hundred kilos. Suarez must have been about sixty kilos, so the upper part could still support him, along with the corpse. Though it was made from a strong magnesium alloy, it wasn't designed for grown men to hang from. Of course, there were other, much stronger, heavy-duty antennas that could hold the weight of at least ten men, even in the most powerful windstorm.

He started climbing upwards, dragging himself slowly on the ladder, panting and snorting at each step. He had to stop after every strut to connect the safety karabiner one section higher. The antenna was now swinging out by about one and a half metres, even though Peter had yet to reach the highest point that he could safely climb to. Meanwhile, the warm air created by the colony's air generators and solar-collector started its evening migration in response to the dome's sudden cooling. This phenomenon whipped up strong winds that swept along roguishly between the high-rises. Winter set in slowly on

Mars, as the planet distanced itself from the sun. At such times, not even the *Umbrella*, the giant solar-collector, could generate enough heat to alleviate the nightly frosts.

Suddenly he felt as if he had been touched by drizzling water. Only Suarez' incessant cursing could be heard after that. What caused him greater anxiety than that was the fact that the antenna was constantly moving, shaking, and producing ever greater oscillations.

'This is unreal, the guy is still alive!' he heard the agitated voice on the radio. 'He just spewed something all over me. And he's talking, too, he won't stop talking and signing! I don't know what to do with him; he's struggling too much, he could break the antenna. I think you'll have to risk it and climb up!'

'Alright, Kid, pull yourself together,' said Peter soothingly, but he was getting nervous too. He had no idea how to handle the situation. He'd sent up the most inexperienced—and at the same time, the lightest—of his men in a difficult situation, the likes of which he himself had not come across before.

'You stay there and calm him down,' he continued his instructions. 'In the meantime, I'll call for a doctor. The situation is different now—we need a doctor, not a coroner.'

Whilst communicating with headquarters, he inched up the ladder. The sprinkling from above had not stopped yet, it continued to fall, sometimes as a drizzle, at other times in heavier drops. It covered his protective clothing, leaving purulent spots. Most of it fell onto his knuckles and into his face, as he looked up trying to estimate how far he could go without the antenna breaking under their combined weight. The bus driver, who had been taken for dead, was shaking convulsively. It seemed that he was conscious, his head turned toward Suarez, grabbing his shoulder and gesticulating repeatedly.

'You are joking, aren't you?' asked his local colleague, who had examined the corpse only half an hour ago and pronounced him dead. 'I haven't seen a man more dead. That huge iron rod stabbed his heart exactly between the ribs, through one of the chambers, and now you're saying he's talking and letting out some discharge from his body?'

'I'm in no joking mood, believe me,' said Peter, panting. 'The antenna is shaking like it could tear loose at any minute or break in the middle. My youngest man is up there, and I don't know how much longer he can stand it. It would be helpful if you came back, because there's something very strange going on here. I keep feeling like I'm seeing a ghost.'

'If you ask me, that's exactly what you're seeing, alright, because I'm sure the bloke is still the same corpse,' said the doctor on the other end of the line. 'I'm coming right away.'

'Alright. Thank you for being quick. Meanwhile, we'll try to calm him down, to stop him moving so much.'

'There's a tranquiliser in the medicine pack, force it down him.'

They disconnected at the precise moment that the shaking stopped. The man had stopped struggling and the sprinkling ceased, too.

'Peter, listen,' Suarez's voice came over the radio. 'He's mumbling something. He's staring, he doesn't blink, but he's watching me and still talking. I'm holding the radio to his mouth so you can hear it too.'

At the other end of the line there was a muffled murmur, like someone was winding a two-hundred-year old tape-recorder slowly forward. The words came out slowly, some wrapped in an unintelligible fog, obscured.

'The cake . . . don't let the cake . . .' here followed a long pause. 'The man at the terminal . . . he caused it. . . .'

The voice sounded as if it came from beyond the grave. It was frightening and eerie.

'Push the recording button on the radio,' Peter told the boy.

'It's been on the whole time. I might be a beginner, but I'm not naive!' Suarez's sounded slightly offended.

At that moment the antenna shook again and, as Peter looked up, he saw the bus driver starting to struggle again frenziedly but now he was clutching Suarez's throat as well.

'Help!' he rattled on the radio. 'He's strong, very . . . strong!'

'Patrol number twenty-one,' Peter called out to the policemen waiting outside the cordon. 'We're in urgent need of help! We require immediate intervention with a stun gun. I repeat, immediate intervention with a stun gun!'

The waiting patrol car flitted quickly over the antenna; a uniformed colleague appeared in the open door with a stun gun. After aiming at the target for a few seconds, he fired the gun but was too late.

Suarez couldn't breathe; in a last desperate effort, he kicked himself off the bus driver's body, bracing both boots against the antenna. He plunged backwards into the deep, almost sweeping Peter along with him. Three metres down, the safety rope tightened and stopped the fatal fall. The momentum, however, flung him onto the lower part of the antenna, hitting his shoulder and his arm, leaving him dangling at the end of the rope. His face twisted in pain, but at least he was alive.

'This is Technical Rescue Two! We request medical attention, one of our men is slightly injured,' Peter called to headquarters. He took a deep breath and started climbing upwards. No matter how risky the action, it was up to him to finish it.

By the time he reached the top, the bus driver was no longer moving. His nose and his mouth were spewing the same foul discharge that had been drizzling down earlier. He didn't look at all likely to return to consciousness again. In fact, he no longer looked at all human.

By the time he had finished cutting through the antenna, the coroner and the rescue unit had also arrived. Of course, neither the coroner nor the doctor believed that this man had been talking just a few minutes ago and had been moving his limbs about. They just laughed and teased them that the kid was going to have trouble proving that he hadn't skidded down the surface of the antenna accidentally, as a result of the slimy discharge. Perhaps the sound recording would convince them.

This green substance was quite strange, covering his face, knuckles, and jacket with small dots. Perhaps the bloke had suffered from a cold recently; the secretion looked like something a flu might produce.

It was time to gather up their belongings and pack away the tools. The descent would take longer than before, seeing as Suarez had been taken in for observation and Peter was left on his own.

He hoped he would have time to tidy himself up; he might get back early enough for the social dance class that evening. Miriam would help him forget today's horrific rescue mission.

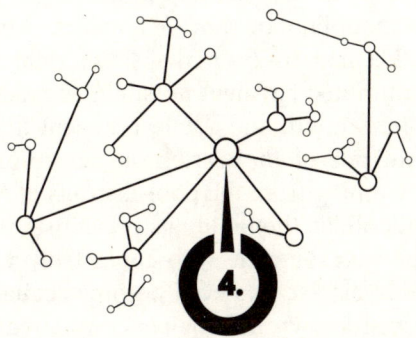

Noah Simpson was feeling in great form. He would never have thought all that suffering, which had surely left a deep impression on the unfortunate bus driver, would pass so easily.

He was already on his second plate of food, consuming it with a ravenous appetite. He felt like he'd lost a lot of energy, maybe for the first time since using the implant. The continuous retching, the accelerated heartbeat, the increased blood pressure, had all had such an impact on his constitution; it was like he'd just run a marathon. Not to mention the loss of fluid. They had only been en route for half a day, but he had already drunk three litres of liquid—water, gin, and beer.

His fellow air travellers all knew his name by now—they had never seen a man eating or drinking so much immediately after boarding. And he still had a card up his sleeve, which made everyone fuss over him: he paid with a Golden Aura card. This type of card trumped all other cards in the Solar System. There wasn't a single store or service that wouldn't open its gates to seventh heaven upon reading the chip. Actually, the card's name was meant to allude to this effect: whoever flashed it found his aura fantastically enlarged. Many people would have liked to get into this aura.

He couldn't be more grateful to Chu Jun, the head of the foreign trading company's southeastern branch, who had put this wondrous bank card at his disposal. He had said as much: 'Until the signing of our contract, you should not be short of anything, Mr. Simpson.'

Nor was he. He had used—perhaps the right word would be 'exploited'—the unlimited payment possibilities practically on a daily basis during the first month and a half. He spent three weeks on the Mother Colony, in one of the Caribbean Sea resort complexes, in complete luxury. Coming from the poor districts of New Cloud York, the cloud-city built above the buildings previously submerged in the New York Sea, he was someone who could truly value this chance to jump up a few levels. He had even become acquainted with a few super-rich, very well-known billionaires considered as being 'Croesus'-rich, even by Solar System standards. There was, for instance, a magnate named Hugo Chivanas, who manufactured fusion reactors for the energy sector. They had become good friends at an evening poker party, that the man even lent him his girlfriend. The woman had no objection either, and they ended up spending a number of nights together. This Hugo considered his woman as little more than merchandise. But Noah had seen this sort of thing before; for him there was nothing unusual about it. Though it was also possible that the woman was not Hugo's girlfriend, but only one of many hostesses. The nights, however, were unforgettable; Vica was a considerate lover, straight out of a fantasy novel. The Golden Aura had the same effect on her as on everyone else. After the third night, however, she complained of a cold and headache, and went back to her room. They didn't meet again after that, as Noah's three-week escapade had unfortunately come to an end and he had to return to Mars. He had promised Sarah-Jessica that before leaving for the Moon, he would still spend a week with her.

Jess was the girl he'd grown up with under the cloud-city. The ideal girl, the blonde teenager who was not only pretty but rightfully determined to get out of the ghetto. Jess, unlike him, studied, applied diligently for various scholarships and schools, until finally her perseverance paid off—she became a biochemist for a famous pharmaceutical producer. At first she worked on Earth, then, after the new type of influenza had increased in numbers on the Mars Colony, the firm transferred her there, temporarily. Just when something was developing between them. Something that was growing out of their old friendship, something that they both needed to heal the wounds of the ghetto: tenderness and, maybe, love.

Noah's path had followed the traditional ghetto track: petty thefts were followed by more serious robberies, and then came drugs, of course. In this 'profession,' a gun was needed for everything, so sometimes that cropped up, too. But after the mostly-bad acquaintances, the wars and battles, there was nothing left but emptiness. He remained a petty thief and a petty junkie. A dependent and a shivering slob. The ghetto highway led to a dead-end with a tombstone. That's where it ended, with his name already outlined, ready to be carved.

That's when the turning point came: the implant and, with it, the hope of climbing out. He had heard of many types of implants—implants to correct vision, implants for hours-long sexual experiences, implants for deep and restful sleep, but he had never read about this type of implant before. It was at the night drug emergency post and asylum that an attendant came up to him, saying that someone had left an envelope with his name on it at reception. 'Futura Respondis—the answer to your future,' it said, with a phone number When he called, a helpful female voice answered. She thanked him nicely many times for calling her back and assured him that this would be the call to put his life back on solid ground.

He had no other choice but to believe her. And so, he went to the personal meeting a few days later at the Futura Respondis office. Near Rio de Janeiro's sandy beach, Miss Stockwell, the same lady he'd spoken to on the phone, received him in the luxury office block built on the sea. She had told him that she would be his contact and if he had any problems in the future, he should dial that same number.

After this meeting, they watched a forty-five-minute film about a young man who had been living with this implant for a few months by then. He was a businessman; Noah could not be certain what language he spoke, it could have been Russian. He travelled widely, usually to far-eastern places, but often to South America and also to Africa. He recounted stories of startling things: since receiving the implant, he never slept. His energy renewed itself from an inexhaustible source. Though it was not shown in the film, Miss Stockwell often referred to the fact that the gentleman spent his nights with the same vigour, and usually not alone. Noah had spent so many nights in a light sleep and a drugged torpor that he knew very well what the woman was referring to.

That was exactly why he thought that this capsule was some kind of drug. 'A product to keep you vigilant and energised,' as his contact had mentioned. 'This will soon be the future of all mankind.'

The film reinforced the needs of the human mind and body for adequate rest. Sleep served the purpose of making humans go on with their lives the next day, armed with renewed energy. The implant, however, replenished the human batteries in the waking state. No longer would they need the various phases of sleep: the muscle-relaxing, calming stage, and the active phase, parading their dreams, were all contained in the capsule. They no longer needed dreams: they could experience them in a waking state, and what's more, they could now make them come true, as well!

The man in the movie looked positively happy and carefree. According to the narrator, he grew his business considerably—there was no mention of what kind of business it was—becoming one of Europe's biggest merchants. Noah had no head for business but, according to Miss Stockwell, the implanted capsule would be helpful, particularly in making learning easier without wasting time, and in raising him up amongst the rank of the top students. Futura Respondis not only offered the implant—entirely free for an unlimited trial period—but also, they would guarantee employment with a real estate and land-concession company, which, at the moment, was offering wealthy businessmen long-term leases for properties on the Moon. Noah was not interested in the land-leasing business, but this opportunity for breaking out and this new type of drug-like business offered a real chance for him to give it a go.

His contact had also told him that he would have to come off his current synthetic drugs immediately because the interactions with the implant could be fatal. Even in this, they had helped him; he spent almost a month prior to receiving the implant in an exorbitantly expensive drug-rehab clinic, which normally only the celebrities could afford. After that came the week-long 'refresher course' where he had been told all the important stuff about the implant. All its positive points, of course. Very little was said about the negative points, these figured at the end of the contract, in the fine print. Only the emergency number was mentioned; and all that was said about the rarely occurring, mild 'side-effects' of the capsule, without going into detail, was: 'could cause leaking.' One more dribble in the life of someone slowly dribbling away would not make any difference. Thus, the decision had been easy.

Although, somewhere deep down inside him, in his lucid, still-drug-free consciousness, he felt that all this was nothing more than an irreversible, lethal experiment. He also knew exactly why they had chosen him, a convicted felon and hard-drug addict; he couldn't say no. The perpetual waking state, the dreamlike existence, and the whirling was the staple food of the addict. What dependant would refuse such an offer, with all the same benefits as dope, but without having to resort to crime to obtain the substance?

At the new workplace, the Moon Concession Corporation, acclimatisation was easy. His boss welcomed him with open arms, as a good-humoured, ever-motivated and steadfast man, keen to prove himself. His rising through the ranks, then, was assured; he quickly acceded to the position of marketing assistant. He would be more qualified to sell grandiose land and real estate than anyone else before him, at least that's what they told him. This position not only gave him financial advantages but other worldly gifts as well; he welcomed these and was soon overdulging. His contacts led him into the upper echelons, amongst the most powerful. That's when his biggest business prospect presented itself, in the form of the Chu Jun World Trading Company.

He wasn't at all concerned that this company was trying to launder its enormous fortune on the Moon—funds made from human trafficking and the sale of arms and narcotics on Earth—using an entertainment complex to be built on long-term leased land. Money was money, wherever it came from.

It was clear from the start that wherever this money came from, it was being amassed in inconsumable amounts in Chu Jun's bank accounts. That Golden Aura card, placed at his disposal, was most likely only one of the countless accounts to cover his expense allowances.

Noah admittedly disliked eastern mobs, but his love of their money outweighed his concerns. His commission on the upcoming 2.5 billion

New Dollar account amounted to 2.5 million. With that, he could take as much as an entire year's unpaid leave. He would bring Jess over from Mars, and they could go to some expensive place and finally get some real leisure time together.

Well, yes, Jess. He should give her a call. Maybe even before the first gravitational acceleration, to make sure the line was clear.

'Jess'—he enunciated her name and waited for the communicator to make the connection. The device was flashing, signalling that it was ringing, but no one answered at the other end of the line.

Surely she wasn't in trouble? He worried for a few moments, only to wash down the rest of his supper with an enormous gulp from a frothy vanilla milkshake. It was impossible that she had caught something due to his indisposition caused by a defective capsule. Noah could never forgive himself if that was what had really happened.

They had spent a marvellous two weeks together, and no matter how attractive and desirable Jess was, Noah did not want to spoil their burgeoning love with a session in bed. Especially because his indisposition, however much he tried to conceal it, was becoming more and more frequent, with hideously foul consequences. Obviously, she suspected something. Luckily, she hadn't seen the worst phase, so she hadn't dragged him off to a local doctor. As a flu specialist, she probably found the symptoms strange. Noah did his best to avoid Jess coming into contact with the greenish discharge, mainly because she would probably have taken a sample of it.

Meanwhile, on-board, everyone was getting ready to retire for the night. The trip only took three-and-a-half days, even with just two jumps. One jump could have covered the distance in less than a day, but in the inner Solar System this was considered a risky undertaking, so most folks chose to stay with the less-accurate two jumps. After that, they covered the final couple of ten thousand kilometres on fusion power. Pilots didn't want to hand over paying passengers to their relatives, pressed into pancakes after flying into one of the planets or the Moon. This technique was still new and unperfected, having only been put into service on the scheduled lines about three years ago, since these jumps used the recently discovered unravelling of the macro-gravitational effects of an anti-gravitational drive around the celestial bodies.

He rang Jess once more. After a minute, there was still no answer. It must have been about nine thirty; she had probably gone to bed. It was the weekend, so she hadn't gone to the lab, unless she had something urgent to do.

Unless some new virus had suddenly appeared.

*

4 hours earlier

Jess had really come to like this kind, playful young man, who had come back to her out of the blue about three months ago, from out of her past. The meeting had churned her up, of course, pulling her back, vortex-like, into the ghetto world under the cloud-city, but the memory of teenage love had soothed her at the same time. During these two weeks, she had discovered her old self again. Perhaps the years spent on research had made her somewhat withdrawn, severing her connection with everyday matters. The umbilical cord with the macro-world had been cut, throwing her mercilessly into the micro-world, into the chemical bonds of molecules. That's why she had been doubly delighted with his visit.

Noah was not the pushy type, and this impressed her a lot. Contrary to most men who wanted to drag her straight off to bed, he was kind, attentive, and restrained. Nevertheless, towards the end of the second week, Jess had already been sending him unambiguous signals, with the result that he moved two or three steps closer but had not taken the final step.

Perhaps, after all, it was better this way. The dreams could remain until the next meeting: the screenplay of imagined kisses and amorous nights. At least she wouldn't be bored for the next four months. They had agreed to a joint summer vacation, when she would take a month off and travel to Earth.

However, there was obviously something to worry about. Noah was not healthy. He said that it was an inherited trait, a genetic disorder, which manifested itself in him, from time to time. He refused any medical treatment, assuring her that he had his own regular doctor. He even showed her the telephone number that he had, to call in case of emergencies.

The telephone number always answered with an automated message: 'Thank you for your patience, please wait for the agent,' but Noah didn't seem worried. He said that worse things had happened to him. Jess tried to assure him that medical science was continuously developing new antibiotics, and that medications were being discovered every day, not to mention the latest results of genetic surgery. She was convinced that if Noah had such a great job, his insurance would cover his treatments.

Noah, however, resisted constantly, minimising the vomiting and runny nose, rushing to the washroom as soon as these symptoms arose. He would lock the door behind him and refuse to accept help, even when he was visibly in distress. He was sweaty but his body remained ice cold, while his blood pressure and pulse went sky-high. Whenever the symptoms finally eased up, he looked like he had been reborn, along with being granted a ravenous appetite. Jess laughed a lot at the way he stuffed himself with food. Noah played on it; he loved to make a comedy of it.

His biorhythm and diurnal cycle were also very strange. When Jess woke up, Noah was already awake, preparing breakfast. In the evenings, however, he went to bed late, retreating to the guest room, saying that he had to read the draft of the contract for the next business deal. Seemingly he slept well, or so he said; he was well rested after only a couple of hours' sleep. Perhaps that was the reason he got over those awful vomiting fits so quickly.

Jess was currently examining the paper tissue that she had found in the guest room, near the bedside table, after Noah had left. He had thrown all paper tissues immediately into the disposal chute in the apartment, confirming that he didn't want to leave any traces of his illness behind. Jess's concern about it had disturbed him.

However, he had overlooked this one.

The tissue was stuck together with a dried, greenish mucus. In the centre of the thin paper, there was a dark green lump visible, dried to a stone's consistency. It was probably about two to three days old. Jess put on a glove. One could never know, this disease might not be of genetic origin after all. Noah's resistance to medical examination had made her slightly suspicious.

She placed the tissue onto a sterile plate and took it over to her home lab, installed in the study. She switched the portable electron microscope on and sat down behind the table filled with solvents and test compounds. Taking out a pair of tweezers and a glass plate, she cut a slit into the fossilized material wedged in the centre of the tissue. Using a scalpel, she carved thin slices from the stone-hard particle in the handkerchief and placed each slice onto the glass plate. She sealed the samples with another glass plate and rolled her chair over to the microscope. Then she adjusted it to the strongest possible magnification and placed the glass plates into the blazing rays of the electron gun.

She was about to look into the lens, when her communicator rang.

'Sarah-Jessica Thompson,' she announced into the speaker.

'Jess, it's Clifford.' Well, it wasn't so unusual for her boss to call her at home. Although it was after working hours, during the past year the same scene had repeated itself many times over, especially when there was some urgent work to be done. The agitation lurking in Cliff's voice indicated it was precisely something like that.

'Jess, you have come to the centre immediately. We've received an orange alarm call from the dissecting room of the Colony Police headquarters. We're facing a disease of unknown origin, indicating a combination of strange signs and symptoms. For the time being, there are two men in isolation chambers, one of them is the judicial coroner performing the autopsy, and the other is an investigator. We've a good many samples, too. We have to prepare the mobile lab. Please leave immediately.'

'Alright, Cliff, I'm on my way.'

She quickly turned off the microscope. Noah's genetic disease would have to wait.

The thought of ringing Noah suddenly occurred to her. But then she changed her mind, as he could be in the middle of a jump already.

If that were the case, she would have no chance of talking to him. Perhaps tomorrow she would try again, before a new jump near Venus.

With a warm glow, she looked at a photo in an alcove as she passed by, a photo of the two of them taken just the previous week. A lovely, exciting future with Noah awaited her . . .

But for now, nose to the grindstone.

She picked up the laboratory bag, prepared for emergencies, and set off towards her car, which was floating on standby in front of her balcony.

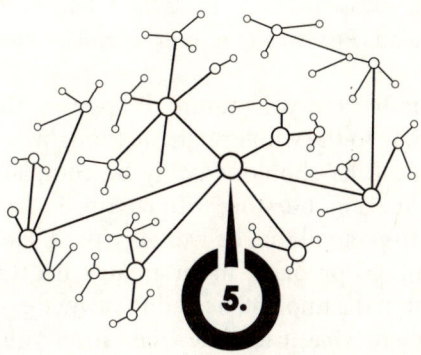

These past few days Alexei was already being treated as a member of the crew. He made friends with everyone, from the engine room to the deck. During the storytelling that took place at the card parties that stretched well into the night, he could finally let himself go in the midst of all the guffawing and banter. To a certain extent, he was able to forget the madness of the previous weeks and Okan's questionable hospitality. He wasn't even bothered that the much-anticipated business deal hadn't materialised in the end. The main thing was that he had survived the episode. He had overcome what had been his longest-ever period of unconsciousness, and not just in any old place, at that: in the middle of the Indian Ocean, with his foot caught in a broken anchor rope. There was a lot to forget!

The bouts of sickness had diminished, only the mildly runny nose and the sweating remained. He tried to make himself scarce when it happened; he tried to avoid having to be examined by the ship's doctor, blaming a slight cold he had caught in the storm, if anyone was inquisitive about it. He threw the dirty tissues into the incinerator, where all the grunge immediately disintegrated into atoms.

He tried several times to reach his contact person, Miss Stockwell at Futura Respondis, because he was running out of the tablets he had to take when he felt sick. But the communicator kept repeating the same message: 'All our operators are busy at the moment, if you wish to leave a message, please press...' *Press the F-button*, Alex finished the sentence in his head. *Piss on them, they're nowhere to be found when they're needed!*

'Futura Respondis, and your future disappears,' this slogan would be more appropriate to the whole affair, he thought.

But to be honest, he shouldn't really be complaining, as he was back to his old self again, bursting with energy. In front of the others, however, he had to pretend that he was very tired. He faked a yawn at four in the morning—probably in an amateurish way because, ever since they had put in the implant, he hadn't yawned even once. He only remembered vaguely what it felt like when it hit you. Sometimes, he fell facedown on the card table, as if alcohol and sleepiness had got too much for him. When that happened, he waited until everyone dozed off or went to sleep around him and only then did he return to his cabin.

Afterwards, he spent hours on the GlobalNet. He was researching what kind of business deals he could make at the landing place. East-African piracy had been continuously active for thousands of years. If he hired a forty-strong mercenary army—there was no way that he would venture anywhere alone and unprotected, as much as he trusted his own resourcefulness—then perhaps he could reach agreements with the local leaders. A good number of African mercenaries had participated in the battles of the Asian wars, so he could easily recruit a personal army. If he could get to the nearest terminal alive, where he could pick up a few hundred thousand New Dollars, then he would have no problems. The captain assured him that he would put his personal escort at his disposal until he was able to hire his own guards.

Port Qoriga (the name meant 'weapon' in the ancient Somali language), the port of the East-African Republic (which united former Kenya, Somalia, Ethiopia, and Djibouti), was comparable to a beehive: members didn't work together in order to survive but gathered the pollen up into their own personal hives. Smaller groups buzzed and whirred around the docks, waiting for a propitious moment when some precious nectar might trickle out of the containers holding secret merchandise.

Mega cruisers, gigantic amphibious hovercrafts, surrounded by smaller but adequately armed gunboats kept arriving at this chaotic port. Only those ships—like their own gigantic hovercraft, the *Lev Tolstoy*—that had the necessary firepower and their own guards to ward off any type of violent act, were willing to undertake unattended docking.

For the last stretch of nautical miles, the piloting was taken over by a convivial Boer, a licensed pilot of South-African origin. They needed his services because the local administration had not been entirely successful in eliminating the mine blockade left after the second Asian conflict. Along the navigation route, wrecks broken in half and vacant phantom ships were mute monuments to the memory of those fearless—or, rather, reckless—souls who had tried the impossible without the help of a licensed pilot. Throughout the zigzagging route to the port, the licensed pilot recounted instructive, and at the same time frightening, stories of human stupidity and pigheadedness.

Captain Rigoriev's friendly handshake felt as good now as it had the first time, right after his escape. Alex assured him that the promised arms would be at the ship's next port of call at Cape Colony within three weeks. At the same time, he reiterated his sympathy for the loss of one of their sailors, who had disappeared off the ship the night before. He thought that he had seen him on deck, as he was checking the lifeboat. Perhaps he had not been careful enough and had slipped on the deck's wet surface.

The captain's trust seemed unbroken, he bid him farewell like an old sea bear, with a broad smile on his face.

The imposing three-man bodyguard team cleared a path for him through the crowded port. The nearest terminal—according to the data given by the communicator—was three streets south of their berth. The narrow streets were filled with an unbelievable multitude of people milling about, giving them a hard time in making headway. Grigoriy, the tallest of the guards, pushed people out of the way, sometimes too vigorously. It was an African characteristic that served him well in cities where people still walked on the ground for transportation, outliers in a world of floating cities and antigravity engines. Most of them shied away from modern paid means of transport, preferring the New Dollar and the New China Empire currency to the biometric methods of payment built into the body, legal tender for settling a bill in the surrounding stores. This rabble, stuck in the past, wanted to feel the coolness of the banknotes, printed on platelets, and loved to hear the sound they made as they were slapped down on the counter.

The terminal was at the end of the street, the only modern-looking structure among the buildings left unchanged for millennia. The pillar, with its glittering golden Solar System logo, could be seen from afar. A network of United Colony 'SunBank-System' bank terminals covered the entire Earth, as well as the colonies established on the Moon, Mars, and Jupiter's Europa moon.

Alex would have stayed with Moscow Maxima, but the little Russian bank only had terminals on the old Continent and in America. During the Asian wars, they withdrew completely from Asia and Africa; but SunBank, on the other hand, was strong enough to survive even in the war zones. Thus it had become an autocratic monopoly in the region once a shaky peace had been established.

Stepping into the brilliantly lit terminal, Alex was enclosed in a cold plasma sheath—preventing anyone from looking or penetrating into it. Unlike hot plasma, its temperature was low enough for someone conducting a transaction at the terminal to be enveloped in a pleasantly cool-to-the-touch, but secure, wall. The biometric scanner shown on the holographic screen processed his identification and the introductions, and as soon as he had completed all the security procedures, Alex could finally get started on the required financial transaction.

First, he cashed chips worth twelve thousand New Dollars. He thought this would be enough for a thirty- or forty-man recruitment. The chips were the size of his thumb—a total of six, in denominations of two thousand each. It was dangerous to walk around with so many chips in such a crowd, but the guards would do whatever was necessary.

He transferred the rest into his biometric chip. This was by far the safest method—no one could rob him or take it from him—it only worked in his own body; more importantly, his living body. That way, his dead body could not be used for monetary frauds. The willingness to pay was governed by his thoughts, he simply had to touch a reading terminal with his hand and think of the amount to be paid. The terminal, of course, asked him back in clear, mother-tongue vernacular, a question audible only in his brain as an inner voice: 'Do you really wish to download the amount in question, totalling two thousand credits?' The answer, in this case, had to be said not only mentally, but also verbally, as double corroboration. There were news reports sometimes about how kidnappers robbed wealthy people this way. But in such cases, the developers placed ever-newer security portals into the system. The latest was the stress identification program, measuring stress levels in the brain. In the event of a sudden increase in stress hormones, the transaction still apparently took place but, behind the transfer, there was no actual credit movement. Alex was constantly amazed at modern technology and how immediately solutions could be devised to fix its failures.

There was a lot of discussion about whether to allow the user to give permission to read his chain of thought, in addition to the reading of thoughts referring strictly to the transactions—that way it would be easy to find out if the account holder was under any kind of pressure. This solution set off averse feelings amongst the users and many had broken their connection with the central bank of the SunBank-System, returning to their traditional cash and card settlements. They ended up returning, once the bank had undertaken, in writing, to withdraw this software. Nobody wanted a bank to take on the role of mind-police.

The transaction completed, the cold plasma retracted to the terminal's dome, and Alex found himself once again back in the commotion of the street. His guards surrounded him, and they set off towards the prearranged destination.

Surfing the GlobalNet, he'd found two bars where an official 'recruitment of bodyguards' was taking place. One of them was directly on the street under the terminal, deep underground. They had to take an old-fashioned freight elevator in order to get to 'hell'—as the place carved in red sandstone was called—to arrive at the shady-looking joint called Borgia Tavern, via winding, cavernous pathways.

Howling techno music vibrated the dust under their feet; on the suspended stages, gladiators fighting with animals, and women and men mimicking wild, unrestrained love, inflamed the already overheated mood. The bar counter was also mounted on anti-grav floaters, circling above the capering, dancing crowd and, if one or two hands swept upwards calling for drinks, scantily clad barmaids rushed about with the hastily concocted beverage.

According to the bouncers, the recruiting was taking place in the back saloon. Alex signalled to the Russian guards to follow him behind the huge ancestral iron gate.

In the stable-sized saloon carved in sandstone, well-built men sat around numerous tables. Their weapons were strapped to their sides or laid out in rows on the tables. The collective firepower would have been sufficient for a small army. They were all—at least according to the ad seen on the GlobalNet—professional, trained, certified, and licensed mercenary soldiers.

The recruiting officer was standing on a dais, scrolling through the current list on an old keyboard attached to a tubular monitor. Customers had to climb up onto a hanging balcony, from which they had a view of the entire hall and could hire the soldiers by holding up the corresponding table numbers. As a rule, people sitting together at a table were usually accustomed to one another and contracted jobs together—mostly guarding ships in the port and acting as coastal escorts. There were groups that had gunboats at their disposal, at least that's what one could conclude from the pictures of small ships laid out on the table.

Alex approached the terminal reserved for customers and spoke into the communicator connecting the buyer with the recruiting officer.

'Alexei Sverlov. I need forty men made up as follows: all the men from Table 1, four from Table 2, six from Table 4, twelve from Table 6, and all of Table 8; I think that makes about forty men.'

'But, sir,' the recruiting officer turned towards him, glancing up at the balcony, 'unfortunately that's impossible. Those sitting at the majority of the tables have been together for a long time . . .'

'I know, and I understand your rules, which, incidentally, I already read about on the Net,' replied Alex. 'But can you tell me, what happens if somebody wanted to hire only three men, and, say he wanted to choose from the seven men sitting at Table 1? Would he have to hire the entire group at that table, or would you direct him to a table with three men?'

'No, not at all. I would look at the master list to see when was the last time that each of them worked, and I would send those for the assignment who have been unemployed the longest.'

'In that case, based on what you have just told me, there would be no problem if we were to select my men according to the system I proposed.'

The officer looked at his list. Alex thought he must be annoyed, thinking it would have been much simpler to send the first three groups together for the assignment. But for Alex, the important thing was precisely the fact that the men wouldn't know so much about each other, so that they wouldn't start to group together or organise any individual activity. They had to remain professional soldiers, ready to carry out orders.

'All right,' stammered the recruiting officer finally.

'Tell them that I'll double their daily allowance,' Alex added, 'and your share as well, naturally.'

'Why didn't you say so in the first place?' The officer switched to a brighter tone. 'What kind of work is it? Port escort?'

'No, somewhat different. It will be a jungle mission.'

There was silence once more at the other end. The recruiting officer took a slow step towards him.

'Then allow me to choose the men myself. Most of them don't like to move too far away from here. In these uncertain times after the war, old tribal coalitions have become strong again; not too many dare to fight in the land of demons. These tribes sustain themselves with privateering and pounce on the ships of the New China Empire and India.'

That's it! Alex thought. He could arm a new privateering group and send it to war against his father's murderers.

'I'll stick to the selection method that you suggested, and I'll try to send the most experienced men from each of the tables, overturning priority for the longest unemployed men.'

'All right,' said Alex contentedly. 'You can expect a decent bonus to supplement your biometric chip at the bank. I hope the reward will be commensurate with your excellent performance.'

'Without a doubt, sir, I am confident, as well. You may count on my services at any time.' The recruiting officer nodded respectfully, turning towards the men. 'Slowsky, Friday, Sokolov, Bianco: Group One. Matamo, Shrywer...'

One by one, the men came forward. The sight of the growing pack of mercenaries in the middle of the room filled Alex with a feeling of security. He may have survived the previous business negotiation, which had belonged in a nightmare, but from now on he would not leave it to fate. Or maybe the feeling of immortality emanating from the implant gave him an exaggerated self-confidence in the affair. Hopefully his prospective customers wouldn't take this trained and experienced group as an attacking force or as militia.

After brief introductions and appointment of the leaders, the hired mercenary troops were ready to move. Alex picked up three tracked transport vehicles. He didn't attempt to get the most recent model because only the Army or the supervising maintenance had modern transportation vehicles at their disposal, and those were generally blown to smithereens as a form of salutation.

He paid off his three Russian guards and sent his regards to Captain Rigoriev with them. He watched the three men for a while as they faded into the continuously surging crowd of Port Qoriga.

He stepped into the control cab of the first tracked vehicle and issued the command for departure. Four days of being tossed about still lay ahead on the road ruled by anarchy, leading toward the interior. Alex knew he would be blessing the continuous energy of his implant when everyone else started to wilt, with the exception of the designated guards.

Belying its ready-for-scrap condition, the caterpillar launched itself at high speed into the tribal territory of the jungle. There was only one, single-car track leading into the thicket. The old, familiar road network had long since ceased to exist; the clock had been turned back about two hundred years in this place.

High above, the aerial expressway strip heading toward the South-African Republic was still visible, glimmering like a sparkling string, but the foliage quickly thickened and intertwined, and soon their only travelling companion was darkness.

*

2 days earlier

Stepan Koroliov, mechanic, started to become suspicious of the behaviour of the newly acquired passenger—and fellow countryman—when he ran into him during his third nightshift in the ship's kitchen. The man was munching a ham sandwich and sipping black Russian tea. The indicator of a communicator was flashing before him; he was probably reading something on the net. It was three thirty in the morning; the card party had finished at two. Everyone had seemed very sleepy at the time, Alexei included, but here he was, as alert as if he had just woken up from a good, long sleep. Even though only an hour and a half had passed and, if he drank that huge mug of tea, he would be unable to sleep all night.

'Hey, Alexei, you can't sleep?' the mechanic asked, waving to the man.

'No, not really. I've had enough stress in the past week to last me a lifetime,' said Alex, waving at him with the sandwich, as if raising a glass for a toast.

'That's exactly why you should get as much rest as you can.'

'I could use a rest, but I cannot. It's post-traumatic stress. I'm plagued with terrible nightmares, I twist and turn and my heart keeps hammering in my chest,' he shook his head.

In contrast, though, he was completely lively and was gobbling the food like someone who had no worries, either with his appetite or his general condition. During the card parties he was the mouthpiece, to the point of telling seemingly tall tales. He laughed, drank, and—not least—played brilliantly. He deprived them of many weeks of pay with his exceptional winning streaks.

Still, something was not quite as it seemed with this man. Stepan, experienced observer of human nature that he was, could see this. This guy appeared to be a sly one. Like someone who was hiding something.

He said he had an arms business and had already wandered the entire world. He squandered his money in a worldly fashion, at least judging from the places that he had been—those trips required loads of money. That was perhaps the reason why he was kidnapped by the

Malaysians, to be held for ransom. As a millionaire or even a billionaire, he could possibly buy anything he wanted—and more than one of most things. For Koroliov, this was inconceivable. He had lived the whole of his life as an employee, he could never break free from this existence, in fact, he didn't even want to anymore; but there had been a time when he would have liked to.

Now, here was this man before him, a mere mortal, with no escort or bodyguard, who 'made his own luck,' as his father used to say so long ago, when he had first sent him to be a seaman. That was exactly his farewell sentence: 'There you will make your own luck, my son.' He wasn't lucky all that often; but, on the other hand, he did have a decent job. That could be considered as luck in many ways. In any case, he was luckier than an unemployed person.

The day following the meeting in the canteen, he was no longer on duty, but he decided to observe what the man did at night, after he had fallen asleep, snorting, with his head on the table. But, as it turned out, he was faking it. After the others had dozed off for real, Alexei stood up and went back to his cabin. Within half an hour he appeared at the door, heading for the middle of the deck. There was no one on duty there; darkness reigned all through the night, with only a few navigation lights illuminating the doorways and the angles. In all probability, he had sussed the places where he could spend time without being disturbed. To Koroliov's huge astonishment, Alex spent the time jogging and working out on this deck, from three to six on the dot. Not merely half-heartedly but with all-out effort. He sweated profusely and, according to the heat sensors in the prow, his body was totally flushed—glowing red-hot in the blue background that symbolised the cool night atmosphere.

Stepan had no idea what to make of this enormous surplus of energy. At first he thought that the man slept during the day—well, when he himself was on the night shift, he couldn't see him during his rest period before noon. Perhaps that's when he rested. But when he started observing him on his days off as well, he came to realise: this man never slept.

To his biggest consternation, no one on the ship seemed to take any interest in the matter. The cook, Gregorij, dismissed it in an offhand manner too, and blocked up one of his nostrils, imitating someone snorting up drugs from a plate.

Maybe it was drugs that kept the man alive. Perhaps that was what his real business was, not arms.

He must have a talk with Captain Rigoriev. He was determined to speak with him before landing. They had been working together for more than twenty years, always on the same ship, so he knew he could count on him. He might find all the things revolving around this character strange as well. Nightly observation of the arms dealer would not pose a problem, as the monitors in the captain's cabin covered the entire ship, consequently the entire deck and even a large part of the cabins could be seen from there. It would not be good for Captain Rigoriev to let such a dubious figure get too close to him.

That night, Stepan waited once again for Alexei to retire to his cabin. The others had already dispersed by then; those on their day off took a nap in the common area, whenever drowsiness hit them. Today, the first officer was passing his time with them, which meant the captain was on duty on the bridge. Now the time had come for action.

He hid in an unused exterior stock-room recess, not far from Alexei's cabin, where some of the flares and the life jackets were stored. Through the ventilation grate, Koroliov had a clear view of the man stepping out of his cabin door, communicator in hand, talking to someone. As Alexei passed by, he overheard the conversation: he was asking for information about the port of arrival.

He watched in silence as Alexei walked past again and reached the top of the stairs leading to the centre of the deck, where he disappeared into the night. Koroliov stepped out into the corridor and set off in the same direction but remained on the lower level of the open deck. This level was also wrapped in semidarkness, only the beacons on the hoists of the lifeboats lit the contours of the corridor. He quickly broke into a run, wanting to reach the bridge, so that he and the captain could see this strange nightly ritual together, as soon as possible.

Koroliov heard Alexei's steps rhythmically pounding on the plated floor above his head. He sprinted back and forth four times, while Stepan could only cover half of the ship's length. Then the pounding stopped, and the usual stretching exercises followed.

As he surged forward, the wind blew a large canvas cover onto his face. It had been torn off one of the lifeboats, fluttering wildly in the early morning wind, mixed with saltwater drizzle.

Perhaps he would still have time to put it back if he hurried, he thought. Tucking the canvas under his arm, he climbed out into the lifeboat. The boat deck facing him was protected from the rain with the canvas cover secured in all four corners; the part that he had carried back was only the bit that covered the outside of the boat, over the water. Normally, he would use the karabiner and the safety rope to work on the boat suspended twelve levels up in the air, but now he couldn't risk being careless and making any noise with the karabiner.

'That's your fault, too,' he muttered to himself, thinking of Alexei, and proceeded to secure the canvas.

Everything happened in a fraction of a second. As if an invisible hand had shoved him over the side of the lifeboat or a strong wave had splashed into the side of the freighter, but all he could remember was his shoulder hitting the side of the hovercraft and his hand trying to find something to grab onto . . . after that, only the taste of the cold, salty seawater and the reverberation of the marine engines remained.

He desperately groped for the distress alarm built into his jacket, but it wasn't there. He had dressed in a loose-fitting sports top and shorts in order to accomplish tonight's observations more easily.

He kept shouting for twenty minutes and swam with all his might after the *Lev Tolstoy*. But the ship was merciless, too fast.

His biochip was an older Russian model, the global positioning accessory was an option he hadn't had the money for. He lived for another forty minutes in the icy water, after which his limbs froze up and he went into spasms.

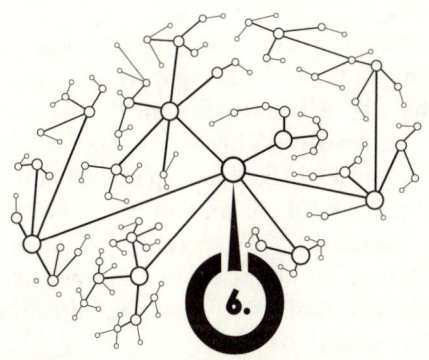

As a result of the incident with the bus, Chris McAllister was summoned to the Centre—on his day off! His boss arrived at the same time, just as Chris was parking in front of the building. Tod Balladero stepped out of the commander's vehicle, impeccably dressed in his steel-grey suit, as always. He was ever thus prepared, even in the middle of the night; perhaps he even slept in that suit. He would be ready to hold a press conference even from his bed, if need be. In his opinion, this was what the duty of a superior was all about. Chris detested this pedantic, rigidly bound life and he could tell that Tod would pick on his tie.

'I know, I know, my tie,' he blurted out, before his boss could say a word. Tod had just enough time to point at it, though he probably wouldn't have wanted to say anything at all, because he'd got tired of instructing a flatfoot who no longer counted as a rookie, on how to wear a uniform.

'Hello, Chris,' the boss nodded. 'I wanted to make a remark, but I'd rather leave it. It's all the same to me how you're dressed, just be here. You are the man who can perhaps tell the most about this morning's bus accident. I summoned everyone who could be of help—toxicologists, virologists, everyone.'

'Virologists? Whatever for?' Chris stared at Tod, astonished, while both proceeded into the building, along the corridor illuminated by emergency lights.

'Because Suzanne, our little pathologist, suspects some virus or bacteria is to blame for yesterday's tragic event . . . she and Cavanaugh, the investigator, have both come into contact with the strange substance emanating from the bus driver's body.'

'What about me?' asked Chris, alarmed. 'What'll happen to me? I was in the bus, too. What if I got contaminated, too?'

'According to Suzanne, there's no cause for alarm. The fluid originated from somewhere inside the brain and was released at the exact time of the brain's explosion. Did you see any greenish, pus-like fluid or discharge in the bus?'

'No, but to be honest, during those few seconds I was looking for the ground under my feet, I had no time to look around,' muttered Chris through his teeth. He wasn't looking for any maddening, boring quarantine. He felt perfectly OK and decided right there and then that he would only go into a sterile room if they handcuffed him.

'Still, someone should be dispatched to see the bus passengers, for safety's sake,' he added, upon which his boss shoved a list under his nose.

'It doesn't contain all the names, only those who participated in giving evidence,' Tod said, dragging his index finger along the list. 'These will be taken to the Quarantine Centre. And look! Whose name would that be, at the very end?'

'No way!' Chris shook his head in disbelief when he saw his own name. 'You won't stick me behind glass, I'd sooner die!'

'Listen, don't give me that crap, you're here now anyway, they'll be quick with the examinations and if you're clear, you can go.'

Chris grumbled something under his breath about somebody's mother and her intimate relations with somebody . . . but just then, they reached the edge of the sealed-off area.

Two armed guards stood in front of the Orange Zone. They were both clad in protective clothing, wearing masks and gloves—one of them was holding a lit-up communicator that verified the photos and names of those who entered. Only his piercing eyes and his thick black eyebrows were visible above his mask as, with an upturned hand, he signalled the men to stop for inspection. The other armed guard—probably an overzealous rule follower, at least when compared to Chris's style—switched his handgun from the rest to the ready position, even though one of them was a uniformed police officer and the other one the Mars New Home Colony's chief of police. They didn't know them personally, at least Chris didn't, for sure. They didn't serve in the Police Force, but as soldiers in the Special Events Containment Group.

'Greetings, Chief Balladero, please proceed to the right, past the door, if you would be so kind, the Crisis Group is expecting you in the banqueting hall,' said the bushy-browed one, having located them on the list from the data shown on the biometric identifiers. Chris automatically followed the boss.

'Forgive me, Sergeant McAllister, but you have to go to the isolation section; just walk straight to the door behind the curtain,' he heard from the armed man standing sternly before him. The other guard emphatically raised his weapon to waist level. Both soldiers towered at least one head above him; there was no sense in starting a dispute. His desperate glance at the boss only got him a spread-out hand in reply, signifying that he couldn't do anything about the situation either.

'I said I'd only go behind the glass if handcuffed,' said Chris, shaking his head.

'If that's your wish, then we can do that too,' said the other guard and, in full view, reached towards his waist where the handcuffs hung from his belt. 'The Orange Alarm is on; we can use whatever force we deem necessary.'

'No need for that,' said Chris, looking up at the overzealous soldier. Though he would have loved to kick him in the balls. If he were just a few centimetres taller, they wouldn't be treating him so contemptuously.

'Where can I leave my service weapon?'

'Over there in the isolation room, in the changing cabin,' repeated the one with the bushy brows. 'Believe me, it won't take long, if the results of the examination are negative, you can go home in just a couple of days.'

Chris bid good-bye to Commander Balladero and marched into the isolation chamber, filled with a brilliant bluish light.

Lousy bus, he thought. He felt that something else was still going to go wrong that day. The skybuses didn't usually perform pirouettes. They were equipped with a built-in multiple collision-avoidance system, an accident prevention system, and all those kinds of gizmos. One of these failsafe systems had not been working on this bus. What was that, if not bad luck?

Not to mention, that if a driver feels sick, or perchance is turning the steering wheel of his vehicle—say with the aim of committing an act of terrorism—towards some building, then these vehicles would automatically switch from manual to automatic control. That hadn't happened either. Making it two lots of bad luck already.

And what about the drivers—all carefully selected, experienced experts? They didn't normally skewer themselves on antennas. After work, they usually dropped in for a good cup of coffee, but they certainly kept clear of high buildings' antennas. And if they died, they did it properly. They didn't revive and spread unknown viruses. This was already orbital bad luck.

The worst orbital bad luck, just four days before the two-week vacation on Earth, when he could have seen the kids. Rotten bad luck, that cut right across their long-awaited leisure time together.

He decided not to continue to aggravate himself and to try and focus instead on the entire affair not taking more than a day. He made an effort to concentrate on the pictures lined up on the board hanging in front of him. According to the instructions, he had to take all his clothes off and hang them on a rack. The rack was to be placed in a closet, which was then drawn back into the wall—perhaps the clothes were to be disinfected but, possibly, they would just be destroyed.

'Serves you right, necktie,' grinned Chris. At least he would get rid of it.

His weapon, his watch, his keys, and any other personal belongings had to be put into a jar that slid out of the wall. Hopefully, he would see them again.

He was ready, standing there stark naked. It was depressing to see the paunchy, rather well-rounded parts of his body, in the security door glass. He had long given up trying to keep himself in shape. Sure, at the time he had been full of love, living with his ravishing, newlywed young wife. Now, divorced, with the occasional relationship every two to three months, there wasn't much to work on. Perhaps next year ... perhaps if he stopped working for a while.

Work was the toughest drug in the world. It's bad if you don't have a job, but the worst is when you find one where you can't get any rest. If you considered the tempo of a cop's life, it wasn't really that different from a criminal's. Both were held on course by the same force: some primitive, profoundly deep excitement that triggered the same euphoric feeling, in both the hunter and the hunted alike.

'Mr. McAllister, please put this on.' A woman with an unfamiliar voice, clad in a safety garment, stood before him. The mask on her face was attached to an air hose, branching off into an air filter on the side of her body. 'Pleased to meet you. I'm Sarah-Jessica Thompson, virologist and biochemist.'

As nothing else was visible behind the safety equipment, it was only the tiny wrinkles in the corner of the woman's eyes that showed that she was smiling.

'I'm pleased too, believe me.' But Chris wasn't pleased at all; he was merely trying to be polite because the woman was being very kind. He didn't know whether to blush at his nudity or let his prudishness go to hell. He took the sterile nightshirt from the woman and put it on awkwardly.

'If I may, I'll tell you what kind of tests you'll have to undergo, so that we can determine whether you were contaminated with a virus or a bacterial infection,' said the woman and led Chris into an empty room. It was bordered by a glass wall on one side—reminding him of an interrogation room—with the other side covered with instruments, tubes, and infusion pouches, all lined up on shelves. A test scanner hung from the ceiling on a telescopic arm.

'Could I ask a question first?' Chris turned to the virologist, whilst half-sitting on the examination table.

'Of course.'

'What kind of virus or bacteria was found in the driver's corpse?'

The woman didn't look at him; she was busy preparing the test tubes needed for taking samples.

'For the time being, tests are being carried out, but you shouldn't worry,' said the woman, glancing at him and turning back to the instruments. 'The results will be ready soon, and I'll be able to say more then.'

Chris wasn't satisfied with the answer.

'Are you carrying out the tests by yourself?' he questioned the woman further.

'For now, only I and my boss are working on the case, but we'll be calling in other experts for the investigation.'

She stopped talking while she prepared the equipment for the scan and for taking the blood sample.

'Mr. McAllister,' she said, turning to the man, her eyes pinning Chris to the examining table like a bayonet, 'believe me, I'm not a novice in this profession. I was involved in containing two worldwide epidemics on Earth, before they transferred me to Mars. Thanks to the effects of my recently completed trials aimed at strengthening the immune system, the number of cases of the new type of influenza disease, the so-called polimutant, with fatal consequences, decreased by ten per cent on Mars Colony. Believe me, I set about my task four hours ago with all the thoroughness that it required. I have taken samples, the analysis of which is currently being processed. For the time being, I can't say any more on the matter, but you can be sure that you will be amongst the first to be notified of the results.'

Her hand pushed Chris's upper body gently but firmly down onto the coolness of the bed. After that, the cop could only feel the prick of the tiny needle protruding from the scanner. The whiteness radiating from the ceiling and the bluish glimmer had quelled his resistance.

'Lousy, rotten bus . . .' he murmured between his teeth, while the woman proceeded to prepare new tools and instruments.

*

At the same time, in the crisis meeting room . . .

'Thank you for coming,' began Commander Balladero, after everyone had taken their seats and the commotion had subsided.

'I'm pleased that everyone has made themselves available right away, considering the importance of the matter. The mayor is presently at a public function downtown, giving his election speech, but he'll be back here just as soon as he's finished. Until then, we have Deputy Mayor Estrella Gonzales here with us. I won't take up your time with introductions, everyone will know one another from work, but if I'm not mistaken, the major part of the group has already been working together for quite a long time.'

Two secretaries entered the room, one brought coffee and placed it on a little table beside the door, the other turned on the agenda recorder for the discussion.

'We are a small Colony, compared to the Moon and Jupiter's Europa Colonies,' continued the Commander, 'more like a big city on Earth. We all know how fast an epidemic can spread in a crowded megalopolis: there have been innumerable examples in the Mother Colony over past centuries. We have not yet received a detailed analysis of today's case; the samples are only just being examined at our premises, although we have sent some of them to the Moon and Earth as well, in the interests of further investigation. For the time being, we are standing by on orange alert, until such time as we have the results, or until we receive no news about further incidences of the illness. Our aim is to get hold of everyone who could have come into contact with the bus pilot. For the moment, the search for the bus passengers and their relatives, and their subsequent transportation to the temporary Crisis Centre, continues. Bear in mind that we are talking about more than four, perhaps even five, thousand passengers in the course of this day. I shall now call upon Claude Brademe, director of the Special Events Containment Group, who will outline the steps contained in the safety protocol concerning serious epidemics affecting the entire colony.'

A tall, slender man in uniform stood up and walked up to the hologram. He pulled out a pair of wire-framed glasses from his top pocket and looked at the communicator.

'Greetings, everyone,' he spoke in French, since this was one of the official languages on the colony besides English, Spanish, and Chinese. Those who had a language module embedded in their biometric chips didn't have to use the automatic translator on the table. A few reached for the headphones, while the man waited patiently until everyone was ready.

'My mission, as the Special Events director, is to draw up a security plan for events such as this one, or to use the general safety plan that already exists. In this particular case, I have modified the general security plan, since there has not been any major epidemic on Mars, including in the Old Colony and in Chinatown, for more than four years. As we know, the Old Colony has its own independent governing and administrative institutions; therefore, this plan does not affect them. In the event of an orange alert, the underground expressway connecting the Chinese quarter remains open; nevertheless, the Special Events, or SE, personnel have been put into position on our side. If we raise the orange alert to red, then the tunnel traffic will be halted immediately and the tunnel hermetically sealed.'

The two Mars settlements, built close to each other, appeared on the hologram screen. The Old Colony had been founded by China in 2072, the first Mars Colony besides the Delta Base, which had been built jointly by the European Space Agency and NASA. Later, the settlements continued to expand with international aid. After the discovery of the aquifer water supply under the surface, construction had been shifted northwards and the new colony, Mars New Home, was established. The two colonies had not always been on good terms with each other; in fact, the Old Colony continuously beleaguered the United Colony Council, the UCC, the successor to the United Nations, with ambitions of independence.

The underground expressway was bathed in orange light, which turned red at a gesture from the director. He then proceeded to move the stereoscopic view to the middle of the table. He pointed to the building where this meeting was taking place, switched to orange, and closed the boundaries of the area.

'As you can see, at this precise moment, only two sections remain orange areas: the dissecting room, the four isolation rooms, the lab, and the lab service areas. On the lower levels, we can create isolation rooms at any time, even for several tens of thousands of people. Outside of these sections, the building is marked in blue, which means that only staff or individuals possessing special permits may enter the building.'

He marked out a new area, which encompassed the inner city and a few smaller, residential districts further away from the city. He marked these as well, in yellow.

'We have set up an alert squad in these areas. We have dispatched our personnel to the police stations and have started to prepare police officers in the event that it becomes necessary to spread the orange alert to larger city districts as well.'

'This is where the private dwellings of those people who were travelling on the bus, and their kin, live. These areas have already been designated as orange. At this precise moment, our colleagues are descending on the area—in civilian clothes, of course, thus minimizing the chance of panic. The only thing worse than a city-wide, uncontrollable panic, is the virus itself . . .'

'And that is something that we can really do without,' interjected Commander Balladero.

'I marked the places that these people may have visited during the past few hours: workplaces, metro, department stores . . . it's unfortunate that this covers a rather extensive area.'

'This is frightening,' Deputy Mayor Gonzales spoke up. She was a middle-aged, blonde woman who wore her hair gathered into a chignon. 'Restaurants, bars, entertainment spots, sports centres, hospitals, schools, retirement homes?'

Director Brademe nodded, with a worried look.

'You are quite right, Madame Deputy Mayor.'

'Estrella,' said the woman gently, 'I suggest that we call each other by our first names, the discussion will go much faster and will be a little less inhibited.'

'Yes, thank you, Estrella,' said the Director, 'you are absolutely right, but don't forget that this is only an orange alarm, localized on the most important points. Until the arrival of the analyses or an unexpected external incident, we don't have to raise the level of alert and section off public areas of the city. If no new event appears here or perhaps on the Old Colony, then we don't have to widen the circle. If, by the end of tomorrow morning, we can transport the passengers of the bus and their relatives into this sectioned-off building, then I don't think we'll have any major problems. Not even if some new virus or bacterium is behind the event.'

'I think that's a splendid plan,' said General Jack Simons of the Special Army Unit. 'Have they started coordinating with the colonies in order to work out an integrated plan? What does the UCC think?'

'It's too early to make any arrangements at this stage,' said the director. 'We know only too well that the media has innumerable contacts within the Council. Any such question or suggestion could trigger off an unnecessary wave of panic, engulfing the Colonies. Therefore, if it proves to be a severe infection after all, then we must prohibit all outward broadcasts. We have already made contact with the Special Events directors on the Mother Colony, the Moon, and those working on Europa. They are aware of the emerging situation. Not a single SE unit is dependent on the Council, so we can trust them. With them, we can start to develop a common strategy, in the event that this infection should become serious. We shall make sure that we let as few people as possible in on what's going on, so as to prevent the information from getting to the news channels. But I hope that this is merely an isolated case.'

'Claude, in today's world, where it only takes three days to jump from one colony to the other, we can't talk about isolation,' said the Deputy Mayor. 'Do everything you need to, but plan in terms of the Solar System as well. This incident, if I may say so, is most unfortunate, but it's nevertheless a splendid opportunity for setting our affairs to rights as far as local and public safety of the colonies is concerned.'

'I agree,' said General Simons. 'I would like to have a detailed report of developments up until now, and I offer the full assistance of the Mars Garrison military units for any such events in the future . . .'

Just then, the door swung open. An officer clad in the Special Events uniform entered. He strode up to Director Brademe and whispered something in his ear. The director's face clouded over.

'Thank you, General Simons, I accept your assistance; that is to say, now, right this minute.'

He changed the channel on the screen.

'One of the stations is broadcasting these unfortunate events live, something that has only just come to my knowledge.'

The holographic wall filled with the chaotic sight of people of every sort running, fleeing in every direction, trampling one another. The location was some kind of nightclub; the sound of people screaming and yelling drowned the music blaring in the background. The centre of the image wasn't clear; the small robot-camera lens hovering over the scene was misted over. Someone was jumping or dancing in the twilight. The self-cleaning lens of the camera slowly cleared the layer of mist.

A terrified shudder passed over the faces of the crisis crew.

'Unfortunately, the worst has happened: I must place the city centre under military control immediately,' said Director Brademe. 'I am changing the orange alarm level to red. I shall set off the distress sirens and order a curfew across the entire colony.'

The city centre, the public areas, the metro, and the isolation ward switched to red on the slowly turning holographic model floating above the table. The tunnel connecting the two colonies was also closed off. The rest of the city switched to orange, which meant a first-degree curfew.

'The mayor was delivering a speech in the sealed-off section.' Claude expressed his thoughts aloud. 'I think, Estrella, you'll have to take over the city's management for a while.'

*

Half an hour earlier . . .

People surrounded him; he was now the centre of attention, of course, the hero who had swung the cop over the gaping hole in the bus, like some kind of trapeze artist. His interview was broadcast all night long on the news channels. The stocky fellow had plenty to say; he didn't just simply tell the story but embellished it a bit, gingerly polished it and even dared to play-act it. All the news channels were after him for new details. He became a popular, much-loved media hero, and he admitted that's what he had always wanted to be.

Guy Schneider, the hero of the Mars Colony, in his present, post-traumatic state, became an unbridled party animal. When he walked into the Pulse Bar, his usual venue—after having signed his deposition at the Central Terminal Police Station—there was barely a soul in the place. Small groups sat around at the tables; some of them sipped at drinks. But as soon as the evening news came on and Guy's face came into view, his popularity soared sky-high. Thanks to the giant holographic advertising image outside the bar, on which the shrewd owner displayed Guy's photograph with the inscription 'the hero of the day is with us to tell his story,' the inquisitive onlookers started to swarm in from the street.

Guy beefed up his role as much as he could. He recounted the whole story all over again, with the same zest and enthusiasm every time. He even found someone to take the cop's part and swung him from one table to the next—all this, while hanging upside down from one of the floating stages. He was a wild success. People kept surging into the bar. A long Mars week was ending, and everyone wanted to let off the steam that had accumulated during the week. And, at last, they had a hero. Not just any hero . . .

Guy had been dancing for half an hour on one of the floating stages with a beautiful black woman, who was incidentally a head taller than him. The disparity in height didn't bother him; instead, he was emboldened to shake his big belly in a fiery tempo for the woman, like in some Latin carnival scene. On any normal, hero-less day, it would be a pretty dancing girl or young man writhing here, without having somebody the size of a fully-grown grizzly bear, totally drunk, next to them.

'Yah, yah, yah, yahoo!' howled Guy at the crowd, beating the rhythm on the stage railing. 'Who is your hero, who is your saviour?'

'You are!' the choir echoed back at him, as one voice, sounding out the rhythm and bouncing around to the music. Arms reached up; everyone wanted to shake hands with the latest scion of the classic comics' heroes. The crowd was sucked in by the music and the vortex created by the spectacle.

'You're a real barnstormer!' said the black dancing girl. She snatched Guy's necktie and clamped it between her legs, steering him around the floor like a Pekinese dog. Guy clutched her bottom, which was clad in a skimpy skirt, and followed her around and around with a lecherous grin. The audience was delirious.

'Superman, superman,' they chanted to the rhythm of the music. Guy accepted this role, extending one arm and pulling himself forward.

They were on their second round, when Guy suddenly felt dizzy. His dancing partner, not having noticed, kept on pulling the wobbly hero along. But suddenly the necktie became taut and, with the same movement, slid out of her grasp. The weighty body of the man toppled over the railing and fell headfirst into the crowd.

His devotees scattered to right and left, shrieking, but he still managed to bury two youths beneath him, who dragged themselves onto their feet with aching arms and necks. The hero, however, remained lying on the floor.

'He passed out!' somebody shouted. 'Get him some air, step back!'

The mob formed an increasingly widening circle around Guy. Someone stepped forward and knelt down by the motionless body, turning it over and pressing his ears to Guy's chest. Hand raised, he signalled a request for silence. Someone warned the DJ and the music stopped.

'There's no heartbeat! Call an ambulance immediately!'

Murmurs spread through the crowd. The office door swung open; the owner, with defibrillator in hand, pushed his way through to the injured man. Two heavy-set bouncers followed, directing everyone to step further back. Flashguns went off and communicators and cameras rolled, as self-appointed reporters took videos and sent their shots directly to the public news channels. By the time the bar manager had the resuscitator ready, the live image streaming from the bar projector high above was already visible on the screen. Since the mayor was just giving his campaign speech on the square in front of the bar, film crew units only took a few minutes to arrive on the scene with their cameras. Here, they had a more exciting subject to shoot than empty political platitudes.

The screens displayed shockingly enlarged images of the resuscitation process. The owner attached the device to Guy's chest and gave loud orders for the strikes. The man's body flinched and then slackened again. After a pause, the defibrillator loudly announced that there was no heartbeat, asking everyone to step back, only to strike down on the man again. At the end of a renewed silence lasting for a few long seconds, the device repeated the horrible news: 'There is no heartbeat, please call the nearest medical unit.'

The manager shook his head in disbelief, then stepped over to the DJ and took the microphone from his hand.

'Could everyone please step back, the ambulance is on its way...'

'*Ambulance? What for?!*'

The crowd broke out in wild cheers. The reason for rejoicing was Guy, who had just smashed the defibrillator to the ground and started to jump on it, up and down. The device wasn't cheap, but the owner didn't mind, he was grinning from ear to ear. He could buy at least fifty units from today's takings. He ran up to the resuscitated hero and hugged him. Guy picked him up and twirled him around in the air at least four times. A little giddy, the manager cheerfully beckoned the DJ to cancel the ambulance and start the music again.

Once again, the techno-sound bellowed forth, people started to jump up and down rhythmically to the beat. The floating bar counter set out on its way again.

'Hey, guys, get me to the washroom, I'm still feeling a bit yucky and don't want to throw up in here,' Guy warned the two gorillas. One of them ploughed forward like an icebreaker, the other one covered him from behind, but even so it took five minutes before Guy could eventually grab hold of the white porcelain of the toilet in the men's washroom.

'Disgusting,' said one of the bodyguards, 'what's this green grunge? Have you been eating spinach?'

'What's it to you, buster?! I'm a hero, and heroes aren't supposed to be questioned about what they eat!' Guy snapped, while hurrying to clean his jacket at the washbasin.

'Stay cool, man,' the other bodyguard motioned conciliatorily, 'It's OK to have your day, but think of tomorrow too. Don't pick a quarrel with anyone, because next week, when you're not such a big hero anymore, they might consider smashing your nose.'

Guy was about to respond with something colourful, when the door opened. It was the owner.

'Guy, you should come back, everyone is waiting for you. You see, I didn't send you to the hospital. What you do with your life is your business, but since you started the show, you have to finish it, too. I'll promise you free drinks for the next three months, just come on,' and he pushed the swinging door open a slit so that the rhythmic shouts of 'Superman, Superman,' could be heard.

'OK, Enrico, but don't forget your words, keep your promise, otherwise I'll start a smear campaign in the media against you,' he said, in a rather serious tone. He could do it now, he had become a popular media star.

'Guys, two beers for me and a Tequila,' he motioned to the bodyguards, '. . . without making faces!'

One of the bodyguards spoke into his communicator, and by the time they were out of the washroom, the floater was already rocking gently before them. A pretty bargirl was holding the tray with the order, but Guy didn't take it; instead, on a sudden impulse, he stepped behind the bar counter and just whispered 'Let's go!' into the girl's ear.

The bar floated gracefully out over the crowd. The people tried to reach it, to touch Guy's hand, as he sat on the lower steps, dangling his feet and strutting his stuff for his devotees.

'Superman, Superman, Superman . . .' The crowd went into ecstasy again. On the screen, Guy was headbanging, rolling the Tequila and a beer down his throat, and, on a sudden impulse, he jumped onto the stage.

The crowd roared frantically, egging him on, waving, and he gave as good as he got. He threw himself back and forth as if possessed, or like someone under the influence of drugs.

By this time, he no longer felt anything, as he was no longer himself. His old, conscious ego hadn't even noticed that his heart had stopped beating about half an hour ago. His body was being controlled by extraneous entities, which had taken over control of his brain for a common goal, towards which they worked continuously: the successful reproduction of their own entities.

They set Guy's body into motion, compelling him into a wild dance and raising his body temperature in order to reach the point of detonation that was programmed into them. Reaching the point of detonation was one of the most effective methods of freeing themselves from the confines of the body, but that choice was their last resort. The primary route led through the stomach to daylight, the secondary route was through the lymphatic system, coupled with perspiration. They found access to Guy's body through the secondary route, swimming in somebody's sweat.

Scattered beads of sweat flew outward from the man, moving convulsively in a St. Vitus' dance, covering the crowd that was swaying and writhing beside him, continuously touching his heated body. There was plenty of drizzling mist left for the fascinated fans jumping around him.

The DJ changed to a new tune, the rhythm took charge. . . .

Guy's body heated up to detonation point. . . .

A moment later, Guy's head exploded, scattering its greenish substance in all directions, as seen on the news channel, broadcasting live. The body continued to wriggle, dance, and gesture, eerily following the rhythm of the music. The intruders controlling his insides didn't leave it at that—they continued to spray the crowd, thus propagating further into the new hosts.

The revellers, who had been in an ecstatic mood earlier, now fled the bar frantically, trampling madly over one another.

Their screams were soon drowned by the central distress siren.

The giant screens displayed Guy's possessed, gyrating body for a few seconds longer before replacing it with the following message: 'Mars New Home Colony—emergency telecast to follow within twenty minutes. An immediate curfew is in effect in the city. We shall inform you of further steps to be taken in the next few days.'

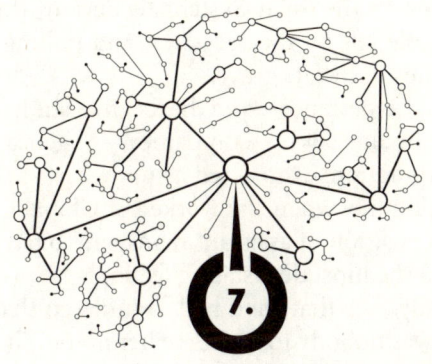

Angelica Stockwell's usual office desk paraphernalia was still in boxes, stacked up against the wall. She had been forced to leave the Rio office in a hurry, with no word from management as to the reason. But she wasn't really interested anyway; when she had originally signed up with Futura Respondis, she had accepted the fact that she could be relocated at any time, at short notice.

She remembered clearly the day when her stock exchange career went up in smoke—it had been a wretched day for the planetary economy. At first, the second Asian conflict had exploded the Earth's markets to a fulminating peak, only to bring them crashing down later. Although the American Dollar hadn't been swept into the streets by the wind—as it had been at the time of the global market crashes centuries earlier—it quietly vanished, along with other currencies. The recession, which had lasted for many long years, had been sustained by the great financiers, the plutocrats, working in conjunction with the oligarchs who pulled the strings behind the scenes in the New China Empire. After New China's victory, the Earth's economy had been slow to tip back into balance. In the end, the tenuous markets were saved from total extinction by the colonies. Most of them had been unable to stay afloat; it was sheer economic necessity that had slowly nudged the

Earth back onto an even keel. On one of the colonies set up for self-sufficiency, the Old Mars Colony, Chinatown had minted official coins that entered circulation in the Solar System's economy, thus rushing in to fill the gaping hole left by the recession and pulling the dying economy back from the edge of its grave.

Despite her financial experience—and the fact that she had formerly been hired by some of the largest companies—Angelica had been shunned by those corporations who acted as midwives at the birth of the New Dollar. At one time, when she worked at Global Capital, she had even attained the position of assistant manager. To fall from such great heights had been the most devastating feeling.

The worst of it really, was that she'd had to undergo that suffering all on her own, there was nobody to welcome her home. She had lived alone all her life. To be more precise, at the age of forty-two, she was married to Money.

She had shares in the 'Legendary East'—as the upwardly mobile Eastern markets were called. Those who had no investments there were idiots. The time bomb was ticking down, triggered when New China occupied half of Mongolia, Russia, and a part of Oceania during the first Asian conflict, and the restricted nuclear strike that followed. This had strengthened New China's position, at the same time giving economically strong New China investors the opportunity to seize power by forming an alliance with the New China Army. The formation of power was moulded into an oligarchic system that divided the Empire into seventeen territories. By then, a weapons-and-metal embargo had taken effect against the oligarchic New China, a mandate handed down by the UC Council.

The economy had borne up remarkably well under this embargo. In fact, when the oligarchs turned against each other—splitting into two camps—and soon thereafter involved the whole of Asia into the conflict, the markets began to soar. North and South America abandoned all caution, pouring arms into the rioting areas, kicking over the arms embargo—in spite of the United Colony Council's warnings. The arms lobbyists, having learned their lesson from the first conflict, reckoned that this latest war could also be outlived; in reality, the formerly allied parties would weaken each other and the oligarchic New China would later disintegrate.

The oligarchs, however, knew very well what they were doing—they stockpiled colossal reserves of weapons, capitalizing on the breaches of the arms embargo. Within a few months, they had reunited their forces and extended their borders westward to the Urals, northward to the Barents Sea, eastward to the Pacific Ocean, and southward to Japan.

Thus the New China Empire came into existence, with the wealthiest oligarch at its helm: the emperor.

It was there, in that exasperatingly deep, black postwar hole, that Mr. Yakizima had found her. His business card said: 'Futura Respondis—perhaps the answer to your future, too.' Angelica had been through at least a hundred job interviews when the man received her at his agency, in one of London's business districts teeming with office buildings.

'Have a seat, Miss.' Angelica took a second, longer look at the immaculate dark suit, the impeccably ironed, clean shirt, the golden cufflinks, which she had first spotted during the handshake. He politely pulled the chair out for her, just like a perfect gentleman.

Only when she sat down facing him from across the table, did she noticed the unmistakable slash on his face. It ran straight down from his left eye to the edge of his mouth, making the facial muscles on the left side of his face immobile as he spoke. The sight of the deep wound shocked her, held her gaze so that she couldn't even observe the other features on his face.

'Please, don't be concerned about the wound,' the man started with a smile, "I know that it shocks everyone, so I usually tell them in advance that it's a war injury. It was caused by a grenade splinter at the time of the first Asian conflict, during the Chinese bombing over Tokyo.'

Angelica tried to pretend that it wasn't there, but the scar was so intrusive that she couldn't take her eyes off it. The man, on the other hand, continued smiling pleasantly; his manners were so engaging that within a few minutes she started to get used to the sight.

'So, Miss Stockwell, you would like to be one of our colleagues?'

'Yes,' nodded Angelica. She wanted to remain cool and controlled. She had tried many different approaches over the past few months: she had been enthusiastic, she had praised clever projects, she had assured everyone that she would be the best person to carry out these projects, she had complimented the interviewer's attire to high heaven, she had probably put herself in a better light than she should have, however, sometimes she had feigned modesty.

This time, she only wanted to be herself. She'd had enough of role-playing. If they were going to hire her, they should take her on as she was.

'Where did you hear about our company?'

Angelica seemed to ponder.

'To be honest, I really don't know if I should tell you . . . I found a letter in my mailbox with your company's name on it. It was addressed to the previous tenant, but he had moved. I confess that I opened it because the man had disappeared into thin air, and hadn't left a forwarding address. The letter said he was being offered a job.'

'Oh . . .' Mr. Yakizima was somewhat surprised, but he soon got over it and his broad smile returned. 'Very interesting story. May I ask the name of this gentleman?'

'Of course: Nick Page. But that's all I know about him. I rented the apartment after he moved away.'

'Ah, yes,' the professor shook his head sadly. 'Unfortunately, we couldn't reach him either, he left in such a hurry. But the gentleman had been with us for an introductory meeting. However, let's be happy that you are here. Some coffee or tea, perhaps?'

'That's very kind of you. Yes, I would enjoy some coffee.' *Good Lord, how I would enjoy it!* she thought to herself. For months, she'd had no money for coffee. The price of coffee had skyrocketed after the collapse of the Asian markets. South America had remained the bastion of coffee production but had really pushed up the price.

Yakizima turned aside to call his secretary on his communicator. Within a few minutes, a steaming black coffee was in front of Angelica. It had been worth opening that letter, if only for this.

'Do you know anything about our company? Are you aware of our trade?'

'Not exactly,' admitted Angelica, 'but the slogan in the letter was very inviting—promising that your firm may be the answer, even to my future. My future could definitely use some answers right now. I have heaps of questions.'

'I understand, Miss Stockwell,' said the man, taking a sip of his coffee. 'What are your academic qualifications?'

'I'm a qualified broker of the highest degree. My business licence is valid on any of the colonies in the Solar System.'

'Really?' Yakizima's squinted his eyes at her. 'Why don't you look for a job in your profession? The stock market will skyrocket again soon. It's always been like that, for the past few centuries—after the fall comes the recovery, slowly but surely.'

'They don't want me,' Angelica admitted. 'They wouldn't want to start anything with someone who had been involved in the placement of Asian stock certificates. They're looking for fresh young workers and, in all probability, ones that haven't been involved in any fiascos.'

'Still, young people are going to commit the same mistakes as their elders, because they don't have experience,' the man leaned forward on the table. He appeared to have taken a liking to the woman's candour.

'It's exactly like you say. We made mistakes and learned from them, but they can only learn from books, what not to do and how not to do it.'

'I think we can now get down to the details, Miss Stockwell.'

Angelica was delighted to hear this. *Honesty above all, honesty always wins out . . .*

'Our firm, Futura Respondis, has been working in the biotechnological industry for twenty years now. We're not a public company, we don't even advertise ourselves in the media, at least we haven't done so until now, but we are omnipresent in many areas. One of our most recent products is a synthetic form of coffee, simply displayed in test tubes. We can even change the taste of the roast. What do you think?' and he raised his cup high. Angelica looked with surprise at the mahogany-coloured, fragrant liquid. The effect on her palate was like that of the finest South American roasted coffee.

'Fantastic,' she said. She had never traded coffee before, but whatever she had to sell made no difference to her. Sell she could, and how.

'We had just started working on a new project at the time of the first Asian conflict. The goal was to try to extend the limits of human productivity. Our aim was to create a tool that would increase human capacity for work many times over, and conversely, reduce leisure time.'

'Interesting,' Angelica nodded approvingly, 'just like a hyped-up, strong black coffee.'

'Something like that,' said Yakizima and transformed one of the walls into a screen. 'The implant consists of a capsule. This capsule actually has to be integrated into a certain section of the brain, where the hormone melatonin is produced, which is responsible for initiating the sleep process. If this is deactivated, or its effect is reduced, we can make the user sleep less or not sleep at all.'

'Wow!' the woman gaped in astonishment. Such a thing could have come in handy lately, during her job search when she had been undertaking odd jobs.

'And what's this about leisure time? Don't the brain and muscles in the body need to take a rest from time to time for certain periods?' she added, since even she could recall it from her biology classes.

'We were able to solve that, too. In fact, the muscles and the brain are at rest, as the capsule takes a considerable weight off both, and this in a waking state. There is no more need for a sleep-type rest.'

'That's fantastic,' Angelica's eyes widened, 'I think I wouldn't mind being a user myself.'

'Oh, no,' said Yakizima, smiling, 'the way I see it, we'd rather count on you to procure new clients.'

'But with this thing, I could do it without taking a rest.'

The man burst out laughing. By now, he appeared to really have taken a liking to the woman's quick mind and style. Angelica held herself back, but what she most wanted to do was to hug the nice little Japanese man, or to dance him around the table. Although, judging from his behaviour towards her and the impression that he gave of being a gentleman, the dance in question could only have been a waltz!

'Miss Stockwell, I see that you're interested in the job and in our products. There's a lot to discuss. First of all, the implant is still in the experimental stage. This means that too often it could result in unstable conditions for the users. This is why we can only introduce the implant into the bodies of test individuals designated and selected by us, that we know are able to endure these tribulations as well as the work overload resulting from the advantages of the implant.'

He paused for a while, only to flash his faultless smile again. 'This is why I wouldn't recommend it in the least to a beautiful and delicate lady such as yourself.'

Angelica didn't speak; she just took a sip of the genuine-tasting, fake coffee. She had to admit, she felt flattered by the compliment. She hadn't received a compliment from anyone in months.
Maybe from now on everything would change.

And change it had—the present reinforced the previously obscure future. She'd had to pass a genetic test before she finally got the job. Futura Respondis had, indeed, been the answer. She had a great job; her income was three times her previous salary. The offices were attractive, her working environment was terrific with a knowledgeable staff, and . . .

. . . and a boss who was an excellent communicator, always up-to-date, and who couldn't be reached for the past three weeks now!

Though now was the time he was really needed. The 'helpline', the telephone emergency line, kept ringing continuously. She had been given instructions exactly thirteen days ago to switch the line to automatic response and not to reply to any calls whatsoever. But she could only listen to it ringing for two days; on the third night, she finally contravened the order.

One of the callers was Alexei, the arms dealer. He said he was beginning to run out of the pills to counteract the side effects. He was calling from some bustling Far-Eastern place; there was a lot of buzzing around him.

'I'd only need a couple of packs,' he said into the communicator, visibly embarrassed by the continuous murmurings of a lady. 'Stop it, will you . . . go ahead, I'll follow you in a minute . . . I'm sorry. So, what I mean is that I'll need two packs, which should help me out for this cycle. Lately, I have been getting these attacks every two months and I only have enough of a supply for about two or three weeks.'

'I understand,' said Angelica patiently. 'Look, I can't send you a doctor now, or the pills, because we're just in the process of replenishing our stock.' She knew this was a huge lie. In the next room there was a stockpile of a yearly dosage, enough for a hundred men. But this is what she had to say. She didn't dare to break that rule.

'Please call me back if things take a turn for the worse, I'll try to do everything to help you . . .' and with that, she disconnected the line.

She started having pangs of conscience. She had seen the implant's side effects on internal films, that was the reason why she had taken the call. She didn't have the heart to let her clients down. She was too good a contact person.

The other caller that night was Noah, that nice kid from New Cloud York, who wanted to break out of the gutter he'd been born in. Without the implant, a coroner would have scraped him up off a back-street alley a long time ago, but with it he soared. Maybe the motivation to say yes was like using drugs. And his history of drug addiction was precisely the reason he had been selected for the experiment, at least that's what Angelica assumed.

'This is filthy shit, Miss Stockwell.' He spoke in a despairing tone of voice. He happened to be in Paris, in the European offices of the Moon Concession Joint Stock Company. 'They said that this would only happen rarely, but now it's happening almost every other month. And sometimes it throws me into an even more rotten state than the most squalid, mangiest drug concoction.'

'How many pills do you still have?' Angelica's mind, meanwhile, was on how she could help the young man.

'Enough for about two, three weeks. But even with it, I feel wretched.'

Angelica took a deep breath and uttered the inevitable phrases. 'Very well, Mr. Simpson, I'd like you to calm down. Please hold out, at the moment we don't have enough pills, as soon as we get a new shipment, I'll mail some to you by express post . . .'

She hung up. She unplugged the communicator and left the Rio office to go home.

More than a week had passed by since she had broken the rules with these two conversations. She had an excuse if, by chance, her boss decided to question her as to why she'd done it: by taking these two calls, she had raised the spirits of her clients. She didn't have the heart to leave them to their fate.

The Rio office had since closed, and she had moved to Ulan Bator, the former capital of Mongolia. The city had been completely transformed under the rule of the New China Empire. The metropolis, that had previously only stretched out on the surface, now reached up towards the sky. Skyscrapers and floating islands could be seen here, as well. On the vast plain, where nomads had once roamed, herding their cattle, horses, and reindeer, new air-conditioned residential districts were now being constructed, to welcome immigrants arriving from China and other countries. The population of the Earth had undergone the umpteenth great migration after the end of the second Asian conflict.

She had just been watching from the twentieth floor office window how the giant floating cranes were lifting up the old gate of the Palace Museum and installing it onto one of the new floating islands built as a Pleasure Park. The Pagoda-style building could no longer be left on the surface, the larger buildings would have crushed it, at least now it would remain for posterity. In the distance, one could see the barren mountains of the Bogdkhan National Park, as well as the lights of the Genghis Khan National Airport, with the surrounding yurt cities and the reflectors of the machines mopping up the last remnants of the slum districts.

Somewhere southeast of there, on the faraway coast of the East-China Sea, the first Chinese Emperor of the second millennium, who had been the one to finance these constructions, was stationed in his new palace, in Suzhou, capital of the Jiangsu Government-General. The New China Empire, with its imperial rule, had been unstoppable; they could administer enormous multitudes and finances and, in turn, the new economy flourished after the war, becoming the prime mover of all changes. The oligarchic governing body not only ruled with an iron fist but had also secured prosperity for its subjects. The average population had slowly grown accustomed to their lives; originally oppressed, they were satisfied with their fate and had become contented citizens who enjoyed life. The losers in the war, the poverty-stricken destitute, had been quickly absorbed by the underworld, the minor groups and the gangs. These groups were controlled by the provincial leaders and, in the end, every thread, every life, converged into the hands of the local oligarchy.

The head of the Ulan Bator governorate, Ulanbataar, controlled every major enterprise and company applying for an operating permit for public work, through his civil servants. Futura Respondis was not a large enough company to have piqued the interest of the higher echelons. For Mr. Yakizima, it was enough to meet with the manager of the city's contracting department to obtain the necessary permits.

Yakizima probably threw in his usual smile, though it was possible that more could have been needed, and he would have had to reach deep into his pocket, too, because Chinese officials disliked Japanese immigrants. But, perhaps because this province had not been a part of former China, and the Mongols had no ancient hostilities against the Japanese Empire—or perhaps because Mr. Yakizima was gallant and generous—the permits were issued within three days and they were able to lease this superb, panoramic office immediately.

"New China is the world's strongest market; this is where we'll carry out our business from now on; for us, the answer for the future is in New China, and the Chinese have their future in us." That was all that was in the letter that she had received from management at the time that the Rio office had shut down. She acknowledged it, packed up, and said good-bye to her friends—a new environment, new friends, and new assignments awaited her.

The one thing she didn't know was what would happen to the old ones. She still kept one eye on the telephone receiver, waiting for it to ring. Even though her former clients didn't know this new number, deep down she hoped they would find her. She felt deeply sorry for them. This was not what she had promised them, when they had accepted to receive the implant—she had told them that they "would receive full support and, in case of any problems, we would send out our medical team. Although we only have a limited supply of pills to alleviate or entirely stop the side effects, production is ongoing."

She hadn't been lying at the time, since she had never imagined that this current situation would ever happen. But now she felt immense sadness and pain. As if she had been cheated, too. She knew that every experiment had its losers, but they didn't deserve this—they had already lived a life full of defeat and suffering.

Whatever fate held in store for them now, they could only rely on themselves.

At that precise moment, the phone rang. *Oh, no . . . not just yet*, she thought. *No, it can't be . . .*

'Hello?' she answered half-heartedly, not even identifying herself.

'Miss Stockwell, this is Yuuna Joshida.' Angelica let out a big sigh at the sound of her secretary's voice. 'I know that we only really started working this week, but I just wanted to remind you that you have a meeting tomorrow with our most recent, and also our first, Chinese client, Mr. Long Xu Wei, at ten in the morning. There will be an additional four clients after him, on the very first day.'

'Yes, Yuuna, thank you, I deeply appreciate your thoroughness and the high quality of your work. I know it isn't easy for you either, as we have only just moved. I won't forget.'

'OK, I'll be there tomorrow as well, very early in the morning, to make sure that everything is working properly for the presentation. The technicians have already installed the projector walls; there won't be any problem with projection.'

'Thanks again. You can go home now.'

'I'll be off and thank you, too. I still have to find the new apartment; I've no idea where everything is.'

'The Centre will help you. I wish you a good night!' Angelica said in parting. She imagined that she would have to grill the Centre, the intelligent control system that came with the apartment, for quite a while as well, until she got the hang of everything.

Tomorrow was a new day, with new challenges. The old clients would survive somehow; she tried to suppress her incessant, accusatory feeling of guilt. That was no longer any of her business.

*

Four days earlier

SpaceJet5 had slowly reached the uppermost point of its parabolic orbit. Its departure from Rio had been delayed because monstrous storm clouds, measuring half a continent, had been raining over the skies of Brazil. The Met Centre had promised that at least a small area of the firmament, the size of a pocket handkerchief, would be made suitable for flying. And so it was: the meteo-robots soon opened up a safe window to the cosmos. These automated, remote-controlled robots dispersed the clouds by forcing out the precipitation with an explosive blast. The airlines offering parabolic flights and private planes would almost immediately fill up and, in fact, even clog up this emergency exit but the Brazilian air traffic controllers managed to keep a tight control of the traffic.

Parabolic flight was still fast and cheap; there was no need for anti-gravitational engines, considerably more expensive in times of war. An aircraft equipped with a new version of the time-honoured drive could reach the opposite side of the Earth within two hours. As a bonus to atmospheric flight, there was also this fantastic view of the Earth and of bustling outer space.

Nujo Yakizima's plane aimed to avoid the afternoon traffic between the Earth and the Moon. He flew it himself; he was a licensed pilot and had served in the Japanese Air Force at the time of the second Asian conflict. Sure, he had been patrolling in a fighter plane then, a somewhat smaller machine than this one. With this new model, the SpaceJet5, it was so much easier to fly that virtually anyone could do it; there was no need for preliminary pilot training. Even though they wouldn't allow anyone off the street to sit in the cockpit, with a week's training—and handing over a few ten million New Dollars—you could own this graceful grandchild of the Learjet of olden times.

'YKA1, this is America Space Control, keep your current altitude. According to the flight schedule, the entry point over Asia should be reached in twenty-seven minutes. Until then, stay on autopilot. Before re-entry, tune in to the Asia Space Control frequency.'

'Thank you, AmSpace Control. Automatic switched on. I'm staying below Lunar traffic, switching to Asia frequency, thank you.'

After switching to autopilot, he got off the seat and floated into the back section. He deliberately avoided activating the artificial gravity; he had grown to enjoy weightlessness. Right now, he wanted to think over the past few weeks' events in weightlessness, something that, in a normal gravitational environment, would perhaps weigh on his mind even more.

He took out a boiling hot tea bag and floated over to the panoramic window. Through the skylight, he saw the ferries and private spaceships pulling away above him to the Moon Colony and back. Those who had found refuge on the Moon when war broke out had only moved back a few years ago, causing a manifold increase in traffic, as compared to previous years. Affluent families and dynasties had left Asia, fleeing from the rattle of guns and the bombs. For the Moon—and of course in the case of Mars and Jupiter's moon, Europa—the war had been beneficial. The amounts that had been lost by the destitute millions had been won by the relatively few wealthy, perhaps a few hundred thousand of them, together with those criminals who always fished in troubled waters. For them, the war had been a blessing.

In the past few weeks, Yakizima had had to make a number of difficult choices concerning the fate of Futura Respondis. He had been preparing for this for months on end, reviewing all the experiments currently running, weighing the positive results—as well as the failures, of course—in order to arrive at a wise decision. Due to the many elements of uncertainty, the experiment and the future could now be in serious danger.

In weighing the results of past years, he came to the conclusion that the scales came down on the positive side. The implant project had started off with animal experiments: the tests, conducted on various different species—mice, dogs, and horses—had culminated in perfect results. The test animals' constitutions had accepted the implants, which were given by means of injections with hypodermic needles, to start with and, compared with their fellow species, they had achieved thirty, sometimes sixty, per cent greater success. The animals had not shown any side effects. They had been manageable all along, not having shown any signs of strange or altered behaviour. The energizing effect of the implant had appeared to be frightening. The trial subjects had lived without sleep for several years.

During the next phase of the animal experiments, the implants' micro container in their bodies had been activated, and they became infected within hours as a result of the pathogens streaming into their system. They would then contaminate subjects they came into contact with, via the lymphatic system and by means of perspiration. If the carrier of the implant or the infected animal wasn't given the antidote to reduce the pathogen into its component parts, then the biological process initiated in their bodies would become irreversible: the immune system turned against the intruder, which in turn, started to reproduce itself by using the immune system, taking possession of and using up all the vital organs, tissues, and cells. Subsequently, the pathogen would break up again and then re-assemble itself once more in the body of the new host.

And so the transfer functioned perfectly. The human phase of the trials could begin.

The implant worked splendidly in twenty-two test subjects. Here, the artificial chip was controlled by the human brain, opening and closing the micro-container with the components of the pathogen. The carriers would therefore be required to take the antidote regularly every other day.

The subjects were living full, active lives, feeling ill to a greater or lesser degree. At first, they reported to a medical group whenever the implant 'misbehaved', which was how they referred to the unstable period when, in spite of the capsule's sealed state, leakages occurred. This was what they had installed the emergency telephone line for. The participants in the trial would order the antidote or ask for urgent medical assistance. They had a similar aircraft to this jet, in the event that they had to reach someone at the other end of the world quickly, at short notice.

Such a rescue operation was only possible if the trial subject didn't leave for an adventure trip to the Amazon, as Nick Page had done, into whose apartment Miss Stockwell had subsequently moved. They had searched for him for twelve days in the depths of the jungle but they had found neither him nor his tour guide. In all probability, it was the infection that had finished them off because, if a wild beast had attacked them, they would have found their remains by following their biochip's GPS tracker. The pathogen had devoured them from the inside, even to the extent of consuming their biochips.

Page hadn't asked permission before making the trip. He was a druggie from Rio, with whom Yakizima had come to an agreement, in spite of being assailed by doubts at the time. He was an unruly guy with a mind of his own, full of wild dreams, just like every drug recidivist. He was unmanageable despite the fact that he had been sent to the usual rehab. Futura had paid for four months in one of the best European institutions; at the end of it, he had come out totally clean. At least that's what had been presumed. He had a perfect opportunity to start a normal life. At the very beginning, he had gone into a new venture with tripled energy: he had set up a travel agency. He organised adventure tours, he launched tropospheric bungee jumping—from a dope addict, he had turned into an active and determined individual.

But later he started doing drugs again, the proof of this was that the three-month supply of antidote was finished within one week. He became sick more often, so he needed the antidote much more frequently.

The implant, in itself, was a revolutionary mechanism, built into the body and controlled by the brain. The mechanism serviced and provided the brain with energy, which in turn operated the capsule: they become mutual symbiotes—theirs was a total harmony. This interdependence, however, couldn't be violated with impunity.

If it happened that someone thumbed his nose at the rules, used alcohol or drugs, took other illicit substances, it resulted in sweating, vomiting, and diarrhoea. In extreme cases, as must have been true with Nick Page, the situation could just as well have turned fatal. One step before the end, only a larger dose of antidote or a specially equipped medical unit could have helped. The implant was a complex system that transformed into a sustainable energy-supply within weeks. If anyone still shot himself over and above it, it could easily cost him his life.

Yakizima knew that, in Page, he had chosen a man who was not fully suitable for the job, but he had wanted to test the implant in the most extreme conditions as well.

The third phase of the trials on humans followed immediately after the disastrously unsuccessful case. The goal was to control the activities of the pathogen concealed in the implant and thus to be able to influence the course of the infection itself.

The two new clients, Noah Simpson, the former small-time criminal, and Alexei Sverlov, son of the arms dealer executed by the Chinese Mafia, seemed to be perfect subjects. They had become obedient and purposeful men. They didn't have to be reminded: if they had to travel somewhere, or wanted to leave the area designated for the trial, they would report and check in according to the prescribed orderly procedures.

Until two weeks ago . . .

At that time, both had left the designated area without reporting and checking in.

By doing so, they had caused considerable upheaval. Alexei had probably gone to arrange an arms deal—according to the GPS data—in a Far-Eastern port occupied by New China and had turned up recently in Africa. Most importantly, he was still alive, if they could trust the data beamed onto the satellite from his biochip.

Mr. Simpson posed the bigger problem. Firstly, he had travelled overseas and following that, he had made an even greater leap: he had left the Earth. According to his contractual undertaking, he was not allowed to leave the Mother Colony. Yakizima nevertheless knew that Noah had never bothered to read the contract. In fact, he was also certain that when this travel restriction had been mentioned to Noah, he had acted as if he had understood everything perfectly. But in his imagination, he was already somewhere else.

During the past three weeks, both had called the emergency line practically non-stop. Most likely they were getting short of the pills or had got hold of drugs or alcohol, the effects of which could only be counteracted by greater doses of the pills.

Their excesses escalated the risks of contamination to a considerable degree.

He ordered Miss Stockwell not to answer the calls because there had been an obvious contractual violation. He knew that she wouldn't be able to resist picking up the phone, he already knew Angelica very well. In the end, she had transgressed the order, as expected—according to the internal listening devices on the line—but she had remained loyal: she had only encouraged them. She hadn't sent a doctor or the pills.

Both trial subjects had been provided with pills for at least two to three weeks. How long this supply would last depended on how many times they would contravene the rules. In the ideal—improbably optimistic—case, if they didn't take anything to excess, then the prospect of contaminating anyone was small.

What a bizarre paradox it is . . . considering that the implant itself incites one to abnormally exaggerate everything, we request moderation from them, thought Yakizima worriedly to himself.

But they're not soldiers, they're civilians. We can't demand too much of them.

And now the risk was enormous, almost unbearably so, thanks to Mr. Noah Simpson, who had taken the pathogen off the Earth.

Yakizima was surprised at his own naivety: How could he have imagined that this wouldn't happen again, especially after the incident with the previous trial subject, Page?!

The trial subjects had to be chosen more carefully. There would be no more room for blunders . . .

If the two men returned, the implants would have to be removed from both and their contracts terminated. Disobedience didn't serve anyone's future. It only destroyed.

He didn't call Miss Stockwell to task for breaking the rules, but he had liquidated the Rio office immediately. He didn't want to leave any tracks. It had been an economical office on a small island, with a staff of five, so it had been easy to relocate it to Ulan Bator.

Actually, this entire imbroglio had effectively resulted in some good, as they could now take the long-planned big step—seemingly impossible and far-fetched for a long time—whereby they could penetrate the New China Empire. *Even misfortune can be used to your advantage,* the ancient Japanese proverb sprang to Nujo's mind.

The final outcome would be positive, and all the bad things would slowly be left behind. Like a river, breaking over the rocks and hitting snags along its way down but in the end reaching the sea just the same—bringing many tons of silt along with it, of course. *The silt is deposited, the water rushes on.*

Slowly, the spatial phase of the parabolic orbit came to an end. The Earth below appeared to have turned, saving flight time and shortening the eight-hour flight by conventional plane. According to the onboard timepiece, he had seven minutes left of his trip into the limits between space and the exosphere, the uppermost layer of the atmosphere; he had to prepare for re-entry.

Using the handholds, he propelled his way back to the cockpit and strapped himself into his seat. He attached the communicator to his ears and switched over to the frequency of the Asia Space Control Centre. At that precise moment, the small lamp flashed on the dashboard panel, signalling an incoming call. There was still just enough time left to deal with a short call. If they were looking for him while in transit, it could be important.

'Yakizima here, go ahead.'

'This is Arai Kazuki.'

'Greetings, *Koutaishi-denka*[1] Arai.' Yakizima's voice was smooth and polite.

'Professor Yakizima, we have received your most recent report. We would like to express our concern with the developments.' The voice at the other end of the line was calm, in total contrast to the contents of the sentence. This seemed to be a courteous call but one calling for accountability.

'I can assure Your Highness, that everything is running its proper course.' Yakizima even inclined his head respectfully whilst speaking, as if he were actually standing before the high-ranking official.

'You know, Professor Yakizima, we in the Court don't know much about biology and biochemistry, but leaving trial subjects on their own entails immeasurable risks. It could undermine the entire project and the work of many long years. Not to mention the dangers of an interplanetary infection.'

'That's a very wise and precise observation, however modest Your Highness tries to remain.' Yakizima's words were ruled by humility, but the humility contained no exaggeration. It was deeply felt and came from the heart.

'Your Highness must surely be well aware that the basis of the latest developments will be how we can stop the spread of the infection in the event of any danger, by means of signals sent by radio frequency waves,' said Yakizima. 'However, we can only employ this method in extreme cases because the signal is omnipotent, that is to say, it's effective in every direction. In the course of our experiments so far, we have been

---

1   Crown Prince

unable to concentrate the signals on a selected area. With an incorrect command, we could even jeopardize the pathogens stored inside the implants. Consequently, it could happen that we are no longer able to keep the carrier of the implant serving us. The implant becomes dead in his body. He will not be of any further use for controlled contamination or for the transmission of the pathogens.'

There was silence at the other end of the line. The imperial prince took several long seconds to reflect.

'My father, *Tennouheika*[2] Arai Noburu, expressed his concern about the present state of the project. I also find it difficult to think positively with regard to the future.'

'Your Highness need not to be worried. With the emission of the aforementioned radio signal, the project can be permanently stopped at any moment. You must have faith in the future, as you have done so far. Your support and continuous trust has always meant a lot to us.'

'I trust you, too, Professor Yakizima. Don't let me down!'

'I won't, Your Imperial Highness, this I can certainly promise you,' said Yakizima. 'I was honoured with distinction by His Highness the Emperor Arai Shinobu, your grandfather, for my services in the course of the second Asian conflict: I'm obligated to his memory and his name.'

'I am pleased with our conversation, Professor Yakizima. I can now convey reassuring news to my father.'

Prince Arai Kazuki, the firstborn son to the Japanese Emperor and heir to the throne, disconnected the line.

Yakizima took a deep breath and blew it slowly out of his lungs. He had been worried about this conversation, and the fact that the Imperial Court would terminate the experiments once and for all. He feared for his efforts of the past twenty years, in which was also invested the work of many like-minded professionals.

'YKA1, this is Asia Space Control, a minute and a half to entry. Heading 113, number two glide path authorized; Genghis Khan International Airport is ready to welcome you. Leave it on autopilot, it will complete the approach on your behalf. Have a safe landing.'

The flight controller's words jolted the professor back into the present.

---

2   Literally *His Majesty the Heavenly Sovereign*. The emperor.

'Roger, thank you, and good-bye.'

The autopilot aligned the craft onto the glide path, and slowly the cold darkness of space receded behind him. Next to the aircraft, scraps of ionising plasma matter danced all around, painting everything in the cabin red.

During descent, he thought about the two deserters . . .

. . . that they would remain sober and judicious, and that they would return to him before they ran out of the antidote . . .

. . . and that they would not cause any problems, either on the Mars Colony, or in Africa . . .

. . . and that the project would continue according to plan . . .

Because, should anything go wrong, Emperor Noburu would give the self-destruction order. Now, at the very moment when they were standing before the gate of success.

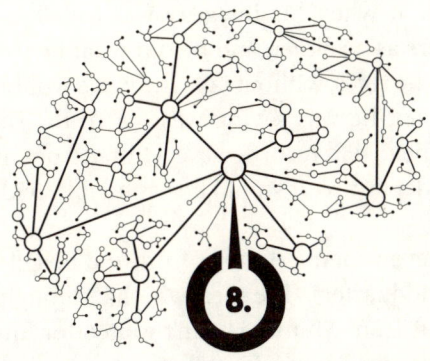

8.

Rusti Kadam, the officer back from the Coast Guard mission, hadn't been in the observation room for long; he had perhaps spent a mere three hours there in all, tests included. Come what may, they wanted to see if he had any problems caused by the muck that the dead man had sprinkled all over him.

To his surprise—and to the satisfaction of his doctors—they couldn't find anything abnormal, the sample proving to be a totally clean human salivary gland secretion. Although the colour was somewhat different from normal, it didn't contain any virus or other microorganisms apart from the usual bacteria occurring in the mouth.

Despite the good result, Rusti wasn't at ease. How could he be, since, when he was finally able to leave the smugglers' ship after a lengthy wait, following the arrival of the Coast Guard amphibian, the Malaysian once again looked as if he had been dead for days. The crew of the patrol boat had found him tied up to the banister, exactly as Rusti had left him: the soldiers that had come on board had lifted the corpse of a man with a blown-open skull onto the hovercraft. Now Rusti's superiors were demanding an explanation from him.

So, after discharge from the hospital, he was going to have to go and face an interrogation.

He didn't like it when his integrity was called into question. He carried out orders as a soldier, and he did what he was told to do. He always followed the rules, without fail. The video would surely convince everyone that what he was saying was the truth. The small camera mounted on his head had recorded everything, from his descent down the cable, to his departure. It would be irrefutable evidence.

There were seven metro stations from the hospital to the Indian Coast Guard headquarters. The men who had brought him in on the service hovercraft from Mumbai hadn't waited for him because Rusti himself had sent them home. His colleagues were tired and this thing looked like it could end up being a lengthy business and, in any case, they would be meeting up again tomorrow during the night shift. Only if the examination ended in a satisfactory manner, of course, and if they didn't find some crazy reason for suspending him.

He had seen enough crazy things occurring over the past few years. Why shouldn't the next one happen to him?

Delhi greeted him with bright, midday sunshine and close to 40°C, when he stepped out onto the open street. Even in short sleeves, he was sweating profusely. He was used to hot temperatures, but he was not usually so exhausted—it was probably the examinations that had worn him out and the fact that he had missed his usual four-hour morning rest. He could recuperate completely in four hours and wake up refreshed. Without it, he was listless and depressed, as he was now.

It may well have been fatigue but, all the same, there was something unnatural in the extent to which he was sweating, he reflected, and took out a handkerchief to wipe his forehead.

The metro departed from the third level. In the course of past centuries, the 'metro' name had stuck to the robot-driven hover-train. Like its predecessor, it still slipped under the earth in places, especially in the northern highlands, near the source of the Ganges.

New Delhi had become one of the megalopolises of the East during the middle of the third millennium. It straddled the Ganges in the north, reaching the southern slopes of the Himalayas, and, in the south, it had swallowed up the former cities of Agra and Jaipur, tearing off chunks of Uttar Pradesh and the Haryanan regency, thus transforming itself into a new and large protectorate—The Regency of the Eternal Light. It got its name by becoming the brightest jewel in Asia viewed from space, outshining all other eastern cities. Even in the New China Empire, it had no rival.

Over thirty years ago, the expanding metropolis had been smashed to pieces by the bombardments during the time of the first Asian conflict. Even now, the rubble was still visible, especially in the northern regions. After the inability of the New China oligarchy to cope with India's strength, New China quickly signed a peace treaty and turned towards the south, annexing each formerly independent state: Myanmar, Cambodia, Thailand, and Vietnam.

The exploding of the atomic bomb in the Bay of Bengal had put an end to the invasion. India, as a great nuclear power, primed its rockets, but never got around to firing them—a quick peace treaty put an end to the conflict that had lasted for seven years.

In the second Asian conflict, New China had simply evaded its greatest Eastern rival. The oligarchy had concluded a non-aggression pact with the Indian government, meanwhile advancing further into the south, occupying Malaysia, Singapore, Indonesia, and the Philippine Islands. They surrounded Japan, but the hitherto neutral Europe and America had formed an alliance with Japan and India, breaking the blockade. In response, the New China Emperor's army had landed on the shores of Western Australia, which was where Rusti had fought in the local allied forces with his men.

And so, New Delhi had escaped, without any further destruction. It was the soaring space industry that had pulled India out of the doldrums caused by the dying economy: all of a sudden, orders for electronic and space engineering techniques arrived in increasing numbers from the Colonies. The New European Confederation (the successor of the European Union, a much looser federation of states), as well as the North American Union (which comprised the former United States of America, Mexico, and Canada), had ordered the latest equipment and instruments from India, in an effort to stimulate the Asian market. Not long afterwards, the first Indian Space Consortium was formed, building the Delta District on the Moon Colony and thus entering the ranks of those states that had their own individual, self-built settlements on the colonies. India had never before seen such unexpected development.

For Rusti, this was not only history, but a part of his life: he had fought in a good number of battles and, having been injured, he had felt firsthand just how much that long lost-word *freedom* really meant. He had been spending less and less time reliving the battles and, thank goodness, he didn't come too often to this megalopolis, which bore most of the scars—and memories—of old battles.

He was about to change onto the next moving walkway in order to reach the third level, but he became aware of a big commotion in front of one of the stores. Everyone had been watching the space projectors and viewing screens. People slowed down or stopped in front of the store so that, in the end, the crowd blocked the traffic. A man in uniform tried to get the people to move on, but then he too became rooted to the spot in front of the newscast.

Rusti stepped back from the walkway. He was curious to see what was attracting the gaping crowd. He had more than two hours in which to make the short distance to the Centre; he wouldn't be late.

On the split screens, seven channels were broadcasting the news. Actually, they were all talking about the same subject: connection with the Mars Colony had been broken off that morning.

'Mars is not responding! Mars is silent!' These and similar captions were running along the bottom of the screen, while pundits and the reporters questioning them were conjecturing about what could have happened.

In one of the programs they were just saying that, 'in all probability, something terribly serious must have occurred on the Mars New Home Colony. They are now implementing the protocol that had been worked out in the event of disaster.' The man who had formulated this opinion was an independent risk analyst and, according to him, 'they will lift the embargo within a few days and then we shall know everything. This is only a precautionary measure, which they generally implement for just a short time.'

In the other program, they were stiffer in their wording. 'I don't think that we should be apprehensive but, in any case, one would expect someone responsible for emergency situations in the United Colony Council to stand up and finally tell us what is happening,' protested an expert dealing with UCC matters.

'I don't know what's happening with my grandchildren,' the worried face of an elderly man appeared; he had been caught by the reporter at a Mumbai shopping centre to speak into the microphone. 'It's worrying enough that they aren't telling us anything. Surely someone could finally give us some information of what has happened. I've already fought through two big wars in this millennium, I've seen enough horrifying things. Of course, I don't mean to say that's what's happened now, too, or that a war-like conflict has developed, but, whatever it is, I'd like to know.'

'My husband is on his way home, he's been working on a construction job for more than two years,' a middle-aged woman cried. 'He was already sitting on the homebound ship, and we were just in the middle of talking when the line was cut. It's terrible . . .' she sobbed, taking out a hankie, 'you know, just like when a plane crashes and the line goes dead . . . oh, dear, I can't believe it.'

Gloom also spread through the crowd watching the rotating pictures. No one said a word; some of them reached for their communicators, perhaps just remembering an acquaintance living on Mars, a few were shaking their heads in disbelief.

Rusti was also taken aback by the news, although the situation wasn't new to him. In times of war there were often communication blackouts, first of all because of the enemy—since they were also watching the same broadcasts, they could easily obtain information that way without having to send reconnaissance planes to enemy territories. That's why he understood it only too well and felt that, if broadcasting suddenly stopped, it could only be for a serious reason. There were many forms of communication nowadays, the Earth or the Colonies could be reached by any number of means: there was the SystemNet, covering the entire Solar System, a wireless computer system free of charge, the long-wave communication network, and the fleets of mail and supply vessels . . .

Information can't simply stop just like that. Someone is blocking it intentionally.

'Believe us, we are doing everything to restore the channels of communication,' said the man who, according to the captions, was the director of the Mother Colony Special Incidents Unit on Earth. 'I don't believe that the situation will last for much longer, perhaps a day or two and you will know everything. I would ask everyone not to conclude and fabricate theories, and this applies even more to you, the sources responsible for information.'

At this point, the reporter asked her colleague to play a video that had been taped that morning. A blurred picture appeared in the upper right corner of the screen, clear in some parts, more visible in other parts. At the dark end of a tunnel, soldiers in uniform stood holding primed energy weapons. They were turning back vehicles—trucks and hovercars.

'Where do you think we got these shots?' the woman reporter asked, without really expecting an answer. 'They were beamed to us from the Old Colony on Mars, Chinatown, by using an old transmitting system believed to have been obsolete for two hundred years, bypassing the blocked information system. According to the narrator's text, the man who took the shot had been proceeding from the Old Colony to the Mars New Home Colony but the tunnel was blockaded by armed soldiers. What do you think of this? What could have happened? A terrorist attack? Accident? Natural disaster?'

The director became visibly agitated.

'You see, this is exactly what I was talking about,' vexed, he drew a deep breath but he didn't want to shout at the woman. 'About your responsibility. About the media's responsibility. This thing doesn't mean anything. It could be simply that there was an accident in the tunnel. How do you know that this shot is genuine and credible?'

The woman didn't appear to be convinced by the answers, and she didn't care about the retort flung back at her either.

'An accident in the tunnel? And do you think they would close down the entire telecommunication system because of it? Please, sir, don't leave, sir . . .'

The man disappeared from the screen and was lost to view in the thick of the reporters chasing him.

By now Rusti knew for sure that there was trouble on Mars. The official's confusion was a dead giveaway.

He was about to leave, to extricate himself from the crowd, but he felt dizzy. He grabbed hold of a well-dressed young man's shoulder.

'Whoa, easy, my friend,' said the man, catching him quickly, before he could lose his balance completely. 'It's the heat, isn't it? You're not very used to it . . .'

'No,' Rusti shook his head, 'I'm used to it. But I've been on night shift, and I couldn't get any rest. I'm exhausted.'

He was sweating terribly. The man gave him a handkerchief to wipe his forehead. Rusti thanked him and gave it back. The man wiped his hands in it.

'You see, I'm sweating too, despite having lived in the tropics for years. It's because of the humidity. Take care of yourself, get some rest somewhere!'

'Right,' Rusti finally nodded and started walking toward the moving walkway. Leaning against the handrail, he climbed to the third floor, up to the metro platform.

His eyes were burning, he felt as if they were protruding two or three centimetres out of their sockets, and he was shedding tears continuously. As if all the taps in his system had been opened up at the same time. To top it all, he had to go for a pee and his bladder was hurting, probably due to the drugs he had been given that morning. If he didn't go now, before the metro set off, he wouldn't last until the

Centre. He spotted the sign for a men's washroom not far from the platform.

The door was hard to open, and his hands were slippery with sweat. On his way in, he stumbled into a youth who looked at him indignantly. The fellow was irritated because their collision had left a big sweat spot on his polo shirt.

The light flickered in the washroom. According to a placard, the power supply was intermittent due to renovation work.

He pushed open one of the lavatory doors. The fans and the pumps were out of order, and—in his unsteady condition—his urine didn't all land in the toilet but also dripped profusely onto the floor, where it would later stick onto the shoes of others, who would then drag it along with them.

The colour of the urine was quite dark and bizarre; he'd never seen it like that. Perhaps he'd caught a cold overnight, there couldn't be any other reason, he thought, since he hadn't caught anything from the Malaysian; he'd been assured of that this morning.

Finally, he washed his face and his hair, to freshen himself up. As he shook his head, millions of tiny droplets of water rained down onto the washstand. Without power for the dryer and the disinfecting machine, he was unable to clean the counter and dry the drops.

Looking in the mirror, he saw that his eyes were like two cherry tomatoes: they were completely reddened. They weren't even red, but yellowish-brown, burning like mad. Later, he noticed that the yellowish-brown spots were actually high viscosity teardrops, hiding the whites of his eyes. They stuck to his hand, giving him the impression of rubbing rust-filled water.

He stepped back out into the heat and he wasn't so dizzy anymore. The sweating had decreased, too.

I could still turn around and go back to the hospital. It would only take five minutes to walk back, and I could have myself checked out by one of the doctors . . . but no, better not. Everything will be alright. It's been a rotten night; I'm just tired.

Meanwhile, the metro going towards the Centre had just pulled in. Seven stops in the air-conditioned cabin would surely do him good.

The door opened before him, and a huge flood of people spilled out. He found his way into the cabin on the side of the doorway while the huge flood of people spilled out in the middle .

He sank into a seat. A mother with a tot sat beside him. The child, about three years old, was mesmerized by the small badge paraded on Rusti's breast pocket. It represented the crest and the copters of the Coast Guard. He wore one with all his clothes, he had quite a few at home, in a drawer. He smiled at the boy and unclipped the pin. The child's eyes widened as Rusti placed it in his little hand. His brown face flashed a smile as he sheepishly hid under his mother's arm.

'Say thank you to the nice man,' said the young mother.

'You're welcome, little man,' said Rusti as he stroked the boy's black hair. He remembered how horrible he must look, so he tried to look at the world through as small a slit as possible, that way perhaps no one else would see his eyes.

'Don't put it in your mouth!' the mother admonished the boy, who, like every normal child, wanted to taste the pin. 'Give it to me, I'll pin it on your shirt, here,' she added, wiping the crest with her hand. 'There, now you're one of the Coast Guard soldiers too!'

A happy smile crossed the little boy's face. He looked up proudly at Rusti, who was beginning to forget about his annoyances. The thermal balance of his system slowly returned to normal, the sweating stopped completely. His eyes weren't burning so much anymore; occasionally, he squeezed out a brownish teardrop. Within five minutes, he was his old self; his strength had come back too. Whatever had caused this earlier attack, his strong powerful constitution, worthy of a soldier, had overcome it within twenty minutes.

The metro pulled away at high speed from the hospital complex's trapezoidal-shaped block and submerged itself into the jungle of Delhi's skyscrapers. With steep turns, but still holding securely, the automatic vehicle sped along: two, three, four stops and he was already in another environment, a residential district, interspersed with low buildings. In the distance, the office-island floating above the city was already visible; that's where the building in which the Central Military Headquarters, controlling the Coast Guard, was housed.

He gathered his thoughts together, organizing everything in chronological order. He became so deeply engrossed, that he hadn't even noticed that his little friend had his head in his lap and had fallen asleep. His mother picked him up and put him on her shoulder, smiling at Rusti as he stepped to the door.

He pushed the button to get off and grabbed the handhold.

With his last beads of sweat, he unknowingly left behind hundreds of billions of tiny, live mechanical components that had broken loose from his body.

*

On the border of the East-African Republic, somewhere deep in the jungle...

Alex Sverlov ordered his men to set up camp. It must have been around two in the morning, at least that's what he reckoned, because his watch had given up the ghost from the salty seawater, it had stayed stuck on Far-Eastern time. The communicator was whimpering in the depth of the tent, in the throes of some sort of self-maintenance program. He was too lazy to get up and fetch it.

He was totally satisfied with the mercenaries. They were quiet, did their job without a word, like true professionals. If only he had men like these back home in Russia. Even though, in Moscow, he paid his Russian men much more than the local wages here, he used to have constant arguments with them. Although, truth be told, they couldn't keep up with his pace. Unlike him, they still had to sleep sometime.

In spite of the fact that they were far from civilization, the jungle was just as noisy as a big city. The leftover menagerie of animals that had been squeezed into the centre of Africa, were all hooting, squealing, growling, and hissing around them.

The image of Africa had changed significantly in the last two wars. Before the two Asian conflicts, major investments had been flooding into the states lying in Africa's coastal regions. The East-African

Republic, the South-Western African Union (the grouping of former small states—starting in the north with Senegal, Guinea, the Ivory Coast, all the way down to the south, including Namibia and Botswana) and the strong Central-African states that had remained independent, such as the Congo, South Africa, and Chad, had all experienced an equally strong economic boom. The East African states joined the Arab Fusion, and with the help of the more than one-hundred-and-seventy-year-old economic superiority, broke off from the African economic block, joining the near-East. Thus, Africa's successor states had to secede from the global stage and go onto the public economic system scene. Because of the population explosion, coupled with the increasing number of capital investments, the cities spread inland from the coast, towards the hinterland. Alex could still clearly remember his father speaking about those times, when life in Africa was still liveable and enjoyable. The old man, when he was young, had been in business, dealing with lawful products such as energy units and fusion foundries and had travelled a lot in the regions that were now falling into decay.

The first Asian conflict had not touched the continent geographically, but had done so all the more socially: the entire world had been recruiting mercenaries from here. The workforce had migrated into private armies, development had stopped, and the centre of Africa once again sunk back into the pit out of which it had started to climb over the past few years: the territories had become lands open to exploitation by militant tribes and armed groups.

The states, that is to say, the East-African Republic as well as South Africa, attempted to eradicate the criminal gangs, with very little success. To foreigners, the centre of Africa became a veritable hideout. The territory resembled a cage full of booby traps. Well-armed units arrived with copters and group-transport machines, but they barely had time to land; those hiding in the jungle had been expecting them with heat-seeking missiles and shield-destroying energy weapons. These were obtained on the black market from dealers like Alex. It was a good world for travelling arms dealers: they arrived with full trucks and containers and went home with full pockets.

The powerful seek-and-destroy invasion that had been planned quickly ran out of steam because both East-Africa, as well as South Africa, withdrew their troops—the military operation, labelled "African Freedom" drifted along for all of three years, in between the two Asian conflicts, and had entailed great losses. It developed into trench warfare. The allied, state troops fell into ambushes in the unfamiliar jungles. Surrounded units that could not receive support from the retreating squads, held on for months; eventually—exhausted, short of ammunition and provisions—they had surrendered. The resistance units, based on loose, tribal alliances, did what they usually did at times like these: they had demanded ransom for the soldiers, at least of those for whom the family could afford to pay. The others were simply slaughtered.

The obvious question made Alex reflect: what had brought him here? To these cruel warlords? What could they offer that other, weapon-hungry clients could not offer?

Perhaps the satisfaction that, with the weapons bought from him, they would ransack the ships of the New China Empire on the Indian Ocean. New China crew would be taken captive, and they would demand ransom from the New China oligarchy. And if it was not paid, they would shoot the hostages like dogs ... like the Chinese arms mafia had done to his father, at the time.

He felt that, somehow, he would have to overcome this. The anger and rage that had settled in the place of forgiveness had burnt deeply into him; it was festering in his mind like corrosive acid, sometimes causing him literal pain.

When would it end?

He comforted himself by thinking that Africa was dead anyway. He couldn't cause any further deaths with his weapons, as that which is dead cannot die again.

The world of arms is not a world of equals: it is weighted on the side of the strong—the strong press the weapons into the hands of the weak, to go off and die with them. . . .

The problem was that death was exported; they took it far away. Every single bullet, energy recharge packs, was a deadly new message manufactured by Alex, irrespective of who the deliveryman was.

He had become Death's agent. His father's legacy...

But the conflicts in which these weapons were used, had not been caused by him—that wasn't his problem.

Not to think, not to worry, just to rest for a little while...

Oh, dear, if I could only sleep for an hour...

It was strange, this breakaway thought about sleep. In the past, he had wanted nothing more than the continuous whirl and activity, he wanted to feel that he was living his life at breakneck speed... now he had become its slave.

He had taken three-and-a-half weeks' supply of the pills with him, to Malaysia, but Okan's men had taken them away. Then they had plied him with that foul-tasting liquor, which had made him feel even worse. But they had all croaked from some poison: yet he had lived, and what's more, had managed it without medication.

He had tried to order medication from Port Qoriga but there had been no reply on the Futura Respondis Rio number. It seemed that his future was not replying, as if it had been discouraged, just like him. Still, the woman, Angelica, had been such a pleasant and kind figure in this muddled-up future. He was almost sure that she had been instructed not to answer the phone.

He called his brother in Moscow, who found three boxes of the antidote in his apartment, about a two-week dose. He mailed it; it could arrive in Qoriga any day now. He would send someone to pick it up because he had already made up his mind not to renounce the trip just to pander to this damned implant.

There were one and a half tons of old weapons lying in one of the North African warehouses, left over from the second Asian conflict, still in serviceable condition. In any case, he wanted to sell them. And he still had a couple of new sharpshooter weapons with him, as a sample.

Otherwise, since his arrival in Malaysia, he had been trying to figure out how to survive the loathsome—so-called active—periods of the implant, that were appearing every other day, without taking the medication. He realised that there was only one possible way to do so: by knocking himself out with a large quantity of alcohol. The same thing had happened in the Malaysian camp; he had been drinking heavily, eating a lot of rubbish. He had knocked himself out and had regained consciousness in the water. He couldn't remember anything, absolutely nothing, but he had survived the adventure.

Now he was experimenting with the same thing again. He would sit down on a collapsible chair and stare at the stars, a keg of beer, two bottles of vodka, and three cigars beside him. If everything worked out, by morning he would faint again, and he would be able to avoid that horrible vomiting episode. That's what he hated the most. He would then be left in peace for the next two days.

Those rotten creeps at Futura, he thought to himself. To use them as experimental mice and then, after obtaining the results, to abandon everyone. No question, that was the objective. The truth was, however, that no one had forced them, no one had held a gun to his head, he had said yes of his own volition. And then there had been all those undeniable advantages, to which anyone would have said yes—but these, unfortunately, could only be enjoyed by the living.

He thought about the fate of that extreme sportsman, whose film had been shown at his first Futura interview. He had lived life to the hilt, a truly energetic young man, although it was obvious that he had used drugs before. Anyone who had moved in those circles could pinpoint them, from even just a few frames. Not even the implant could change a drug addict's compulsive movements.

It could be that the guy had blown his mind with drugs because the constant buzz afforded by the implant had not been enough for him. Or, perhaps he hadn't taken the pills on a long trip and had finally fallen asleep forever. *Just like me, soon,* he thought, as he took a big drag of his cigar.

What wouldn't he give for a fifteen-minute, short snooze! Even without dreams, just like that, he wouldn't care; he would have jumped at the chance.

Just to escape from the world for a short while.

He was at the end of his first bottle of vodka, mixed with two beers, but was still feeling perfectly well. He had no idea how this 'knockout' would come together again. No nausea, no retching, no greenish gunge either. If the plan didn't work, he would be vomiting for two days and, on top of that, it would be exactly at the time when they would be reaching the rebels' camp. Shitty deal. Then the same thing would happen as it had at Okan's Malaysian camp. However, because he had taken care of his own safety, this lot here wouldn't be able to finish him off and abandon him. He couldn't even understand how he'd had the courage to venture into Okan's camp by himself.

It was the implant; it gave the bearer a sense of indestructibility by taking control of his hormones and, with it, his sense of fear.

The only positive thing he could see in this desperate situation was that the mercenary guys were very well organized. They had built the camp in a semicircular shape, backed against a rock. They had posted fully armed guards at all four points of the compass, leaving nothing to chance. They would relieve each other at fixed intervals, smoothly, in a professional manner. Within the camp's hundred-and-twenty-metre perimeter, they had installed sensors. They were well worth what they cost; every single cent had been well spent.

Their commander, elected by themselves, was a mercenary by the name of Bianco. Born in South Africa, of Italian descent, the two-metres-tall fellow had a fairly good sense of humour. They had been sitting together in the cabin of his lead caterpillar for the past three days, that's how they'd had the time to get to know each other. He was a pleasant conversationalist, even allowing for the inhuman fact that his hand never trembled on the trigger—this was how he put it. One could well believe him, though; the deep scar on the right-hand side of his face was living proof. He was one of the most ideal customers that an arms dealer could wish for.

His hard, Italian profile, which looked like a rough pencil sketch, was recognizable, even in this pale moonlight. He walked up to Alex with an energy gun on his shoulder.

'What are you doing, boss?' His accent was that of a South African Boer, it sounded strange coming from the mouth of a descendant of Italian stock.

'What am I doing, my friend? I'm about to prevent big trouble.'

'Well, well, what kind of trouble? A love affair?'

'Not exactly. Rather, something of which I can't speak, as much as I'd like to.'

Bianco nodded slowly and took a puff of his cigarette. 'Is it something to do with insomnia?'

Alex was taken aback by the man's question. He had done everything in the preceding days and nights to make it look as if he slept splendidly. He had put up his tent, made his bed, lain down, but had gazed wide-eyed at the tent cloth until morning.

'The breathing of someone who is properly asleep is totally different from the way you were breathing in and out. Deeper and longer,' he added, in reply to Alex's inquiring look.

'I passed by your tent several times last night, when I was on duty. It was obvious to me that you weren't sleeping.'

Alex was impressed by the man's powers of observation.

'You sure know your business, my friend,' said Alex, snapping his fingers in acknowledgement. 'Now I understand why you are the leader of the mercenaries.'

'And you sure are a strange bird,' smiled the beefy mercenary. 'I haven't seen anyone like you. You never rest, you sleep little or not at all...'

'That's what I want right now!' said Alex and raised the bottle toward the soldier, 'Let's drink to sleep!'

'As you wish, boss,' blinked Bianco, the better to see Alex's face, 'but be prepared; as soon as the sun rises, we enter tribal territory. By tomorrow we shall have crossed the remains of Lake Victoria, over the Victoria Arch, and from then on we shall be in Silaha territory. If you're going to feel sick there, and you're not going to be at full strength, we may have serious problems.'

Alex knew that the mercenary was right. The entire arms-sale project would end up in a bloodbath, if something didn't turn out as planned. If he happened to feel like death, right at that time, like he usually did every other day . . . and this was due to be one of those days, but it didn't want to start. The alcohol may have upset everything, perhaps he had started to drink too soon.

It would be great if that parcel arrived from Moscow.

And it would be great, as well, if that lousy lot at Futura would finally pick up the phone.

Bianco's figure was slowly swallowed up in the darkness, as he walked towards the farthest lookout, to relieve his partner. Strange, how clearly this man could see everything.

Alex had never imagined how obvious it might be from the outside that he was using an implant. There was never a problem about it with screening devices—at airports they always asked him to confirm what type of implant he was wearing in addition to the biometric and localization chip. "Implant E4—epilepsy chip—FutRes" that's what was marked on the document.

A perfect pseudonym for such an encapsulated monster that cannot be knocked out, not even with alcohol.

Bastard Futura Respondis . . .

But that woman, Miss Stockwell—she sure was pretty . . . and it would be great to finally dream about her.

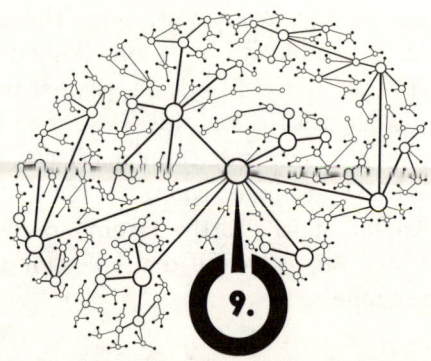

Noah Simpson packed up his personal carry-on and slid it into the wall storage, to keep it secure for landing. The cabin was incredibly comfortable, luxuriously outfitted and spacious. This had been his first trip where he could drink, eat, and spend freely . . . he was enjoying every minute of it. Chu Jun's Golden Aura card of dubious origin, filled to the brim with an inexhaustible supply of mafia cash, was well-known currency on an interplanetary scale as well.

That one week spent with Jess on Mars had been worth more than anything. True, he had broken the rules: he had smoked weed and drunk heavily, but he hadn't done so for ages—until then. He had gone off the rails but, because he'd had to keep away from these pleasures for so long, it was good to just let things slide a little. Consequently, he'd had to take double, sometimes triple, doses of the antidote to compensate for the side effects. The usual runny nose and nausea had been there too, sometimes together with a bit of mucus coughed up, but he had finally survived it all.

At the New Home Central Terminal, he shouldn't have accepted the invitation from an old acquaintance; this had been highly irresponsible of him. Robert Ridderhelm had been his buddy from the New Cloud York elementary school, they used to hang out a lot together. He could really drink! He had become a chauffeur to one of the big cheeses on Mars and he just happened to be waiting for his boss to arrive by ship from Europa, when they had run into each other. He had kept the booze flowing, despite Noah's claim of not being allowed to drink for health reasons—he had even shown him the epilepsy implant certificate—Robert just continued to order new rounds of drinks. There were four hours left before departure, so Noah had knocked himself out completely at the end. That's when the worries started. Especially since the remaining box of pills was lying in the checked-in luggage.

No matter, he had survived it, as he had so many times before. And now he would strike his life's biggest land-leasing deal: two and a half million New Dollars! *My God, what a huge amount of money,* he thought to himself.

He would move to Mars and marry Jess. He must have made a good impression on her and something must have stirred in her too, that was almost for sure, because she had spoken a lot about children, the family—perhaps she felt that her biological clock was running out. It would appear that everything was happening at just the right time.

If this deal came through, he would have the implant removed. He was already annoyed enough that Futura didn't answer his phone calls. They knew very well, of course—and probably kept tabs as well—how many pills they had sent him the last time, and how long they should last. They knew that he had started drinking or doing drugs again, so they had left him on his own as a punishment. This recklessness would certainly mean a breach of contract, although he had never had the patience to read that document through to the end. It was possible that, as far as they were concerned, they considered the agreement unilaterally nullified.

But that didn't really matter. His life would change completely without the implant. Though he did think about it a lot and was often plagued by uncertainty as to whether he would accept life without it. But he always ended up by concluding that, if he continued this crazy life with the implant, Sarah-Jessica would sooner or later notice that something wasn't right. It was possible that she already had but hadn't mentioned anything about it.

He could still hide in the guest room and pretend to go to sleep, feigning exhaustion. But later on, when they were man and wife—*oh, how nice that would be!*—he wouldn't be able to keep secret the fact that he didn't need any sleep.

The constant momentum, the endless spinning, would then cease; instead, peace and family would take their place. And the moment that they fell asleep after some good sex, he wouldn't have to toss and turn all night, with eyes wide open.

Physically, he didn't feel any need for rest, but perhaps that would still come. Who knew when the implant would become too old, or when his body would fall behind in this mad race with the implant.

Right now, what he wished and yearned for so very badly, was simply peace of mind.

He couldn't understand how he had managed to survive the incidents at the terminal, how that awful vomiting, the extreme sweating had stopped: that's what an attack was. Perhaps because he hadn't just been drinking but had actually drunk inordinate volumes that night. The other explanation was that the festering infection had drained out on its own from his system. Whatever the reason for the mysterious recovery, there was no doubt that he was well again. Soon he would get his baggage, where his last pills were. Provided he didn't contravene the rules again.

One thing was for sure now—if there was still no one at Futura to pick up the phone, he would fly to Rio and personally turn the tables on them.

The Trans Terra Travel Agency's luxury spaceship, holding seven hundred passengers, started to slow down. This could be detected by the way the objects left loose on the table starting to slide down towards the bow. With the artificial gravity, he wouldn't feel much more than that, since the ship had been continuously compensating for the power impulses resulting from deceleration. There was also a comfortable, belted armchair, into which he should have been fastened, in principle, but there had been no need for safety belts at takeoff, so he wasn't very concerned about it.

He had visited the Moon once before, sometime back in his childhood. There was a missionary aid organisation in New Cloud York, in the districts under the cloud, taking poor children on trips to Earth and sometimes to other parts of the Solar System. All that he seemed to remember from that trip was that they had seen the instruments left on the Moon by the Apollo mission, almost four hundred years before. A gigantic glass dome had been placed over them, to protect them from visitors. He had read in one of the brochures that they had built the space station on that precise spot, in memory of those space pioneers.

It was thanks to a New China Mafioso that he would get to see it again. Chu Jun was a rather odd character. Affected, gentlemanly, and over-refined, yet a delusive power emanated from his every step, his every move or action. He loved to charm people and to bring them so far under his spell that, figuratively speaking, they would go down on all fours and bark happily at his every command. Noah wasn't afraid of him; on the contrary, he felt a certain inclination to compete with him: he, the small-time gangster-turned-land-broker wanted to show the Mafioso that he was somebody as well. Nevertheless, he had to admit that Chu Jun could twist him around his little finger: acceptance of the Golden Aura card wasn't exactly the most suitable way to preserve his self-respect and autonomy. He couldn't stay the course this way. In the interests of a promising future, he'd still have to learn how to keep a tight rein on his momentary wants.

Again, his thoughts drifted to the future . . .
Oh, Jess, little girl . . .
Rotten Futura . . .

The ship was already perceptibly leaning to the left, although the computer-controlled fine-tuning of the artificial gravitation was trying to keep everything in its place—including Noah. Meanwhile, the opposite wall and the floor changed into a continuous screen and the image of the approaching Moon came into view.

Breathtaking, Noah thought. Just as if he were standing in open space. The travel agencies certainly knew how to attract and hold clients. Whoever saw this panorama just the once, would only want to travel in such a luxurious cabin from then on. The vision of the crater-covered celestial body approaching across the infinite silence of space, like an island in the unpopulated, icy cosmos, was unforgettable. With its squat mass looming grey, it emphasized the minuteness and insignificance of man.

The blue Mother Colony appearing behind the Moon, the Earth was an even more wonderful sight. It reminded him of his childhood—mother, father, buddies, sweethearts, street battles, everything. . . . The Earth is the past; the Moon is the future, the materially safe future.

The map of the future, wallpapered with two and a half million New Dollars.

The Earth had slowly slipped back behind its companion, thrusting its child into the foreground like a conscientious, mindful mother. The regolith's grey mass slowly covered the entire wall. The lights of the regolith mines operating on the dark side were already visible, the colonies extending to the northern pole, extracting the water enclosed in the rocks.

The ship slowly reached the Lunar Earthside, and the image of the row of ship traffic between the Earth and the Moon, glittering like pearls, presented itself to the traveller. Metal bodies of transport and tourist vessels, private spacejets and ferries sparkled in the blinding brightness of the Sun, in the background. With a slight manoeuvre to the right, his ship entered this line of traffic and started its descent toward the surface.

Beneath Noah's feet, the Moon Colony system, comprising forty-two domes, continued to emerge. Branching out from the largest, central dome—like caviar around a boiled egg for breakfast—were the smaller districts: housing settlements, service buildings, industrial units and factories, hundreds of life-sustaining systems. The colony was continuously expanding with the addition of newer settlements. Viewed from Earth, the bubble-system growing on the equatorial region surrounded the celestial body, appearing as a belt-like cluster of brilliant light.

He would also be contributing towards the sale of newer terrains on this resplendent jewel. It was a wonderful thing to participate in the efforts of humanity's colonization. Noah felt important, perhaps for the very first time in his life. He was now personally involved in the establishment of something new, something that would not merely remain new for just the next twenty-four hours. He would now no longer live his life just from one day to the next.

Moon Concession Corporation had made its appearance on the market as a fresh, energetic firm, and he was one of its youngest employees. He couldn't understand why they saw such big potential in him, why they had chosen to hire him, in particular—someone who knew nothing about real estate business nor had any pertinent academic qualifications or experience. Futura Respondis, however, had taken care of everything he needed to take on the job. Before he could come to his senses, he had been hired and not just as any old employee but one with a fabulous, well-paying job, fit for a fairy tale.

His first business deals had been done with the boss, a fellow by the name of Eric Kovacevic. He didn't look at all like a boss, or even a real estate agent, but rather like a commando, or a training officer. True enough, he had been versed in land deals, but he was a foot and a half taller than Noah and his upper arm was as thick as Noah's thigh.

The study period resembled a military drill. They sat opposite each other in the London office, while Eric questioned him on the paragraphs and he had to answer everything by heart. If something didn't go right, the next day he would be made to walk up to the forty-second floor on foot. Ultimately, he welcomed it, for it did his rather un-athletic frame and leg muscles a great deal of good, and the implant gave him enough energy to cope.

Besides himself and Eric, there was only a secretary working in the office. Nevertheless, they were renting seven premises on that floor. After the first deals, Eric mentioned they had hired another group of young men straight from the university. He had chosen the best of the successful graduates, but Noah had never met them. They had become employees of the most recently established branch office set up on Europa. "We'll make a meal of the Moon, between the two of us," Eric used to say. Noah's appetite and ambitions were continually growing, so he hadn't protested against the proposed plan to invade the Moon.

Shortly afterwards, Eric introduced Chu Jun. He said that he wasn't sure whether the guy was on the level. "But we in the real estate business aren't too interested in that," he declared. "We're only interested in how much money the customers have lurking in their pockets, and if they want to spend it with us, then we're happy to accommodate them."

He also added that Noah could accept any gifts, as this was an old-established custom in this business. The New China Empire was the hotbed of corruption. "You either give yourself over to the opportunities, working and adapting, or you never conclude any business deals with them," he explained. This was a necessary evil, as he always called it. He showed Noah his own little gift, too, a floating island, or ship—Noah had never been able to determine the proper term for it—in the South of France, which he had apparently been given by one of his influential business clients.

Noah picked up the rhythm easily enough and didn't spend too much time worrying if he occasionally had to look up seedy contacts from his past. Eric, however, was fascinated by his pace—he might well be because, while he was sleeping the sleep of the just, Noah was hard at work.

There was no question about it—the implant was a blessing, especially for a young beginner in the trade. If they could eliminate the side effects, then this would prove to be a fantastic and inexhaustible source of energy for humanity.

The waving young flight attendants on the live image covering the wall of his cabin brought Noah back from his thoughts to the present: this meant that the ship had docked safely.

Come on, let's get on with the adventure, sweep in the first few millions, then live a normal life again—all this kept running through his mind while they took the reading off his biochip at the gate. The officer watched the monitor with a stern expression—he asked for the papers certifying the implant, before indicating that Noah could now step onto Moon Tranquillity Base territory.

Great God in Heaven! That was all that he could think as he looked down from the fourth level gallery of the Neil Armstrong Terminal. What changes had taken place here over the past twenty years! The building had grown tenfold! The crowd surged and flowed about nauseatingly—he had experienced this same feeling on Mars, as well. Interplanetary travel would always be a gut-wrenching experience for a guy coming from the ghetto.

Chu Jun had promised to send his chauffeur, who would wait for Noah at the Apollo 11 landing site, not far from the old United States flag. It wasn't hard to find, as the carefully preserved scene of the first landing on the Moon was located in the centre of the terminal. This perfectly preserved landing zone was clearly visible from the descending elevator, with the abandoned lunar module's descent stage, the instruments and, of course, the flag, all under a giant glass dome.

The elevator door quietly glided aside and disappeared into the wall, opening the way for a group of newly arrived school children, about twenty-five teenagers, running toward the scene of the lunar landing. The countries that had started the colonization based on the decision by the United Colony Council, all considered the first landing areas on the Moon and on Mars as Interplanetary Heritage sites; their modification or removal was forbidden. They had thus preserved everything in its original location—even the footsteps of the astronauts remained intact in the dust of the Moon. Noah had read somewhere, perhaps in one of the pamphlets, that in preserving a slice of the Moon's soil, the Neil Armstrong Terminal had actually been built around the site of the landing. He found it interesting that anyone who wanted to could even walk under the landing spot, as it was the departure point for taxis and the rapid transit railway towards the outer domes.

The most interesting experience—and not just for kids frolicking around it—was that, in the area around the landing site, there was no artificial Earth gravity, you could check out what the original gravitational circumstances had been at the time of the first walk on the Moon. Children were accompanied by stumbling adults—but only until they were able to stand on their own two feet. By jumping off the ground with both feet near the duplicate of the flag, an automatic camera that was installed there could produce the famous "salute to the moon" photo that John Young, the Apollo 16 astronaut, had devised—this picture had been repeated later by some astronaut or another, on every moon and planet conquered by man!

'Mr. Simpson?' a podgy man came up and addressed him. He had been so mesmerized by the sight of the children playing, that he hadn't noticed when he had left the American flag, the meeting place.

'Yes, Mr. Chu Jun sent you, right?' he extended his hand towards the man. Either the man didn't know this form of greeting, or he simply wasn't allowed to accept the extended hand. He bowed politely and waved towards the moving walkway leading to the parking blocks.

'Please, come with me. Mr. Jun is waiting impatiently for you. We were expecting your arrival a few days earlier.'

'I hope that Mr. Jun will forgive me. I had an urgent matter to attend to on Mars, as we have some interests there as well,' Noah lied. They had no interests outside of Europa, but he hoped that a chauffeur wouldn't involve himself in his boss's dealings to the extent that he would want to be informed about it.

The man didn't say a word after that. It seemed that, after transmitting the message, telling him that they had been waiting for him, his authority ended. They gathered his belongings and walked over to the limousines waiting in the parking area. The chauffeur asked for his bag, and Noah remembered the small vial lying inside.

'My pills,' he explained, disconcertedly, fishing out the last box of antidotes from deep within the bag. 'I always feel rotten after travelling, you know . . .'

The chauffeur either believed him or not but he didn't really seem interested in anything. He shoved the suitcase into the back of the floater and walked heavily over into the driver's seat. The right door at the rear opened automatically in front of Noah to indicate where he was supposed to get in.

They drove through an endless tunnel of trees. The flickering lights appeared pale through the limousine's darkened windows. Cackling youths in an open convertible running alongside were trying to figure out what kind of celebrity could be coming to visit in a darkened luxury car.

I'm not a celebrity, Noah thought, *hard to articulate, but only the favourite guest of a Mafioso.*

His hotel, the Sheraton Moonlight, was glaringly bright and overly decorated in the Rococo style. He should be getting used to this pomp, he thought, as the bellboy came rushing to take his luggage. Human assistance meant rank and exclusivity; there was no sign of any service robots on wheels.

The chauffeur—who apparently had no desire to communicate verbally with him—just pressed a card into his hand as he was leaving.

The message on it said: 'Meeting in 3 hours' time. Be punctual, the chauffeur will wait for you in the hall. Regards, Chu Jun.'

He'd be punctual. And how! He had an appointment with two and a half million New Dollars . . .

*

Three-and-a-half hours later, in Chu Jun's house, in the Moon Colony . . .

'No, please believe me, I didn't bring anyone here! I don't work for the United Colony Revenue Office!'

Noah was shouting. He had been doing so for half an hour now, intermittently, ever since they had tied him up on this fitness machine. It had been done in such a way that his hands, tied behind his back, were attached to the weights of the machine by means of a short rope, so that if he didn't hold the heavy counterweight with his legs—which, in his estimation, weighed more than one hundred kilos—it pulled his arms up high, so that only his toes touched the ground. The implant gave him energy but didn't provide him with invincible superpower. He had never liked physical exercises; his moderately developed musculature didn't fare well with being overtaxed. This training was becoming ever-increasingly painful.

The driver, who had struck him as being friendly and rather quiet when he arrived at the terminal—had apparently been instructed to practice his other favourite occupation, that of torturing—was increasing the weights by a couple of kilos every five minutes. He wasn't packing old-fashioned iron discs onto the machine: this was modern equipment, the virtual weights were increased by pressing a button, and these were not just virtually heavy—Noah's legs could feel them. The stocky man carried out his assignment in the same taciturn but effective manner as he did the driving.

Chu Jun was sitting behind a glass desk. Every object, office accessories and knick-knacks, on the table, were also made of glass or some transparent material, as if he wanted to emphasize that the man working here had impeccable morals, someone who had nothing to hide. He must have been around sixty, wore glasses, had a receding hairline with black, shoulder-length hair, a gold ring on each finger, and wore a flawlessly cut, Chinese-style, black jacket. Playing with a glass pen, he was tapping a heartbeat-like rhythm on the table. But he was probably just counting the seconds so he would know when the next weight should be added to the machine.

'Mr. Simpson, you are surely not so naive as to think that we don't watch with whom we go into business?' he smiled, but didn't stop tapping on the table. He looked at the chauffeur and raised his index finger, at which point the weights became one push of a button heavier.

Noah's legs trembled from the exertion. He decided to give them a break, he would relieve his pain with the other painful feeling in his arms and shoulders, letting the machine-driven virtual weights pull his arms up behind him. It didn't make a great deal of difference, it felt just as bad.

'Damn you! Can't you understand that I don't work for any government or colonial organizations?! I was a criminal, too, for many long years; the last thing I would do is to become a cop!'

Noah didn't even understand why he was pouring abuse on the Chinaman; he knew this would incense him even further. Neither did he understand at all why he had mentioned his criminal past. Perhaps to prove that they were on the same side . . . or that they had once been on the same side.

'Mr. Simpson, first of all, you upset me somewhat with that statement and, secondly, you admit that you think that I'm a criminal. As a matter of fact, this just serves to reinforce my notion that you were sent to check on us by some criminal investigation outfit, perhaps the United Colony Revenue Office or the UC Intelligence Agency Organized Crime and Gang Section. . .'

'I'm not reinforcing anything!' shouted Noah in despair, pushing the weights out with his legs. He would hold and bear it for another five or seven minutes like that.

'My employer is the Moon Concession Corporation, the name of my superior is Eric Kovacevic, you spoke with him, too . . . ah . . .' he continued, struggling. 'We have three offices—one in London, one here, and one on Europa!' he struggled to stammer out the end of the sentence.

'But just the same, perhaps because of a stupid preconception, you conclude that I haven't made my fortune in a clean way?'

'I'm not concluding anything! The Golden Aura card provides inexhaustible resources for you; its replenishment is perfectly legal and can be accomplished by honest work, but—'

'But perhaps not in these poverty-stricken times after the war,' Chu Jun interjected. 'That's what you were thinking, right?'

'But I came here to do business, not trouble. That's what I was thinking.'

The tapping seconds signalled the arrival of another weight of two-kilos. *Rot in hell, you squalid, filthy pig*, Noah thought, and his legs began to shake uncontrollably again. He felt the lack of the antidote; those two pills he had swallowed at the hotel weren't enough. Perhaps that was the reason why he had to make an enormous effort to tighten his trembling leg muscles.

He needed those two and a half million New Dollars, he needed them badly. So that he could stop with all the lies and self-delusions, so that only Jess would fill his everyday life from here on. He was enduring all this just for her.

Chu Jun raised his hand. The weights suddenly ceased to exist. Breathing heavily, Noah drew his tortured legs up under his body. He would have massaged them, but his hands were still tied behind him.

'You are extraordinarily strong, Mr. Simpson,' Chu Jun went on. 'Perhaps I could succeed in making you talk by another method. The medication, if you would, please.'

The driver fumbled in Noah's bag and put the antidote-filled vials on the table.

'My chauffeur told me that, when you got off the plane, you took two of these pills. According to what you said, this was to lessen the discomfort from the flight, but you must know that nowadays there is no longer any discomfort in flying. You either tell me the truth, or I shall throw this lot immediately into the disintegrator and you'll never see them again.'

Noah felt that he was sinking deeper and deeper, starting to fall headfirst into the abyss of despair. He wouldn't last without the medication.

'It's a drug against epilepsy. I'm an epileptic, and I have an implant in my body in order to prevent the attacks. If I don't take it, I'm plagued by spasm attacks every second day.'

'I understand, Mr. Simpson. It was a very honest reply. Therefore, these pills are of vital importance to you, without them you could even lose your life?'

Bingo, you ass, Noah thought. *Unfortunately you now have a new weapon in your hand.*

'Please look at this picture. Do you recognize this gentleman, talking to another man?'

Noah stared at the picture that Chu Jun had propped up in a transparent folder in front of him.

'It's my boss, but you know that very well: Eric Kovacevic. The president and principal shareholder of Moon Concession Corporation.'

'And who is that man next to him? Have you seen this gentleman in Mr. Kovacevic's company, or perhaps you have already met him?'

'No, I have no idea who that man is.' Noah was telling the truth, he had never seen him, either with or without Eric.

'This man works for the UC Bureau of Investigation Organized Crime and Gang Section, his name is Richard Enderston. The photo was taken over seven years ago, at the conference against organized crime in the North American Union. One of my friends sent it over the day before yesterday from Earth. Unfortunately, it was blocked for a long time under interplanetary security, but we found something in the multi-billion-photo depository collection, cracked open by hackers. The cops had managed to get rid of almost everything.'

Noah didn't understand what it was all about. *Seven years ago? And so what?*

'And what do I have to do with all this? I didn't even know Kovacevic at that time . . .'

'That's right, Mr. Simpson, but now he is your closest colleague. And here you are, right now, sitting facing me, in order to strike a twelve billion New Dollar land-lease contract. Do you know in what field the gentleman in question, Mr. Enderston, specialises?'

'How the hell should I know?'

'The tracking down of money-laundering in the Solar System...'

Noah had never been so lost in his life. 'So?' he asked, uncomprehending.

'So, Mr. Simpson, land purchase in organized crime circles is the most favoured money laundering technique. You must know this, if you yourself were involved in criminal activities. In many cases, the gangs look for smaller companies, such as yours, in order to conduct the transactions safely.'

By now, Noah was beginning to have an inkling of what Chu Jun was driving at. 'So you are accusing me and my boss, Mr. Kovacevic, of lending a helping hand to the investigating authorities?'

'More than that, as this is not just a simple lending of hands. I believe that Mr. Kovacevic set up this company three years ago in order to set a trap for me.'

'You've gone mad...' Noah really meant what he said. The man had obviously been living from crime; he was on record as being one of the largest arms-and-human traffickers, this was an open secret, even in Asia. But he couldn't fathom this lunacy about Eric.

'Nevertheless, he did it in a most professional way and, until this moment, we didn't know about it either. He hasn't left any traces, I repeat, no traces at all, behind him—just this single photo. His recorded academic background fits his profile; he finished Economics with distinction at Harvard. There is no information to be found on him on the Public Inter-System Net, at least nothing of a personal nature. In one of our earlier dealings, he had presented himself to us through a real estate broker, curiously enough, precisely at the time when we were looking for a company that would help us in procuring larger land areas for purchase.'

'That picture from seven years ago doesn't prove anything,' said Noah, hoping that this was really so and the whole thing was just a nightmare.

'Do you really think so, Mr. Simpson? It would appear that you don't require any medication after all,' he said with a smile, picking up the small box from the table and holding it up over the mobile disintegrator in the wall.

'No, don't! Wait!' Noah shouted at him. He wanted to gain time somehow but had no idea how. 'Call Eric now, at once! Here is the number of his communicator on my handset; you'll find it in my left inside pocket . . .'

It was a spur-of-the-moment inspiration but he couldn't think of anything else. He had to save the last box of antidote by whatever means. He could then track down Futura Respondis, wherever they were in the Solar System . . . but if he lost this last box of antidote then there was little chance for survival, perhaps just a couple of days. If worse came to worst, he would have the implant operated out by someone, provided he could escape from here. Although, for that surgery he would need that two and a half million, which, under the present circumstances, seemed to be a somewhat remote possibility.

The wall of flesh that was the Chinaman took the communicator out of his pocket and handed it to his boss. Chu Jun started to tap on the keys and quickly found Eric between the contacts and dialled the number. He gave the communicator back to his man to hold the handset to Noah's ear.

Noah heard the long, deep, buzzing signal of the call. One, then two . . . then five . . . then ten . . . but nobody answered.

'Try again, but now the London office. The number is below Eric's on the list,' Noah said hastily.

Everything repeated itself, exactly as before. The hulking chauffeur handed the phone over to his boss again; it was obvious that he couldn't handle the communicator, he was only familiar with driving and torturing. He looked at the handset with the idiotic expression of a technical illiterate.

The communicator didn't ring this time. On the line, an automated voice repeated that there was no subscriber at this number. Noah couldn't believe his ears. Immediately upon his arrival, he had talked to the secretary, confirming the latest details prior to the transaction of the deal. *He had to be there, damn it!*

A very loud, imaginary warning signal set off somewhere in his head, one that he hadn't heard for years—probably the last time he had heard it was when he was still hanging out with the boys in back-street alleys under New Cloud York and some situation had become seriously rough. He was in trouble; what's more, in big trouble. It could be that he had been sent as a decoy, after all. And he had lured the big fish to the hook, as he was supposed to.

Futura Respondis had arranged the job! Didn't they know anything about this either? Or were they in on the act as well? Hard to believe that Miss Stockwell would have done such a thing. Or perhaps they had become incommunicado because of this, and the whole thing was interconnected? *Impossible*...

'You see, Mr. Simpson, often truly incredible things can appear to be real,' said Chu Jun and, smiling, he turned to the box of medication, which he placed on the edge of the disintegrator's open lid. 'On how little it all depends. If the delicate balance is upset, it's all over,' he said with malicious pleasure, making a flicking motion with his finger a few centimetres from the box. The box could have fallen into the disintegrator from this little gust of wind but, thank heavens, it didn't move.

'Now that all your carefully prepared traps appear to have collapsed, would you elaborate on the method you had planned for my downfall?' he asked and signalled to Noah's torturer to increase the load. Noah's shoulder began to turn inside out. He wanted to avoid letting it dislocate, so he started pushing the machine with his legs.

'Look, whatever you think or whatever you deduct from that picture, however you torture me, destroy my medication, or kill me, I'd be unable to tell you anything else but what I know: I don't have anything to do with the whole thing.'

Chu Jun was visibly reflecting on Noah's statement. He was trying to fathom whether this man was either genuinely not involved in the police activity or whether he was such a pro that he would continue to play his role to the bitter end.

The next moment a huge explosion shook the building. All glass objects—including the colossal office desk, document holders, pen and pencil cases, glass statues—were blown into millions of fragments. The flying pieces of broken glass cut into Noah's face. He couldn't even defend himself with his hands tied tightly behind him. The training machine fell over on its side, tearing the rope to which Noah was tied out of the wall. Chu Jun and his chauffeur dove onto their bellies on the floor—seemingly it wasn't the first time that this had happened to them.

Through the imploded pieces of the door, commandos came flooding in, with a clatter of heavy boots, fanning out in a star formation to cover the office from all angles. Stinging teargas came pouring in: the guards had probably been neutralized this way.

Noah's eyes were burning from the gas, he was choking but he was delighted that his nightmare had ended, whatever happened afterwards. If Eric was a member of the agency against criminal activity, then he would be exonerated, and if he wasn't a cop after all, then he could surely be counted on as a friend. Anything was better than the situation at hand.

If only the medication could be saved . . .

As he looked up at the lid of the disintegrator, by some sort of a miracle, the little box was still poised in the same spot. Despite all the flying door debris and glass splinters, nothing had toppled it into the atomizer.

'Off the floor, up on your feet!' One of the soldiers pushed the barrel of his gun into the nape of Noah's neck. He was wearing the uniform of the UC Police Quick Intervention Unit. Noah knew them well; in the past he used to find himself in situations where the uniformed guys were on the other side of the barricade!

'Find the signed documents! We need the contract!' one of the masked officers ordered another private.

'They're nowhere, not on the floor, either.'

'Look in the disintegrator, perhaps it got stuck on the brim!'

In the disintegrator . . . the words seared through Noah's brain.

The soldier stepped over to the open lid and, with his free hand, reached into the inside of the lid and felt about. The little box continued to dance about on the narrow ledge.

'Nothing, lieutenant,' said the soldier, quickly withdrawing his hand from the opening. The air pressure from the movement of his hand caused the little box to spin around again.

'My medication!' shouted Noah into the face of the soldier helping him to his feet. 'It's on the disintegrator!'

The soldier who had checked the atomizer turned around, but he was too late. The box tilted over one last time, first toward the outside, then, turning around, toppled into the opening.

The End, Noah thought. Filthy, crappy days are on their way, and then the slow end.
Especially if he couldn't find Eric to clear himself.

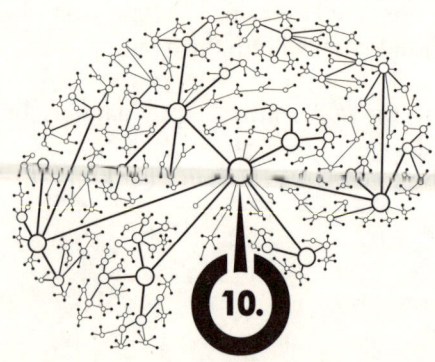

Claude Brademe, director of Special Events, was cruising around the closed-off area below the Mars New Home Colony Central Dome in an antigravity car. He was watching how the work on the quarantine section was progressing, on a holo-tablet. The red block on his picture indicated the part where the mayor, who had been holding his election speech, was stranded. Of the seventeen smaller domes attached to the Colony's Central Dome, four were glowing red; the infection had already reached those. Security level orange was in force for the rest.

'What's the current situation, Jack?' he asked General Simons, the Mars Special Forces commander sitting beside him, who was leafing through a long list.

'There are seven thousand people in the closed-off area of the centre, directly below us. Two hundred and twenty-four who were contaminated have been isolated; according to the latest reports, their condition is continuing to deteriorate. The symptoms are consistent in each case: sweating, nasal discharge, cough, strong secretion in the mucous membranes. If the amount of mucus in the stomach increases, it is expelled by vomiting. For the time being, there have been no deaths; they're trying to alleviate the symptoms with antihistamines and the latest antibiotics. The virology experts have taken samples of the substance and have begun their analysis.'

'What about the mayor?' asked Deputy Mayor Estrella Gonzales, sitting behind them. She too was observing the camp erected in the closed-off section beneath them.

'For now, he's still symptom-free and healthy, but he can't leave the closed-off area. You'll have to continue representing the city, Madam.'

'I'd have preferred some other choice instead. I don't want to end up in the mayor's chair this way,' the woman said, shaking her head.

'There's both good and bad news arriving from the outlying districts,' the general continued. 'In the first district, two clusters have formed: one in an evening dance school, the other on the twentieth floor of a high-rise building. The original starting point in the dance academy was a man called Peter Köpke, who works at the Special Technical Unit of the Police Department. He was infected by the bus driver, Jim Kingston—the "Alpha-person"—as he is often referred to, on the night of the accident, when they wanted to lift the dead body off the antenna.'

'How many people have been infected at the dance school?' asked Brademe.

'Seven altogether, a mix of women and men,' answered Simons. 'The other cluster is in the same district.' He turned a page in the report, 'One of the men travelling in the problem bus is our starting point. Apparently, he only infected one person, his wife, on the twentieth floor of a high-rise. We have hermetically sealed the floor and the tenants have been evacuated.'

'Were those infected taken to the Police Station that's been transformed into an emergency hospital?' asked Brademe.

'No, they were treated on-site; even the medical team at the emergency unit would be unable to do anything with them, they couldn't receive better treatment there either, not until the pathogen of the infection has been found. They can be cared for more or less adequately on-site, and they are safely quarantined there. In any case, the emergency hospital will be completed within a day; the more seriously infected can be transported over at that time.'

'In the second district,' continued the general, 'the bus driver's wife and daughter were quarantined; it was the little girl's birthday. The father bought the cake at the terminal, before he went to work and had it sent home. Ten children were invited; they were placed in quarantine, together with their parents, in the same building on one of the evacuated floors. They are all OK. They didn't touch the cake, as they would only have served it once the father had come home.'

'In the seventh district, two men from the bus, father and son . . .'

Simons went on and on, enumerating the information, whilst the emergency camp being erected on the closed off area beneath them slowly lagged behind.

Estrella looked with a worried expression at the deserted streets, the floating islands, the restaurants, the hanging corridors, and the sky beneath the empty dome. Two days had passed since the bus accident and the entire colony had become paralysed.

A quarantine of this magnitude had only happened once before in the past two hundred and eighty years, at the close encounter of the Martina Comet, one hundred and ten years ago. Before her inauguration, the deputy mayor had watched one of the most staggering incidents in Mars' history on old news clips, of how they had vacated the Central Dome and the way people had been ordered to the outlying districts. At that time, there had still been good contact with the Old Colony, the Chinatown, so a large part of the population had been sheltered there.

During the preparations for collision, they had even opened up the giant Solar Mirror, *The Umbrella*—which, in the cold season during the Mars winter, focused heat onto the colony, whilst on hot days it served as a protective shield against the heat—assuming it could somehow lessen the force of the impact slightly. According to calculations, the collision was going to be inevitable. Although the dimensions of the comet's nucleus weren't at a destructive level, it could have caused significant devastation with its forty-five metre, asymmetrical core. The space protection system now in operation, which could divert any interplanetary body from its course with the help of special tractor beams, had not existed then.

'. . . So, the total number of those infected is eight hundred and seventy-two from the entire population of almost four hundred thousand,' General Simons concluded his review of the report.

'The projection of these numbers wouldn't sound bad,' said Brademe, 'but if we look at the fatalities, it's horrifying: so far, all those infected in the first wave have suffered a horrible, cruel death. Right now we don't see any prospect of our stopping, or even slowing down its propagation; who knows how many latently infected persons might come forward over the next few days. The analysis of the samples is currently ongoing, but the investigators had not found anything much up to now. Therefore, these numbers could change daily, and unfortunately, they are most likely to rise.'

'How is that possible? There's hardly any infection or virus that we haven't been able to vanquish during the past centuries. With today's technology, today's equipment . . .'

'For the time being, we don't know what we're facing. We've sent the samples to Earth and to Europa; they'll be there within two days. The ships are just waiting for the second gravitational jumps. By combining forces, we might be able to come up with something then.'

'And for how long would we be able to keep it under control? How long will this news ban last?' Estrella spoke up behind them.

'I don't know how long we can keep it under wraps but, according to the current protocol, we'll have to stay isolated for four weeks,' explained Brademe. 'If we were to lift the embargo, and interplanetary traffic started up again, then the contamination could spread to other parts, as well, during the incubation period.'

'What do we know about the incubation period?' asked Estrella dispiritedly, even though she had suspected what the answer would be.

'We still don't know anything for certain but perhaps during this evening's meeting we'll hear of new results. Anyone catching the infection could be dead by tomorrow. But if we take the survival time of those contaminated by the "Alpha-person" as our criterion, then the average period could even be reduced to twelve hours.'

Shocked silence settled over the cabin. Only the humming sound of the floating antigravity motors and the low sounds of fragmented radio communications from inside the pilot's helmet could be heard. The colony's leaders were overcome by a feeling of hopelessness and despair.

The antigravity car slowly descended onto the parking lot on one of the terraces of the Central Police Station building, which had been organized as a crisis centre. The strong Mars wind buffeted it about pretty violently. The units producing the artificial atmosphere regulated and purified the Dome's airspace but, even so, the brisk evening movement of air swept along some red sand every now and then. In these cases, the buildings became covered in a thin, reddish-pink film. They were cleaned regularly but, between two cleanings, children usually scribbled messages into this flour-like, delicate layer. Now, the words *help* and *do something* could be seen everywhere, written into the dust.

The Crisis Unit was already awaiting their arrival. A few red writing pads were set out in front of the chairs around the table, with the infection's currently accepted designation on the cover: the M-pathogen. In front of the projector wall, two white-smocked investigators were waiting, preparing to present the latest developments to the Crisis Unit. Once the women and men had taken their seats, one of the men began his presentation.

'Greetings, everyone. Allow me to introduce myself: I am Professor Clifford Mills, director of the Mars Biotech Laboratory and chief investigator, next to me is Sarah-Jessica Thompson, our eminent chief virologist.'

In the middle of the room, a three-dimensional holographic map appeared. The professor rotated it around with the help of a light-pen.

'Here we have the Central Dome of the New Home Colony and its seventeen attached districts, and there, farther away is the Old Colony. The history of the M-pathogen began at the Central Dome Terminal. According to the information available to us, this was the starting point of the contamination. The very first carrier of the virus is reckoned to be James Kingston, pilot, age forty-seven. Hereinafter, we shall refer to him as the "Alpha-person" so as to illustrate how the contamination spread.'

The image above the table changed again, displaying a schematically rendered human figure with red markings.

'And so we see the "Alpha-person" going to work, with the infection in his body. He seated himself in the driving cabin of the scheduled service vehicle and went through his almost eight-hour driving shift, before he started to feel sick. During that time, according to the ticket sales recorded and onboard biochip registrations, there was a turnover of three thousand five hundred passengers on the bus, although this figure doesn't include children and the elderly, who either didn't yet wear biochips or no longer wore them. Therefore, this number could be about two to three per cent higher,' he said, while the picture of the bus came into view on the holographic monitor. The 'Alpha-person' and the figures representing the three thousand five hundred passengers were connected with lines.

'The search to find them all is ongoing; could you please confirm, Chief of Police, that this is so?'

Tod Balladero nodded his affirmation. 'Probably not everyone among them became infected, which is why these pictograms are marked orange. Since this is the second level of infection, the figures are all marked with the number two.'

'Those forty-two men, who were on the bus at the time of the accident, were placed in the second level of infection,' and new orange circles appeared at the push of a button.

'The following among them were certifiably infected with the M-pathogen: Guy Schneider, Stephen Perkins, and Gustav Schmidt. They all got red circles; two of them are no longer alive. One of those is Guy Schneider; he is the one that suffered the ominous incident in the bar. All three had been sitting in the front of the bus, from which we have been able to conclude that the pathogen only exerts its influence over a certain distance, most likely only through bodily contact, or, even more likely, through contact with bodily fluids and perspiration.'

'The reason why we can affirm this,' the image changed, with new schematic human figures appearing, circled in red, 'is because these are the second contamination level individuals, namely Peter Köpke, police technician; Suarez Pereira, his colleague; Suzanne Blanchart, prosecutor; and Steve Cavanaugh, investigator. They were all contaminated by the abdominal discharge emanating from the "Alpha-person." As we speak, barely two days after being contaminated, their condition is critical.'

'Here we can see the third level of infection.' Yellow human figures appeared, scattered across the map in the outlying districts but with the majority grouped together on the main square of the Central Dome. 'These people caught the infection in the third wave.'

'The largest cluster,' he continued, while the image changed once again, 'was the result of the contamination that occurred in the Pulse Bar, where Guy Schneider came into physical contact with a great number of people before he died. They had brushed against him, touched him, danced with him, drunk from his glass, etc. This resulted in the infection centre with the largest number of contaminated people, two hundred and twenty-four cases. And I stress the fact that we're still only two days after the contamination. According to the reports received five minutes ago, the situation has deteriorated further: already, one hundred and seven have lost their lives in the past half hour—and the number is constantly climbing. What is remarkable, if I can use that word in this particular case, is the fact that almost all of them turned from their serious condition into a life-threatening, critical situation, within the same five- to ten-minute period, only to die just a few minutes later. And the process hasn't stopped; we're slowly losing all the infected individuals that are still floating between life and death.'

'This means,' Cliff took a deep breath, 'that the unknown microorganism achieves its objective within two, maximum three days and the host body gives up the fight.'

A shocked silence fell upon those sitting in the room. It was clear to everyone just how harsh and ruthless the contagion was.

'What can you tell us about how quickly the M-pathogen is spreading across the colony and our prospects?' asked Director Claude Brademe.

'I can only talk about the propagation speed at an assessment level. If the pathogen continues to present a fatality rate of this magnitude at the current propagation speed, and we're unable to stop it, then the Colony would perish within a month and a half.'

A murmur passed around through the audience, many winced. They were visibly counting on more time than a month and a half.

'What is the incubation period of the virus, if any, and how is this mysterious "Mars-pathogen" classified? Is it a virus or a microbe?' The deputy mayor threw her questions at Professor Mills.

'We can't talk about definite incubation period, as there was a victim who died within twelve hours, but there are also those who have remained in grave condition for two days. This period could therefore vary, perhaps depending on the host's metabolism. I'll let my colleague, Sarah-Jessica, answer the second half of the question. Jess, who has been working around the clock for the past two days, has been trying to uncover the nature of the pathogen. Jess?'

'Thank you. Hello, everyone.' Jess stepped forward and took over the light-pen from her boss. 'I would start by saying that, much as I'd like to see fast results, virology and epidemic research are not fields where fast results can be produced under any circumstance. This epidemic is entirely different from any other contamination observed up until now. Its estimated propagation speed, coupled with such a high fatality rate, has no equal in history.'

'Let's consider what we have managed to learn up to now about this M-pathogen,' continued Jess, changing the holographic image. A clump, composed of organic, spiral forms, appeared on the screen. 'These were the strange formations that we were able to extract from the victims' secretions. They are neither viruses, nor bacteria. In fact, they are long chains of unknown proteins, which are invested with hitherto unknown functions.'

'What does that mean exactly? How is the infection being transmitted?'

'We don't know. At this point we have no idea how they operate and how they reproduce themselves. In fact, unfortunately, I have to say that we are already sure that they are not the actual pathogens themselves. These are just white protein chains produced by the pathogens. These polymer chains are not known to science, there is no known living organism in the Solar System that produces such protein chains. Still, some hitherto unknown living organism, supposedly a microbe—let's use this classification for the M-pathogen—produces these in huge quantities in the human organism. Until now, we have found eight different proteins in the mucous solution, and none of them relates to any other.'

'So we're still groping in the dark?' Director Brademe wanted to know.

'I can't say that there's a great deal of light at the end of the tunnel. Nevertheless, we do know something. Those men who were in contact with the protein complex—and we have found these in the nose, saliva, sweat and stomach secretions—constructed this protein in their bodies and, by as yet unknown means, have reproduced it.'

'Then it is the pathogen after all?

'It is possible that its protein could be part of a microbe, for instance, or that a microbe could produce it by following a command encoded in its genes, but even the living human organism itself could produce it. In any case, it could cause pathogenic activity, like, for example, certain altered proteins, let's say prions, which are the genetic mutation of an existing protein. As we know, these were the cause, centuries ago, of spongiform encephalopathy, until we eventually found the source of this genetic trigger. In general, these differ so little from their known protein form, that the immune system doesn't perceive them as invaders, so they don't turn against them. But now, the proteins they have found, don't at all resemble the proteins in the human organism, therefore they couldn't be their mutations either. Normal proteins are produced and used in many different ways by our metabolism—at the cellular level or as messengers between cells. Perhaps we are facing a new type of message carrier that transmits the information related to the infection. The most interesting fact is that, although the proteins are unknown, the human organism nevertheless participates in their reproduction and doesn't cast them out.'

'So, it seems that we have encountered something that transcends our present knowledge,' said General Simons in a somewhat awkward, soldier-like way.

'Not exactly, since even today we're aware of a number of proteins that encourage communication between cells,' Jess continued, 'but it could also be that we are standing on the threshold of an impending revolutionary discovery: we may have to change some of our previous notions about the possible forms and functions of proteins.'

'We still have another very important observation,' Jess turned to Director Brademe, 'which fills us with hope with regard to discovering exactly what the pathogen is: we have found an individual in the third contamination level, who is carrying these proteins, these long polymer chains have got into his body, but he doesn't show any symptoms of the infection. This means that there are carriers who are symptom-free and don't become sick.'

'Would there be a possibility of producing some kind of antidote from the carrier's body?'

'This would be possible if we knew the pathogen. Without the pathogen, we only have mucous cells, where these strange new types of proteins are to be found,' answered Jess.

'We'll examine the person presumed immune to find the spots where these proteins are embedded, and why they behave differently in the body of an infected person,' Cliff interjected. 'Right now, we have to concentrate on finding this difference in the three infected persons lying in the isolation room and the immune person. The key, in any case, is somewhere within them. We have to get to know why and how they're activated in the majority of bodies, how they start to reproduce, and the reasons why protein production doesn't start in other bodies—such as the immune person's body. He has no symptoms or activity whatsoever.'

The lay people sitting in the room tried to understand this hopeful explanation.

'Is it possible to know who this lucky immune person is?'

'Yes, of course, his name is Chris McAllister, one of the colony's police officers. He was the one who brought the bus to a halt Friday evening. Incidentally, he had shaken hands with Guy Schneider. It's possible that Schneider was the one that transmitted the substance to him, the proteins carrying the infection.'

'If Chris's immune capacity is confirmed, we could ask him to lead the investigation, since he can't fall sick. It also means that we'll have someone with influence in places where others can only work at great risk,' said Balladero, the chief of police.

'That's exactly it,' said Cliff, reinforcing his words, 'but now we'll need more tests to be able to state with one hundred per cent certainty that Chris McAllister is immune to the M-pathogen.'

The lights came back up and the two investigators took their seats at the table.

'We really appreciate the work you are doing and we can only urge you to do everything within your power, whatever it takes in resources, financially or otherwise, to stop the spread of this infection,' the police chief continued.

'I would briefly like to outline what our men have found in connection with the primary virus carrier, as we had already started the investigation ourselves at the same time as the research by the biology unit. Prior to his shift, Jim Kingston, the bus driver, had entered the service manager's office, where he requested a new jacket, as he had left the other one at the cleaners. According to the workers at the cleaners, there was a dry, green stain on the jacket, which they had removed with a clothes brush before the cleaning process. This is an important observation for you, researchers, that this substance in its dry state doesn't contaminate, at least there's no evidence that this may be the case, given by those who came into contact with it. This newly uncovered fact means that the pathogen had already been in his system prior to starting his shift or, if we look at the rate of survival so far, then he could have come into contact with it sometime before, during the preceding two days. However, the question remains: why would he go to work in a stained jacket? If he had indeed been sick before, why hadn't he turned around and gone straight home? According to eyewitnesses, he arrived for his morning shift in good humour and smiling, just as he always did. Another very important observation is that one of the men's restrooms at the terminal had to be closed down due to the filth found there—which was already dry by then, so the cleaning staff clearing the dirt were not infected. This restroom, however, is located on the upper level of the interplanetary passengers' area; in other words, in exactly the opposite direction from where Jim arrived every morning to his workplace.'

He took a deep breath and continued, 'All this could have disturbing implications: those being that, at the airport terminal, Jim Kingston met the person, a guest in the interplanetary passenger lounge, who was the actual source of the discharge on his jacket.'

The chief of police made a brief pause for effect and glanced around at the crisis crew members.

'If this is really so, then we have to voice it: we must revise our current conclusion, that Jim Kingston is the number one spreader of the disease, the "Alpha-person." If our assumption is correct, then there must have been someone from amongst the passengers arriving from off-planet who had brought this disease from elsewhere or who happened to carry it away as a passenger in transit. A curious bit of information was that inside his jacket pocket they found a business card soaked in mucus and rendered illegible, from which not even a microscopic analysis could produce a dye sample, and thus it was impossible to establish its source. Perhaps this could prove that he had met someone.'

'I recommend that the full departing and arriving passenger list for that morning, and perhaps also for the previous evening, be examined if it hasn't already, and the colony's health organizations and the United Colony Council Epidemic Institute should be contacted immediately,' interjected Claude Brademe, as he had the final word, being the prime person responsible in emergency situations. 'We'll keep the blockade and the news ban until the UCC decides otherwise, but we have to start the collaboration and exchange of information immediately. There is a strong likelihood that the Mars-pathogen has not only spread to our colony but is spreading elsewhere at this very moment, as we speak.'

The functionaries considered this as the concluding warning and reached for their communicators: they began the coordination effort instantly. Jess was tapping her nails on the table; she was tormented by bad forebodings. She thought of Noah, his strange cold symptoms, and the fact that he had left Mars the morning when all this had happened.

'Jess . . . Jess!' She barely heard Cliff's voice. 'We have to go back to work. If we don't start right now, the colony is finished.'

Jess stood up dazedly, she knew her boss was right. With this mortality rate and without significant research results, the colony wouldn't last much longer.

'Perhaps we have one thing on our side: if it dries out, it doesn't contaminate,' Cliff added wearily, obviously trying to provide some encouragement.

Jess hadn't got around to examining the handkerchief that Noah had left in the guest room under the microscope. Looking at it, there was a dry, greenish-yellow secretion on it, identical to what they had found on the people who had become infected. Up until now, it hadn't occurred to her that Noah could be connected with the current happenings . . .

Still, it couldn't be. If he were the Alpha-person, then both of them would be dead by now, since they had been together the whole time.

She couldn't reach Noah now, because interplanetary communication had been blocked.
She would have to wait until the blockade was off, only then would she be reassured that he was OK.

*

18 minutes earlier under the Central Dome, in the designated quarantine section.

Ruth worked as a nurse in one of the outer district's private clinics, with a district doctor. A few hours ago, however, a blue and white helicopter had come to pick her up. They weren't looking for volunteers, there wasn't time anymore, and they simply gathered specialists together for the emergency hospital and quarantine section, set up in the centre of the city. They were in uniform, didn't ask any questions, and just flashed a paper with the seal of the Police Department. Even if she had wanted to, she couldn't have said no because three years ago, as an immigrant, she had signed the declaration of support for the Special Events Directorate. She could be called in at any time in case of emergency.

The copter dropped her off at the edge of the quarantine zone. From there, she was guided through an air-inflated foil tunnel, the end of which led to the inside of the cordon. She had already seen this closed-off area from above, it spread over almost the entire main square. Unlike some hours ago, when the mayor had been giving his speech, the area had already been vacated, as the population had been housed on the ground floors of the high-rises and in the metro stations. Everywhere, uniformed and armed soldiers of the Special Events unit patrolled around. The situation was as serious as they had described it in the emergency news reports broadcast by the city management.

The sterile tunnel led to a bar, at least that's what it looked like; Ruth had never been there before. The place was hermetically sealed off, with rows of air purifiers and disinfecting units everywhere. The nurses and doctors on duty lived in the area in front of the bar, this was where they had arranged their quarters as well. As soon as she saw this, it became clear to her that she wouldn't be allowed to leave this place for a while. A glass wall separated them from the emergency hospital; on the opposite side, employees dressed in special sealed suits were busying themselves around the bedridden figures. No details could be seen, only shadows moving about in the foreground of the dim light, as all the treatment rooms were curtained off.

'Dr. Anton Spinelli,' a young man extended his hand towards her, 'you can call me Anton. I'm pleased to meet you, Ruth. You'll be working with me. We alternate shifts every seven and half hours with the others, in eighteen-strong teams. At the moment, we have over two hundred infected patients. Forgive me if my explanations seem hasty, but we'll have to start within twenty minutes.'

Ruth didn't have a chance to say a word, she just followed the doctor into a room with sterile clothing and helmets hanging on the wall.

'Under normal circumstances you wouldn't have to jump in at the deep end but the nurse assigned to me fell sick,' the doctor said. He was about ten or twelve years younger than Ruth, around thirty-five. His dark, Italian complexion was in deep contrast with the blinding white of his protective garment.

'Don't worry, the nurse wasn't struck down with this disease,' the man started to explain himself worriedly, as he saw the look of alarm on Ruth's face.

'That's OK,' said Ruth, 'I was beginning to get scared because, even though I signed up as a reservist, if our lives were endangered, how can I put it . . . well, then I wouldn't know if I would dare to do it.'

'But, dear Ruth,' said the doctor, with a slight scolding tone in his voice, 'this is our calling. That's how we've accepted it, that even in danger, we would heal others, isn't that true?'

The doctor only had his helmet left to put on, having slipped quickly into his outfit. Ruth tried to emulate him, follow the steps, but was soon left behind.

'Don't be afraid, believe me, these clothes are perfect protection. They have been tried and tested during countless tropical diseases and epidemics on Earth. You just have to be careful not to get caught on anything and to avoid tearing it.'

By now, Ruth had pulled all the clothing on, too, and was just holding her helmet, twiddling it around helplessly. Dr. Spinelli helped her to clamp it on and connect it up to the cylinder on her belt that guaranteed her air supply.

'Excellent, very clever,' the doctor encouraged her. 'There is a knob on your cuff, it's the radio, we can use it to talk. I'm putting my helmet on, try it out.'

'OK, so . . . testing microphone.' Ruth smiled timidly, she didn't have much flair for these technical things.

'Very good! If you have any worries or feel sick, just let me know, and you may come out right away. There, you can see the showers; you must stand under one of those when we've finished our shifts. It zaps every bit of pathogen off the clothes, it doesn't operate with water but with tiny ray beams that bombard the clothes.'

'Follow me, please,' and the doctor set off along another plastic corridor, which led them through to the other side of the glass wall where they would be working. Ruth was already feeling ill at ease, in her anxiety her head was suffused with heat, her ears were burning.

'Are we going already?' she asked, despair lurking in her voice.

The doctor sensed it and turned around to face her. 'We must go because we have to relieve two people who've been on their feet for quite a while now. Please calm down, because I'm counting on you.' His face was frightfully serious.

Ruth felt she would see things that she would never have the chance to see at the district clinic. She was uneasy with this whole thing, the clothes, the gear, and the preparations.

'Forgive me, I'm fine. Let's go.' She tried to pull herself together.

Meanwhile, the doctor stepped into the area that had previously functioned as a bar. The beds were arranged in groups of ten, each group partitioned off by curtains between them. At the foot of each bed, patient monitors were beeping and flashing, and bags filled with solutions and medications were hanging on infusion stands. Nurses walked from bed to bed, squirting syringes into the patients. If all of this hadn't been in a bar, then it wouldn't be any different from any emergency unit.

That's exactly why she wanted to block out the disturbing factors and look on it as an everyday job that she had taken on in a completely mundane hospital.

'Hi, Anton. I'll tell you briefly what's been happening in the past eight hours,' a female doctor stepped up to Dr. Spinelli; judging by the signs, she was the one about to be relieved. 'In our thirty-member group, everyone's state of health deteriorated in the past three hours. The amount of secretion in the mucous membranes has grown, this hampers their breathing, and many cough it up. The secretion samples must be kept fresh because, according to the latest report, contamination only occurs immediately after the sample is taken, once outside the body, it will dry within 20–50 minutes. This way, we have to take a sample from every patient and place it in a special solution that mimics the inner environment of the human body. According to observations, there is some kind of protein chain multiplying in the mucous secretion.'

'What's the situation with the tested antihistamines and antibiotics?'

'No results, that's why we stopped the dosages. It's almost certain that this is not an allergic reaction to these proteins, and it's also been ruled out that we are dealing with proteins produced by bacteria. Therefore, they are only being given salt solutions now.'

'Have you tried replacing the blood?'

'It was a totally useless torture,' the woman doctor shook her head. 'The proteins exit through the mucous membranes, through perspiration, or through stomach secretions. They're not only in the blood.'

'I understand. Then we can only alleviate their suffering by caring, we have no other alternative.'

'Unfortunately...' the woman bowed her head, a blonde lock of her hair brushing against the glass of her helmet as she shook her hair out of the net.

'Let me introduce you to Ruth, she is our new nurse,' the doctor stepped to her side.

'Pleased to meet you,' said the woman doctor, smiling. Deep behind the wrinkles from her smile, lurked sadness and tiredness. 'I wish you a lot of strength for your first day. Don't be alarmed, this is certainly a horrible sight at first but, believe me, these people were once just like you and me, and they're in great need of your help.'

'Thank you, I'll do everything that I possibly can.' Ruth drew strength from the young woman doctor, who said good-bye and left the emergency hospital with her assigned nurse.

This is where it really begins, thought Ruth. *Oh, my God . . .*

'Ruth, let's go and make the rounds of all the patients, starting at the beginning. Let's see how we can alleviate their suffering. Stay beside me, we'll read the case histories together, and then we'll decide what we'll do in the next few hours.'

Doctor Spinelli stepped over to the bed of the first patient. A middle-aged man was lying in front of them, eyes closed, at times coughing while gasping for breath. A green discharge was drying on his nose.

'Mr. Seymour, sir, how are you feeling?' the doctor wiped his face with a sterile cloth. The man opened his eyes to a slit.

'Water . . .' he moaned, 'Water! I'm thirsty.'

'You can't have any water, sir, because you're going to feel even more nauseated,' said Anton, with sympathy. 'That's exactly why you are being given this saline solution. I can give you a wet towel, to moisten your mouth, that will help to stop your thirst.'

'Alright,' said the man, resignedly. He could only lift the towel with a great effort. As soon as he put it to his mouth, he started to retch, vomiting right away.

'Quickly, hold his head, so he doesn't choke. I'll bring a vial for the sample,' said the doctor and rushed over to the medical cabinet. Meanwhile, Ruth was having trouble holding the man's head because the patient's hands and feet were shaking violently. He started to sweat profusely, thick, greenish perspiration drops making his skin slippery, so that his neck kept slipping constantly from her hand. To top it all, Ruth was having a hard time enduring the event; her clothes were covered with the secretion. This wasn't simple indigestion but some horrifying attack.

'I'm here,' the doctor returned and took a small sample of matter from the soiled bed sheet and put it into the vial. 'Good, you can lay him back now, perhaps the urge will pass.'

Ruth tried to do what the doctor said, but the man kept gesticulating, his extremities were fidgeting uncontrollably.

Suddenly, the woman in the next bed also started to shake.

'Water . . .' she moaned, too, 'I'm so thirsty.'

Ruth looked at the doctor helplessly.

'Go, Ruth, try to calm her. Don't give her anything, because she will start to vomit. If there is a secretion, take a sample of it. The vials are over there in the cabinet, and don't forget to write the names on the samples.'

Ruth felt herself becoming submerged into this unusual and terrible situation. She had never worked in a hospital ward either; she had only handled general cases with her district doctor. She had been mercilessly thrown in at the deep end, and soon only the tip of her nose would show above the surface as she slowly drowned in an unknown torrent that belonged in a horror movie.

Forcing herself to remain composed, she started talking to the woman, while Dr. Spinelli was still trying to calm the man, who, however, was shaking ever more vigorously. The doctor went over to the cabinet and drew a sedative into a syringe.

'We have to give them some sedative, or else we'll have to tie them down, otherwise they'll drop off the bed!'

He was just taking the plastic top off the needle, when three other patients also started to shake. The monitors for two of them signalled that their hearts had just stopped.

'Here, give it to them, quickly!' the doctor handed the syringes over to Ruth and ran to one of the patients whose heart had stopped. 'No, this can't be true! Why at the same time?'

The beds of the two patients in crisis were not side-by-side, so he had to decide with which one to start. He rushed to the nearest dying patient and pushed the revival button on the monitor. The electrodes connected to the patient filled up with current, his body arched up and fell back onto the bed again. The doctor then rushed over to the other patient on cardiac arrest, pushing the revival button.

Mesmerized, Ruth watched the convulsing bodies, as they arched up and down, then again, up and down, like dancers in some bizarre modern ballet. The syringe was still in her hand.

'Give it and come and help here!'

She recovered from her torpor and turned towards the patient—at the same, precise moment as the cardiac arrest whistle sounded beside her. She didn't give the sedative; she dropped the needle and looked at the young doctor, startled.

'Push the revival button—quickly! It's right there, on the console!'

The voice didn't get through to Ruth. It had all become too much for her.

'For God's sake, don't be so scared, you're totally useless like this!' the doctor admonished her rudely, because he had already lost patience. He stormed over to another unit, divided by a curtain. He pulled it aside and shouted to his colleagues, in an urgent tone: 'Could someone come and help? We have an emergency!'

There was no response from the back of the room because both the doctor and the nurse on duty there were rushing from bed to bed, with the same desperation. They already had five patients in convulsions and, just then, a sixth and behind him, a seventh, started off in the same way. The vital function monitors shrieked in succession, a garish song in the round, whistling through the place like a pitch pipe concert. Behind him, Spinelli heard more and more alarm signals coming from his unit as well. Now, he was the one standing as horrified as the substitute nurse who had been assigned to him earlier. Petrified, he listened to the symphony of death.

When he turned around, Ruth was no longer there. He saw her figure disappearing around the bend in the corridor, heading toward the sterilizer room. She was desperately rushing out of this madhouse.

Outside, soldiers were pulling on sterile clothing; an officer was giving orders around them. One of the groups had probably asked for help, although it seemed that they were only coming to clear away the remains. Doctor Spinelli walked along the row of squirming, choking patients and pushed the revival button wherever there was a cardiac arrest. The bodies were rising and falling rhythmically as the machines tried to restart their circulation by means of artificial heart massage. In the case of the patients who had received resuscitation first, there was no longer any audible heartbeat; the only sound to be heard was the continuous whistling squeal from their monitors.

Spinelli went over to one of them. According to the heart monitor, the elderly man no longer had a heartbeat, although his chest continued to rise and fall rhythmically. The doctor bent down closer, to make sure whether he had really seen it or was only hallucinating from the shock.

'My grandson . . .' the man suddenly whispered and grabbed the doctor's hand covered in protective clothing. Anton got such a scare that he staggered backwards, but he soon braced himself and bent closer again.

'Don't let him near me,' he said in a hoarse voice, and the green secretion trickled from his mouth. 'I'm terminally ill . . .'

At that moment, his body began shaking again, but he wouldn't let go of the doctor's wrist. Anton tried to hold him down on the bed, but it was a totally useless effort—he couldn't handle it, it was too much for him and his hand cramped up. He pulled himself back from the body as best he could, stretching as far back as possible on his arms. It was good timing: the man's head suddenly exploded, covering everything with the greenish substance.

By the time Dr. Spinelli had prised the man's fingers off his wrist, the chain reaction in the room had already started. On his inside radio, he heard the nurses' screaming voices in the adjacent isolation room, and the desperate cries of the doctors echoed in his ears.

The whole thing was so cinematic and surreally distant, it was as if it weren't happening to him. He stopped approaching the beds, knowing only too well that there was nothing he could do. He walked amongst the convulsing patients, between splashing mouths, the talking dead, in death row. This wasn't a hospital, it was the place of the Last Judgment.

Soldiers clad in protective clothing came swarming into the room, carrying black bags . . .

*

Eight hours later, on Earth—Japan, Japan Sea, Unmei Island

Ayame Oita became quite restless when she saw the special newscast on the TV set left turned on behind her. She had completed today's experiments at the Futura Respondis Marine Research Establishment on man-made Unmei Island. As one of the researchers in the Futura Unmei Machine project, she had been living here for almost ten months already.

In the special newscast interrupting the nightly talk show, they were reporting about a ship. They showed the *Lev Tolstoy*, marked with the Russian insignia, drifting on the Indian Ocean. The huge carrier flagship had been drifting at the wind's mercy on the open sea southwards from Port Qoriga. According to its black box, it had deviated forty-two nautical miles from its route and was tossing about, abandoned, on the surface of the great Antarctic Ocean. After the one-and-a-half-kilometre-thick ice caps had melted, the open water surfaces had grown larger, while the dimensions of the continent receded—in many places, the water dominated. Thus, the ship could have drifted undisturbed for quite a while, if the secondary distress signal hadn't come into play. The primary distress system was broken, or it may have been turned off, they weren't certain yet, although this automatic system could have navigated the ship to its destination—the American continent—whilst, at the same time, informing the global naval authorities.

The ship was swarming with the men of the United Colony Army, the Blue-Caps units. Gunboats circled around it, protective uniform-clad figures climbed onto the deck—the TV channel brought the events in virtual close-up, with its artificial satellite equipped with high performance optics.

But what irritated Ayame were not these images, it was rather the few minutes-long amateur video that the captain's widow had handed over to the TV channel. 'They threatened me,' she said, fighting back tears, 'they said that if I told anyone what had happened to my husband and the forty-five-member crew, I'd be in trouble. But I decided that I wouldn't keep quiet, because Kolya wouldn't have either. He sent me this video so that everyone would know about it and we would be able to defend ourselves against it and that somebody could find out what it was. I don't care what this or that government has to say about it, I am not going to be ordered about, either by the Russian Naval Authority or the United Colony Council.'

After that, the reporter solemnly stated that he recommended that the material to follow should only be viewed by those with a strong disposition. The recording was somewhat dark but in high resolution and sharp; it sometimes cut off, probably because the communicator that took the shots switched over to another satellite. The video showed a man, according to the captions, Captain Rigoriev, walking from corridor to corridor on the empty ship, while continuously commenting on what could be seen on the video. His voice was muffled and barely intelligible. First, he entered the sickbay, where black, packed body bags towered to the ceiling. They were fastened down by wide straps so that they wouldn't move about as a result of the billowing waves.

'Twenty-one dead,' said the Captain, 'just within the last seven hours. The government of the South-African Republic wasn't too concerned with our distress signal; I'm not surprised, given the current state of affairs there after the war. I've also informed the Russian Naval Authorities, and they said that I should keep away from ports and harbours, they would send units later to our rescue.'

The captain went to another room, where men were lying on tables, covered with blankets. They were coughing, choking, and having trouble breathing.

'This is the canteen; we're now using it to provide for the sick, because the sickbay is filled with our dead. There are twenty of them here, in a terrible state. This disease is like some kind of tropical fever. Those ill are very hot; no painkiller or fever reducer alleviates their suffering. After giving them immune strengtheners, the deterioration process picked up speed, as if the immune system wasn't impeding the disease, but rather, on the contrary, helping it to proliferate. It was only because of this protective equipment that I have been able to remain at a milder symptom level,' he said and turned the camera on himself. He was wearing strange, home-made protective clothing made of some transparent material consisting of wide adhesive tapes. A gas mask covered his face, which was why his voice was muffled. The gas mask probably wasn't filtering out all the pathogens but it slowed down their penetration.

'Grigori, bring a cloth, go and wipe their faces,' he told a sturdy man. 'He's my bodyguard. He is still in relatively good shape, as are the other two in the back. But they are also beginning to show mild symptoms. We don't know how long we can hold on; we're waiting for the Navy or any other help.'

'31 degrees 57 minutes south, 52 degrees 22 minutes east—this is our current position. I turned the primary distress system off on the ship because if we don't move position within a certain period of time, the robotic pilot would take us to the next port. In view of the present circumstances, this would be fatal for any populated area.'

At this point, the transmission broke off. Not only the amateur video but the entire TV broadcast. The screen was only filled with the static notice of a breakdown in transmission. According to the caption, there was an error in the satellite relay and a channel crew was already working on eliminating the problem.

Ayame thought about another morning newscast: The communication satellites on Mars had also come to a halt, the relays and boosters broadcasting to Earth had also failed. Perhaps the solar wind or a magnetic storm . . .

The Japan Sea had also been plagued by strong winds and storms for two weeks now; a large typhoon was passing by above them just then. It was a wonder that the machines stabilizing the island were able to compensate for the power of the water and the wind.

The picture suddenly came back, just as unexpectedly as it had disappeared, and another reporter from another studio took over.

'We apologize for this inconvenience, but the technical unit is informing us that we have lost one of our satellites. The satellite serving the broadcast relay has deviated from its path, and it will take a while to correct the error. Our broadcast is now being sent from the antennas positioned on the Moon back to Earth, therefore we ask for your understanding for the resulting technical problems.'

The amateur video continued. Again, the camera showed the canteen on the *Lev Tolstoy*.

'Captain! Come quickly!' Grigori shouted in the background. 'The men have started to shake all at the same time! We can't handle them!'

The surging figures of the remaining crewmembers still alive, wallowing in pain, filled Ayama with horror. The captain quickly put the camera down on one of the tables and it settled on its side, turning 90 degrees to the right. In spite of this, Ayama could see that the four men were rushing from one sick man to the next, trying to calm them. Meanwhile, more of the sick tumbled off the tables, onto the floor, and continued to quiver as if driven by seizure attacks.

'Bring some ropes, we have to tie them down!' the commander yelled to one of the sailors, who was deploying his full weight in order to keep a convulsing body on the table but he obeyed the order, letting go of the sailor and running to the other end of the room.

The sick man left on the table suddenly sat up. Turning to the commander, in a barely audible voice, he said: 'The man . . . the man who got off at Port Qoriga . . . don't let him go any further . . .'

With that, his head vanished off the screen, or rather, disappeared in an explosion, and the camera was covered in mucous liquid. At that moment, the picture froze and, with it, so did the clock in the lower right corner: it showed the exact time eight hours earlier.

The system still continued with audio recording for a time, while the ongoing turbulent horror could only be imagined without the image. The chaotic hollering and thudding noises painted an even darker background. Again, another breakdown in transmission. The screen showed the same error message as before.

Ayame waited another half a minute and, when the channel wouldn't come back on, she started switching them; but no other channel was carrying this information—all that was showing everywhere were movies or commercials.

The sight penetrated her optic nerve and paralyzed her insides. The image resembled the results of the experiment to a tee. Everything had unfolded in exactly the same way with those unfortunate victims as with the rats during that morning's experiment.

Three days ago, she had pulled out twenty entities from among the animals and prepared them for the test. She had then attached the scaled-down copy of the implant to the appropriate part of the brain of the selected rat marked '20-A.'

Then she had separated the other nineteen rats from the one fitted with the implant and proceeded to study their behaviour one by one. The one marked '20-A' didn't sleep during this time and consumed three times as much food as those in the isolated group. Since fitting the implant, it was being given the antidote every hour, so Ayame didn't perceive any side effects in it. After bringing the two groups together, transmission of the infection occurred within about seven minutes—she could verify this later from the blood samples. The speed of propagation was much higher than in the previous tests, meaning that the tiny molecular mechanisms had improved as a result of the development work over the past few months.

However, the goal of the current test wasn't the increment in the speed of propagation but the verification of the functionality of the so-called terminator command, long awaited by management—and the control function promised by the researchers. This was a radio signal broadcast in every direction, which would cause the implanted pathogens, the Unmei Machines, to stop working, stop self-reproducing too, stop everything. The receiving system built into it by the researchers was actually a nano-sized cone, imitating an auricle, a receiving membrane that would translate the radio signals into biological information. She had been working on the development of such a radio signal for several months now. Today had been the first live test.

But the experiment hadn't brought about the expected result: the rats had perished within two minutes, instead of registering a slow but steady improvement. The Unmei Machines—instead of coming to a halt—began to intensify their performance, this process leading all the way to the death of the host body, leaving a horrible mess behind, with the usual greenish liquid. The reproductive phase, the last phase of the infection, had somehow been revved up to such a point that the body could no longer hold the mucous containing the Unmei Machine protein constituent within itself.

The host of the implant marked '20-A' hadn't been hurt, as this process couldn't start due to the immunity secured by the antidote. Nevertheless, new experiments would be necessary, in order to perfect the terminator command, so that those infected could be freed from the invaders, without problem.

Ayame felt awfully bad. She had the feeling that the machines had already escaped, in one form or another, into the world and because of the faulty terminator command given by her, the entire crew of that ship had perished. It couldn't have been an accident—the known crisis situation, as seen on the screen, had occurred during the firing of the signal.

Only the hosts with the implants could have committed an error, they had been the ones propagating the Unmei Machines, as they had obviously contravened the conditions stipulated in the contract. She didn't know these men, only the doctors who had carried out the implantations had met them. Futura had only allowed partial insight into the complex network of the project, she was only doing her job and she never questioned anything.

Until now . . .

She decided to call Professor Yakizima, whatever the consequences. She knew that the professor wouldn't be happy with her coming forward, because this conversation would be stepping well outside her sphere of authority as a researcher. It would also be contrary to the strict rule that had come into force in the current, strategically sensitive phase of the project. In this final phase, only in the most imperative of cases could she initiate an outbound-directed conversation, because of the constant eavesdropping by spy satellites. This current state of affairs could, however, justifiably be regarded as an emergency situation.

The communicator rang for a long time. She started having second thoughts and almost gave up when she heard the professor's voice at the end of the line.

'Yakizima here.'

'Professor Yakizima, this is Ayame Oita, with your permission.'

'Hello, Miss Oita. Excuse me for being so tardy in answering your call, but I'm just in the process of settling in my new home here in Ulan Bator. It must be something serious if you're calling me on my direct line instead of leaving a message through the Unmei System.'

Ayame felt the annoyance in his voice.

'I'm very happy that you finally answered the phone. Yes, this could be serious trouble; I don't even know where to start. Did you have a chance to look at the news in the past few minutes?'

'Unfortunately not. The New China government is rather strict in filtering the information to which we may have access here. We cannot see Japanese channels at all.'

'This wasn't a Japanese newscast but the independent news channel called "For Asia."'

'Sorry, that wasn't accessible either in Mongolia, for obvious political reasons. You must be aware of the fact that the proprietor of the "For Asia" news channel is a businessman who originates from an old Russian region and who regularly organizes anti-New China demonstrations through the channel. He's not popular around here.'

Ayame fell silent for a minute. She tried to collect her thoughts.

'Today was the first time that I sent out a terminator command to the lab rats.'

'I hope you carried out the experiments under the shielded mode...'

'That's exactly the reason I'm calling you. The newscast I mentioned showed a report about a drifting Russian ship on the Indian Ocean, where a severe disease had exterminated the crew. They just showed the images in the news,' she let out a big sigh. 'The symptoms were remarkably similar to those caused by our Unmei Machines.'

Professor Yakizima couldn't get his breath. Alexei Sverlov crossed his mind...

'Good God, Ayame, where did you get this idea?' The professor was so shaken up that he forgot all social courtesies, addressing her familiarly.

'Because everything occurred in exactly the same way as with the lab rats when I gave the order. The experiment...' her voice faltered, 'I mean, the experiment failed, the Unmei Machines didn't stop, they turned against the host bodies and destroyed them. It can't be a coincidence that I saw the same on those images as what I've seen here in the lab.' She was stuttering, all worked up.

'But this is absolutely impossible!' she exclaimed suddenly, as she looked at the indicators on the verification panel. 'The shield on the transmitter is still switched on!'

'According to you, is it still possible that, in spite of this, the antenna's shielding system wasn't working?'

'I don't know, it could have been damaged in the raging typhoon last week...'

Professor Yakizima knew that he would have to regain control over his thoughts, because he could easily be led to make a mistake by his increasingly overwhelming nervousness. His undisciplined conduct could result in giving Ayame the wrong information. Any further impatient and unguarded questions would only reinforce the fact that the Unmei pathogen could indeed have caused contamination on that ship.

But he had to admit that the breaking loose of the Unmei Machines was a very realistic and possible explanation for what Ayame had seen. According to the tracker, Alexei Sverlov was now somewhere in Africa, and it would be quite conceivable for him to have used a Russian ship for the trip. What could be happening with his implant now? If the terminator command had escaped from the research island due to a fault in the shielding unit, then his implant would now be a useless piece of metal.

Perhaps it was better this way, he thought. Perhaps much better, if he didn't have to worry about the two deserters. The Unmei project was now in its final phase, and in this phase one could do without wayward adventurers.

'Look, Miss Oita, there's no need to be alarmist right away. In all probability, some hideous bacterial infection on the ship caused a violent outbreak of food poisoning. It had nothing to do with your experiment.'

The girl remained silent for a long time at the other end of the line, her struggle was disconcertingly evident, even from such a distance. Perhaps it was the first time she had realized what the possible final outcome of her experiment could be, thought Yakizima. But she couldn't back out now, she was a volunteer as well, as were so many in this project.

'And what happened to the lab test animal bearing the implant?' the Professor asked. He wanted to know what the fate of the two deserters would be if the failed command had indeed escaped from the island. If the lab test animals were intact, then the two carriers would also be safe.

'The carrier is intact and healthy. The earlier predicted result that we had feared did not materialize: the implant continues to function, the carrier is capable of causing new infections. The Unmei Machines are active and functional.'

Yakizima suppressed a sigh, he wasn't sure whether to be pleased with the news or not. Perhaps now, before the start of the next phase and the placing of newer implants, the two men should be eliminated. They had already breached their contracts much earlier, by leaving the area to which they had been assigned, without giving prior notice. These areas had been specifically established so that they would be able to intervene in cases of implant failures or any other complications. If they had run out of the antidote, then they would soon lose their immunity, and the machines would exterminate them mercilessly.

Suddenly, he felt ashamed for his thoughts. Despite having chosen them well in advance, those men had volunteered for the research, and for that reason he couldn't abandon them. They were warriors, too, in their own way. They were fighting with the shadows of their past—but perhaps they hadn't chosen the proper weapons for this fight.

'Have the shielding system checked out by the technicians, and don't worry. I'll report your excellent work to my superiors, that is to say, directly to the Imperial Delegate. They won't forget about you, you may rest assured of that. Continue with your experiments until the terminator command causes the Unmei Machines to come to a halt. Thank you for your call.'

Ayame remained seated, and stared at the '20-A' rat, which hadn't slept for the third consecutive day and was the picture of health. The cage next to it was empty; the rat carcasses had ended up hours ago in the disintegrator.

Perhaps the same thing was happening right now on that ship . . . with those that had previously been human beings. They had not been volunteers; they'd had no idea that they would be the victims of a research experiment.

As much as she tried to, she couldn't believe in the professor's explanation. The coincidence of the two events, the similarity of the symptoms, was more than a simple random happening. Uncertainty ate away at her, deep within her, and she could only have shared it with the two other researchers working in parallel with her, at another project site.
But would it interest them at all? Or had they broken away from the outside world and already sunk irretrievably into the nanoworld?

What would happen if she now violated her obligations of secrecy as pledged, by calling Youko? Her sibling had always been a good listener in their childhood, whenever she'd had problems . . .

In one of Ulan Bator's recently opened, modern buildings, Professor Yakizima knew exactly what was currently passing through the woman's mind. As a former soldier, he had experienced the fact that the conscience surfaces in even the best of volunteers, when it was a matter of the innocent victims of war.

'Hello, Commander?' he spoke into the communicator calling the Unmei Island. 'Please turn off every outgoing line, as well as the incoming TV channels. Starting today, the island is an entirely locked down object. No one may arrive, no one may leave, until my further orders. Thank you.'

Nujo Yakizima rendered homage to the ancient gods of self-sacrifice and heroic death with his tireless work. Perhaps his biggest mistake was that he also expected others to fall to their knees and adore these ancient gods without a murmur.

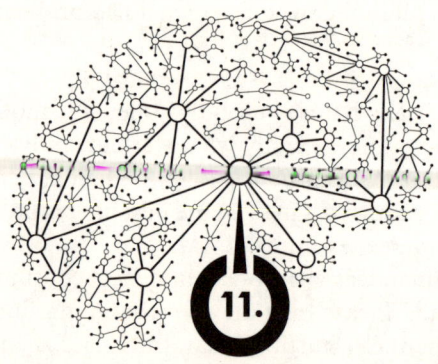

11.

Alex realized that he was tied to the back of a pickup truck. They had bound his hands to the back of an old bentwood chair, with a rope twisted from the leaves of some kind of plant with incredibly sharp edges, which cut like a razor. His prolonged struggles, since who knew how long, had caused it to bite deep into his wrists; his sweat was running into the wound, burning him dreadfully.

But he could only find a vague explanation, based on hazy recollections, as to where he was and what this was all about. He must have drunk his way through two entire shifts at the camp one night, sometime in the past. The mercenaries had been shouting back and forth to him now and then, he vaguely remembered them cracking jokes with him, and he had to endure Bianco's disapproving glances, as well. He had warned him that this would end up in trouble.

However, he had no recollection whatsoever of the dawn.

And then they must have tied him up here, otherwise they couldn't have transported him . . . but Bianco and his mercenaries wouldn't have done it in such a cruel and painful way. He would have been dumped in one of the half-track stockrooms.

They weren't the ones who had done it!

With a jaundiced grin, he acknowledged having succeeded in knocking himself out and surviving it all. He had drunk himself into a coma and weathered the nauseous period! *He had managed to screw the implant, after all!*

Or maybe not, he thought, suddenly alarmed at the sight of his appearance. He was covered all over in the usual yellowish-green, dried mucus. There wasn't much to be seen of his camouflage clothing, as his entire body was covered with some linen-like fabric, seemingly torn out of some sheets.

But at least he couldn't remember anything. Not even the nastiest period. *Where the hell is that rotten antidote?*

May Futura rot in hell . . .

The pickup truck was standing in the middle of a clearing in a settlement that had perhaps been desolate for centuries—probably lively enough in its heyday—now simply full of rubbish and ruins. The jungle had slowly reclaimed the terrain usurped by houses: roots snaked in through the windows between the glazed bricks, breaking through the flat roofs, encircling entire rooms and pressing upwards toward the sky, ripping them out of the blocks of one or two-storied houses. Some of them looked like those ancient tree-huts that fathers built for their kids between the branches. Tiny quadrupeds, perhaps small monkeys, were playing with the rust-encrusted hairdryer hoods in the hairdressing salon. In the display window of the variety shop on the opposite side, backwoods plants, ferns, and lianas had taken the place reserved for the day's special item. Over on the other side, the crumbling column of an energy pump was standing in splendid isolation—at some time in the past, floaters could come and fill up here. On top of the pump, a cell lamp was still flickering, but the energy connector and the hose were missing—they had probably landed up in some scavenger's stockpile or been pilfered by the looters that abounded everywhere in these parts.

In the middle of the square, over Alex's left shoulder, someone had made a firing range out of a dried-up old fountain. From within, firearm barrels stuck out, pointing into the four winds. On the fountain's cement ledge, bags, metal scraps, and appliances—doors, fridges, air conditioners, and metal furniture—were all piled up against the wall. The door of one of the fridges was missing, so the body itself, stripped of its back, served as a firing slit. Through it, one could see the inside of the bunker devastated by a fire or an explosion, with jet-black dust covering everything. Alex watched the rifle range for a good two minutes but the barrels of the firearms didn't budge, and he didn't see anyone behind the firing slit either.

Minutes passed without any event occurring that would indicate a human presence, which finally made him realize that he was there all by himself. Except for the birds perched in the neighbouring stores and monkeys playing noisily, there was nobody around. At the end of the street, he saw a shadow, suggestive of a stooping figure running across, but it was only a pronghorn with an injured leg. A few minutes later, its fawn followed.

This could only mean one thing: that they had crossed the Victoria trench, along the banks of the dried-up Victoria Lake, because the hoofed, plant-eating mammals were only to be found in the reservation to the south of the Kampala metropolis, which was located on the western side. They had long been driven out of Africa's remaining territories by humans. Of course, wherever they were still to be found, those reservations had fallen into the warlords' hands. Most of the animals had either been hunted down or had broken out when the fences around the reservations had been destroyed.

Therefore, he was now on the West side, in a ghost town near the reservation . . .

He tried in vain to loosen the rope on his hand. Whoever had tied this knot, knew his business, because it was ruthlessly tight, causing burning pains whenever he moved even a little. Funny, how the daintily curved back of the bentwood chair offered such strategic fixing points for the knots, it must have been in good condition to stand up to it all—at least compared to the crumbling and disintegrating furniture lying all around in the surrounding area. He also tried to move his legs, but they were tightly fastened to the chair's legs. That mysterious stranger had made sure that the rope made of lianas wouldn't cling to his pants or his boots; he had even pulled up Alex's socks, so that they could cut sharply into his shinbone. He felt it, too, when he tried to move himself a bit sideways with his toes.

The sky was covered with clouds, so he couldn't establish the time and where the sun might be in the sky. It could possibly be the afternoon. But what day was it? How much time had passed since he'd been knocked out?

The small truck, a Chrysler pickup, was still the ancient, wheeled version. The motor might have been traditional, or perhaps it had been converted to fusion drive. Painted in camouflage colours, it was designed for local conditions and, as he saw from the corner of his eye, it had been transformed into a well-equipped mobile fortification, because behind it protruded the barrel of a heavy automatic weapon. He couldn't make out what type of machine gun it was—it might have helped him to determine how well equipped and prepared his captors were. Looking over his right shoulder, he noticed that the door of the driver's cab was open, and that the torso of a man was hanging out of it. Most likely he was dead—his hands had drawn a long stripe along the dusty road, showing the direction from which they had come, for about twenty-five metres. This man must have been driving him somewhere, when a sniper's bullet had finished him off. If only he could see who it was. It could have been one of his own mercenaries who had wanted to liberate him. Someone must have abducted him while he was knocked out.

The truck's platform—and Alex, too—were pointing in the direction of a building that was a replica modelled along the lines of a Victorian country manor. In Africa, even in the high-rise era, they still continued to build these, obviously with super-modern interiors in line with state-of-the-art technology, merely retaining this archaic exterior. Alex tried to remember what it was that had happened to him when he had been inside—as there was no doubt that was where they had arrived from, it being the only building in the town area still in good condition. But nothing came to mind. A totally black void swirled around his brain.

The manor was enclosed by a wall built of miscellaneous bits of scrappy household items and pieces of furniture, just like the wall encircling the fountain. There was just one, single opening in the middle of the wall, with barbed wire mounted on both sides, showing the way. In its own way, it was a real fortification.

For Alex, there was no question about it: this had to be King Silaha's palace. The residence of the dreaded lord of the tribal territories.

If only he knew for how many days and, above all, under what circumstances he had stayed there as a guest. The deal hadn't gone through, that was for sure—at that thought, he broke out in reluctant, rattling laughter. This damned, arms-trade-tour around the world never made it. The implant didn't give him infinite and invincible strength as had been suggested by the programme at the time. Futura . . . had used him as a guinea pig.

While he was brooding over this, he saw a faint flame flare up through the opening cut into the wall around the manor. The small flame flickered, lurching back and forth, as if someone were brandishing a votive candle.

Alex couldn't believe his eyes but he couldn't wipe them, though it would have made him feel better: both eyes were continuously shedding tears. He shook his head, to clear the picture, but the light didn't die, it continued to swing back and forth. After a minute or so, it became obvious: the light was a flickering flame, from a torch or something similar, being held by a distant human figure. The figure was walking unsteadily, as if he were injured, or rather like someone who had just given himself a shot, or was simply drunk. Whatever caused his unsteadiness, it was apparent that he was heading for the pickup truck.

Things were becoming urgent for Alex; he had to find a way to escape somehow. He no longer had the time to speculate on his past blunders, neither did he expect to be picked up by any of his remaining men—that figure there was continuing to approach ominously. He tried to move his hands again. Clenching his teeth against the pain, he jerked them up and down; perhaps the lianas would tear off on the back of the hardwood chair. It seemed hopeless, because the chair's back was smooth, the lianas sliding easily over it. But his hands reacted all the more to these movements: his blood flowed out like a bubbling stream. So he relinquished the struggle, deciding instead to wait out what would happen to him, rather than bleed to death.

The figure was taking its time in approaching, stumbling somewhat, stooping at times, so Alex had enough time to observe him. A slightly paunchy man of average height but with a smaller frame than Alex, with Creole skin and mutton chops. Alex was rather surprised, as he didn't look like one of the locals, nor even like someone born on this continent. He had heard earlier that King Silaha's forebears were of

South-American descent, so perhaps this chap also shared the same origins.

Or it could be the King himself, blind drunk . . . although this seemed the least likely option.

As he approached, it became clear that he was holding a Molotov cocktail. The burning wick was a long piece of linen, exactly like the one twisted around his own body. The piece of linen was trailing behind him in the dust, he was trailing the fire as if he were walking a dog. Judging from the length of the fabric and its rate of combustion, he had a maximum of about five, perhaps eight, minutes left.

'I don't like this whole situation at all,' Alex murmured between his teeth and set his limbs into motion once again, but his bonds didn't loosen one iota, they remained just as tight as before.

He knew with cold certainty that the man intended the bottle for him . . .

'Well, well, Mister Alexei!' shouted the man, raising the Molotov cocktail up high, as if he were proposing a toast. 'The outing with my man didn't last too long, thanks to the superb weapon you brought me as a gift! The aiming device on it is splendid; even such simple and untrained men like me can handle it easily!'

Holy cow, thought Alex, *he put his own man to death with my gun!* Not a good omen. The guy had snapped completely.

'No, don't take it seriously, it wasn't me, but whoever did it, was using the same excellent gun as the one you have. I hope he's not watching me through his binoculars,' he said with a devilish smile and pretended to duck down behind the vehicle. But, in fact, he was obviously only pretending that someone was watching him. He was completely stoned.

'I think we'll be able to strike a deal if you can bring me such superb weapons,' he said, smiling roguishly. He spoke the regional African language, which had evolved from the two main ubiquitous African languages, Swahili and French, over the previous centuries, with a Spanish accent. Alex didn't speak this composite language, but the translation module of his biochip helped him out immediately.

'Your Majesty, right?' Alex asked cautiously. Since he didn't remember anything, he wasn't too sure about the matter.

'Yes, yes, I just happened to leave my delegation behind,' said Silaha, who called himself king, although he was nothing more than a petty warlord. He had taken advantage of the chaotic situation and had ripped off large chunks of territory from the countries feuding with each other. 'The fact that I'm forced to show up without my attendants, is all due to your mercenaries' blasted activities. Unfortunately, my household has been considerably diminished.'

'I'm sorry. I have no idea what may have happened; in fact, believe me, I don't remember anything,' said Alex, and he wasn't lying.

'Oh, of course, I'm well aware that you don't remember it. In the state you were in at the time we made the raid on your camp, you couldn't have remembered much.'

Right, thought Alex, *then it was a raid*. They had probably surprised them at night with a larger group, so that his mercenaries hadn't had a chance to defend themselves. And yet, someone had still come to get him—or perhaps Bianco had organized the campaign for his escape—and had shot that gink out from under the wheel.

'Are you sitting comfortably, my friend?' Silaha inquired, pointing to the chair. 'Unfortunately, this was the only place I could find for you to sit.'

'You could loosen the ropes,' requested Alex, although he didn't believe he could persuade the man.

'Of course, my friend, of course,' laughed Silaha, 'I'll do it right away. Although I had spent a long time braiding them, as is written in our formal ceremonies. But for you, I'll do it!' he exclaimed, laughing. He didn't look at all like someone about to do something.

'What formal ceremony are you talking about?' Alex asked, alarmed.

'Why, the one we use when tying up those that are still moving, when they should have been dead already.'

'What the heck are you talking about?'

'Why, about you, Mister Alexei Sverlov!' Reinforcing his reply, he threw his arms-dealer ID card at Alex's chest. ' Or do you prefer to be called *Ángel de la Muerte*?'

Alex knew that the Spanish expression meant the angel of death, but he didn't understand anything about the whole thing. This man was probably insane, or he was so inebriated and stoned that he had no idea what he was talking about.

'Why should I be the angel of death?'

Silaha broke out laughing. He shook so much from laughing, that he almost dropped the bottle. The flame was very close to setting fire to his clothes but, even drunk, he was still lucky enough to narrowly escape that fate.

'What do you mean *why*? Because wherever you go, you bring death with you!'

Alex was genuinely taken aback by the man's words. Although it was true that many had died around him in the past few weeks, he had thought that had been a consequence of his dangerous occupation. If someone sells death in bulk, it was inevitable that sometimes men die in his surroundings.

'Oh, you don't remember, of course. How could you?' Silaha laughed again. 'A ship, what was it called again? That famous writer . . .'

'The *Tolstoy*? What about it?'

'Yes, that's it, the *Lev Tolstoy*! Everyone is talking about the ghost ship that was found near the Antarctic, drifting out of control! You came off that ship. And yet, on that ship, everyone had perished.'

'What do you mean, everyone had perished?' Alex didn't believe his ears. 'And how do you know that I came off that ship?' even as he asked, he already knew the answer.

'Your communicator disclosed a lot of secrets to us,' the warlord smiled and threw the small device onto the platform. 'The coordinates scrupulously follow the ship's path.'

'Concerning the deaths, well,' Silaha stopped for a small pause, pointing at Alex's clothes and bindings with the burning flask, 'they unequivocally bore the exact same symptoms as this vile green monstrosity that is visible on you as well, and which finished off nearly my entire household.'

Alex tried to assimilate this new information. They had found the ship drifting at sea, with everyone on board the *Lev Tolstoy* dead, all showing the same symptoms that the lack of antidotes had caused him . . .

Damned Futura Respondis, frig their blasted experiments! He was furious. Whatever this thing was, it was propagating something deadly. This meant that Okan's men hadn't died from food poisoning in the Indian Ocean after all.

Without the antidote, the implant is spreading something that's causing people's deaths!

'Oops, my friend,' Silaha laughed again, looking at the burning wick in his hand. The linen was dwindling down noticeably, with possibly enough left for half a minute, 'pity that our time is up.'

'Wait, I'll explain everything!'

'No need! In any case, I wouldn't believe you anyway!' he yelled, no longer convivial, but blinded with rage. 'Why would I believe a dead man? Why, even this linen, I had torn off your mortuary cloth,' he said, pointing with a smile at the burning wick.

'What are you saying? I'm not dead!'

'Not right now, but about six hours ago, you were lying in a coffin, wrapped up in a linen cloth, waiting for burial!'

'What?!'

'I know you are the angel of death! And so, you must perish by fire!' and, with that, he raised the flask in order to throw it at Alex. At that precise moment there was the sound of a soft thump.

He knew that noise only too well; it was as if a thin membrane had been punctured by a projectile.

Silaha's hand stopped over his head. Blood flowed out of his right ear, running down his neck, then his other arm and hand, all the way down to the ground. At that point, the bottle slipped from his hand, falling onto his head. The blazing body crumpled like a sack, into the dust. The flames slowly covered him, the stench of burning flesh and black, suffocating smoke rose into the atmosphere.

Alex saw movement in one of the portholes of the bunker built up around the fountain. The sniper's rifle retracted, and soon a figure climbed through the opening built from the old fridge. He recognized the man's Italian features, muscular upper trunk, and his light, athletic gait: it was Bianco. *So not everyone had perished in the raid!*

'Thank God,' was all that he could stammer out when the mercenary jumped onto the platform and cut off the liana ropes. 'I thought I'd been left all alone.'

'Thanks to you too, boss,' said Bianco, 'When you decided to knock yourself out with booze early that morning before the raid, you sent me back to the port, for this.' Bianco was holding a package, with a box inside. *The antidote arrived from Moscow!*

'Bianco, I have to tell you something. It would be better if you didn't come too close to me.'

'I know, boss,' said Bianco, nodding with that mischievous gleam in his eyes, like when he used to sense something, just like a clairvoyant, 'I already knew that night that something was troubling you. But you needn't worry: whatever it is, I'm immune to it. I would have caught it much earlier, since we were travelling in the same cabin.'

There could be something in that, thought Alex. If this condition really was contagious, then Bianco would have been its first victim.

The mercenary helped him down from the platform and sat him in the right-hand seat of the pickup truck. He dragged the corpse out of the driver's seat and covered it with a tarpaulin.

'This is a shaman's badge,' said Bianco, pointing at the ceramic pendant he had torn off the dead man's neck. 'He probably put you on the vehicle to take you into the jungle and execute you in a ritual ceremony. But I shot him from there,' he pointed to the spot where the antelope had crossed the road earlier, 'from the end of the street. Unfortunately, it took a while before I could get any closer to him but I got here just in time. Now we're going to hit the road back to the camp and give our partners the funeral rites. Try to relax, though I know that a certain something doesn't let you rest. But you can tell me the story later, if you feel like it.'

He stepped over to the burning body, put out the fire, and searched through Sooty's pockets. He found seven thousand New Dollar chips there and two other cards, which they might be able to use. Fortunately, modern currency was made out of fireproof material.

'This may have possibly been yours, some time ago,' he tossed the chips into Alex's lap.

The pickup truck started up smoothly. Bianco stepped on the gas pedal. It was unusual to sit in an old car with an ignition motor, although any vehicle would have suited Alex right now. Despite the fact that it belonged in a museum, the four-stroke engine purred comfortingly in his ears.

He had been Futura Respondis's guinea pig, but he decided to rebel against his role. He wanted to know the purpose of this experiment.

And now he had a bodyguard, as well.

*

Seven and a half hours earlier . . .

Slowsky had been the last one to relieve Bianco, but the boss, the Russian pipsqueak—as Slowsky called him—had sent their leader back to Port Qoriga at dawn, to fetch him some kind of medication. But it must have been some drug, which kept this strange bird awake. Because, how else would he be capable of doing all of this without any sleep at all? The naked truth was that he didn't sleep a wink. Someone who sleeps doesn't go out jogging at dawn and doesn't go for a leak in the bushes every two hours. Only those who drink all night long out of sheer boredom from not being able to sleep have their bladder full all the time.

Consequently, he had relieved Bianco sooner, as the man got into a caterpillar and set off in the direction of the harbour. The postal authorities had sent a message saying that they would bring the package as far as the border, but no further, and would turn around there, as they were not prepared to take any risks bigger than that. They didn't dare to penetrate deeper into the jungle, which was why Bianco had to make the two-hour round trip back in order to meet them at the border.

Now Slowsky had to walk around the camp, as he had become the leader of the mercenaries. There wasn't much for him to do, everything was quiet, the sensors placed around the camp weren't registering any movement. They might just scrape through the entire thing without confrontation and their reception wouldn't be hostile.

As he approached the Russki's quarters, he saw their employer sitting in the chair in front of the tent, with the bottle of vodka that had fallen out of his hand lying on the ground beside him. It was rolling back and forth, empty, clanking loudly each time the wind blew it up against the leg of the camping chair. The beer cans scattered all around were lying in a half-circle before him. *The little idiot*, thought Slowsky. He had just thrown everything about, all over the place, even though the cans represented a significant security risk by kicking up a row in the wind. He picked up an empty sack and, one by one, picked up the half-full carton of cans, practically without making a sound.

As he picked them up, grumbling to himself, around the Russki's feet, he noticed a strange liquid between the man's legs. At first, he thought that the idiot had pissed himself in his sleep, but this substance was somewhat thicker. He had seen blood and other bodily fluids, especially when he had to find someone's trail in the jungle, but this material was entirely different from any of those. He got to his feet and switched on the lamp mounted on his vest.

'What the bloody hell?' was all he could mutter when he saw his employer's face. The same greenish-yellow, pus-like substance trickled out of every orifice in his head. The same coloured drops ran down his face, oozing out of the corner of his eyes, via the tear ducts.

'Hey, everyone! Slowsky here. I think we have a major problem. The Russki doesn't look too good,' he broadcast over his radio. 'One guard stays in the north and in the east; as for the rest, a meeting at the central tent, at once!'

He was no novice at his trade, he'd been forced to deal with strange cases in the past, but he had never seen anything like this. He'd had a boss who had shot himself up with some crap or another and run around naked during the entire campaign; then there was the one whose strange nightly habits caused him headaches: he sang loudly during the secret mission on which they had been sent out. But this Russki had this urge to croak at this precise place in the middle of nowhere. And of course, this raised the question of the squad leader's responsibility—God forbid that this puny little man should kick the bucket during his watch! Why, oh why, wasn't Bianco, his little favourite, here now to save him?

Sokolov was the first to get there. Without thinking, he gathered up Alex and laid him on one of the fold-out beds. He unbuttoned his bulletproof vest and pulled off his jacket. Meanwhile, he got himself stained, his hands and clothes got covered with the strange stuff. Seemingly, he wasn't too concerned.

'It's bloody beyond me, what this grunge is that's pouring out of him,' said Slowsky, and he plunged his finger into one of the spots on the rim of the camping chair. 'Like snot, or rather, like spit. But the colour is even more bizarre. The smell is totally neutral. What would it taste like?'

'I don't know, man,' said Sokolov and disengaged Alex's chest, 'but if you ask me, my brother is dead.'

'But his chest was definitely raising and falling, while he was still sitting in the chair,' Slowsky said, uncomprehending. 'I even bent down closer to him to make sure.'

'Maybe then,' the Russian mercenary lowered his head to Alex's chest, 'but now I tell you, his heart is no longer beating.'

'Wait,' Slowsky spoke, picking up a dried leaf from the ground, and wiped away the secretion with the sleeve of his jacket, to free the nasal passages. He put the leaf under Alex's nose, but it didn't stir.

'He couldn't be more dead,' said Sokolov and started to pump Alex's ribcage. Through a piece of fabric torn off one of the mosquito nets, he blew air into Alex's lungs via his mouth. This wasn't easy because, at each blow, the phlegm-like fluid came gushing unstoppably through Alex's nose.

'This is horrible!' he tried to wipe off the stuff that had landed on his face. 'It's blocking his windpipe completely.'

'So let's wait for the Doc, surely he'll tell us something concrete.'

Doc Shryver was his nickname; he was the most skilled among them in medical matters. Although each mercenary was capable of dealing with wounds, suturing a cut, reviving a colleague, or alleviating pain, still it was Shryver who had served two years as a medical orderly for one of the units at the time of the second Asian conflict. The final opinion in this case would be his.

'He's dead, no doubt about it,' said Shryver, when he finally arrived. He took out a small instrument, a portable test scanner. The device whistled continuously while he held it over Alex's heart. 'Dead. It must be an allergic reaction to something, food or the large amount of booze. His system is producing this liquid as a defense mechanism. I don't believe he can be saved any longer. Perhaps if we cleaned the air passages, we could still revive him . . . how long has he been lying here?'

'No idea, but Bianco left about ten minutes ago to pick up the medication arriving at the port.'

'What kind of medication?'

'I don't know, the Russki needed something,' said Slowsky, trying to avoid Sokolov's disapproving glance. He knew that his Russian colleague loathed it when he called him by that name. 'Perhaps he's in this state because he didn't get it in time.'

'What now?' Friday, the giant Congolese mercenary who had arrived with the Doc, intervened. Everyone looked at Slowsky, he was now the leader of the pack.

'It'll take Bianco two or three hours to get back with the stuff. Even if he were still alive, it's doubtful we could stabilize his condition until the medication arrives, whatever that thing is,' Slowsky thought aloud.

'So tell us what we should do: turn around too? It's dangerous to stay here with a corpse at the border of the tribal territories,' said the Doc. 'Not to mention the crate full of sniper rifles that we're carrying as samples. Our employer got hold of them at the harbour, who knows what the source was, and if the authorities were to catch us, we'd all be up the creek without a paddle.'

Slowsky lit up, even though it wasn't permitted. The cigarette glowing in the dark made an excellent target. He was well aware of that, but now he couldn't dispel his nervousness any other way.

'Right. Rip up some linen, wrap it around his corpse to hide that load of muck. Put him into the caterpillar storage space, we'll take his body. His family will probably want to bury him on his own property. Break camp, we leave in twenty minutes. When you're finished, I'll call Bianco not to come back but to wait for us there.'

The three men quietly set about the task, covering Alex's body with ripped fabric. They tied his limbs very tightly, his arms beside his torso, so that the body would be easier to carry. When they finished, it looked like a mummy exhibit in a pre-colonization era museum.

Slowsky was pretty annoyed. It was anybody's guess as to who would be paying them now. They had only received thirty per cent of their soldier's pay in advance; perhaps the rest would come from the family out of gratitude for returning the body. Eerily, this was exactly the same situation as a few years ago during that campaign in Shanghai, where they had to bring out a high-ranking general from a Chinese prisoners' camp, a pajama-clad Indian with a big red stripe on his overalls. Of course, in the midst of the gunfight and all that chaos, the chap had been hit, and died a few hours later in the copter. And so, they hadn't gotten anything after delivering the corpse, the family said it was the unit's fault, that the campaign hadn't been properly organized. The hell it wasn't, but the officer started to fuss, ordering this and that to be done, and that from then on he would take over the command, and some such similar stupidities ... of course, he had been jumping around so much that his pursuers had finally shot him in the end.

A mercenary operation required brains, not just military rank— Slowsky thought to himself and, forgetting all precaution, took a big puff from his cigarette.

The next moment, the sniper's bullet tore away half of his face, tossing his tell-tale, smouldering cigarette far away. He could no longer hear when the sensors, mounted in the outer perimeters, started squealing from all directions at once: his body fell into the mud with a dull thump.

*

20 minutes after the attack, in King Silaha's Palace

Everyone was toasting the scout who had been able to nail that glowing point from such a distance, in the thick of the jungle. He had seen it with his bare eyes during a night watch and had sent word to one of the snipers, who, looking through his telescope, had confirmed his hunch: a well-equipped mercenary unit was stationed on the border of their territory. Silaha had given the orders for an attack, he didn't want to wait until they broke camp and perhaps jumped them. With forty of his men, he quickly concluded the action, thanks to the major mistake that the smoking mercenary had made, thus leading them onto their tracks.

They gathered up everything in the camp: tents, beds, weapons, caterpillar vehicles. They stripped the fallen mercenaries naked and even put on their clothes. They scalped some of them, attaching the hair tresses to their belts as talismans. The victory was a major feat of arms:

the paid mercenaries were state of the art 'war machines,' extremely well trained and equipped with the latest technology, they almost never made mistakes. But they had made one now.

Silaha looked complacently at his men, who were happily hauling in the loot from the caterpillars parked in the palace garden. They weren't a very bright lot but, by contrast, they would do anything for the reward and the money. Their other quality was loyalty and he loved this and valued it highly. They weren't like those *mercenados* in South America, who stood by whoever offered them the most. For them, he really was the King. They had conferred the title to him, and he truly wore it with pride.

'Look, here, Your Highness!' shouted one of his men. Two large-sized, locked crates were standing in the cargo hold of the caterpillar. Excited, the men surrounded the mysterious crates, with their hidden secrets, promising big profits.

'Great!' the King shouted contentedly, 'bring them into the large hall, we'll open them together!'

His words were followed by cheering. Each crate required about ten men, who carried them above their heads, as if they were the spoils of victory. They walked in step, or rather, they danced as they made their way through the wide entrance hall all the way to the great hall, with its locked double doors.

The walls displayed looted paintings; antique pieces of furniture were crammed into the room into any and every possible available space that could take them. From worthless, gaudy junk, to the latest in communicators and everyday household items, everything could be found here. The entire house looked like a shoplifter's nest piled up with everything useful or useless.

The two crates occupied the space in the middle of the big salon. The soldiers stood around and waited for Silaha to order them to be opened. He waved to one of his men, who started to force open the lid of the smaller crate with his dagger. After removing a few nails and snapping open the metal clip, the lid loosened. Another soldier stepped over, and they finally pried the top open together. In the crate, there were weapons for precision distance shooting, working with focusable energy bursts—the most up-to-date on the market. Silaha had seen such a weapon previously, during the course of an operation somewhere with some rival tribe. A rhinoceros that had been targeted in the reservation had its backside turned into fog at a distance of about one and a half kilometres, upon shooting it with this type of weapon.

'Well, I never...' he said appreciatively and walked over to the crate. Strangely, the weapon was cold and metal-like, even though the frame was of a man-made composite material. But the old foxes on the arms market knew that every maniac user liked to feel the coolness of good old metal under his fingers.

'Bobate, bring the macaque!' one of the men shouted over to one of the youngsters, practically a child. They were the ones who served him most faithfully, his best, most talented men came from amongst these youngsters. Bobate was strutting about in one of the dead mercenary's bulletproof vests, which was obviously too big for him, but he didn't really care. He was trying to remove a greenish mucus that was covering the entire vest, from his new acquisition. A few of the others were also struggling with this substance, trying to rub it off the looted clothes.

The young man looked up upon hearing the order and rushed out into the next room, returning within a few moments with a monkey on his arm.

A mixture of hushed whispering and idiotic giggling could be heard from the throng; everyone knew what would follow next—the King was going to test the gun.

'Open the doors and take the monkey into the farthest room. Sit it down on the chair's armrest, tie the chain up well, so that it can't escape.'

The youngster nodded and proceeded to open up the doors of the interconnected rooms, up to the last one. The very end of the seventh and last room was about twenty-five metres away. He took a well-decorated chair but then changed his mind, picking one that was much simpler—after all, the Ruler shouldn't smash up the finest looking one.

'The vest, put the vest on it!' yelled Silaha. 'Let's see what it will protect!'

The young man obeyed and stepped aside, at a distance well removed from the chair.

Silaha examined the gun, put it to his shoulder, tried to feel its weight, then lowered it again. He was looking for the safety switch but couldn't find it; however, as soon as he placed his hand on the stock and on the trigger, the gun automatically cocked itself.

'Ah-haaa!' he looked around with a smug grin, imparting his satisfaction to everyone. The weapon was very sophisticated, *perhaps even excessively so for this dirty lot*, thought Silaha.

He raised it up to his shoulder, took brief aim, and fired the gun. A blinding beam shot out of the muzzle, sped through the open doors between the rooms and, missing the target, blasted the wall partition of the mansion's kitchen. Bellowing and yammering could be heard from the kitchen through the three-metre-diameter hole; one of the young cook's stump could be seen: his body above the hip bone had disappeared.

At first, a stunned silence fell over the soldiers but then someone guffawed and it spread to the others. *The idiots*, thought Silaha, *they don't realize that any of them could turn into a practice target at any given moment.*

The startled monkey fled, pulling the chair with it. Bobate's face was visible through the doorway, looking alarmed; he eyed the gathering, trembling. From there, the situation didn't appear to be all that amusing.

'Alright, now the other crate,' Silaha directed his men once again, who set about forcing open the lid. This proved to be easier than the first crate, as it hadn't been nailed down at too many points; one man, alone, was easily able to manage the operation. As soon as he had prised off the lid, he threw it down in the same movement, and jumped backwards into the gathering.

'*Muerto, muerto!*' he pointed to the crate. Looking at King Silaha, he had lapsed into Spanish. Silaha had succeeded very well in teaching a few of them to speak his ancestral language.

Silaha reached for his pistol, approaching the crate slowly. Who knew what was in it, the whole thing might be a trap. These guys had probably come to exterminate him with these modern weapons, perhaps this corpse was part of the script.

There really was a human figure in the crate, wrapped up in white linen. He was lying absolutely motionless, turned against one side of the crate. There was no doubt that he was dead, since he couldn't even get any air through the linen.

'*Muerto, muerto*, of course he's dead!' said Silaha with indignation. 'He's dead just the same as those you killed half an hour ago. They're dead as well, aren't you afraid of them, too?'

'We killed their spirit, with a rite, but the spirit of this one could return at any time and finish us off!' said one of the soldiers, gesticulating nervously. They were all scared; the circle widened. Silaha was the only one who didn't move. He then burst out laughing.

'Alright, enough of your nonsense, with your beliefs, you're tiring me out. You two, pick him up and put him on the table. We have to find out what kind of guy this is!'

The chosen soldiers reluctantly carried out the order. They still had the two bodiless legs in the kitchen dangling in front of their eyes. They knew that when the King got angry, he showed no mercy. They would rather be haunted by the soul of the dead than suffer their ruler's punishment, if they didn't carry out his orders.

Silaha took out his knife and carefully unfastened the tape. He started at the ribcage of the figure, this way the linen could be peeled in two directions. Slowly, the man's jacket emerged, covered with the same green substance as that which covered the mercenaries' clothing. With the blade of his knife, he picked up a dried piece. In disgust, he smeared it back onto the jacket.

'Step back, people, step back!' a danger alarm started screeching madly in his head. Perhaps they were trying to introduce a mortal disease among his men. Perhaps they had dragged the Trojan Horse itself into their camp, after all.

'This man is contaminated; he died of some kind of disease. Everyone who came in contact with this material through the looted clothes, must take them off immediately and burn those clothes. And you, wash yourself thoroughly.'

His men flocked in panic towards the exit, throwing the soiled clothes off themselves on the way. Many went to the garden taps where they started to shower themselves.

'Not good, this is not good at all,' said Silaha, thinking aloud, and walked around the crate. He went to one of the drawers, took out a pair of gloves, and went back to the body. Carefully, he unwound the linen; he would like to find out who this man had been. He didn't look like a mercenary; he was of medium stature, without big musculature. What could he have been looking for in Silaha's jungle? Perhaps he was the employer? Could the whole thing have been his plan?

He slowly peeled the linen off the upper torso, only his head was still covered. He cut those pieces off even more carefully, practically one by one. He wasn't superstitious, he had seen enough dead people, he himself had finished off hundreds of them, but he still had a strange feeling.

'*Demonio . . .*' he hissed, more to himself. *You little demon, you've managed to smuggle yourself in here, directly into my palace.*

The corpse was that of an average, Central Asian, middle-aged man, with a full beard, hair cut short. He looked positively repugnant, his whole face was covered in dried mucus. Silaha found the man's wallet in his upper pocket, with heaps of cards, none of which he could use here at all. He didn't even know the symbols, and he had no idea which bank had issued most of the valuable chips. There were perhaps two that he might be able to use locally; he put those into his pocket. He found another seven thousand New Dollar chips; he was delighted about that, as these were happily accepted in all parts of the world.

'Mr. Alexei Sverlov, in person, at my place for a posthumous visit . . .' he murmured to himself, while looking at his various club membership cards.

'Well, well!' he raised his eyebrow at the sight of the next card. 'Mr. Sverlov is a practitioner of a trade that touches me very closely . . . you're an arms dealer!' He was examining the United Colony arms dealer certificate, which contained the name of the issuing organization in many languages, including Spanish. UC Arms Trade Organization.

'Secretary!' he shouted. In the meantime, many of his men had finished washing; the clothes were being burned in a huge bonfire by the old fountain not far from the manor, which was also filling the role of an advanced lookout post. The man who served as secretary came running in through a back corridor leading to the rear of the building. He was half naked; he had probably thrown his shirt into the fire.

'If there's a clearly visible pirate satellite above us, to which we could connect, then take a look at the Global-net, to see who that man is. He is probably an arms dealer, he didn't come here to kill us, but to strike a deal, of this I'm almost sure. Look him up, where we could find his kin, with whom we could come to a compromise, perhaps they would continue any arms trade deals that he had implicitly negotiated. If not, his corpse would be worth a couple of ten thousand or even a couple of hundred thousand New Dollars.

The short, emaciated man took note of everything, took the certificates, and returned to his office.

'No one enters this room, except with my permission,' Silaha turned to one of his soldiers. 'You will be responsible for whoever goes in here.'

He had no real reason to worry because the soldiers, filled with superstitious fears, they wouldn't want to go near the corpse.

'I'll be in the office, I have important business to attend to, don't disturb me,' he said, starting to walk up the wide, richly adorned staircase, encircled with gilded replicas of ancient statues. He wanted peace, to think over his strategy, what he would do with this seemingly valuable corpse.

He had been searching the net for an hour and a half and kept switching TV channels, when one of his men knocked nervously on his door.

'Many of the men are feeling sick; the same liquid is running from their noses as that on the looted clothes! Come, Your Highness! Many are leaving the palace, they're fleeing!'

'What? Shoot all of them! Shoot all the disloyal, lousy dogs!' yelled Silaha and stormed down the stairs. In the smaller rooms that served as the soldiers' quarters, there were already about a dozen men shaking with the strange fever. Two or three soldiers were running back and forth between them, the most effective remedy was a wet cloth and a washbowl.

'Isolate them! They can't stay in the building! Take them all to the outbuilding! Immediately!' ordered Silaha, himself stepping back from the sweating and shaking men. The healthy ones were reluctant; they didn't want to touch the sick.

'Get going, or I'll put a hole in your skull!' he shouted at one of the soldiers who was staring mesmerized at the writhing sick, holding a pistol to his head.

Stretchers were brought from the storeroom; reluctantly, the soldiers laid their colleagues on them.

At that point, they heard a scream behind them:

'*Demonio! Demonio*! The demon has risen!' The soldier responsible for guarding the Russian arms dealer's corpse was fleeing through the hall to the entrance. Tossing away his gun, he ran outside, but Silaha brought him down with a single shot. His lifeless body stopped before the entrance door, sliding a few metres on the marble floor.

As soon as they entered the room, they saw that the corpse of the Russian was no longer on the table, but on the floor, on his belly. He was trying to scramble to his feet, without success.

He was visibly alive and he was moving.

'Tie him up!' said Silaha to those standing nearby. Many of them were backing away; there were those who rushed out through the door, into the garden. Silaha shoved aside those standing nearby and started shooting once again, twice, three times. One of them got away, but two of them collapsed, dead in their tracks, before they were able to reach the garden. Others no longer dared to take flight.

'I'll tie him up,' it was the shaman, stepping out from the crowd. 'I've seen guys like this. After the rite, they try to flee frantically; everything has to be done exactly as our ancestors told us. They have to be tied with ropes braided from palm leaves, which have to be soaked in a special infusion. The demon weakens from it.'

Silaha just looked at him, stupefied, too many things had happened in the last few minutes.

'Alright, but make it fast,' he said, after mulling it over briefly.

He let the shaman do his job, at least the mood would ease. The soldiers could see that the spiritual forces were being restrained. Silaha thought, if the Russian arms dealer was really alive, and wasn't an otherworldly figure, then he would question him as to what all this was about, and what it was that was happening to them. He took the communicator that he found in the Russian's pocket and looked at any accessible, non-encrypted data.

He thought that the worst was over, but half an hour later all hell broke loose. His soldiers were running away, screaming, from the makeshift lodgings for the sick. By the time he reached the place, all he could see were mangled corpses, writhing, disfigured zombies. They had all breathed out their souls at the same time, in this insane dance of death.

He torched the outbuilding himself. Some of his men were still alive in the fiery furnace, more dead than alive, screaming something in Swahili.

His soldiers were gone. He didn't have the energy left to order them back; he let them run. If they were contaminated, the strange disease would finish them off anyway, within a couple of hours.

Only the shaman stayed with him. He was squatting by the unconscious but live Russian, chanting magic spells.

'I'll have to take him out into the forest and set him on fire,' said the shaman, 'otherwise we'll never get rid of the curse.'

Silaha thought of the ransom money and the unexploited sources resulting from the trading of his body. But then he looked around his property crumbling into ruin and nodded his approval. He raised the flask containing a self-concocted brandy to his lips and took a long swig from it.

'Alright, let's tie him to the platform of the pickup truck. Then you can take him and do whatever you want with him.'

Having finished the work, he returned to his room and turned on the TV. With Alexei Sverlov's—this mystical man's—certificate and the remote in his hand, he fumbled through the channels.

Night was falling, when one of the newscasts aroused his interest. They were showing the captain of a Russian freighter who was reporting about a raging infection on board, in a self-shot amateur video.

It showed a ghoulish similarity with the events at the palace . . . but the broadcast suddenly stopped.

This man was also Russian, the ship was Russian too, pondered Silaha. This ship had moored in Port Qoriga, where this man had probably hired his mercenaries. According to the Russian communicator, he had crossed the ocean to come to Africa, therefore he had probably travelled on that ship . . .

The Russian was the angel of death . . .

He overheard the cross-country vehicle starting up. Slowly, it moved away down the alley.

This would be the angel of death's last journey . . .

At that point, the jeep's motor roared loudly, only to impact on something with an almighty crash. Looking out the window, he saw the shaman hanging out of the driver's seat. In all probability the disease had finished him off, too.

He had to do something. He looked for a bottle and some gasoline. He picked up his brandy and started walking towards the stranded vehicle near the fountain.

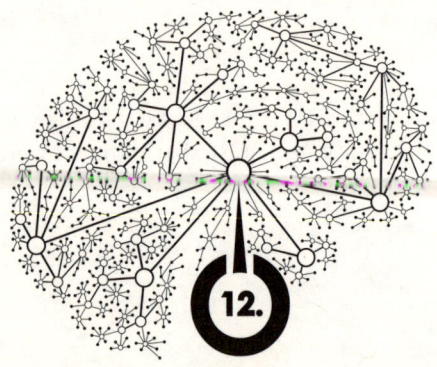

12.

Exhausted, Jess was sitting in the off-duty corner of the well-equipped lab in the crisis centre of Mars New Home Colony. She had been working incessantly for three days running, and the Colony had also been locked down for exactly three days. The quarantine would last until she or Cliff produced some sort of result. The samples sent to the colonies were only now being studied by the researchers; it would therefore be too soon to expect any help from that quarter. Jess and the others had the advantage of being ahead by three days. This business, however, was proving to be much more difficult than she had originally thought. They had carried out all the exhausting, useless experiments—none of which had produced any kind of result at all.

She was sipping coffee and looking at the samples that she had taken from the protein strings on the large projector. These were a result of the 'simultaneous-explosion-incident,' or SEI—as it was recorded—that had occurred in the main square yesterday. She was keeping them alive in a special solution. For the past four hours, however, the protein strings hadn't moved. They showed no activity, and they weren't reproducing themselves. The enzymes in the nutrient solution had not produced any effect on them whatsoever, even though she had experimented with all available enzymes so far.

Among the protein-producing amino acids there were two entirely unknown molecules, never before synthesised in nature—they didn't contain the alpha carbon atom. The molecular structure, similar to that of an amino acid, was held together by an unknown tetrahedral structure. That's why Cliff suspected that these two amino acids held the key to the mystery. They were probably not naturally derived amino acids.

The proteins also showed strong diversity in their shapes: most were in the form of a long, annulated polymer chain structure, but the protein consisting of the two amino acids of unknown origin created a divergent, three-dimensional body, along clearly defined lines. One resembled the shape of a brick, the other, an open-mouthed pyramid or, rather, a horn, as though a membrane were fastened onto its wide end. They appeared to be synthetic precisely because of their shape. And yet, it appeared as if they had been deliberately hiding up until now, since they had only been discovered in the latest samples and had not been present in earlier ones. An explanation was found for this phenomenon: the unknown proteins, once removed from their host body, only stayed whole for a few hours, after which they dissolved into simple amino acids.

However, in this environment that simulated the host body, they were still being held together: she had caught them at last! They floated about in the nutrient solution, just like the tiny paper boats that she used to fold and float on water as a child, which used to give her so much pleasure.

But these are causing everyone pain and torment, spreading doom in their path, sweeping along in torrents of blood . . . But how?

At this point, Cliff stormed into the room. Generally, he always knocked first but didn't bother to do so this time—he was too excited. He was holding napkin strips in his hands, in various colours, rolled into ring-like spirals, just like the protein molecules on the screen. He threw them onto the sofa.

'I see you've found something,' Jess smiled, glancing at the pile of paper strips.

'Yes! And you won't believe what!' Cliff was positively beaming. He didn't show any fatigue, even though he too had been on the go for several days. 'Here, let me show you.'

He pulled up a small table on wheels and cleared away the test tubes on it.

'These are our proteins,' he said, laying out the paper strips before them, 'and they're all self-contained, independent polymer chains. They're visible on the display monitor as well, side by side in the solution, as independent, self-sufficient chains. There's nothing special about them. There are many small protein chains floating peacefully before our eyes. Nothing happens to them, as the protein containing the foreign amino acids, comprising the two funny brick-and-funnel-shape catalysts, is missing. What happens if we join them up, too?'

'Nothing!' Jess slapped her knee indignantly. 'I've been waiting for a good couple of hours for something to happen but nothing happens! They float side by side with the same, undisturbed serenity! And I've even pumped up the solution with enzymes . . .'

'Yes, because the solution is only a nutrient, but not the host itself! For some reason, the host acts differently on these proteins. If they land in the host, this is what happens!' he said, joining the diversely shaped napkin strips together by the hooks placed at their corners.

Jess gaped in astonishment at the newly developed shape.

'You're not saying that this is what it turns into? This appears to be a very serious, higher-level system. How can you prove it?'

'For the time being, I can only prove it in theory. I looked at the possible connections that could evolve and this is the result. Of course, there are still three different forms, but each one conforms to the brick-shaped protein string in the centre. The rest, including this strange, membrane-covered pyramid-shaped formation, are all linked to this central protein.'

'How can you prove it in practice?' Jess kept repeating the same question because that was really the theory's stumbling block.

'I have no idea. I'll need your help with this.'

Jess put the coffee mug down and rotated the disconcertingly genuine-looking, interlocked group of molecules.

'Cliff, if they really bind together, then this is something colossal.'

'I know. This has to be how they bind together; there are only a very limited number of ways they can bond.'

'We'll have to inject the proteins into the lab animals, simultaneously—like this,' said Jess, 'only then are we going to know how they function.'

'Yes, but we have very little test material left, where we can find this key protein; we only have enough for about three tests.'

'That's better than nothing . . . have they brought the SEI corpses into the isolation room yet? We might find enough suitable material in those.'

'If the tissues start to disintegrate, the mucus providing the protein quickly dries up and we don't have much chance of finding active proteins.'

'What's the situation with the spread of the infection, how many cases do we have now?'

'According to the latest reports, we have about two hundred infected cases; they're all in a satisfactory condition. They're generating the mucus, but they're far off from yesterday's SEI state,' explained Cliff. 'It's questionable whether the proteins in their system have produced this hypothetical formation. It's also possible that this situation will develop later, when the infection becomes fatal.'

'We'll have to bring one of them into the isolation room next to the lab,' said Jess. 'If he or she contains the key protein, then our case is as good as won. However, one thing is strange about these patients; they aren't suffering the acute SEI state yet. Their symptoms are milder, for some reason. As if the pathogens were following a well-defined cycle and, after the peak point, this was now the time to gather strength. Nevertheless, these proteins should be acting the same way in them as well.'

'Taking this into consideration, we need to start new animal testing with the remaining test material too,' said Cliff, pointing to the rats running around in the cage.

'And we also have to test the cop, McAllister, but only if he agrees to be brought back here, of course, because he hates this glass cage,' Cliff added. 'So far, he is the only one contaminated whose system hasn't reacted to the effect of the proteins. Baffling. But he could be one of the keys, apart from these peculiar proteins.'

'Go, talk to the management,' smiled Jess. She had been waiting for this Eureka-type feeling for a long time now. Her researcher's instinct was telling her that her boss could be right.

'The CliM-protein,' said Clifford, turning back from the door, laughing, 'that's what I'm going to call it.'

'Oh, go away!' Sarah-Jessica waved her hand dismissively. 'You'll be lucky if you're allowed to name even one of the unknown amino acids. The rest will be registered by more renowned scientists than you, anyway, somewhere on another colony! Or they might be doing so right now, if you don't hurry up and get in there before them!'

As soon as the door shut behind Clifford, Jess was left alone with her thoughts. The excitement caused by the intellectual pleasure abated and was replaced by personal misgivings.

She thought about Noah and the fact that she still couldn't reach him.

And that the sample originating from his handkerchief, which she hadn't had time to look at so far, was waiting for her at home, under the microscope.

Dear Lord, please don't let him be the Alpha person!

*

At the very same time, on the monitor next to the Moon Colony Police Headquarters' cross-examination room . . .

Eric Kovasevic was complacently looking over the scene unfolding before him, coming from the three cross-examination rooms. The walls of those rooms only let light pass through from this particular angle, enabling him to see and hear everything from this central position.

In the first room sat the target of his investigations over many years, the crowned chief of the Mafia, Chu Jun himself, the Mother Colony's well-known drug lord and dealer in human flesh. He conducted his activities mainly in the New China Colony, with the knowledge and permission of the ruling warlords and often with their support. He had aroused the UC Bureau of Investigation's interest when his crime organisation started to work its way up to Solar System proportions. Since the authorities on Earth had been unable to pin anything on him, he was able to increase his power in Asia with complete confidence; hence the matter had to be raised at a UC level.

Three years ago, when they had become aware of Chu Jun's plans to set up an entertainment centre on the Moon, they entrusted Eric with setting up a discrete, apparently low-budget office, as a front. In the back of the office, members of the UC Bureau of Investigation Organized Crime and Gang Section worked steadily and painstakingly to set up their ambush. They registered one of the empty domes of the Moon Colony in the company's name. Then, they dangled the bait in front of the Mafia leader—they entered into a plea bargain with a business involved in a suspicious money-laundering case: if they recommended Eric's company to Chu Jun, they wouldn't be prosecuted.

In the central cross-examination room, the man accused of multiple murders, Chu Jun's bodyguard and chauffeur, leaned against the table with a bored expression on his face. He visibly wasn't afraid of anything because, if anyone could be sent down following the investigation, it could only be his boss. As long as no one presented damning testimony against him, or unless they could convict him of some of the earlier murders, the cell doors would open to release him after just a few weeks of detention under remand.

Noah, Eric's former employee, was sitting in the third room. He was in bad shape, which caused Eric some concern. According to Enderston's order on how to proceed with the investigation, Noah couldn't be released as yet either. The United Colony Epidemics Institute had decreed that every passenger on the Trans-Terra TT225 line from Mars had to be taken to the Quarantine Centre. Mars New Home had been closed for the third day now and could only be reached via the highest level of communication; every other connection was being blocked. Noah couldn't be approached until the quarantine section picked him up. What's more, whoever had come into contact with him—including the Mafia chief, his bodyguard, and a few commandos—would also have to be isolated.

Eric had been worried about the young man's health because of the camaraderie that had developed between them over the past two years.

Although he knew about Noah's past, the young man's desire to learn, and the efficiency with which he threw himself into his work enchanted Eric. He regretted the fact that he'd had to use him as a decoy in the operation, but if they had told Noah the office's real purpose, the preparatory work of many years would have been wrecked by the young man's past record coming to light. That was exactly why he had been so concerned about him and—he had to admit, about the operation as well—when he found out that the Noah had accepted The Golden Aura card offered by Chu Jun. The 'business's preparatory work' was an old-established custom in Mafia circles, but it had been too great a temptation for Noah. Finally, after spending a few days at a luxury resort and a week on Mars, he had decided to stop the spending. According to reports, he had strengthened ties with his long-time girlfriend, Jess. In all probability, that's what had kept him on the straight and narrow, saving him from temptation.

It was also certain that he would be getting the two and a half million New Dollars that would have come from this deal—the investigating authorities would pay it to him gladly, since the Mafia organization had acquired many thousands of times this amount of money by crippling human lives.

But now it would no longer do so.

The door opened behind him, and Richard Enderston, the chief investigator, stepped in with a wide grin on his face.

'We got him, we finally got him!' he gave Eric a high five. 'I congratulate you, Eric, after so many years of hard work! It wasn't easy to coax him out of New China, where we couldn't have done anything with him, but over here their jungle laws aren't valid anymore.'

'Thanks! It wouldn't have taken much to destroy everything. That picture from seven years ago of the two of us would have really put the kibosh on the entire operation. You'll have to pay more attention to your tidying up operation in future.'

Enderston stopped at the transparent wall of the Mafia chief's room.

'It looks like he knows he's finished,' he made a movement as if to grab Chu Jun's neck.

'That's still not certain; we can't find the signed contract . . .'

'But he signed the agreement while he was still on Earth and paid ten per cent of the full price. That ten per cent tax-free New Dollars of such a huge amount would be just enough to withdraw him from circulation for twenty years.'

Eric stepped up beside Richard.

'Alright, I'd like to talk about him now,' and he pointed toward Noah. 'I hear we can't let him go. This epidemic affair has put everyone that travelled on his line under quarantine. Mars New Home has not been responding for the past three days. What do you know about what's going on over there?'

Enderston turned toward Noah's cross-examination room.

'The United Colony Council isn't saying anything for now, I only know what they're saying in the news, as there's a total security blackout. The Epidemics Department may know more, but all I got from them was a restraining order with Noah Simpson's name. But you have to realize that if the sterilization people are taking our man away, the problem is probably not with the communication satellites, as they explained in the newscasts two days ago. An epidemic has broken out on Mars, we can be quite sure about that.'

'Yes, there's no doubt about that!' Eric nodded. 'But we can't let it go just like that. We'll have to tell him that he'll get his reward for the unselfish work he's been doing for the past two years. We can't do this to him. We got him involved in a dangerous situation without his knowledge. I feel personally responsible for his fate.'

Enderston appeared to be pondering.

'You remember how we came across him?'

'Yes, we hired him through a private Japanese agency. We placed job announcements to keep up appearances, but of course we threw away everyone else's, as we wanted to install our own man. On one of these occasions, they applied too. Perhaps that was the reason we accepted their candidate, because it was a rehabilitation agency, the "Back to Society" organisation, if I remember the name, and they were engaged in looking after those who had served prison terms. We thought that their candidate would be an "experienced veteran" in these circles. We took a big risk, but the guy made good; in fact, his capabilities even surpassed those of our own men.'

'Yes, that was the agency's name. We checked it out. It was a regular, licensed, private agency in Brazil, with headquarters in Rio. The manager was a nice lady, Mrs. Yuuna Joshida,' said Investigator

Enderston, scratching his chin. 'I verified it myself. She had previously worked as a person in charge of social affairs at the Japanese Ministry of Health ...'

'How does this all tie in?' Eric didn't understand why his boss was concerned with the past.

'Because I had to look after your friend's personal data, because that too had been mandated by the Epidemics Department. While I was doing the research in the United Colony Registry, I noticed that the headquarters of the "Back to Society" outfit in Brazil had been liquidated exactly a week ago.'

'And what's so strange about that? Organisations are being formed and liquidated every second in the Solar System.'

'Actually, it could be a coincidence,' Investigator Enderston agreed, 'but don't you find it odd, that all this happened at exactly the same time as we liquidated our own offices, that had been serving as a front?'

Eric started to think it over. Perhaps he was beginning to understand where Richard was going with this.

'Did they know that our office was a front?'

'I don't know, but it's possible. Or, that the office was not what it looked like from the outside, at least.'

'Are you insinuating that our Intelligence Service wasn't functioning properly? If that's true, then we'll have to re-evaluate our reporting methods, considered effective up to now.' Eric became increasingly surprised.

'I am merely stating the facts: our office ceased to exist in the same week as that Japanese office and in the same week—based on our suspicions—as a Colony-wide epidemic broke out on Mars. And here, sitting before us, is an apparently seriously ill man who had just returned from Mars ...'

'These are pretty far-fetched conclusions; your imagination is livelier than ever.'

Investigator Enderston turned to Eric, smiling.

'You're a cop, you know that we have to set off from bold and far-fetched premises when we're faced with something unusual. It's in somebody's interest to let this epidemic blow up, and this chap has brought it right to us, too.'

Eric listened to his boss in disbelief. He had his own far-fetched ideas sometimes, but even he would never have dared to imagine something of this magnitude.

'I'm not leaving it at that,' Richard said, pointing to Noah. 'I'll have a word with a friend of mine in the Intelligence Service and ask him to find the manager of "Back to Society," Mrs. Joshida, based on the coordinates of her chip, to establish her whereabouts.'

'You know you can't do that if there's no arrest warrant against her,' said Eric in a serious tone. 'You could lose your job over that.'

'Come now, Eric,' said Richard and looked at the investigator with a mischievous smile, 'you know that in the end I'll be given praise and not a reprimand! It was the same with the Chu Jun affair. The whole thing came off the top of my head and, as you see, it ended up as a complete success.'

Eric knew that his boss was right. Richard had incredible flair. In the Chu Jun affair, even the uppermost echelons had looked at him idiotically at first but the seemingly impossible plan had come good.

Enderston paused for a moment and turned towards Noah again.

'I feel like there's something in the background behind all this, and I'm going to track it down by whatever means I have to. If Mars is in trouble and this guy is the cause of it, then I'll get the Heroes' Cross, not my dismissal.'

He shook hands with Eric and left the room.

No one could have seen what followed as the men in their white security overalls arrived, because the walls had turned opaque again. Eric had to wait for the Epidemics Department personnel, who took all three men—the two gangsters separately, under special police support and surveillance—into quarantine.

*

Simultaneously, on the Sea of Japan . . .

The high-speed luxury floater raced along, a few metres above the sea's surface. The pilot cabin's window was being splattered by a strong spray of water, driven by the storm-force wind that had suddenly arisen from the South Pole. At times, the crest of a wave hit the bottom of the floater full force, but Nature's raging energy was dissipated by the streamlined structure, and rivulets of water ran, unhampered, along the hull. Upon reaching Japanese shores, the pilot had already activated the concealed device, which deflected the light and the radar beams away from the vessel, with the help of electromagnets. He was on a highly secret mission; he had to look out for safety and invisibility even more than usual. That's why he was moving so close to the surface and that was why they had only left well after sunset.

Rain was to be expected, they could practically count on it. Since the ice caps had melted, ever stronger and more frequent storms kept breaking out, almost weekly. Every two or three months, they had to weather continental-sized typhoons, too.

Luckily, this was one of the smaller ones. If this had been a large storm, they would surely not have set sail, since it was forbidden to jeopardize the life of the Crown Prince of the Japanese Empire, even for such an important meeting.

They soon reached the ocean liner designated as the venue for the meeting. The pilot gave the password over the radio and, at the stern of the ocean liner—which was, incidentally, disguised as a cargo ship laden with containers—the floodgate doors were flung open for them, allowing ingress into the ship's bowels. After stopping the engines, the captain's last remaining job was to secure the gangplank to the inner walkway. And, of course, he had to bow down to the floor before the Prince.

'We thank you, Captain Shimizu. It was a safe and speedy journey, as always,' the Prince said, as he passed by him. He sported a black, fashionably cut suit, and a white shirt with a large, turned down collar. He was hope itself—the future, at least as far as Shimizu was concerned. He was the incarnation of the once and perhaps the once again, glorious Japanese Empire. And lastly, the Prince—even in men's eyes—was a very handsome young man.

The Japanese Empire had ceased to exist as an institution three centuries ago, when the Emperor of Japan died without a successor. The colonized Japan no longer needed an emperor, his role had slowly faded away, and so they didn't bother looking for an heir to the crown within the family members of the collateral lines of descent. The young generation was pushing outwards, towards new territories in the Solar System, while the elderly were busy worrying about the seething chaos across Asia. With the death of the Emperor, Japanese awareness and pride seemed to have been lost. The island hadn't lost any wars in two and a half thousand years apart from that one, single occasion: in the worldwide cataclysm of the second millennium, when they had been beaten in the Second World War. After that defeat, the Emperor was no longer a distant, god-like creature, but a person like everybody else, with human features. With the rupture of the ruler's mystique, the necessity for the gloss of centuries-old tradition was torn away from the people. They could exist without the Emperor, after all.

It was in this unusual state, radiating defencelessness, that the first Asian conflict struck Japan. The nation that had previously buried their ideals did not participate in the counterattacks initiated by the allies (India, Australia, Mongolia, and Russia). It had retreated, cocooned itself and waited. Waited for someone to step forward out of the past.

The Arai family was not related to the former imperial family. The head of the family, Arai Shinobu was a talented businessman. He was a strong leader, causing many to see the vanished legacy of the former emperors in his accomplishments. And yet, he was one of them, not a carrier of noble blood, which made him even more likeable. And so, the legislators didn't waste much time: they enthroned him by modifying the constitutional law. He, in turn, showed his gratitude by strengthening the island country before the second Asian conflict. Thanks to this, the New China firestorm, intended to set the entire Eastern world ablaze, was forced to come to a halt on the shores of Japan.

That's why Captain Shimizu felt gratitude for the past and the possible future, and bowed down to the ground once again. He watched the departing Prince, who had inherited the dashing physique of *Tennouheika* Arai Shinobu, his imperial grandfather. Two older men followed him, probably government officials, although he had never seen them before.

A European-looking man came to greet them, someone that Shimizu didn't know either. The man bowed, in the proper manner, probably aware of the strict greeting protocols. They may have met before, because the Prince extended his hands towards him and they talked as if they were old acquaintances.

But this was no longer any of his business. He could return to the commander's cabin to look over the system and prepare the ship for a safe return.

'Greetings, *Koutaishi-denka* Arai,' bowed the man who had arrived to welcome the imperial prince and his entourage.

'I, too, am honoured by the renewed meeting, Mr. Afanasiev, but allow me to greet you in your own customary manner,' Prince Arai extended his hand for the informal greeting, 'although it would be better if this meeting had taken place somewhat later and in somewhat happier circumstances.'

'That's true, Your Highness, I agree with you,' said Artyom Afanasiev, who led the way for the delegation along the corridor that had been created between the containers. The ship was owned by the Russian Independent Republic, so he felt at home in its interior. 'Unfortunately, this is a rather important and, judging from the signs, unavoidable meeting; we now have to discuss some very difficult questions.'

After a few turns, they entered a well-lit, comfortably furnished room, equipped with projectors. Three men were waiting in the room. They all stood up and rushed forward to greet them.

'*Koutaishi-denka*, let me introduce to you Mr. Boris Sobrilov, Head of the Unit in charge of Asian Affairs of the Russian Secret Service and his Assistant, Mr. Andrei Volkov,' the two men bowed politely, 'and the Attaché of the Immigration Ministry of the Mongolian Republic, Mr. Batzorig.'

To their surprise, the short Mongolian man didn't bow before the Heir Apparent to the Imperial Throne, probably not aware of the protocol rules affecting him. None of this appeared to disturb Prince Kazuki, who took his cue from the man acting as host, Artyom Afanasiev, who was the Special Attaché to the Russian president, in charge of military matters.

Afanasiev offered the prince a seat and waited until they had all taken their seats around the tables.

'First of all, I thank you all very much for coming to this important meeting. As a result of the unexpected incidents that started the week, we were unable to discuss this matter either over the telephone or by any other electronic means,' said Afanasiev, by way of introduction. 'In the name of the president of the Independent Russian Republic, Mr. Semenov, I would like to convey our sympathies to his Highness, Prince Arai's father, *Tennouheika* Arai, for his illness, hoping that he may return as soon as possible to his official duties.'

'Thank you, Mr. Afanasiev,' said Prince Kazuki, bowing his head, 'I myself hope that my father may soon return to the helm of his country, since now it would be of paramount importance that his wisdom and experience were there to guide us all in the forthcoming difficult decisions.'

'Indeed it would be,' Afanasiev took up the lead again. 'The events of the past few days have raised questions: Are we indeed heading in the right direction? Is this really what we collectively want? Accordingly, I call upon Assistant Volkov to acquaint us with the current situation.'

'Thank you, Mr. Afanasiev,' the young man looked down at his notes, 'I am holding this morning's reports here in my hand. Regretfully, I have to say that, after three years of uninterrupted success, now that the Unmei Project has entered its final phase, we are facing serious problems. The direction of the project has slipped away from the leader of the investigation, Professor Nujo Yakizima. Our task is therefore to judge whether we have only lost direction partially, or completely.'

He looked up from his notes and let his glance move around his audience.

'Mr. Afanasiev, I've received every report myself in the past few days,' said Batzorig, the Mongolian liaison officer, 'and if I remember well, at the time when we agreed to support the project, there was already talk about a certain amount of "collateral damage," to be frank, the project's possible civilian victims. If my calculations are correct, we are still well below the estimated figures.'

'Indeed, there was word about collateral damage to civilians,' Afanasiev continued the discussion, 'but these cases—which, according to preliminary estimates, could reach between one and two per cent—should have happened during the final phase of the project, and even then, only in war zones and not on the colonies.'

'At this point, what we know for a fact is that the Unmei Machines escaped from the Mother Colony,' said Sobrilov of the Russian Secret Service, 'and they got as far as the Mars Colony. The management of Mars New Home has completely and hermetically sealed off its borders. It's almost certain that the infection has started to spread and has already claimed victims. The Epidemics Institute of the United Colony Unified Council hasn't provided any official information but our Secret Service has ascertained the number of victims as being one thousand to twelve hundred strong, and this number is growing despite the probable quarantine measures. We also know that the day before yesterday, an armoured vessel arrived from Mars, bringing samples for analysis purposes on Earth. Our Unmei Machines are in these samples, too. At the same time, samples also arrived on Jupiter's Europa Moon. We have to sort out two questions: how much longer are we going to endanger civilians in the interests of the Unmei Project's success, the second being, how much longer can we remain hidden, or, how long before the Unmei Machines are detected?'

'In Japan's opinion, as well as in that of the project's leader,' Prince Kazuki began expounding his point of view, 'in a war, we have to allow for innocent civilian victims, in any case. However, I believe that those unfortunate events, where the project was inadvertently transferred to another planet, puts the onus on us to ensure that this cluster is neutralised. If we're not successful in this, then the project, irrespective of the colossal amount of work that has been put into it, would have to be terminated, however distressing this would be for us.'

'Your Highness, if you please,' Batzorig interjected again. 'I believe that we must consider the situation in light of the numbers as well. If we only look at the cluster on Mars, the probable number of those critically infected is perhaps less than ninety hundred-thousandth per cent projecting on the total population of the Solar System. In the agreement, we talked about one ten-thousandth per cent.'

'Let's leave out the numbers because this is only speculation, Mr. Batzorig,' said Afanasiev. 'Don't forget, we don't have any kind of numerical information from Mars, we don't know the exact figures. As per international conventions, there are no spy satellites around the colonies, therefore, we're completely blind and deaf.'

'But we have pretty reliable data on the cluster that evolved here on Earth,' Volkov chimed in. 'We all received the announcement from the *Lev Tolstoy* about the contamination that occurred on board the ship, caused by Alexei Sverlov, according to the investigation. The infection spread remarkably fast, and the fatality rate was ninety-seven per cent. If it were to proliferate elsewhere at this rate, Mars Colony would become depopulated within a month's time.'

'Thank heavens, we were able to block that satellite channel quickly, the one that was broadcasting the captain's amateur video. One of our military satellites was able to divert the *For Asia* free news channel satellite from its course. After that operation, they immediately switched over and continued to broadcast with the help of one of their antennas placed on the Moon,' said Sobrilov, 'but we intercepted it just in time before the clip could produce a greater reaction. To be sure, rumours are still flying about in the wind throughout Asia, but perhaps we were able to calm the waves. We subsequently sequestrated the video, citing reasons of national security and strict secrecy. You received this material, as well, and we are presently analysing its content. The Blue Berets, the men from the United Colony Council, have taken possession of the ship, as, unfortunately, the Russian Navy was late in arriving at the scene. The request for extradition is still being considered; until then, the ship is being held in quarantine in a port in the Antarctic. Of course, this answers the second question right away—according to this, we can't remain unnoticed for long, since the Epidemics Department would quickly find a connection between the events on Mars and the case on the *Lev Tolstoy*. Perhaps the best thing would be if we quickly managed to take the ship back into Russian hands again, before they find out about this connection.'

'This was the first time I had seen shots of the Unmei Machines in action, or rather I should say, of what they leave behind,' interjected Volkov. 'Based on the sight, our professor had designed a rather effective "fate-machine." Am I saying it correctly, Your Highness? The meaning of the word *Unmei* in Japanese is fate, is it not?'

'Indeed it is, Mr. Volkov,' said Prince Kazuki, 'and they are indeed very effective tools, which is exactly why we've developed them. And, true to their name, these machines become the guiding force of our destiny, they lead us on to our fate. However, this fate has to be programmed by us and, in order to be able to truly proceed towards the desired future, we'll have to bring all contamination resulting from our mistakes to a halt and we'll have to terminate the clusters.'

'Well, I believe we are all in agreement on this as well,' Afanasiev spoke up again. 'The only question is, how are we going to achieve this? We can't just send the pills out to the Colony, it would be very remarkable if new medication were to be ready within a few days after the arrival of the samples...'

'Yes, that's true, that isn't the way to deal with it. According to Professor Yakizima, there is a termination order that can be transmitted by means of a radio signal, which disconnects the machines,' said the prince. 'If we can direct this order towards Mars with the help of an antenna, then we can contain the contamination. And so the other parts of the project may continue and the work of many years won't be wasted, while, at the same time, we'll be preventing an increase in the numbers of civilian victims.'

'Russia agrees,' said Sobrilov, 'but only if we can get hold of the implant carriers on Earth. According to the testimony of the chaotic state of affairs left behind in their tracks, they're still alive; moreover, they continue to thwart our plans.'

'I agree,' endorsed Batzorig. 'This is a good solution for Mongolia, though I think that, even in this dubious situation, we could continue the project, since the collateral damage following the activities of the two fugitives, even at colony level, doesn't reach what is laid down in the agreement.'

At this point a low-tone warning signal interrupted the conversation. Afanasiev's and Sobrilov's communicators were signalling simultaneously. Both men picked them up and listened to the message.

'You tell us, Artyom,' said Sobrilov in Russian to Afanasiev.

'Alright, so we have some good news,' he began, turning towards the others. 'The United Colony Council handed over the *Lev Tolstoy* an hour ago to the Independent Russian Republic and all this was accomplished without any samples being taken from the corpses on board; they were simply placed under military quarantine. This is very auspicious news for us. The Unmei Project will continue to be undetected on Earth. Of course, there is the danger of failure in the samples arriving from Mars, but their examination will certainly take some time.'

'However, there are two items of bad news as well,' he continued, after taking a breath, 'one is that new clusters of the Unmei Machines had formed in India, in New Delhi. For the time being, we're scrutinising how this could have come to pass; there is probably a connection to the Lev Tolstoy and Alexei Sverlov. One of the men from the Coast Guard could be the starting point of the source of infection in India.'

'We must involve India immediately in the project, not only due to its connection, but also because of its strategic importance,' retorted the prince, practically without thinking. 'We mustn't procrastinate any longer, or else we shall have to take the decision to stop everything. In India's earlier military successes—better said, conquests—in the second Asian conflict, the honesty of their intentions was called into question, which was why we hadn't included them in the project. Thanks to the new borders drawn after the war, theirs became contiguous with the borders of the New China Empire for several thousands of kilometres. If an unknown epidemic broke out in India, then the New China Empire might respond with the immediate closure of its borders, which could well mean the end of the project. It is in our fundamental interest to have an ally, along whose borders we can move freely.'

'But Futura is already in New China, in the occupied Mongolian territory,' interjected Batzorig, 'so our access doesn't present a problem.'

'That's true, Mr. Batzorig,' approved Volkov, 'but a possible internal border closure could also affect the Mongol territory where Futura has its headquarters. That would mean that Futura could no longer move about freely within the country. We can't afford to take any chances.'

'Well then, everyone agrees that we contact the Indian authorities via the Secret Service channels?' Sobrilov asked. 'We'll help prevent the propagation of the epidemic in the country, and we'll offer them our alliance.'

'I'll vote with an unconditional yes,' said Prince Kazuki.

'So will I, so be it,' voted Batzorig.

'Then I'll tell you about the other disturbing news,' continued Afanasiev. 'A few hours ago, the investigators of the United Colony Organisation against Criminal Activities arrested our number two implant carrier, Noah Simpson.'

'We should have been more circumspect in choosing the implant carriers,' Batzorig said indignantly, 'their criminal records determined the fate of the entire project, setting us up to have problems with them later.'

'The selection of the implant carriers came entirely within Professor Yakizima's remit,' said Prince Kazuki, 'and I think I understand and see what his purpose was. If the implant could be kept under control even by individuals with such chaotic pasts, then we wouldn't have any problems in the last phase either.'

'But it couldn't be kept under control,' disagreed Volko, 'we're in the process of rectifying the mistakes right now.'

Prince Kazuki sat absorbed in thought for a moment, trying to formulate his words in the clearest possible way.

'Allow me to expound my personal views regarding this matter. Professor Yakizima was a fighter pilot at the time of the second Asian conflict. My grandfather, Emperor Arai Shinobu, honoured him with distinction for holding his ground in defence of Japan, as evidenced. I have a feeling that the currently evolving situation is the result of his conscious choice. The oft-mentioned collateral damage—leaving out the cluster on Mars, of course—would have unequivocally stemmed from the circles of those criminals. Alexei Sverlov's Far-eastern arms business had obviously been aiming at New China, Chu Jun is also one of New China's affluent criminals. You must see, yourselves, that Professor Yakizima would have liked to do a full dress rehearsal, with isolated events, thus also liberating himself from these circles of criminals.'

The men silently digested the Imperial Prince's reasoning, which seemed logical.

'If that is so, we, as the leaders of the operation, should have been informed about it,' Sobrilov started to speak. Indignation lurked in his voice.

'We were all aware that the carriers of the experimental implant were, clearly, a source of danger to the entire Unmei Project. We had already lost someone in an earlier phase, even his corpse remained undetected,' said Batzorig. 'I recommend that we leave these questions, it's already in the past. We should concentrate on the future. My opinion is that we should definitely provide Noah Simpson with medical care and take him out of quarantine, if possible. This is also very important because the Unmei-Capsule is registered as an epilepsy implant, which perhaps wouldn't arouse the doctors' attention, but we mustn't give the Epidemics Department the slightest opportunity to somehow get near him.'

'Alright,' Sobrilov nodded. 'We have men on the Moon Colony, and I'll make immediate arrangements for his removal.'

'I suggest that we start getting India into the Unmei Project,' said Prince Kazuki. 'We hope that, this way, we'll have a new ally in the final phase, and India won't want to use it to expand its land-acquisition efforts.'

'So we can now say that a decision has been made concerning the future of the Unmei Project,' said Artyom Afanasiev, closing the discussion.

'Your Highness, are your men, the future implant carriers, ready?' Sobrilov nevertheless asked.

'Yes,' Prince Kazuki nodded, 'all of them, since early childhood, are faithful warriors of the Japanese Empire and followers of the glorious Kamikaze heritage. Gentlemen, when the Unmei Project enters into its final phase, a "*divine wind*" will sweep through the New China Empire within a short space of time.'

Part II

Divine Wind
(Kamikaze)

Wei Xu Long was kneeling before a portable homemade altar in the back corner of his study. He hadn't opened it for years, hadn't even looked at it, and spirituality had disappeared from his life ever since. But in the past few hours he had been praying steadily, practically nonstop. The words streamed out of him in a torrent. The accumulation of repressed, unspoken thoughts and feelings finally took shape and united with the spirit world. His soul was in misery.

The homemade altar was full of *Emas*, tiny painted boards, plaques on which he had written his prayers and wishes to the *Kamis*, the spirits. They were hanging from small nails, on fuzzy, coloured embroidery threads. His childhood requests were all still there, at the very back: a little dog, the picture of a toy, school-related requests. The subsequent teenage years had been skipped; that had been the empty period, when he had turned away from the spirits, and then there were the prayers during college exams, all stacked up. He remembered how the exam situations had weighed down on him, that was when he had returned to Shintoism—the ancient creed that embraced spirits by the millions.

He had written his last request two hours ago, at the beginning of his prayers. '*Wisdom*,' that's all he had written down. He was almost sure that wisdom also had a Kami among the eight million spirits. He had been praying to it for the past two hours.

'Don't take anything else along with you as you go through life, except wisdom. The rest will follow, one by one.' Those were his father's words, when he had turned him out of the house and sent him on his way, two years ago, to take up his first job. He was quite right; Wei had come to realise that. His decisions were greeted by some Kami or another, who took him by the hand, pointing towards Shinto, the trail unfolding before him, leading to the way of the spirits. His father was not a believer, but he had instinctively felt that he had to let his son turn to wherever he would feel safe. He knew very well that Wei would distance himself from him, looking for peace elsewhere, but he also knew that once he had found that peace, Wei would return to him. He was very well aware of it, since Wei was only his foster child. At one point, he had to leave, in order to find himself.

Wei was in high school when he found out that the members of the Long family were not his blood relatives. He had already noticed differences, especially the way his stature and build was different from that of his two brothers. As he grew up, his face also became different, more elongated than his closest relatives. They had ridiculed him later in school, calling him 'Jap' or 'Jappy.' He had run home, beside himself with anger, demanding explanations from his parents. His mother just cried and said that they should have told him sooner, but that nobody had the courage to do so. They only wanted to help him, so that he could become part of a family once again. He was a Japanese war orphan; he had lost his parents in the first years of the second Asian conflict.

His father had come home to a big row in full swing, with the boy storming out, banging the door behind him. He had run after him for a while, along the corridor of the high-rise block, but couldn't catch up with him. Later, he confessed he had been afraid that the boy would jump off the seven-hundred-metres-tall building, or go down to street level and start roaming about in Suzhou's darker sections, which would have equated to a suicide as well.

But Wei hadn't done it.

After two weeks of truancy—the better part of which he had spent in movie houses and wandering through shopping centres and terminals—he'd returned to his foster parents. No one had informed the police. They knew that the police disliked 'Jap foundlings.' They had hoped the boy would eventually find his way home.

So, on the altar, there was only one end-of-adolescence *Ema* request: *'father and mother.'*

The answer hadn't been long in coming, and he had finally found his way back to his foster parents. He felt that a spirit had guided him back to his true, loving family.

Still, in his childhood prayers, he had searched many times for contact with his biological parents, by trying to follow Buddhist traditions and praying to the spirits of his ancestors. But the only response that he got was a void. The past was silent; the Buddhist *Avatars*, the spirits, were letting him suffer in torment, remaining in the background. The *Kamis*, the Shinto spirits, however, had guided him along the way. At least that's what he felt.

If only those awful attacks . . . if only they hadn't happened . . .

They had started during his teenage years. At first, he only felt as if a few minutes had been eliminated from his life. Later, he had disappeared from the world for hours, involuntarily spending the time in a void. Because of this, he'd had to discontinue school. They had gone to every department of the Jiangsu Governor General's office, to every hospital, but no one could help him. They had suffered through the most hopeless period of their lives. At their lowest point of despair, a letter had arrived from a Japanese institution, a certain 'Futura Respondis' biological laboratory. In consideration of the boy's Japanese origin, they offered him free medical treatment.

Wei had been looking forward to the trip very much, so he was extremely disappointed when he wasn't allowed to land on the Japanese island. His sponsor, a certain Miss Yuuna Joshida, told his parents that it would be better, for diplomatic reasons, not to step onto Japanese Empire territory, which had not been recognized by New China. Hence, the treatment was carried out on a ship, or rather, on some manmade island. The intervention hadn't lasted too long and had rendered his life free of complaints. The epilepsy—they said it was a certain form of it—had almost completely disappeared. Subsequently, only two or three short attacks a year had occurred. Later, the company had even helped him with his studies; he couldn't have finished university without them.

And then, yesterday, almost twelve years later, a familiar voice came over the communicator: it was Miss Joshida. She said that, as a result of the recent easing in political relations, they had obtained their permit and could finally open an office within New China. They were in Mongolia, in Ulan Bator.

Wei could also feel this easing, because nowadays the 'Jappies' were addressed considerably less in that way. In fact, the Emperor of China, Jin Qin *Huangdi*, had announced that, a decade after the war, he wished to conduct negotiations in a peaceful manner and that he was ready to officially acknowledge the Japanese Emperor proclaimed during the war, and with it, the Japanese Empire. Miss Joshida also mentioned that she would be coming to the Futura headquarters in order to exchange the previous implant with a newer model. 'It won't take long,' she promised over the phone, 'the whole thing is done in half a day, through the previous implant's channel.' Wei was already used to the implant, the tiny, match-head sized cover of the metal opening to the implant channel at the back of his neck was a familiar, everyday feeling.

The reason he agreed for the capsule to be updated was because he hoped that his attacks would stop altogether. And, what's more, he wouldn't have to leave New China to do it; they would send a car for him, door-to-door service.

'That's enough!' Two fragile, fragrant hands covered his eyes. It was Nuo, whose name was also concealed among the Emas. When he had seen her for the first time at university, he had prayed to the Love Kami for weeks on end, to make it possible for them to meet. She was the very embodiment of a shrine to unattainable desire, beauty, and intellect: that is why Shinto had made him run into her, on his way to the spirits. In fact, she was so ravishing, that surely the way to the gods was through her.

'Your gods have heard you, don't worry,' the girl said, laughing, and laid his head in her lap. She had magnificent, black, laughing eyes.

There wasn't a moment that she didn't brighten up Wei's face. Even now, he just smiled and smiled as the girl gently stroked his face.

'Wei, you absolutely have to go to the Mongol Province, no matter how much you object to the new surgical intervention. The car is already on its way, you can't turn back now.'

The young man just laughed, ever more loudly, suddenly he turned the girl over and then he was on top.

'Why are you laughing now?' the girl asked, surprised. 'Three hours ago you were pacing up and down in the kitchen, completely undecided about whether to accept their offer or not.'

'I was considering it because I knew that the road I'm on is the most sensible route to follow!' he said, with a lingering kiss. A few moments ago she had been on the defensive, but now she flung one arm around the boy's neck, pulling him closer while lowering the other to secretly reach for the altar.

'So what is this then, you know-it-all?' Nuo was holding the Ema, inscribed with the word of wisdom. She quickly broke free from the embrace and ran out the kitchen door.

'Give it back at once!' Wei became really angry. He hated it when anyone reached onto the altar, even if it was his own wife. Nuo's great-grandparents had still been Buddhists, but the girl did not ascribe to any religion and didn't believe in either the gods or the spirits. To Wei's sorrow, she didn't respect Shinto enough, either.

The boy's anger vanished midway through the chase. The girl teased him coquettishly across the table. She was still in pyjamas, which silhouetted her attractive figure to perfection, making her irresistible. She looked at him with an impudent smile, the wish-card in her hand, fluttering it like some sort of bait before a wild beast.

Wei chased her towards the bedroom and then changed course towards the study. Just as he had suspected, the girl jumped through the bedroom door, mixing her screams with laughter, climbing onto the edge of the bed and crouching down at the headboard. She surrounded herself with pillows, like someone preparing for a lengthy siege, knowing that this was to be the place where she would meet her fate.

Wei jumped onto the end of the bed and approached slowly, like a cat. Each movement of his hand resulted in a stifled scream, which ended up turning into a girlish giggle. Then, a sudden leap into the pillows, and he caught her up in his arms.

'The spirit of wisdom claims what belongs to him, as his own!' he announced in a grave voice, taking off his polo shirt. 'Avatar of innocence, give me back my rights!' he said and flung himself onto her again. She was, of course, laughing continuously, hitting him with pillows.

Nuo slowly grew weary of resisting, the laughter stopped, only the barely audible soft sound of kisses filled the room—the rustling of sheets acted like some sort of spiritual music, as the phantom-like bodies shed their clothing and fell hungrily into each other.

That morning, Shinto carried Wei into reassuring, undulating waves of euphoria, freeing him of his earlier, seemingly overwhelming worries.

*

Angelica Stockwell didn't conceal her confusion.

'Yuuna, what's all this?' she asked her secretary on the intercom, uncomprehendingly. 'According to the data on the system, this man that our chauffeur is picking up to bring to us is already our client, and if I see correctly, has been our client for about ten years already. Is this some kind of clerical error, or is it accurate? If I'm correct, our company ad was only posted a week ago in New China and, if I'm not mistaken, so far we've never had a Chinese client. Or maybe I've missed something . . .'

Angelica had come in early, so that she could look over all the new clients' data, the first of which was Wei Xu Long, a twenty-eight-year-old man. The initial surprise she had was when she saw the massive amount of subject matter about him in the system. In it, they had written that he had received the 'Implant A1—epilepsy chip—FutRes' product ten years and six months ago. This wouldn't have been a problem in itself, since Futura had started its operation with those first-generation chips, actually used solely and entirely to treat epilepsy. But the strange thing was that Professor Yakizima had always talked about

New China as being potentially the future and the largest market—and, lo and behold, they already had a New China client, and what's more, for more than ten years.

'Yes, Angelica, what's in the material is correct. But it would be best if you would see the professor, because he could tell you much more about these matters than I could,' said her secretary. It seemed to be a good idea; the professor had been in his office for half an hour already and it would, perhaps, be better if he could clear this matter up before the interview.

'Would you tell him that I'm coming up?' she asked Yuuna and proceeded towards the elevator, with the bundle of files under her arm. The professor's office was exactly above them.

The sharp light of the morning sun was practically scratching the glass wall of the elevator, as its rays pierced through the skeletons of the skyscrapers in the business district. In the distance, scintillating clusters of spaceships and air-cars were ascending over the mountains. In the surrounding forests above the city, a cloud of fumes hung suspended, softly smudging the outlines, making the early morning crowd sleepy again on their way to work. The coils of vapour were only occasionally dispersed by those vehicles that flew up to the floating breakfast gardens and cafés between the high rises.

The professor was sitting at his desk, taking bundles of files from the pile of boxes stacked up next to him and placing them on his table. It seemed that he hadn't completely finished the most detestable part of moving, that of unpacking.

'Ms. Stockwell, hello! How nice to see you this morning. Even this wonderful sunrise couldn't compete with your beauty.'

The reserved man didn't pay compliments often, but when he did, he was an expert at it.

'Professor, are you trying to confuse me,' said Angelica, smiling, 'or, are you anticipating my sensitive questions and you want to sweep me off my feet?'

Yakizima's looked disconcerted.

'Sensitive questions? This morning, when the first New China client is arriving?'

'Actually, that's precisely it.'

'Before you begin, let's go out onto the terrace, in this glorious, warming sunshine that exactly matches your radiant reflection.'

Angelica became more and more astonished. The professor never behaved in this manner, for any reason whatsoever. He was usually polite but maintained his distance. The only time he may have mentioned her femininity and beauty had been at the interview when she was hired. And then it had been because he had wanted to hire her. The reason for this current torrent of appreciation would come to light before long.

They sat down on the comfortable lounging chairs of the rooftop terrace, evocatively surrounded by potted plants.

'If I'm not mistaken, you want to know about Wei Xu Long,' smiled Yakizima. He had apparently been expecting her this morning. Almost simultaneously, Yuuna appeared as well, bringing a steaming pot of tea, with biscuits.

'Thank you, Yuuna, you're very thoughtful. Please stay, since this conversation concerns you, too,' said the professor, upon which the secretary sat down beside them.

'How is it possible that Futura has New China clients?' Angelica hit him directly with the question.

'Look, this is not such a recent story, and it's better to talk things over now, before you meet our first clients. I'll do my best to explain everything clearly and succinctly.'

Angelica sat back, opened the folder, and waited anxiously for the truth.

'Wei, this pleasant young man, was one of our first clients when Futura was established and first started the operation. At that time, our activities were still focused strictly on the medical field, having developed the implants for the prevention of epileptic attacks. We had been working in Japan, but our reputation reached as far as China. Miss Joshida was handling communication and contact maintenance at the time, and then you took over that assignment. In a nutshell, Wei was one of her first clients.'

The professor raised his cup and took a sip of tea. He subsequently looked at Angelica with an expectant smile. She became flustered; she had been waiting for more, a lot more explanations, as this much she could figure out on her own.

'That's all?' She asked in her confused state.

'Perhaps that's all I can say; I don't know what Miss joshida could add to it . . .' said the professor, glancing at the secretary. The woman looked at her notes.

'Not much, except perhaps that his symptoms started in high school, the implant solved almost ninety per cent of his problems, and with this new E-series, his attacks may permanently come to an end.'

Angelica couldn't believe what she was hearing. The E-series chip had been advertised as an 'energizing, performance implant.' Although in the documentation, it said that it was to combat epilepsy, the actual tests being conducted didn't explicitly allude to this. Neither Alexei Sverlov nor Noah Simpson were epileptics.

'Are you absolutely sure that this young man needs it?'

Yuuna looked at the professor, then bowed her head, ferreting about in her notebook. It was clear she didn't want to say anything more, leaving it to Professor Yakizima.

'Angelica, if I may address you this way,' the professor had never been so informal with her, but on this rather peculiar morning it no longer appeared as something blatant. 'The E1-series got its name precisely because this is the first implant that fulfils two functions: for healthy subjects, it imparts energy—they are in the majority—and for epileptics, it acts as a treatment. In other words, it functions as an epilepsy chip. That's why the initial letter of the E-series is not only a serial number but also an indication of its function.'

'In that case, he would live like any other mortal, with normal sleeping periods?' Angelica asked. 'But completely liberated from his earlier disease?'

'Yes, but we're still not completely sure about that,' said the professor, gently stirring his tea. The steam rose, like the haze drifting over the city. 'That was exactly why I wrote about it in the publicity material, so that less emphasis would be put on the energizing part. For them, the relevant part should be the treatment of the disease, not the energizing effect.'

Angelica's ears registered the use of the plural.

'For them?!'

'Yes, there will be twenty-three altogether in the coming days, our earlier clients. They're all in possession of the A-type implant, and we are implanting the E-type in all of them. This will take twenty minutes, and there's no need for a medical team, as I'll be doing it myself via the implant channel after the informative talk initiated by you.'

Angelica suddenly felt lost, as if something had been concealed from her during the years she had spent at Futura. The professor smiled politely. Yuuna didn't look at her, staring fixedly into the greenish vortex of her tea with downcast eyes. It was obvious that there was a great deal that was hidden behind the exposed facts in this affair.

'Alright, I'll try to accept it as it is, though I find it extremely strange that you've never mentioned a word about this during all the years I've spent with you.'

Yakizima only smiled politely, stirring his tea. Yuuna continued to immerse herself in her notes.

'Just one more question, Professor,' Angelica went on. 'What will happen to the two implant carriers? Have you given up on them completely, or are you planning some rescue operation as far as they're concerned? They'll be running out of the antidote . . .'

The professor stood up and walked over to the glass railing, then turned and looked at Angelica. She took the sign as an invitation and went over to him. In the chasm below them, an express train sped through two buildings; the sun covered its frame with golden paint before it penetrated the cloud of fumes, like an arrow out of a bow.

'I don't plan to sacrifice them, even though their recklessness did make me rather angry. We'll soon get in touch with them, and they'll receive renewed antidote material,' the professor explained. 'But only until we terminate the contract with them and remove the implants from their systems.'

Angelica let out a long, very audible sigh.

'I can see that you're being tormented by a guilty conscience because we had to stop holding their hands, but they're just as much responsible for the situation that developed,' said Yakizima, turning to her. 'They have jeopardized a very long research period with their behaviour.'

Angelica thought of Alexei, the Russian. They had met probably about six times, but on the most recent occasions she had hardly behaved in a professional or indifferent manner with him. She had felt attracted to him, and she could see in his eyes that he didn't look on her as a simple support contact.

'They weren't exactly the best subjects for the experiment,' Angelica spoke quietly. 'Their chaotic pasts endangered the entire project.'

The professor shook his head.

'Our standpoint can't always be based on experiences filtered from the tangible world, Angelica. I have to look at the bigger picture, the future, towards which we are advancing, in an arrow-straight line. You are only looking at personal fates, at humans.' He took a sip from his tea, and then turned back in the direction of the table, 'The lesson from these two experiments is that if the implant could withstand two such carriers with a criminal record, then we wouldn't face any problems with future carriers. The E-series passed the test with flying colours.'

Angelica had to agree with the professor because she did, indeed, see the human destinies in this research: souls forging ahead, wishing to improve themselves, who welcomed and considered the energy-giving implant as their last hope. Perhaps she shouldn't be concerned with Futura's future plans. She should just be grateful for her job and accept it for what it was.

'Alright! I'm going, and I'll read through the material,' she said, bowing as she left. The two Japanese remained on the terrace; they were both smiling.

If they're so happy, this is indeed a wonderful day, Angelica thought. *They may well have a good reason, since Futura is writing history: the implant would be marketed commercially, to which end they have selected one of the world's biggest markets.*

'It's hard to know how much she suspects, or what she thinks. Sometimes I find her inscrutable,' said Yuuna, as soon as the elevator closed behind Angelica.

'Just like Europeans in general,' added the professor, placing his cup on the tray. 'But relax. I don't think she has an inkling of the project's depths. She's a pragmatist, her approach to things is from her humane standpoint; what's more, she has never been employed in military service, like you have, Major, working for the Intelligence Service, or like me, a wartime pilot. We're capable of putting the individual aside in favour of the larger picture, or a bigger goal. Europeans lack resolve. I'm not very keen on using them, but we had to hire her. Based on her biotest, she is immune to the Unmei Machines, she can therefore work safely as a contact person. She'll never get infected.'

Yuuna nodded in agreement and proceeded to collect the cups.

'How's the development work on the Terminator Command going?' she asked, picking up the silver tray.

'That's what's worrying me; it should have been finished a long time ago. That faulty command could be of some help to us, as there will come a time when we could use it as a weapon,' explained Yakizima. 'If the Terminator Command can still be finalized today, then it will be ready to launch within two days. We can stop all the unnecessary and unfortunate propagation of the cluster.'

'Let's go, we have to get ready,' said Major Joshida, and proceeded towards the elevator, 'Our first Kamikaze warrior will be here within two and a half hours.'

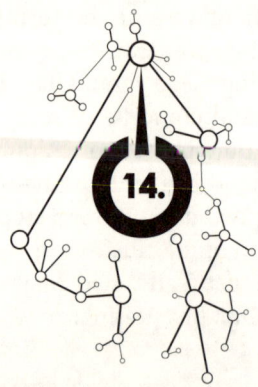

14.

Alexei Sverlov was in great shape again; the unpleasant side effects were gone and the main reason for this was his having given up the booze. He had enough antidotes left, certainly for two weeks, at least; in the meantime, he would find that goddamn Futura and shake the little Japanese professor out of his skull.

His biggest asset was his new friend, Bianco, who always popped up at the right time and in the right place. He watched the big bodyguard, dozing off on the next seat. He envied him for being able to sleep so well without the implant. He deserved the rest because yesterday he had carried out a one-person commando operation.

On the way back, Alexei had already agreed to hire him as a personal bodyguard. Bianco hadn't resisted the offer even though it meant having to leave the continent; he had served far away from Africa before, during the beginning of the war. As he had explained, his task had been to rescue protected people from chaotic situations and to accompany sensitive shipments to awkward places. He didn't appear to be over-enthusiastic either, shaking hands on the agreement with an impassive face. Mercenaries were like that, they'd go anywhere as long as they got paid.

Alex had to engage him because it looked like Bianco was the only one who could stay with him without any trouble. Whatever this implant did, besides providing him with continuous energy, whatever virus or deadly pathogens it spread, Bianco would never get contaminated. It wasn't easy to find someone who was skilled with weapons and who, a week later, wouldn't throw up the same greenish-yellow gunk as he did.

For the past two hours, he had trudged along the trails cut through the jungle, all the way to the old expressway leading to the Kampala metropolis. To his surprise, traffic was heavy. In this ancient cradle of humanity, they were still using vehicles running on wheels.

He got into the lane that led to the city, lost in the distant fog, and took up the slower pace of the convoy. He wouldn't have dared to press down harder on the pedal anyway, there was no way of knowing what state this jeep was in, it had to take them through the hundred and twenty kilometres still ahead.

Above them, the air-expressway, which also led to Kampala, stretched to an altitude of two thousand metres. From time to time, he glanced wistfully up at the air-cars whisking by, he would have loved to speed up the pace, as he had started to feel extremely hungry. In the ravaged camp, they had found hardly any food except for a few energy bars. Although they had searched the entire area, Silaha's men had taken everything with them and had burned what was left to ashes. Before setting off, they had buried the remains of Bianco's companions in a common grave, paying them their last respects.

In the monotony of driving, memories started to haunt him. The silt that had accumulated over the troubled years kept pushing itself into his brain in the form of flashing pictures. The answer had to be there, somewhere, in all that rubble: what had led him to Futura? What had been that magnetic attraction drawing him to Futura Respondis, that had made him plunge headlong into a totally unknown and uncontrolled experiment?

Perhaps the nonstop spin had been the temptation that he couldn't resist. And that movie about that guy planning extreme tours. The performance suggested in that presentation . . . having seen the film, there was no man who would say no to such an offer. They had been chosen because of their addiction. A drug addict and an arms dealer with a criminal record need constant stimulation.

But what was Futura's objective with this experiment? What had become totally evident to him was that the implant's activity increased if he took, or inhaled, less of the antidote. At that point, it would be dangerous not only to him, but also to others. Was that the reason they wouldn't answer the phone anymore? Was that part of the experiment, or was it just a way of getting rid of him?

There were too many unanswered questions, and he couldn't concentrate on any of them for the time being. He closed his eyes for a moment and shook his head vigorously to drive them out. But, nevertheless, one of them kept impudently circling around in his skull: besides the guy in the movie and himself, was there anyone else who had been given the implant?

He recalled what that crazy, self-appointed king, Silaha, had told him: that everyone had died on the Russian ship. It was the implant that had finished off the *Lev Tolstoy* as well ...

Could I really be the Angel of Death?

For some time now, he had sensed that the advantages provided by the implant dwindled away before the wall of drawbacks, grown to gigantic proportions, which surrounded him, isolating him from everyone. He couldn't find a friend or a partner for himself: no one had been able to keep up with his pace. The occasional contacts that had thawed the chill of solitude had been short-lived, and his desires had chased him into having to purchase love.

Those who might have been suitable for longer term relationships couldn't understand his unending struggles, which he often couldn't understand himself: all his actions had been directed towards avenging his father's death. He should have let go of that tragedy long ago, along with his father, and let time carry him away; the farther away, the better.

However, while he was using the implant, he was incapable of working that event out of his system. Something within him had been injured, something had broken; and that made him switch into top gear. His mind had tried to solve the mental tension with light sleep. During those periods, he would relive everything that had happened over previous days, months, and years.

Strange, how every time he thought about Futura, the eyes of that lovely woman, Angelica Stockwell, came to mind. She had always treated him with such sensitivity and consideration. He had to find her because he had a funny feeling that she somehow didn't belong in this whole tangled picture. She was *innocence personified* in this story. Her dyed red hair, her warm brownish-green eyes, her delicate hand . . . the others were just rotten pigs.

Eventually, after an hour and a half, they arrived on the outskirts of Kampala. Typical for an African megalopolis, there was considerable traffic even at ground level. Due to wartime conflicts, Africa had stopped developing, jumping back a few years in time to the era when people still walked on streets. This was no longer typical of the gigantic European cities: the well-to-do had left the street level, leaving it to poverty-stricken pilferers and those who pursued their business in the shadows. That was why the asphalt world was generally ruled by criminals.

'We should get hold of an air-car as soon as possible,' said Bianco. 'We're not safe; kidnapping here is one of the most lucrative businesses.' Alex trusted the mercenary; there was no doubt that he was well capable of deciding that this place wasn't the best for a wealthy arms dealer.

'Fine, my friend. Let's go and find an air-car agency.'

Bianco shook his head.

'That's the problem, you won't find any here. They don't sell such commodities in these suburbs, the stores would be ransacked within a few weeks.'

'So what's the plan, then?'

'We'll have to steal one.'

Alex looked at him, stupefied; he couldn't believe his ears. True, his conscience hadn't often bothered him in the past, especially not when he was selling arms to criminals. Still, this sounded different.

'Don't worry,' said Bianco, 'the majority of these people here have, by and large, stolen such vehicles themselves. Look around, who would be able to afford one of them in this neighbourhood?'

Alex tried to go along with that explanation. His troubled face showed that he wasn't succeeding too well.

'Well, OK,' he agreed finally, resigning himself to the idea, 'but on one condition: you guarantee that you'll steal a stolen vehicle. We'll leave it at the airport afterwards, and the police will then return it to its original owner.'

'But of course, I guarantee it,' Bianco replied, grinning at the idea. It had been a long time since he had heard such arrant nonsense, but the Russki's good-boy intention appealed to him. 'We'll have to wait until sundown, and then we'll look for a casino around the area. We'll find the best gamblers there, the types who can afford something better than a four-wheeler.'

They waited for nightfall in the parking lot of a fast food joint. The food looked absolutely disgusting but, in fact, tasted quite good. According to the owner, the meat patty was made from real meat; he kept assuring them that it came from the meat of the remaining hoofed animals, but its substance resembled some synthetic version far too much for this to be true. Being hungry, they decided it was better not to know what the exact ingredients were in this bizarre place.

Four blocks away, there was an entertainment centre. A huge crowd had already gathered for the evening's gambling in front of the building. For a long time, there were only four-wheelers arriving, even eight-wheelers, huge luxury limousines, but not a single air-car. They had almost given up hope, when three air-cars flew in. Two of them stopped at the second-level terrace of the ten-floor building, the other one alighted on the rooftop.

'The one on the rooftop is ours,' said Bianco and checked his gun.

'Why that one?'

'Because afterwards we won't have to flee through the narrow streets and between buildings. From there, it's a straight, unhindered flight to the airport.'

Alex collected his things and stuffed them into his backpack.

'That hotel there, facing the building. Take the room at the very top, with the balcony looking down on the casino. When you're ready, go to the balcony and wait. You've got fifteen minutes.'

'Fifteen? Have you gone mad? Neither of us can get anything done in that amount of time.'

'Give me a thousand New Dollars, in chips,' said Bianco. 'With that, even I can be on the rooftop in five minutes.' For Alex, one thousand New Dollars as an incidental cost didn't seem that much under the circumstances.

Bianco encouraged Alex by shoving him gently on his shoulder, before they both got out of the car. Alex walked along the sidewalk towards the hotel and, on his way, gave the car keys to a bum on the side of the street, pointing out the vehicle to him. The middle-aged man, dressed in rags, could only believe that the wheels were his when Alex slipped a two-hundred New Dollar chip into his hand, urging him to go towards the car. He only approached it, however, once Alex had disappeared under the arched entrance of the hotel. He probably thought that somebody was having fun at his expense.

In the meantime, on the other side of the street, Bianco had reached the crowd standing in front of the entrance to the entertainment centre. With practised jauntiness, he passed by the queue, right up to the doormen. He kept his hand in his pocket where the pistol lurked, at all times.

'Hey, my friend,' he addressed the heavyset bouncer. Perhaps startled to have come across a guest of such a calibre, he made no attempt to stop him. 'Me and my friend would like to go in and see your program,' he said, extending his hand for a handshake, with his 'friend,' a two-hundred-dollar chip, flattened in his palm, 'and my friend won't be ungrateful if he could have a good time at your place tonight, as well.'

The doorman shook his hand for quite a while, trying to get a feel of the bribe: if he had a biochip, he could probably tell its value.

'Of course, I'm glad you came,' he said, withdrawing his hand with the chip in it, which he slipped unnoticed into his pocket. 'Please, do come in, greetings to your friend, too!'

'Thank you,' Bianco inclined his head and proceeded to enter the building, but suddenly a discreet alarm went off beside the door.

'Sorry, my friend, but you can't take guns into the building,' said his newfound pal, extending his arms by way of apology, 'unless you have another one or two persuasive friends . . .'

'One or two?'

'Make it two,' the big bouncer smiled. His broad grin pushed his thick moustache up, raising it skyward.

Bianco deciphered the coded message and slipped another two chips into his hand. In response, the man disconnected the weapons-scanner. Everything was for sale here, even the safety of those who wished to have fun. The number of guns per head in this place must be pretty high already, Bianco thought, one more or one less wouldn't hurt anybody. This was truly the chaotic world of the street, but it was exactly that chaos they needed right now.

He reached the rooftop with the elevator where, to his surprise, no one was guarding the air-car that they had chosen. The open vehicle was resting on its skids a few metres from the fire escape. *Can it be this simple, leaving it just like that, in these surroundings?* the mercenary wondered. The back of the car was facing him, but he couldn't see the inside because of the high-back seats. So he slowly started to inch his way to the side. He had almost reached the vehicle, when some tawny-coloured object came leaping out at him from behind the red leather upholstery.

There was no time to pull out his gun, although, to tell the truth, he should have had it in his hand a long time ago. The fully-grown lioness aimed for his throat. Bianco protected his throat with his forearm; the incisors hooked into the strong fibres of his armour-plated jacket. They couldn't pierce the fabric, but the bite was crushing his muscles with a half-ton force. Not to mention the impetus with which it threw the mercenary to the ground. Meanwhile, it kept pressing on his shoulder and his chest with its two front paws and then started to hug him around his neck.

With a flash of genius, Bianco suddenly spun around, his speed surprising the big cat, but only enough to let go of his arm and leap onto his neck from behind. Bianco curled up and rolled into a ball, which finally helped him to reach for the gun under his armpit. He didn't even have to take it out of its holster, he raised his left arm a little and three energy bolts knocked the lioness down.

Bianco stood there panting for a while, trying to work off the stress attack caused by the surprise and to calm the massive flood of adrenalin. He was standing next to the corpse of a dying animal, which, a few minutes ago, had still been a fully functional car alarm. This could only have happened in Africa, on his beloved continent.

Before getting into the car, he had to shoot through the thick chain tying the animal to the vehicle. He was still half stunned, shaking his head: the scene that had just taken place was incredible, and the fact that this magnificent creature had to perish . . . He had been prepared for almost anything else—an automatic weapon, a robot, even a human—but not a lioness. He stroked her fur in farewell and to apologize, before jumping into the air-car.

'Come on!' he prompted the vehicle. 'You don't need any other safety system; you've trusted your lion!'

It appeared to have heard what Bianco suggested because, when he pressed on the ignition button, it took off into the air with a whirring sound. The owner must really have trusted his deterrent, the live alarm, and hadn't installed any other form of security in the car. But it was also possible that the vehicle had been stolen and its safety system had been deactivated after the theft.

Bianco slowly guided the vehicle upwards, above the wall bordering the roof, from where he could see all the balconies of the hotel on the opposite side. In one of the doors, there stood the Russki, hands in his pockets, nonchalantly, like someone just watching the traffic on the street. He pushed the gas pedal and, with a quick turn, directed the car to the balcony.

'Well, I'll be damned!' Alex whistled approvingly, while throwing his bags into the backseat. 'The most disgusting pimps in Moscow have machines like this! Nice, and at the same time repulsively flashy. Congratulations, my friend.'

'Careful with the compliments,' said Bianco. Alex settled into position, his bodyguard switched to full throttle and started to ascend towards the clouds. 'I was such an idiot, such a greenhorn, that you almost had a lion to take you downtown, instead of me.'

Alexei looked at him, baffled, as the Italian recounted his adventure.

'I've never seen a live lion, only bionic ones,' Alex shook his head incredulously. 'In Russia's zoos there are only artificial ones. I had no idea there were still some living somewhere.'

'Just a few, perhaps, only on reservations, and even those are cloned. Not that many survived the chaos after the wars,' replied Bianco. 'It could be that I just killed the last one.'

This probability saddened both of them. The war hadn't only been a scourge on humanity but had also damaged the planet's ecosystem. Silence settled between them for the remaining kilometres.

Night had fallen when they reached the first skyscrapers, and floating traffic had also increased. The GPS navigator was functioning in some local, tribal language and it was impossible to adjust it. Alex's translation chip was silently keeping a low profile, as it didn't recognize the words, but luckily Bianco had sufficient experience in handling it to be able to find the right way to the airport. According to the system, they were a bare seven minutes flight time from Kampala International.

That was when—virtually out of thin air—the cop car caught up with them. With its large-sized body, it dominated the space on the left side in an authoritative and peremptory manner. It switched on its blue-red rotating light at exactly the same time as the cop's voice came through the loudspeaker. He was speaking in another African language, and since Alex didn't have it in his translator chip either, he tried to look ahead, with his most resolute and most poised expression, in the direction of the future, or rather, towards the airport, ignoring the cop car completely. As if it weren't there at all.

'I hate language updates, especially in the case of languages that are dying out . . .' he was forcing the words out through the crack between his teeth, 'What's it saying?'

'It says that this car has a warrant for its apprehension and that we should pull over to the side,' said Bianco with a slight smile on his face. Meanwhile, his pistol had come out of the pouch under his armpit and was resting on his knee. 'And don't talk like that about one of the most beautiful languages on the continent.'

'You're right, to you it's beautiful, to me, it doesn't say anything. So what will it be, are we stopping?'

'We can't stop, because the police here have been recruited from the same criminals as the ones they're chasing.'

'I love Africa,' said Alex, following events from the corner of his eye. In the meantime, Bianco had pulled into a side street, with the police car following, running parallel.

Suddenly, Bianco switched to reverse and the car shuddered as the police car shot past. The mercenary started to fire continuously with the gun resting on his knee. Their own side window shattered with a loud crack first, and then the bullets reached the cop car's engines. The cops returned fire with an old, gunpowder-type firearm, but Bianco manoeuvred their car out of the line of fire. Smoke erupted from the cop car and then, leaning slightly to one side, it twisted down towards the ground. The police cruiser ripped off two balconies before crashing onto the ground with a heavy thud.

'An excellent weapon,' said Bianco to Alex. 'Had I known that you were selling toys with such tremendous firepower, I'd have stood by you much sooner,' he added, smiling as if he'd just been trying out the gun at a shooting range.

'But now, everything is urgent,' he pointed towards the airport. 'We have to get there as soon as possible, because they'll be snapping at our heels within a few minutes. Hold tight; I'll have to step on the gas. And at the airport, you'll have to find someone who isn't interested in our biochips and doesn't want to screen us, and won't be bothered by the arrest warrant either, which has probably been issued against us already.'

For the first time in ages, Alex, once again, felt that same rush in his veins that he had felt long ago after one of his shady jobs. Although he no longer liked them, the memory was still great.

Really great.

*

Moon Colony, Epidemics Centre, Severe Infections Quarantine

The black-uniformed men stopped at the reception desk and took out their IDs. They were wearing impeccably ironed, starched white shirts with cuffs, something that even government employees didn't wear nowadays.

'We'd like to speak with the director.'

'Mr. Smith, Mr. Stanton, from the Epidemics Institute on Earth,' the secretary read the names on the IDs out loud, 'I'll call the competent authorities immediately, meanwhile, I'll ask you to please have a seat in the waiting area,' the woman said, pointing to the comfortable leather armchairs. The two men sat down opposite each other, without uttering a single word, and propped their briefcases against their feet. They didn't make themselves comfortable in the armchairs, they were obviously counting on being received immediately. Their business was probably urgent and they were nervous. A good secretary could always suss these things out.

'Sir, there are two gentlemen here from Earth, they would like to speak to you. They don't have an appointment, but I thought it must be some important business,' said the secretary.

'Fine, show them into the conference room next to my office, I think I know what brings them here,' said the man on the other end of the line.

The secretary stepped out from behind the counter and walked over to the two waiting men.

'Gentlemen, thank you for your patience, please follow me.'

The two men reached for their briefcases and stood up at exactly the same time, as if they were twins. *These are either investigators or inspectors*, the secretary thought. *Their movements are circumspect and trained, as if copied from a codex.* Or this whole thing was also connected to that burst of activity, the arrival of those seventy men who had been placed under quarantine just a few hours ago. The security measures were doubled up as well; the quarantine premises were being guarded by armed men of the United Colony Army. As a secretary, she had also had to sign some kind of confidentiality agreement, so she was very intrigued to know what was going on. Everything was connected to the silence of Mars New Home, that was for sure. She had to admit that she was a little bit scared. She had seen a lot in the nature of epidemics over the past few years. There were many who had been predicting the arrival of a deadly super-virus . . .

'Did you have a good trip?' she asked the men walking behind her, perhaps they would be more talkative if she put her tried and tested female wiles into action. She made a point of walking in front of them, so that they would have a good view of her legs between the slit of her skirt, cut off just below the knee.

'Yes, Miss,' the answer was short and terse; it sounded like a response meant to end an unsolicited, prying conversation.

'Oh, it's not as big a deal as it used to be, since the whole thing only takes a few hours. And the artificial gravitation makes everything so much more familiar, doesn't it?' she gave full vent to her smile, which she'd been told was seductive, to the more handsome-looking man, who just smiled back politely. There was no question about it: these men were here on a very important and very urgent mission. She no longer felt the urge to pry any further, her premonitions and fears were intensifying.

'Here we are,' she said and opened the conference room door. The director stepped forward.

'Thank you, Miss Alarie. Would you be so kind as to bring us some refreshments, coffee or tea? As the gentlemen prefer . . .'

One of the men raised his hand and politely refused the offer.

'I'd like some tea, please,' said the other one.

'Gentlemen, please have a seat. I'm Gustav Larson, director of the Moon Colony Epidemics Centre.'

'I'm Mr. Smith, and this is Mr. Stanton,' said the more talkative man, while they showed their IDs. 'United Colony Epidemics Institute, Ontario. We've come at the request of the UC Council to inspect and to take back to our quarantine centre a passenger by the name of Noah Simpson, travelling on Mars Trans-Terra line TT225, if he is in transportable condition,' the man pushed a document across the table, with the Epidemic Institute's large, circular logo on it. The director read the letter attentively.

'Why haven't I been informed about this?' he looked up from the letter, his face showing incomprehension and a certain amount of annoyance.

'We, ourselves, only received information about our mission immediately before our departure. Our scientists on Earth are very upset about the events presently occurring on Mars, and they wish to provide you with their full assistance,' said the man who had proclaimed himself as Mr. Smith and who seemed to be the spokesperson.

'Well, I'm equally upset by the fact that I have no idea what's happening on Mars,' retorted the director. He found the entire affair rather strange. 'However, this is a quarantine, of which you're also well aware. No one leaves here until it's determined whether anyone is carrying some dangerous pathogen.'

'We're in full agreement with you on this point. I'd like to ease your fears by assuring you that we would transport him to the Centre in a special quarantined spacecraft, obviously staffed with competent personnel.'

The director reflected, glancing back and forth from the document to the two men. There was something missing from the picture.

'Why him? There were almost seventy travelling on this craft, why are you after him specifically? Is this perhaps all connected with the earlier Police operation?'

'Precisely,' said Smith, smiling. 'Here is another request from the Head of the UC Bureau of Investigation Organized Crime and Gang Section, Mr. Richard Enderston, who wishes to interrogate the witness further.'

The director read through this letter as well. It was all perfectly in order.

'This is the same order for interrogation that I received for the two detained subjects; they want to transport them tomorrow, if all their tests prove negative. Why don't you take the three of them together?'

'According to our information, Mr. Simpson was the investigators' undercover man, not a criminal. Why should they transport them together?' the man wanted to know.

The director placed the documents side-by-side and reached for the communicator.

'Alright, but allow me to make a call to Investigator Enderston, to make sure I understood everything properly. He gave me his number, to call him in case of problems with the detained . . .'

'No need for that,' said Smith, suddenly standing up. 'We didn't mean to disturb you or to complicate the situation. Go ahead and proceed with the examinations. We can wait to transport this individual once you have all the results.

Both men stood up and extended their hands in sign of their leaving.

'Oh, yes, before I forget,' said Smith, reaching into his briefcase, 'Mr. Simpson is suffering from a severe form of epilepsy. According to our database, there is a chip to this effect implanted into his system. This is the medication that he must take every other day. If he doesn't get it, his condition might become critical.'

The director looked at the box; the name of one of the largest pharmaceutical producers was on it. Although he didn't know the product itself, he intended to check that out as well.

'Fine, I'll have it sent to him,' said the director. 'So, I'll call you at the Centre, after the quarantine has been lifted.'

'Don't worry, it won't be necessary. We at the Centre are following matters attentively and keeping tabs on everything, and we'll be in touch.'

The secretary no longer walked in front, but beside them when she accompanied the men to the elevator. The three of them stood silently, looking in front, as they waited the few seconds it took to ride down to the lowest floor, the elevator being sufficiently noiseless to hear the chirping from Mr. Stanton's, the tongue-tied man's, communicator and the foreign language sentence following it:

'Vi poluchili novie soobshenie' (You have a new message). That was all before the man quickly reached into his pocket and muted the system.

The secretary, who was born on the Moon, only spoke United Colony English. That was why, if she hadn't had her biochip, she couldn't have identified the scarcely audible signal as Russian. It made her wonder why a man in the North-American Union, with a typical English name, living in Ontario, would use Russian messages on his communicator. But the world had become so involuted; the borders dividing one national state from another no longer existed. Why, she herself came from a family with French roots but even her father no longer spoke his ancestors' language.

The two men departed without a word. They left the secretary with a rumbling feeling of fear.

In the meantime, Director Larson returned to his office and immediately went onto the SystemNet, as the enigmatic meeting kept bothering him. He logged on to the internal network of the Epidemics Institute and examined the employees' list. Forty-five Smiths and thirteen Stantons worked for the Centre at a global level. Which two could they be?

He should call Investigator Enderston regarding the requests . . . but, when he reached for the phone, he noticed that the visitors had taken both documents with them.

His hand brushed the bulge that was the box of pills in his pocket. The man called Noah Simpson had been looking quite ill when they brought him in. Perhaps he really did need this.

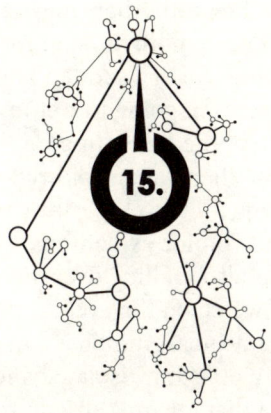

15.

Mars, New Home Colony, Quarantine Centre

Cliff and Jess stood in their hermetically sealed protective clothing by the side of the patient, who had finally agreed to be brought into the isolated section of the lab, so that they could take a sample from her. Against all the odds, the young woman was feeling well, free of pain, had no fever or any other serious complaint. She was only troubled by the annoying nasal discharge—she actually used the very word 'annoying,' as if it were just a little cold—along with the sweating attacks that came on suddenly. Her appetite and mood were good, and she was happy that she hadn't had to come into the Quarantine Centre earlier. She had nevertheless agreed to the test, feeling that it was her duty, in the interests of her family and the Colony.

'Thank you for agreeing to let us take samples,' Cliff started, his voice sounding strange, echoing inside his helmet. 'I'm Professor Clifford Mills, chief investigator; my colleague is Sarah-Jessica Thompson, virologist. What we'll do now is take a sample of that fluid that keeps running from your nose and we'll examine, as quickly as possible, the effect that it has on another living organism—a test rat.'

'I understand,' nodded the young woman. 'My nose generally fills up on a regular basis, I don't know why it does it at that specific time and why at regular intervals but, right now for instance, it's completely clear. When it happens, it really bothers me because I'm asthmatic, and the congestion makes it even more difficult for me to get air. The same happens with the sweating. All of a sudden I'm soaked in sweat, like in a heat wave, and I feel as if I'm going to wet my panties . . .'

'Does all this happen at the same time?'

'I don't know exactly,' the woman said reflectively, 'maybe not, the heat waves are more frequent than the runny nose.'

'I understand. Thank you for explaining,' Cliff nodded, glancing at Jess. He saw that she was also mulling over this statement. 'We'd be well advised to keep a close watch on the cyclical pattern.'

'I've also noted that my breast milk has run completely dry. I have a three-month-old baby, who is now isolated and, thank God, didn't get infected. I was horrified that my milk dried up when I got infected. As if they had closed a tap . . .' Jess and Cliff looked meaningfully at each other.

'It blocks the oxytocin,' Jess said out loud what both had been thinking.

'What's that?' the young woman asked.

'It's a hormone in the human body, produced during pregnancy or during nursing. Is there anything else that's unusual?'

'The fact that my sleeping pattern has been broken, and I'm much less tired now. I found it strange because I should be sick, depressed, and tired, but I feel just the opposite. At first I got very scared when I became infected with this deadly pathogen because, although I hadn't seen what happened to that unfortunate man in the bar, my relatives had, so I pushed the panic button. I thought the same thing would happen to me and that I would die before I could raise my child,' the young woman was getting all worked up, her eyes filling with tears, 'but for the last few days, that's all there's been. Thank God, nothing more serious.'

'We'll do everything we can to make even these mild complaints disappear,' said Jess, smiling. 'That's exactly why you're here, so that we can stop this pathogen.'

'Of course,' the woman smiled back, 'That's why I agreed to go through with this.'

'I'll ask you now to lie down quietly, and when you feel one of the attacks you just mentioned coming on, tell us immediately.'

'OK.'

Cliff prepared the test animals on the table behind them and switched on the nanoscope. They would have to snap the sample in a state where the protein chains wouldn't disintegrate but remain visible in their predicted shape. Cliff felt that perhaps this hypothesis would be the last straw they could grasp at.

Jess watched the woman's changes in condition and measured her pulse and blood pressure. The scanner was monitoring her body continuously, projecting the three-dimensional image it obtained onto the screen. Jess saw that everything seemed normal and healthy and, even though these proteins were undeniably circulating in the woman's bloodstream, according to the signs they weren't causing any damage. This condition could be compared to the silent incubation period in the case of a viral infection.

'I can sense it coming now,' the woman said and started to prepare her handkerchief.

'Blood pressure is rising,' said Cliff, glancing at the scanner.

'We won't need that now,' said Jess politely, taking the handkerchief out of the woman's hand, giving her a sterile material.

'Alright, I can feel it coming,' she said, raising the material for the sample to her nose. Meanwhile, the scanner was displaying red markings and knots. The instrument signalled increased activity around the sinus cavity, the middle ear, and the nasal passages. A milder reaction at the molecular level was visible in the lymph glands. The woman was continuously struggling in the throes of convulsions, trying to get rid of the accumulated mucus. After a few blows and coughs, she succeeded, and then it started again as if a dam had been breached. The cloth for the sample was soon filled up and had to be changed.

Cliff quickly took the cloth, smeared some of the substance onto a sample glass plate with a small spatula, and stuck it under the nanoscope. He also switched on the digital imager so that everything connected with the experiment could be recorded.

The chains formed from the amino acids, the protein spirals, slowly took shape, showing their outlines on the monitor.

'There's no connection between them,' the professor shook his head angrily. 'I don't understand, I thought we could still see what we're looking for in a fresh sample. That beast just doesn't want to show itself.'

Cliff was swept away by his emotions, speaking about the proteins as if they were living beings.

Meanwhile, Jess was already replacing the fourth cloth when the attack finally seemed to calm down. The young woman took a few deep breaths and spread out her hand.

'So much for that.' She appeared worn out by the whole thing.

'How do you feel now?' Jess asked.

'Not in the best shape, a bit like during a bad flu. I'm a little exhausted by the struggle . . .' Meanwhile, the scanner screen displayed red clumps again, the lymph glands were starting to fill up, until a luminescent flash shot through the entire body.

'The sweat-attack is starting,' said the woman, and her face turned completely red. Jess collected the emerald-coloured beads of perspiration from the patient's arm and knuckles with a small swab and placed them on a glass plate, handing it to Cliff, who quickly placed it under the nanoscope.

The image on the screen showed exactly the same polymer chains as in the previous case. The proteins were still not showing the interconnected structure that Cliff had envisioned.

'I don't believe this,' the professor fretted, 'they have hardly emerged from the body and they've already separated completely from each other. They barely spent one second in the open air.'

'If they ever did get interconnected . . .' said Jess in the background, busy alleviating their patient's high temperature with cooling cloths. Slowly, this attack subsided, too, and the woman looked as if none of this had taken place at all.

'Jess, would you accompany the lady to the isolation room? After that I expect you back here immediately. We'll have to continue with the experiment while the samples are fresh.'

Jess took the patient into the isolation room and helped her get settled on the bed. In the meantime, Cliff stored the samples that they collected in tiny vials. He mixed biological nutriments in with the samples, simulating the internal conditions of the living organism, so that they would remain intact, until Jess returned.

He selected four rats, two each for the nasal and the sweat samples. He shaved the fur around their jugular veins and placed four syringes on the preparatory table. He then pulled the body scanner over the animals.

He was just waiting for Jess to inject the pathogens.

Cliff had imagined that this verification procedure would be much simpler. In theory, everything had appeared so obvious, yet this secretive and frightening thing, this silent killer, appeared to be asleep right now. Or else it had somehow disguised itself and was silently laughing at them.

'I'm here, we can start,' Jess said from behind; the professor was so immersed in his thoughts that he hadn't even realized that Jess had returned.

'Alright,' Cliff jolted back into the work at hand, 'I've prepared everything. Here are the samples, sorted into separate groups, according to their origin: this is the nasal secretion and this is the perspiration. Here are the animals, too; they each get a separate number. Number One and Number Two will be getting the first two samples from both sources. Afterwards, we'll wait to see what the scanner signals. If it detects activity in the blood, then we'll take a sample and examine it again under the microscope. We won't inject the other two animals, Number Three and Number Four, yet—not until an hour has passed. Our goal is to see if there is any difference between the two samples, and what significance the elapsed time would have on the infection. Shall we begin?'

'I'm holding the animal,' said Jess and carefully turned over the rat on whose back they had earlier painted the number one. Cliff picked up the syringe marked with the number one.

'For the log, then: Injection of nasal secretion, test animal Number One, 09:18 Mars time.'

The needle went into the jugular vein; the animal resisted a little but afterwards calmed down in its cage.

'For the log:' the professor dictated again, picking up syringe number two, 'Injection of the sweat drops, test animal Number Two, time: 09:18.'

Jess then returned this animal to its cage too. She pulled down the body scanner's ultrasound probe unit, which was hanging from the ceiling, and positioned the four cages in such a way that they would all be visible simultaneously on the monitor. The two test subjects and the control animals were also in the field of vision so that she and Cliff could easily observe the changes.

Cliff collapsed into one of the chairs, he was visibly exhausted.

'Go and get some rest, I know you've spent the entire night in here,' said Jess, stroking his shoulder. 'I saw that you played the rerun of all the simulations on your computer.'

'Yes, and I found two additional connecting versions compared to the previous three. Now we already have five variations,' said the professor. He would have liked to rub his face but his helmet was in the way. 'I was afraid that if I ran another simulation, I would find another five connections, and it would never end. The best scenario would be if there were only one possible connection.'

'Go and get some rest!' Jess urged, even more firmly than before. 'I'll switch them all on: the video, the scanner, the nanoscope's digital recorder, I promise you won't miss anything. If, by any chance, the process were to start up, I'll let you know immediately.'

Cliff just looked straight ahead with glazed eyes.

'You're absolutely right; if I don't get at least twenty minutes' rest, I'll be useless and won't even notice anything obvious right under my nose.'

He stood up slowly and opened the airlock's door. He pushed the sterilizing system's button, whereupon a mixture of chemical compounds, combined with hot steam and a powerful water jet, washed down his contamination suit with a soft whirring sound. As the steam dissipated, he raised a hand in farewell: 'I'll be in the rest area. Call me immediately!'

'Absolutely. I'll call you. Now, go and get some sleep! Don't worry, everything will be alright!'

No sooner had Cliff disappeared than Jess turned back to the scanner. Although the proteins in the samples injected into the animals' bodies could be clearly traced in the scanner, drifting with the blood and into the lymphatic system, there were no signs of fusion or interlinking.

The woman in the isolation room appeared to be totally healthy, quietly watching TV. On the little cabinet beside her, there were already some hankies she'd probably used to blow her nose. In her case, the pathogen wasn't deadly, but it wouldn't let her rest, either. If they were lucky, similar patterns would emerge within the test rats as well.

She stepped up to the airlock and cautiously looked out into the corridor. She thought it was a good moment to perform a long-awaited test. She took a vial from the drawer, containing dried-up pieces of paper tissues. They stemmed from the sample she had examined so many times before under her microscope at home: it was Noah's handkerchief, which he had left behind. This high-performance nanoscope would give a much better image of it and it represented another, new sample available for comparison.

She feared the outcome—her hand trembled as she placed the samples on a glass plate, securing it with another one on top. She inserted it, together with the fresh sample, under the tip of the nanoscope. She took a deep breath and brought herself to look at the monitor.

What she had feared most had happened: the two samples showed perfectly identical structures. The only difference between them was that one was floating in live nutrient solution, while the other was squeezed in between particles of dried mucus. They were the same protein chains, the same frightening monstrosities.

Noah is the Alpha person, there's no doubt about it.

The next moment she was overcome by a frantic panic attack. Never before in her life had such a violent fear fallen upon her. She needed to rip the contamination suit off her body and get out of the isolation room. She was suffocating, she couldn't get enough air; she turned up the volume of oxygen in her helmet. She was hyperventilating, knowing full well that the increased oxygen would only make matters worse. She turned the control valve in the opposite direction just in time, reducing the inflow of oxygen. Eventually, her heartbeat returned to normal.

The adrenaline rushed down into her legs and made her feel suddenly and dreadfully tired. The thought that she was also contaminated because of Noah was terrifying. She wanted to flee, find a way out, no matter where to.

But then, after deliberate concentration, and muttering a few prayers, she slowly pulled herself together and rationalized her current situation. Noah had been gone for a week now, so, if she had been contaminated, she would have been long dead by this time. They had not had any sexual contact, they weren't at that stage yet; nothing had happened between them that could have transmitted the pathogen directly. Noah's symptoms hadn't looked as bad as the woman in the next room, maybe the disease had still been evolving in his system. If that weren't true, he would have died a long time ago, along with Jess. They would have been the first two victims, not the bus driver.

What was happening with Noah now? If the communication ban were lifted, she could find out something. But that was still a few days away. Or, if she got in touch with the Moon Colony Epidemics Centre on some work or research pretext . . . but until the first results came back for the samples that had been sent to the research groups, or until they found a solution, they wouldn't lift the blockade curfew. They wouldn't want panic in the colonies, although the communication silence, irrespective of whatever explanation they invented for it, would generate the same wave of panic. They could also lift the blockade if the epidemic broke out somewhere else as well.

If Noah were to reach the Moon and then take the pathogen back to Earth . . .

The darkest presentiment struck her: if the pathogen had killed the bus driver and the others as quickly as it had, then, at this mortality rate, no one stood a chance. For Noah, who had never had a strong constitution, this pathogen would mean certain death. He wouldn't survive, unlike this woman in the room next door.

She looked up on hearing the airlock open. Cliff stood there, fully equipped, in full gear. For Jess, it was as if this past half hour had been wiped out.

'I could only sleep for thirty minutes,' said the professor, his face still crumpled.

He noticed that there was something not quite right with Jess. 'What's wrong, Jess? You could use some sleep, too, you look awfully run down.'

Jess just raised her hand and nodded, as if in agreement. Cliff walked up to her and put a hand on her shoulder.

'You go now, I'll take over,' said the professor, smiling. He still looked very tired, deep crow's feet extending all the way to his temples, 'I'll also let you know if something crops up.'

Jess wanted to say yes, she would go, and to thank him, when it suddenly dawned on her that she had left Noah's sample under the nanoscope!

'I see you've already taken a blood sample, from which one?' Cliff's question blasted her mind at almost the same time.

'Thhh... the... Number One,' she only hesitated for a moment, all she had to remember was which rat they had injected with the nasal secretion. 'I took it not long ago, the old one had dried up already. They're totally identical.'

Cliff examined the display at length. Indeed, the samples appeared totally similar.

'So, nothing has started yet,' he said and took a sterile needle. 'I'll take a sample from Number Two as well, to see what happened there.'

Jess was more exhausted than ever. She had no idea why she was withholding the true facts, since this wouldn't help anyone, not Noah, not herself. In fact, it could promote the outbreak of an even bigger epidemic if she kept the identity of the Alpha person a secret.

Accompanied by her doubts, she walked out into the sterilizer's airlock and let the chemicals and hot steam wash away her fears.

*

India, Governorship of Eternal Splendour, New Delhi, Centre of Infectious Diseases—Standby Group Session

'Two thousand seven hundred cases per day,' said Navashen Damodaran, chief virologist. His brown complexion loomed in the foreground of the chart projected behind him, which made his face barely visible to the others due to the strong lighting in the background. If they had seen it, they would have known just how grave the situation really was. The man was wearing the ancient *sherwani*, a modern version of the long, buttoned-down, coat-like garment, mandatory for him as a civil servant.

'This is horrible...' the face of Arshia Dalmia, the female president, reflected consternation, 'the infection is spreading at an enormous rate.'

'Unfortunately, this is the biggest problem, esteemed Madam President,' said Health Minister Akram Chudasama. 'We are unable to control it. It's actually a big accomplishment that we were able to trace the thread back to the person that started off the infection, a certain man named Rusti Kadam, who is one of the Coast Guard officers. After the medical examination at the New Sir Ganga Ram Hospital, he had to report to the Coast Guard headquarters, at which time he used the metro system, thus spreading the pathogen to an unknown number of people—perhaps ten thousand or even a hundred thousand. On that line, there are between two hundred and four hundred thousand passengers commuting daily.'

'Nice work that, being able to track down the man,' said Madam President, 'but this doesn't mean that we can stop the infection, does it?'

'No, it doesn't,' spoke the chief virologist, 'but at least we know which way we should go. Rusti Kadam participated in an operation on the Indian Ocean, where he came into contact with a man suffering from an unknown infection. The corpse of this man, who incidentally was the bodyguard of a notorious Malaysian arms dealer, had been transported to the same hospital.'

'That would really mean that he was the true starting point, the Alpha person?' the health minister wanted to know.

'From information available to us until now, he is the one. We have, however, checked into the fact that the Coast Guard was called upon by a Russian freighter named *Lev Tolstoy*. This very ship was in prominence a few days ago on one of the Asian channel telecasts, showing images of the captain, who documented that a raging epidemic had broken out on board. We placed a call to a correspondent of the Asian channel to release the footage to us but they have no knowledge of such material and, according to them, such images hadn't been shown in any of their newscasts. Meanwhile, however, there are persons here, sitting in our midst, who saw it with their own eyes.'

'This is rather strange. Weren't you able to find anything on the GlobalNet?'

'No, and if there was anything, they have long since removed it.'

'And what's the situation with the vessel?' asked President Dalmia.

'We called the Russian Navy; according to official communication, the ship had sunk north of Antarctica in a tempest before they could tow it to the harbour.'

'So there's no other trace? The corpse of the Malaysian being the starting point?'

'Yes,' replied Virologist Damodaran, 'the researchers managed to identify these protein chains based on the samples taken from the corpse. These polymer chains, unknown to us, could be responsible for the emerging epidemic.'

The group, comprised of researchers and civil servants, watched in shocked silence as the strange structure was projected onto the screen.

'And what's the situation with Rusti Kadam, the Coast Guard officer? What did he have to say about the naval operation? Had he seen anything, noticed something, that could possibly give a clue as to where this arms dealer's gang had been and who they'd come into contact with?'

'No, he hadn't seen anything of that sort. If there had been others on the ship previously, then they were no longer there when the Coast Guard arrived. They had either died and their bodies had been thrown overboard, or they had been picked up by the Russian ship.'

'Therefore, either way, they're at the bottom of the ocean,' ascertained Health Minister Chudasama.

'Yes, most likely,' the virologist agreed, 'but the most interesting fact is that Rusti Kadam is in perfect health. In some form or other, he is immune to the disease; his only role consisted in being a carrier in spreading the epidemic.'

The group continued to sit in silence; perhaps they were all considering what the next step would be. India's president was the one to break the silence.

'Ladies and gentlemen, with great respect, I thank you all for your work, and I recommend that we contact the United Colony Epidemics Institute. We cannot remain isolated with our problem. India is a country of many billions; people travel, they come and go, and no longer on just a global level, but among the distant colonies as well. We must acquaint them with the general consensus about this pathogen.'

At that moment, a knock on the door interrupted the speech. The president's personal secretary stepped in and whispered something into her boss's ear.

'Not now, we're about to make a decision in a very important matter,' she said, politely brushing aside the secretary's urging.

'Madam President, the persons waiting for you wish to speak to you precisely about this matter. They are saying that they should be heard before any decision is made in this room.'

The president nodded, excused herself, and walked out of the room.

In the corridor, the guards were waiting for President Dalmia. They escorted her to one of the parking terraces, where the presidential limousine and the escort vehicles were waiting. An air-car with tinted windows appeared from behind the limousine. The bodyguards led the head of state to this air-car. The back door opened and the president took a seat in the vehicle.

'Madam President, thank you for taking the time to see me,' the man bowed his head respectfully, joining the palms of his hands. It was General Nagesh Bandhary, head of the Indian Secret Service.

'By all means, General Bandhary, especially if the matter concerns the current discussion.'

'Yes, Madam, it does. We were contacted half an hour ago by the Russian Secret Service. They have informed us that they know what has caused the epidemic currently raging out of control. If we were willing to sit at a table with them and treat the matter with the utmost discretion, even in the currently tense situation, then they would help us to control the epidemic.'

Astounded, the president looked at the head of Secret Service.

'In your opinion, are they telling the truth, or do they just want to infiltrate themselves in some manner into this chaotic situation?'

'As yet, our Service hasn't been able to determine the veracity of what they are telling us, but it's true they have obtained the data and samples of the epidemic that had been raging on board the vessel that disappeared on the Indian Ocean and which has apparently sunk. Perhaps they have discovered something they wish to share with us.'

'So why don't they contact the Epidemics Centre, as would be their duty?'

'That's the strange part in this entire affair,' said the General. 'They haven't been quite clear and open in their message to us either. This means that they would only reveal more if we were to agree to their stipulated conditions.'

'What kind of conditions?'

'We haven't the faintest idea. We could only find out more if we were to accept their invitation.'

'And we shouldn't inform the Epidemics Centre?'

'In all probability, one of the conditions would be that we don't inform them.'

'But the infection is spreading at such an incredible rate,' the president shook her head. 'India is an open state, a vast number of travellers, tourists and businessmen cross its borders daily. Before long, the pathogen would become a world traveller too, carried along with them.'

'I understand, Madam President, but what would happen if indeed they were to know a way to stop the infection spreading?'

She stroked the embroidery on the hem of her dress, absorbed in her thoughts. She felt it was very difficult to have to make an instant decision.

'Very well, General, go and send them a message indicating our interest in their plan. I shall ask for another day from my group before informing the United Colony Council.'

'Understood, Madam,' said the general and bowed his head again, 'I think this is the wisest decision under the circumstances.'

The president stepped out of the air-car, and the driver raised the vehicle's nose for takeoff and accelerated. The car shot up into a low-hanging cloud, only to emerge from the other side to begin its descent towards the business district of Delhi.

The guards accompanied President Dalmia back to her seat. Once she had sat down again, all eyes turned curiously in her direction. They anxiously awaited the latest news.

'Ladies and gentlemen, I still abide by what has been said, that we shall inform the UC Council about the situation that has developed in Delhi and the region. However, the latest information I have been given, which I unfortunately cannot share with you, has prompted me to wait for one more day. I ask you to continue the work you have initiated. Let's keep fighting this unknown pathogen.'

As she stepped out of the room, she could almost feel the bewildered silence that she had left behind. That same silence accompanied her all the way back to her limousine.

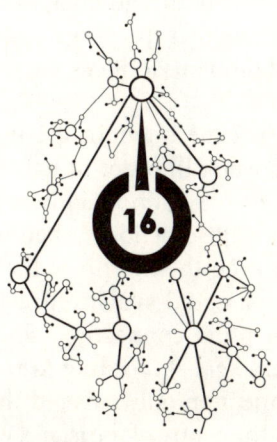

16.

Unmei Manmade Island, Sea of Japan

Ayame Oita, researcher of the Unmei Project, showed her card to the sentry. The guard looked at something on the monitor for half a minute. Ayame didn't understand why she was being fussed over. True, she hadn't put in an appearance since the island had been completely closed down, but there were only ten men left on the island besides her and, on top of that, she was the only woman here. But she suspected that she knew the reason for this lengthy inspection: this was a crystal clear message from management to the effect that, after her last desperate telephone call, they would not allow any information to leak from the island.

It was good to see the fresh, green face of the manmade island once again. The leaves reflected the sun's rays, projecting every possible shade of emerald green onto the footpath woven from soft plant fibres. The walk was very easy on her feet, as if she were strolling on a cloud. Even though, psychologically speaking, she had felt for some time that she was in a deep pit.

Yesterday, the professor had asked about the development status of the Terminator Command. Ayame had coolly stated that she was expecting the results of the latest test this morning. Yakizima had been rather uneasy, remembering the imperial prince's expectations, but Ayame didn't want any part of this guilt trip. She was convinced that if *Koutaishi-denka* Arai knew that the progress of the project was being furthered at the cost of human sacrifices, he would have shut it down a long time ago.

Ayame completed the experiment before noon. She had also made a sensational, new discovery. In order to halt the project, it would be sufficient for only one of the nano-machines to take the Terminator Command, as they were all somehow linked with one another at the quantum level, so that even the machines that were farthest away in kilometres or light years, could synchronize their functions. Ayame couldn't control the quantum connection, she could only observe its expansion and its parameters. According to the images recorded, the current nano-level connection only covered the lab area. Perhaps the dormant intelligence at the centre of the island would decide whether to establish connection with the nanorobots or not. Maybe they wouldn't dare to do it now, because of the recent fiasco.... Nevertheless, today's results had proved that the failure of the previous experiment—when the activity-stimulating command had been transmitted to the far distant nanomachines—had not been caused by the faulty transmitting apparatus. They were in contact with each other, and Ayame had written this into her final report as well.

She walked out of the shaded woodland and set off along the promenade bordered by cherry trees, leading to the relaxation benches on the eastern side of the island. Cherry blossoms were dropping continuously, covering the path with a lush carpet. It was like this no matter what the season, because the modern, genetically modified cherry trees no longer bloomed to bear fruit but were just there for people: so that they could marvel at the uninterrupted pink showers. Pity, that during the last phase of the project only three workers remained, and only the wind would enjoy all this wonder, chasing the petals, sending them into playful swirls. But only when the island's automatic control let it in, just as now, when the sun was shining so nicely. For this to happen, the arch of the dome on the east lounging terrace overlooking the ocean slid to the side, allowing free access to the refreshing ocean breeze.

Her coat was sprinkled with wondrous pink petals. As soon as she stepped out onto the lane strewn with tiny gravel, the wind from the open sea lifted a few of them off her. Seagulls that lived on the protruding flanges of the dome waited for some titbits of food that might come their way. Many of the workers used to feed them, way back, when there were more employees working there. Since then, the birds had remained but the humans had returned to Japan.

They had returned there, some hundreds of kilometres away—no one knew exactly how many, as the island kept changing its position—the place where she, too, would much rather prefer to live.

If only things could be as they had been back then. If only she hadn't applied for this job.

At first, the assignment had heralded an exciting challenge: she would be working as a researcher-biologist on an implant preventing epileptic attacks. That's how this colossal scientific adventure had started. Japan's warlike demons had seized the peaceful experiment and transformed it into a raving monster. The *demon of disease* had overthrown the spirit of healing, converting everything in its proximity into contagion. It was this phantom that had been sucking her soul dry, too. But she didn't want to surrender to it.

This was also the phantom that had been gnawing away at Emperor Arai's soul because, had he been in full control, perhaps he would not have allowed demons to rule his country. Perhaps his son, Crown Prince *Koutaishidenka* Arai, would give the order to halt this mad scheme.

If he should receive a signal . . .

Ayame reached into her pocket. She placed the syringe-gun next to her, where the cameras couldn't see exactly what it was.

The weather was magnificent. Although this was already the stuffy monsoon season, in between two gloomy rain showers both she and the island received a little gift: for her, it was the memory of a bygone spring and for the island, a chance to replenish batteries via its solar cells. To her right, in the distance, the peaks of the Oki-islands were visible and with them the blue-tinted block of Japan's Daisen volcano. Over the last hundred years, its ice caps had disappeared, now only the clouds painted its summit white. Somewhere behind the mountain, in the heart of Japan, lived her loved ones—her sister and her family...

Could I still start a new life in their midst and rid myself of the demons of war?

Slowly, she unpacked a sterile needle and pushed it into the end of the gun. From her right pocket, she took out a vial intended as a powerful soporific for animals and fitted it into the gun.

The wind gained momentum, sweeping cherry blossoms onto her lap. *The ever-renewing miracle of nature,* she thought while slowly unbuttoning the snaps at her collar, *and we're constantly interfering with this miracle.* The *Kamis* were watching in disapproval and the world of spirits with a thousand faces was recapturing its rightful possessions.

She pulled the little catch of the syringe towards her, and the tiny needle punctured the aluminium foil cover of the glass vial containing the soporific. The needle conducted the substance into the gun. With the knob, she chose the highest possible dosage number indicated on the barrel.

She didn't want it to be this way. She didn't want her creation turning into a monster.

Slowly, she placed her finger on the syringe gun's trigger. The cherry blossom petals fell onto the barrel, for a moment it was hidden from her eyes. *It would be so nice to simply disappear,* she thought.

But the demon of war didn't want her to just disappear. It was the demon who lifted the firing end of the gun to her jugular vein...

The water sparkled; the rising wind, with the approach of further rain, ruffled its surface into golden colours. A benevolent cloud, the colour of pink cherry blossom petals, took Ayame into its embrace and laid her down onto the densely flowing, oily sea.

*

Imperial Crown Prince Arai Kazuki bowed his head in silent respect when Professor Yakizima told him the sad news. He was wearing an embroidered topcoat designed from an ancestral pattern, having just paid a hospital visit to the emperor, when the call from the professor reached him.

He was sitting in his father's study; behind him, an array of ancient garments and objects, crown jewels and imperial gifts, were lined up in glass display cabinets, amidst the mix of traditional and modern furniture and faded draperies. *Shinto's* great portal framed the door to the study, signalling that whoever stepped into this place had to reckon with Shintoism, which had once again been declared the state religion, the way of the spirits.

'We shall bury Miss Oita with the highest pomp and honour,' said the prince. His face was sombre as he sat behind the desk in the holographic image projected from the imperial palace. 'We shall bid farewell to her as our first Kamikaze, our first heroine.'

'Yes, *Koutaishi-denka* Arai,' nodded Professor Yakizima, but deep in his soul he considered the woman's gesture as cowardice, for not having been able to face up to the expectations that her country had of her. But he didn't want to admit his opinion to the prince. 'According to the research log, she had completed the final test for the Terminator Command. The test proved to be successful, thus, controlling the Unmei Machines will no longer be an obstacle.'

'This is a very important step,' said Prince Arai, 'because we must correct our mistakes.'

The prince used the plural in a manner befitting an heir apparent to the imperial throne, yet the responsibility for the development of the contamination plexus lay ultimately upon the head of the research project, Professor Yakizima.

'Thank you for your magnanimity, *Koutaishi-denka* Arai, but in this regard the liability is on my shoulders,' said the professor and resignedly bowed his head. 'If you wish, I shall step down from the leadership position and pass it to someone much more qualified than I am.'

'No, Professor Yakizima, there is no need for that,' said the imperial prince calmly, 'what we need most of all now is your wartime experience, your selfless spirit and your endurance. There is no way that we would want to part company with you at this critical stage.'

Yakizima raised his head. The imperial prince had inherited the common sense and level-headedness of his father and grandfather. Despite his young age, a deep determination emanated from his eyes.

'Our Secret Service, including the Russian station, is at this very moment negotiating with India's president and the security organisations, in the interest of involving that country in our plans,' the prince went on. 'The reason we were forced to take this step was because the infection started by Alexei Sverlov's cluster had reached Delhi and is even now spreading at an alarming rate across the giant megalopolis. We must either put a stop to this infection, or India will, within one day, contact the United Colony Epidemics Instiute.'

Yakizima didn't trust the egoistic Indian leadership that had been hastily chosen at the time of the second Asian conflict, but perhaps the woman-president, who had gained a vote of confidence over the past few years, would react more favourably to their initiative.

'If that happens, then New China may close its borders. Not only its borders to the south, but also the internal borders, which would be disadvantageous to us,' the professor concluded the thought. 'It would be tantamount to a catastrophe because, in the final phase of the Unmei Project, freedom of movement within the country is essential.'

'You are right,' agreed the prince.

'I shall order the implementation of the Terminal Command as quickly as possible, in order to stop the unnecessary infection clusters, that way we can prevent a more thorough examination by the United Colony Council, and last but not least we would placate India, thereby possibly placing a great and powerful federation on our side.'

'Let's see how the negotiations with India shape up,' said the prince, 'but whatever happens, you may transmit the order tonight, at midnight.'

The professor sensed that the prince wanted to take up a negotiating stance by blackmailing India, in that the Unmei Machines would only be switched off in case of an agreement. However, this could yet prove to be a double-edged sword. It could even backfire with multiple force and derail the entire project. If India didn't keep the accord and turned to universal public opinion, it could also mean Japan's downfall.

'Understood, *Koutaishi-denka* Arai,' said Yakizima and bowed his head. 'I have just this second logged into Unmei Island's network and could initiate the order at any moment.'

'Thank you, Professor Yakizima. Your work is of priceless value for Japan. We shall not forget your services. My father, Emperor Arai, sends you his personal greetings and would like to meet you personally after the conclusion of the war.'

Professor Yakizima's head remained respectfully bowed until the spatial hologram narrowed down to a dot and faded away to nothing.

The war, the words hit his ears. The prince had never used this expression before now. So far, this last stage had been known as the final phase.

But he was right. This was already war. The war of the Japanese nanomachines against the New China Empire.

*

Mars, New Home Colony, Quarantine Centre

An hour after the experiment had been initiated, Sarah-Jessica administered the delayed dose to animals Number Three and Number Four, when Cliff came forward with a new idea.

'We must open up the skulls of the rats and see what is going on in there. Something happens in the body, but when we take blood samples, the entire process stops and the proteins fall apart,' he was so carried away by the thought, that he set about doing the preparations without waiting for Jess's response. 'The scanner shows vigorous internal activity in different points of the body, for example, the brain, the spinal cord, the lymph glands, pancreatic gland, the nasal mucous membrane, but we can only examine these areas in detail with the nanoscope, if we open up one of them. I'll begin by trepanning the skulls; we'll take a look at what's in there. Help me to immobilize the animals!'

Jess was utterly exhausted, she could no longer concentrate very well. She had already been in the rest area twice, for short periods, but each time she just ended up being even more fatigued. She took out the harness used to secure the rats during surgery. She inserted rat Number One, the first to have received the proteins, and buckled up the straps. The animal let out a yelp; she must have touched it too roughly.

'Jess, we're not far from the solution now, hang in there!' Cliff looked at her pleadingly from behind the helmet glass.

'Yes, right you are, I'll pull myself together,' she forced a smile and stroked the agitated animal. She tried to coordinate her movements and be more careful, but her thoughts were elsewhere. She thought of Noah, what could be happening with him now. She saw him in the test animal's strapped-down body, just as the Epidemics people were examining it, cutting up his body, looking for the cause of the infection, cutting open his skull . . .

'Good heavens, Jess, please pay more attention!' Cliff admonished her again. Test rat Number Two was shrieking in her hands, and in its desperation was already attacking her gloves. 'If you don't pay attention, it will bite through your glove and then you'll be in serious trouble. Not just you, but me too, because I'm responsible for what happens on these premises.'

'Uh, alright, sorry,' Jess blew some air, trying to shake herself back to reality. With a syringe, she applied a local anaesthetic on the rat's head and neck. 'OK, Number One is ready for surgery.'

'Good! Then let's begin. Cut the skin and I'll breach the calvarium.'

Jess cut the skin open on both sides. Cliff cut out a five-millimetre hole with the laser and removed the piece with tweezers.

'That should be just enough to insert the flexible arm of the nanoscope,' said Cliff, approaching the tube to the hole. 'Switch the recorder on, and when everything is ready, I'll start from the cortex towards the deeper parts.'

The rat brain's spongy structure appeared on the projector screen. For the time being, only the image from the camera mounted on the tip of the tube was visible, which helped him find his bearings inside the brain. Cliff handled the apparatus with a steady hand.

'I've managed to cross into the inner cerebrum; I'll soon be reaching the rat's thalamus. That's precisely what this walnut-shaped organ is. In the interstitial areas, the presence of greenish mucus is quite perceptible, so, we'll surely find proteins there. Jess, switch on the nanoscope to the first size range, let's see what there is!'

Jess started to do the enlargement. The projector showed the connected mucus covering the spongy structure of the brain.

'Go farther down,' Cliff said, fastening the tube with a small adhesive tape. On the screen, the long stalks of the proteins appeared, but they were all detached from each other.

'I don't believe it,' Cliff shook his head, 'they're not connecting! I can't see the source where the proteins come from, either, even though the scanner indicates strong activity in this area. Perhaps I should go much lower. I'll go all the way to the hypothalamus.'

Jess loaded the image from the camera again onto the monitor for Cliff to see the path along which he was advancing toward the lower area of the brain. With a firm hand, the professor carefully guided the camera through the furrowed tissue of the brain. As he slid the endoscope downwards, it encountered more and more mucous substance.

'It must be here somewhere. The mucus is flowing in such large volume that I can barely see anything. Here I am now, at the hypothalamus . . .'

Cliff's voice faltered but Jess also noticed the reason: there was nothing on the image except for a web of connecting mucus.

'What I meant to say was, the thin sheet of the hypothalamus should be here somewhere. Turn on the nanoscope so we can see what we've found!'

Jess turned the camera off and switched to the nanoscope. As she increased the size, she just stood there, gaping, with her mouth open. Cliff was absolutely right with his theory.

'There . . .' that's all she could say offhand, then her voice stuck in her throat, 'exactly, as you said. The proteins had joined together to form a single complex structure.'

'I'd correct you, Jess,' smiled Cliff, he seemed very happy, 'they're there, because they're not alone, but hooked on, in the form of millions of tiny mechanisms, to the hypothalamus . . . joining together at exactly those points, as I had predicted,' he was grinning like a schoolboy participating in a secret experiment for the first time in the chemistry lab. Jess wasn't so cheerful.

'Lord Almighty, Cliff, this is a monstrosity!'

Cliff's smile wasn't that sincere anymore either when he saw Jess's face.

'But why?' Jess was still mesmerized, looking at the bustling nanomachines on the large projector screen. Each one kept shooting out newer proteins, which then flocked together and, forming a net, installed themselves in the cellular nodules of the hypothalamus. They grew over them and encompassed them like some kind of creeping plant.

'As to why? Because this was what was built into their programming. They have to take over control of the body . . .' said Cliff, almost in a whisper. He was enraptured by the marvellous, systemic order of the tiny mechanisms.

'This explains the increase in blood pressure and the excessive urine production in our patients . . .' he continued, thinking aloud, 'because the volume of antidiuretic hormones is also regulated by the hypothalamus, which could also alter urinary output and raise blood pressure . . .'

'Breast milk—lactation,' Jess joined in. 'She told us that her breast milk had dried up. This is also where the oxytocin hormone is produced, which releases the milk flow . . .'

'The decrease in sleep requirement and the circadian rhythm, or the shift in the day/night rhythm . . .' Cliff spoke up again, 'here, too, control of this rhythm is by means of hormones . . .'

'Control of body temperature, the sweating, the activity of the lymph glands . . .' said Jess in a somewhat irritated tone, 'it also all originates here, but for God's sake, how much longer are we going to go on enumerating all of this!'

Jess had to turn away from the image; she couldn't stand looking at this monstrosity any longer. She didn't give up as a researcher, but as a woman in love. She thought about Noah, and the fact that now each little clue linked up to form a frightening picture—things that she hadn't noticed two weeks ago, when they had been happening right under her very nose. Noah's exceptional energy level, with very little sleep, his sweat attacks, and the secretion formed in his nose . . .

Cliff was still staring at the image, but when he became aware of Jess's despairing rage, he finally tore his eyes off the screen and took hold of her hand.

'Forgive me, I was being inconsiderate, I know the way you're feeling right now—'

'No, you don't know how I feel!' Teardrops trickled down her face, onto the microphone. Puffs of steam appeared inside her helmet. 'But if you want me to help, then let's go, let's begin now! We have to find out why these monsters joined together in this rat, and why that woman next door hasn't died yet! We also need to understand why some individuals, like for instance that cop, McAllister, have not been contaminated!'

Cliff was stunned by Jess's vehemence, he had never seen his leading virologist in such a mental state.

'Right!' In this situation, this was the shortest and most suitable reply. He looked deeply into Jess's eyes for a long while. 'Get McAllister in here, we have to take a DNA sample from him. We must take a full DNA sequence from the lady in the next room, as well as one of our patients who is in serious condition. We have to find out why these proteins join up into one mechanism, and why they then set up connections with neurons. The reproduction process, on the other hand, is clearly visible: when a protein machine is created and finally assembled, it will start to reproduce itself, while simultaneously linking with another cellular structure, of course.'

'Right. I'll have the police officer brought in,' said Jess in a calmer voice now. 'However, you'll have to see which are the membranes that resemble an ear-trumpet.'

On the image, these ear-trumpet forms were recognizable. They were rising above the outer half of the interlocking units, all looking outwards, seemingly eavesdropping all at once . . .

'Wonderful,' said Cliff, as he enlarged the picture.

'If you say this monstrosity is beautiful or wonderful one more time, today will be the last time you ever see me again!' said Jess in a hard voice and started walking towards the airlock. She was very angry, or rather despondent, and her bitterness now overflowed the bounds of tolerance.

She couldn't help it, even though she knew that Cliff was only driven by his research enthusiasm, and that these functioning machines were wonderfully planned and produced structures in their own way.

No matter how they had come into being, or whoever had created them.

*

New China Empire, Mongol Protectorate, Ulan Bator, four hours later...

By now it would be entirely superfluous to wait any longer, Professor Yakizima thought, sitting down in front of the terminal in his study. News was constantly streaming in from India: a province-wide epidemic had broken out in New Delhi, which would slowly cross over the city boundaries, covering the entire Regency of the Eternal Light. Not only the international news channels, but the Chinese agencies and TV stations too, pounced on the sensational news that was just coming to light. Despite the danger, they dispatched their personnel to the site, who were reporting back with masked faces, from in front of the Delhi hospitals, trying to guess in which direction the infection would spread.

Therefore, India had not come on board the project, as had been presumed, but had laid the fact of the infection before the world at large. Whatever the reason for their decision, it would be revealed in the course of that evening, and Yakizima would be notified about it. If the Russian Secret Service had kept quiet about the project's details in the course of its negotiations with the Indian government, then there would be no obstacle to continuing the Unmei Project.

The professor connected up with the Unmei Island server via an encrypted and secure Japanese satellite. He navigated through the menu items projected onto the holographic screen, to the Unmei Machines' control. He touched the virtual button outlined in the air and, in response, a model of the fate-machine rose up from the surface of the table. Next to the revolving model, on the left, was written the command to boost output: *Acceleration of the reproduction process.* To the right, resplendent in the lovely blue colour of the sea, the newly tested *Terminator Command* lay waiting.

It was Miss Oita's last message, this blue island on the reddish-brown disturbance of the glowing hologram. Oita was not the warrior type. She should have been rejected a long time ago.

'No, I don't think for a minute that the infection that has broken out here has anything to do with the silence on Mars,' said a man on one of the news channels; according to the caption it was no other than Akram Chudasama, India's Health Minister, 'although I, for one, think that the colonies should unite, the full force of interdependence should be shown, in order to defeat such a global infection or, rather, an infection of Solar System magnitude.'

'Nevertheless, from what you're saying, I still gather that, in your opinion, some kind of infection has developed on Mars, too,' a voice called out from amongst the crowd, although the speaker couldn't be seen through the forest of microphones.

'Please, don't twist my words,' said the minister, evidently annoyed. 'I only said that with an epidemic of unknown origin, of such magnitude and with such a rapid spread of infection, it is our duty to report it to the UC Epidemics Institute.'

So, that was the message, thought the professor, India had turned the situation into a moral issue. Earlier, at the time of the second Asian conflict, it hadn't cared about the populations of neighbouring territories, enslaving the inhabitants under the guise of liberation struggles. After their 'liberation,' India hadn't given back the countries' independence but had remained in the territories as the occupier. The professor regarded this attitude, the way they made decisions in favour of their own countrymen but didn't treat citizens of other countries on the same footing, as false and hypocritical.

Yet, if they knew that these afflicted civilians would escape with a single flick of his finger, releasing the impact of a radio signal expanding at the speed of light . . .

Now!

He touched the fluttering, sea-blue button. The membrane on the funnel-shaped formation towering up on the back of the prototype quivered and then disintegrated into the constituents of the protein-composed mechanism.

And so, the end—at least for a while.

He switched off the terminal, walked over to the tea counter in the corner of the lounge, and poured himself some steaming water for a cup of *Matcha*, stirring the powder of the green tea sprouts into the water with a bamboo whisk. He wanted to feel the intense, bitter taste of this peculiar green tea.

Meanwhile, in the newscast unreeling behind him, the local Mongolian government channel was reporting about an emergency session of the New China government to deliberate on how to handle the critical situation that had developed not far from its country's borders.

So, it had come to pass, and what's more, everything had happened as one could have foreseen. The best step had been to bring the move of the Rio office to the Mongol Province forward by two weeks. If New China now closed its borders to the south, they were already inside the walls.

*

Mars, New Home Colony, Quarantine Centre, twenty minutes earlier

Cliff had been asleep for an hour in the rest area; it was Jess's turn to be on duty. She was already at the bottom of the checklist, and the DNA sequences were just about ready. The computer had been working for two hours to find the deviations occurring in the DNA. They wouldn't have an easy task, as even more deviations could show up in the genes of the three men, which could indicate a genetic disease of an entirely different origin. Thanks to the complete mapping of the human genome, and eighty per cent of its function, it was no longer shrouded in mystery and the genome program was able to pinpoint whether genetics had any relation to immunity.

After her boss had left for his last break, Jess had stood in front of the sequencer for a long time, looking disinterestedly at her image reflected from the screen. Her thoughts were pounding so loudly in her head that they inhibited her other senses. If Noah was infected, and if Noah was the Alpha person, why hadn't he infected her? In fact, before that, why hadn't he contaminated others in the colony? They had been together every day, they had walked all over town, been in restaurants and nightclubs, cinemas and theatres—but none of these places had reported any such infectious disease. Perhaps the nanomachines had still been dormant? Perhaps there was a phase after entering the system when they were merely creating the internal network, and didn't start to reproduce?

Or perhaps those pills that Noah had been taking for his epilepsy were inhibiting the nanomachines from reproducing? Still, he was the one who had started the contamination in the terminal. The disease must have turned more severe on the last day for Noah, and still, she had never caught it . . .

She suddenly made a split-second decision: she unfastened her helmet, pulled down the zipper of her protective suit and, freeing her right hand, she slipped it out of the garment. She picked up a sterile syringe, took a blood sample from herself and placed the sample into the sequencer. The other samples had been in the machine for over an hour, so hers would only fall behind just a trifle in the end.

She had to know; she could no longer handle the tension. She had to find out if her genome would show conformity with those of the obviously immune persons.

This helped her to calm down somewhat; it would all be perfect if only they could, at long last, lift the quarantine that had been in force for a week already, and she could talk to Noah. If they could reach a final conclusion and gather useful data as a result of their work here today, then this should happen any day now.

She knew that she had fallen irretrievably in love with Noah. When they were fooling around as children in New Cloud York, she had already had the feeling that she would meet him again sometime in the future. This feeling had died down when she moved to Mars and the emotional rollercoaster had slowly subsided. Later, Noah had certainly shaken things up again in her life, when he announced that he would be paying her a visit. Jess hadn't wanted that week to end and, to be honest, she didn't want to live on Mars either. Perhaps the reason she had moved here in the first place was so that she wouldn't have to face the feelings she had in her youth. Coupled with the fact that they were truly meant for each other.

A message appeared on the indicator display to say that the machine was ready with the three sample sequencings. She quickly put her protective gear back on; she had just finished doing it when she heard Cliff rummaging behind the airlock.

'Let's see what gifts we got from our tinkling wonder machine,' he said, as he entered the door. 'What's the situation with our test animals?'

'The rats reacted the same way as they did for the four samples. It didn't matter at all whether they originated from the nose or from the sweat glands. The same network has developed in all four animals' brains, with the protein-machines spread over the hypothalamus and then, after a certain time, they started the reproduction process. So many changes occurred compared to what we detected earlier, that these formations have now developed elsewhere in their bodies as well, for example, in the lymph glands or around the pancreatic glands.'

'So, the factory has geared up.'

'And it looks like it's switched to full production.'

'Then let's have a look at the deviations found in the genomes,' said Cliff and sat down in front of the monitor. 'The computer has already given out the possible genes showing deviations in the three samples.'

'I can see that we'll be facing a much more difficult task than expected. I must admit that I thought that nowadays everyone profited from having their genes corrected, since genetic engineering can solve well-nigh anything. I thought we would only see a few deviations. But it seems that our sample donors—two sick patients and one immune person—have not taken advantage of this possibility,' said Cliff, who, being a biochemist, considered genetic engineering as something self-evident. 'In this day and age, it's a totally safe procedure, it doesn't pose any risk, but people are still superstitious, they're reluctant to let anything tinker with their system.'

'The three samples all show deviations in around four places,' he continued. 'Two of them are nestling in known sections of the genes, one predisposes to asthma; this is gene number seventeen, marked

ORMLD3. The young lady lying next door is also fighting this disease, according to her own admission. The other one is a genetic iron-storage disease, its hemochromatosis gene, a mutation of HFE C282Y, is to be found in one of our infected patients. What's left are the two remaining faulty genes, and one or both of them could be the cause for immunity, and both of them are from our police officer. Unfortunately, this is still within the genomes' unexplored area, which doesn't make our work any easier. For the moment, we have no idea what these genes' functions are, so we don't even know if they contribute to our monsters' inactivity. We would need a control person, someone who shows immunity, but, unfortunately, McAllister is the only one in the current population who hasn't presented any known symptom so far.'

Jessica suddenly felt that she had to mention her secret, she had to tell everything. She felt a mad urge; she could hardly bear not to speak up.

'We should try to knock out that gene.' This was what she ended up saying, but it wasn't anywhere near what she had meant to blurt out. 'We can't do it with a chemical blocker, as we don't even know the gene's function, much less the substance for blockage.'

'Rats have these genes too, so we could surgically remove the two mitochondria originating from the mother's side, from the rat's ovum.'

Jess looked at him, wide-eyed.

'Now? We've already been on our feet for twenty-nine hours, with only short breaks . . .'

'Jess, if we don't do it now, then we're letting down all those people who are waiting for the results of our work.' Cliff wasn't sure whether what he was seeing in the girl's eyes was exhaustion or some other kind of internal struggle.

'Even with a robot, it would take more than two hours . . . with accelerated embryo development it would be another day before the rat-foetus reaches the size that we can use to inject the proteins.'

'Yes, that's why we should start as soon as possible,' said Cliff decidedly. He opened up the compartment in the wall and pulled out a console. There were three pneumatic arms hanging down from the frame. The professor activated the robot and sent over the rat-genome from the terminal. He punched in the genes' data and hooked the nanoscope up to the robot.

'Jess, bring the rat marked with a B, it's a female. Let's remove an ovum from it and we'll get going,' Cliff said, somewhat annoyed, as he saw her vacillating movements. What he couldn't see was the major battle that was raging in Jess. She wouldn't be able to keep quiet much longer about her immunity and Noah's role, for the whole of this critical period.

She placed and fixed the rat in front of the robot and instructed the automatic surgeon to remove the ovum from the rodent. The tiny motors of the manipulators started to hum, the three arms swung into a synchronized dance. The laser scalpel carved a small incision near the animal's pelvis, stopping the bleeding at once, and a stalk the size of a pipette pierced into the notch. The magnified process was shown on the monitor, including the lethal proteins' invasion of the entire area around the reproductive organs.

'It doesn't really matter if the ovum gets infected,' said Cliff, pointing to the screen, 'because at least we'll find out what impact they have on the developing embryo. If we remove one of the genes, or both, then immunity should be established, at least according to my most cherished dreams.'

The robot kept bowing down repeatedly, suturing the incision with biochemical bindings and placing the ovum on a body-friendly breeding ground.

'OK then, let's start with the surgical manipulation.' Cliff rattled off the instructions to the robot. 'This will take longer, we could take another break, what do you say?'

'Alright.' That was exactly what Jess needed. She wanted to flee from the room.

'It would do us both good,' the professor smiled, trying to cheer up his virology specialist. 'Dr. Jess, you may step down until further notice!' he said, like a commander to his subordinate. Jess returned a pallid smile. Whatever was bothering her, Cliff thought, was quite deeply seated in her soul.

They both turned towards the airlock, when the scanner, which was watching the test animals, gave out a whistling sound.

'Wait . . .' the professor stepped back and read the messages on the projector. 'Quickly, switch on the nanoscope, because something is happening!'

Both revived, as if they hadn't been terminally exhausted. Jess quickly switched to the image showing the test animal's hypothalamus.

'The net is dissolving!' said Cliff and pulled out the tube a little. 'The entire nano-network is disintegrating into its elemental parts!'

'The machines are releasing the neurons?'

'It looks like it, but wait! Increase the enlargement to see what is happening at the machine level!' Jess increased the numbers on the console, until only one nanomachine filled up the screen.

'They're disintegrating! Jess, every one of them is disintegrating!' Cliff was ecstatic, running back and forth in the room.

'Is this only happening here, or is it a behaviour pattern being executed, following a general, internal programming?' asked Jess, while checking the monitor showing the patient lying in the next room. The woman was lying calmly, reading some paper. 'We must call the Intensive Care Unit of the hospital and check if there is any improvement in the condition of the severely ill patients.'

'I'll call them immediately.' Cliff stepped over to the communicator console, but before he could press any of the buttons, three lights started to flash. He looked at Jess, stupefied, then picked one of them.

'This is Dr. McGregor from the Intensive Care Unit, Professor! I don't know if someone has already notified you in the Isolation Lab of what's happening, but the scanners are showing considerable improvement everywhere!' Both heard the euphoric tone of the doctor's voice on their internal radio. 'We have no idea why, but the critical condition of all the two-hundred-something patients being treated here, has been improving! And you won't guess it: all of them at the same time!'

Jess smiled sincerely, at last, and a tear appeared in the corner of her eye. The glass of the professor's helmet was covered with puffs of steam, he was sweating so profusely from the excitement.

'Yes. Thank you, Dr. McGregor. The additional information we have is that we have seen, live, as these beasts disintegrate into their constituent parts and release their victims,' said the professor cheerfully. 'We don't know why, we don't know how long it takes, but it looks like something of major importance is occurring at the nano level.'

The professor disconnected and took the other two calls on hold. Every hospital unit was reporting the same news.

'We can hope that this means the end of something,' said Jess and switched the nanoscope image to the gene-surgery robot again. 'Look, the machines are disintegrating here too, and they no longer surround the ovum. This is some kind of synchronised, coordinated activity. Something is happening simultaneously in organisms that are far removed from one another. This cannot be a random incident.'

Cliff watched as the robotic arms moved in precision in the mitochondrial DNA chain.

'Stop the process, it's totally useless for us to continue,' he said, somewhat resigned. 'If the proteins fall apart now, there is no gene or enzyme or anything that could make them unite again. Without the nanomachines, we cannot prove immunity.'

'Yes, we can,' said Jess and stepped over to the machine. Amidst all the excitement, neither of them had heard the machine signalling that sequencing of the last sample was ready.

'Here's the control sample,' said Jess and pointed to the screen, 'the one you mentioned. From someone who, in all probability, is immune to the infection.'

Clifford looked at her, perplexed.

'Where did you get it from?'

'This is my sample,' said Jess quietly. 'Once this is all over, we must sit down for a long talk.'

Cliff looked at her inquiringly for a while, and then nodded in acquiescence. He sat down in front of the sequencer and looked at the results.

'If this sample is indeed from you, then we can state that you, too, have the same two faulty genes as those we saw in the cop's genome. Therefore, based on the results obtained from the two samples, as yet not considered completely convincing, you too possess immunity against the infection.'

There was no resentment of any sort in Cliff's eyes, yet Jess turned her glance away from him. She was too tired for explanations. She continued to stare in front of her for a minute, and then proceeded towards the airlock. She had to clear her head and prepare for her confession, sure to be a lengthy conversation.

Moments preceding the events, one of the gravely ill patients in India's northern region was being shaken by a violent coughing attack. The nanomachines in his system were working at full force, when one of them—perhaps one micron of a second sooner than its partners working in the surrounding area—was accessed by the Terminator Command's signal. The nano-sized membrane of the receiving unit quivered, coding the vibration of the membrane into biological instructions and inserting it into the system. It relayed the signal in all directions, to all the existing Unmei Machines in the universe, firing it on the strands of the quantum world, after which it followed instructions to dismantle and annihilate itself. The patient's condition improved by leaps and bounds and, within a few hours, he was already complaining about hunger and thirst. Finally, after a three-day period spent between life and death, he was even able to receive visitors.

The nanomachines operating on Mars had already sensed the instructions streaming along the quantum connections, before the Terminator Command, which was spreading at the speed of light, could reach the planet and vibrate their membranes according to the prescribed instructions. The machines came to a halt; the death factory had concluded its activity.

Clifford still spent some considerable time browsing through the research videos, rotating the digital material back and forth. Finally, he found the spot where everything had changed. Barely twelve minutes ago, all the eardrums of the nanometre earpieces had vibrated simultaneously. As if they had captured a signal from somewhere in the distance. As if they were in contact with one another.

Or as if something, or somebody, were communicating with them...

Soon he would have irrefutable evidence in his hand that these machines were manmade creatures.

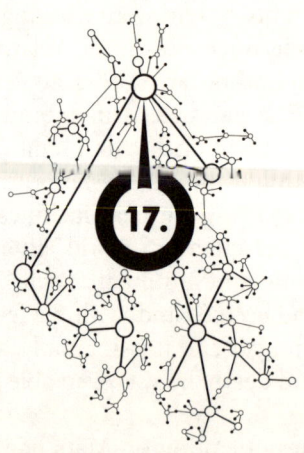

Moscow, Independent Russian Republic

Oleg Sverlov was very happy to have his brother back home. He had been worried that the medicine vial wouldn't reach him in time. The prospect of a small parcel getting lost in a busy African port was very real. But his joy was dampened by his brother's account of his adventures, including the news:

'Sixty per cent of the business is yours, Oleg; I'll sell the rest in the next few days.'

Oleg's eyes widened as he looked at his brother, his moonlike face and thin eyebrows only intensifying his astonished expression. He wasn't as good-looking as Alex, whose face was more elongated, with a full, jaunty beard, like their father's. Oleg couldn't even grow a normal beard.

'You're not serious, you're just kidding, aren't you?' Of course, he knew that his brother always thought things over very seriously. Perhaps he should feel happy to have the chance to carry on the family business but, instead, he felt scared, as if something had suddenly afflicted him. He was only twenty-five, practically a child as far as serious business management was concerned.

'You'll learn, believe me. My colleagues will help you. I'll put Kolya, my assistant, in charge to take over the management for a while until you get the hang of it,' said Alex, already starting to search for something on the GlobalNet. With that, he appeared to have finished the subject. 'He's a nice person; he'll be a substitute father to you. If you pay him a bit more and show him your appreciation, you'll never have to worry about the running of the business.'

Oleg stopped fighting the inevitable; he knew once his brother said something, he didn't take it back.

'And what will you be doing?' he asked Alex, who was ferreting about amongst his messages.

'I'm going to stop this struggling lifestyle, kiddo; I've had enough of this. I have made peace with myself, I reconciled the loss of our father, and I don't want to take revenge for his death anymore.'

Oleg felt that his brother had always been driven by an insatiable desire for revenge, which had led him into all sorts of suicidal actions. They had never talked about this, but he could see that, with every single weapon sold, with each bullet sold, Alex was sending a message to the killers. He was glad that this would be over now, because no one could keep up this pace much longer.

'That's why the business will be in good hands with you, Oleg, because you're so pure-minded, as I once was and perhaps could still be someday. But please excuse me now, I have to check something in a hurry.'

Fiddling in between his messages, he found what he was looking for.

'Here we are! So, I haven't paid for the information for nothing, after all,' he said, pointing to the dot appearing on the screen. 'Mongol Province, New China Empire. That's where we have to go, Bianco.'

The mercenary didn't say a word; he just sat at the table, munching on a sandwich the size of a small loaf.

'You said you had made peace and had forgiven; so why are you going to New China?' asked Oleg, startled. 'It looks like I was rejoicing too soon.'

'No, brother, what I said stands. I'm not going to New China for revenge but to find a man and ask him why the hell he messed up my life . . .'

'So, it's still revenge that's taking you there?'

'Not revenge, little brother,' Alex answered, smiling, 'perhaps love.'

Oleg started to laugh. In the last few years, Alex hadn't been interested in sentiments; no woman could deter him from his drive for revenge. Perhaps this was, in fact, a sign that he really had changed.

'I don't believe it, what's gotten into you?'

'That's it, little brother; it really is a disease that's gotten into me. And not just a minor one, but a disease that took over my entire body. That's precisely why I decided that I'd had enough.' He glanced sideways at Bianco and saw in the mercenary's eyes that he understood perfectly well what he was alluding to. 'That flashing little dot is a biochip locator transmitter belonging to a lady who could perhaps explain to me what the heck happened to me and the world in the last few days . . .'

Oleg didn't quite understand or didn't pay too much attention to this last sentence, he was totally swept along by his brother's determination.

'Terrific!' he said and clasped Alex's shoulder. 'What I still don't understand is how you two intend to get into the country now. Look what happened yesterday evening and during the night,' he said and transformed a part of the wall into a projector screen. He switched to one of the Russian news agencies' telecasts.

'According to the latest reports, New China has closed its southern borders with India and is thinking of ordering a total border closure,' the newscaster was saying. The other side of the divided screen showed one of their reporters, live from New Delhi. 'Yes, Vladimir, that's right, I'm here in front of the hospital where, just about an hour ago, more than two thousand patients with this strange infection were being treated but, according to the latest news, a miraculous improvement has taken place in the condition of all the patients. Relatives, as well as friends, have filled the hospital's entrance hall, all of them rushing to the scene to see their loved ones again after the lifting of the three-day quarantine.'

'What does the UC Epidemics Institute have to say about this?' the woman from the studio inquired again.

'The experts are still being quiet about it, but there is to be a press conference soon. However, as you can see, everyone is rather happy that the whole thing is over with.'

'Have they said anything about the infection being possibly connected to the closure of the Mars New Home Colony? As it is, all we have been hearing about this, across the Solar System over the past few days, is pure conjecture, but we don't know anything concrete...'

'Precisely, there is conjecture, but, according to one of our sources, Mars is lifting the closure as well, and so we shall at last reach the end of this long and mysterious affair.'

Bianco poked at the screen with his sizeable sandwich.

'You haven't been on Mars.'

Alex watched for a while longer, as the news agency's correspondents interviewed the patients' relatives. They were all talking about the symptoms so familiar to Alex, which had become an almost everyday occurrence for him.

'I wasn't there, but my intuitions have proved to be true: I'm not the only guinea pig. There was another person, as well,' said Alex, shaking his head, 'but it's possible that there were many more of us—'

'What are you talking about?' Oleg interjected, his eyes flitting back and forth between Alex and the huge Italian. 'What did you get mixed up in?'

'I suspect this whole thing about your implant is a much more complex issue than anything you've dared to think of,' said the mercenary-turned-bodyguard, between two bites, completely ignoring Alex's little brother.

'Yes, I don't think this is just a simple turbo-chip, as they tried to make me believe back then.' Alex shook his head, pointing to the screen. 'But India, that must certainly be my dirty doing; I must have passed this crud onto them somehow.'

'Would you please tell me what's going on here?' Oleg stood between them, he'd had enough of being totally ignored.

'Baby brother, I don't know how much I can tell you about my suspicions, and I don't want to confuse you too much either, but one thing is for sure—whatever it is that they implanted in me, it wasn't what they said it was.'

'Then you're not an epileptic?' Oleg asked. He was totally lost. 'Why the heck did they put this implant into you?'

'I've never been an epileptic, and I have no idea why they put this implant into me,' said Alex and signalled to Bianco. 'But I have my suspicions. Let's go!' he said, giving his knee a slap.

'You're leaving? Where are you going? You barely arrived an hour ago and you're leaving already?' Oleg planted himself in front of his brother.

'Look here, kiddo,' Alex began, hugging his little brother, who was standing angrily in his way, looking at him exactly as he used to in the past, when Alex had walloped him for something. He had the same woebegone look on his face. 'We're not children anymore. We've grown up, and you'll have to understand this. All of a sudden, everything that I have done so far will come tumbling down on your head. You'll be the one who will have to care for our mother, too; but I won't leave you empty-handed, and Kolya will support you in everything. If you ever need me, my communicator is always on, you can reach me at any time but, for now, you'll have to accept this. I have to untangle the loose threads in my life, and I may have to kick somebody's ass while I'm at it.'

Oleg didn't budge; he didn't return his brother's embrace. His body was taut with anger. Alex slowly let him go and started to pack his knapsack.

'When you left for the Far East, I thought you'd never come back!' Oleg shouted, his eyes filling with tears. 'Now that you're back, I thought you'd never leave and abandon me again!'

Alex looked up. He saw his brother was choking back sobs. Bianco flung his gear onto his shoulders and diplomatically stepped out into the entrance hall. Alex was hit with a wave of emotion; he had no idea how much Oleg loved him. He hadn't even thought about the fact that he had been filling the role of their father ever since they had lost him. He put his knapsack down and put his arms around his brother's neck, pulling Oleg's head down onto his chest, like in old times, when he was smaller.

'I love you very much,' he was surprised at himself that he could articulate the words, as he hadn't used them for years. Perhaps this, too, had been killed in him by the implant. 'You and mother mean the most to me in the whole world.'

He held Oleg's broad face in his two hands.

'You are the future, Oleg. You're no longer "little brother," you've grown up! You've become a big, strong man. Look, you're taller than me!' he said, showing the five centimetre difference favouring his brother. 'You'll learn the ropes of life, believe me. If our father were to see us now, he'd be very proud of you!'

Oleg nodded, sobbing.

'Our borders are still open for now, but we don't know at what moment New China will be closing them,' said the correspondent, who was reporting live from one of the border crossings. 'As you can see, they are getting ready for a total lockdown, using an electro-magnetic shield, which means that entry into the country won't be possible, not even by air; but a decision to this effect is only expected sometime in the near future. All this is being motivated by preparations for the forthcoming festivities . . .'

'We have to go,' said Alex softly, patting Oleg's face, 'take care of Mum and yourself, Oleg!'

Bianco was waiting behind the door that led to the second-level parking space. Their air-car was floating there, filled up with enough fuel for the trip, even to take them as far as the Mongol Province.

'If Borislav Zuppa calls, send him to Kolya, pay him my part, and he'll send me the money later,' Alex called back from the door.

'Drop it, Alexei, I don't care!' said Oleg angrily. 'Just promise me that I'll see you again . . .'

Alex clasped one index finger with the other, like a hook. It was their old childhood signal. The symbol for the brotherhood connection. Oleg answered the same way.

The door closed behind Alex, and Oleg had the feeling that, after losing his real father, he would also be losing his surrogate father . . .

*

New China, Jiangsu Government-General, Suzhou Imperial City

'I can't believe that you're that mad!' Nuo couldn't stop laughing. She looked at the man who meant everything to her, and what she loved most in him was his ability to be so crazy sometimes. 'You're about to fall down and then this won't be a celebration, but a funeral! This new implant has made you far too reckless!'

Wei had grabbed the tail of a giant, floating dragon and, using the ornamental cord hanging down from it, had fastened it to the nearest pole. He climbed onto its back and tried to ride the waves running along the reddish-yellow body. The Dragon Festival was not linked to the Moon's New Year, as usual, but to the investiture of the first New China Emperor, to *Shi Huangdi*; Jin Qin. Suzhou was parading in never-before-seen splendour. The ten thousand papier-mâché dragons were part of this pomp, guided by robots, in a manner intended to frighten the people in the busiest places—the promenade bridges extending between the high-rises and around the floating garden areas. The biggest specimens, such as the one Wei had grabbed, even spat fire once they had reached a safe altitude.

He had seized the tail by stretching and reaching up from the top of one of the stone lions on the promenade bridge, many spectators cheering him on. At first, they thought he just wanted to play with it, but when he climbed onto its back, many shouted for him to come down. But Wei was driven by an inexplicable euphoria.

'Alright, I believe that you love me, I don't need any more proof,' Nuo shouted; she, too, was worried, because the dragon was having an increasingly hard time staying in the air, and had started to drift towards the promenade bridge. 'Come down, the *demon* of audacity is taking you completely into his power!'

Wei had a good laugh then slid down the rope to stand beside Nuo. Some of the passersby applauded, the others just shook their heads, looking scandalised.

'That's Northerners for you,' said one of the men in harsh mockery, loud enough for Wei to hear. '*Shantung bandits*! All these tall lads and adventurers coming down from the North!'

'Including almost all the conquering and empire-building Chinese emperors!' Wei shot back. 'Where would we be today without them, isn't it true? By the way, I'm not a Northerner, I'm from the South, even more so than the Southerners!'

'Leave it alone, he's a fossilized old ape,' Nuo shushed him, 'he's living in the past, thinking in terms of China's ancient regions and peoples.

There are no more cunning businessmen living south of the Yangtze, no more wise men moving the intellectual capital to the South, away from the attacking hordes, no more southern, irascible and adventuresome *Kwangtungs* from Quangdong Province. The southern Chinese, snake-eating *Yüehs*, the blaspheming and trouble-fomenting *Hupehs* living in Central China! That's all history!'

'That's true, the only thing that makes me happy is that he took me for a northern, conquering type,' said Wei, grinning.

'Well, you're too tall to be a Southerner, that's for sure; in this town, you're a real giant!' the girl laughed. 'You would make a better emperor than the present ruler.'

'I'm not surprised that he chose the Qin dynasty family name for his accession to the throne. Who would want a southern rice-eater? What everyone would rather see is the ongoing dynastic reign of a large northern pasta-eater, with a great legacy of conquests.'

'China has always been a melting pot,' explained Nuo. 'We've learned from everyone: the smell of blood and the craft of conquest, from the Mongols, they trained us with their constant attacks. From the Southerners, trade and that cunning mentality. About every eight hundred years, our blood was renewed either through our own conquests or as a result of subjugation. Today, we have the same thing: Emperor Jin Qin and his government annexed Asia and implemented the next bloodletting.'

The young man's brow darkened.

'Do you really mean that?' he asked.

The girl hugged him and kissed his chin.

'No, I don't think so, you know me well. I'm not a partisan of the forced acquisition of territories, except when it's about gaining a bigger part of the conjugal bed!' she said, laughing, and gently punched Wei in the stomach then stepped up the pace on the bridge towards the taxis flashing in the distance.

Wei was head over heels in love with his young wife. He admired her fresh spirit, her intelligence, and that she managed to punch him just when he was exhaling so that it was even harder to catch his breath again.

He only caught up with Nuo next to the taxi, but he didn't have any problem sprinting. He had already noticed that he was in better shape the very first day after the implant had been replaced.

The *Kami* of wisdom hadn't abandoned him in his present decision, as it had done so many times in the past.

'Where are we going?' Wei asked, but she was already sitting in the floating taxi.

'Are you coming or not?' she asked, peeping out from the door, 'you said that this is my celebration, so we're going wherever I decide to go.'

'Alright,' Wei nodded and sat beside her.

'To the Channels,' she said to the taxi driver.

'The Channels? Have you gone mad? We said we would go to a normal restaurant.'

'Don't fret! Yesterday, while you were away, I went to see the area and, if the news is correct, the emperor had completely cleaned up the place. There's no crime, no trash, no rubble. He wants to build a real imperial city on the ancient stones.'

'Alright, but if they start a fight, I'm leaving immediately.'

'Agreed,' said Nuo and gave him a peck on the cheek.

'This is exactly what people like now,' his wife continued. 'For a long time, China has been a country of apathy: "Don't interfere in public affairs, keep hidden in the background, don't interfere with *grande politique*," as the catchphrases go, and now here is a conquering emperor who has turned apathy into courage. Just like one of the former greats.'

'Hang on just a minute!' Wei raised the palm of his hand in protest. 'Don't compare Jin Qin to the great Qin Emperor. If I'm correct, Jin Qin is not a man of impeccable morals. There was a lawsuit against him for Mafia activities back at the time of the Republic.'

'Could be, but that hasn't been proven,' Nuo disagreed, 'he was freed at the end of the hearing. That's how he won the presidential seat after the elections.'

'Rather strange, as he wasn't even running for it,' said Wei, somewhat sarcastically.

'Your sarcasm is misplaced because, whether you believe it or not, this entire thing was the Chinese people's will. I'll spell it out for you. Orthodoxy is among our most important characteristics. It also signifies conservatism, and conservatism signifies the respect of traditionalism. As a consequence, tradition demands a strong China. So there!'

'Wow, I bow before your arguments,' Wei smiled. His wife had lined up a brilliant and ironclad case.

Meanwhile, they left the northern high-rise district and started descending towards the Great Channel. Wei felt extremely uneasy, he wasn't at all happy about the location. As a child, he had accidentally stumbled into it with one of the gangs, down at the forbidden street level, and the harsh memories had burnt themselves into his mind. The stomach-churning feeling, however, quickly vanished when he spotted the lights of the Great Channel. It didn't look at all like his memories of it. Imperial splendour had emerged, thanks to a canal network built by a great emperor.

The taxi parked beside a long floating garden, and the driver opened the door. Wei paid with his biochip and helped Nuo step out of the cab.

'There you are! This is what I asked for today, for the celebration,' she said, pointing to the infinitely long row of adjoining tables on the floating islands. This giant snake, like the tail of the dragon, followed the line of the channel running below. On each island, there was a dragon tree, with stones stacked around it, like in bygone centuries.

'The true dragon festival,' said Wei smiling, clasping his hands on his chest. 'You know, this is really worthy of our evening!'

'Absolutely! The last night before the Dragon Festival is always the most beautiful. Although there is no new year to follow it, perhaps there will be a new era. And let's hope that it'll be in our lifetime, too.'

'Yes, I'm sure it will be.'

They sat down at the first two available places, facing each other. Complete strangers, families, and couples sat beside them in an interminable row.

'Just like in the old movies,' said Wei and smiled back at the people beside them, 'I can't even believe I'm in New China.'

'My dear, wherever you are in the Solar System, you would feel the same coldness and alienation amongst people. Except here! Could this, perhaps, be New China's secret?'

'I wouldn't really know, I'm not Chinese.'

'At times like these, of course you're not,' smiled Nuo, 'when you would have to admit that the other important and famous Chinese trait is contentment. Just accepting what we have. It's one of our characteristics as well. I suggest that we now practice this feeling together. Let's just accept what we have been given for tonight.'

'You're right,' laughed Wei, while the waiter placed two glasses of champagne before them on the table. 'The emperor's gift,' he said.

'To the emperor then!' Nuo raised her glass.

'To your new job!' Wei touched her glass with his.

It was a wonderful night. It remained in Wei's memory as an evening of unique moments, never to be repeated.

The next day, they both got up early. The sun, as a long sunshine-tailed fire-dragon bathed in gold rising over the Dragon Festival, whooshed along their quilt, turning them out of bed. They lovingly held onto each other for a fleeting moment before they hurried to get ready.

'Is this what you'll be wearing?' asked Wei, holding an ensemble cut in the modern style, consisting of a black jacket and red trousers, hanging on the rack. The black jacket had a red belt ending in metal buckles. 'They'll never let you in like this.'

'Don't make me mad—they were the ones who sent me the pattern. When they came to the nursery and selected me, they specified everything in full detail. Pattern design, colour, quality of fabric,' said Nuo in a disbelieving tone. She was still standing there in just her panties in the bathroom. 'They would only accept silk, real silk, nothing synthetic...'

Wei would have liked her to turn around, so that he could see all of her.

'But this is modern! I thought that period garments would be entirely reinstated!' he shouted into the bathroom but only to make her come rushing out. Which was precisely what happened.

'How could you be like that?' Nuo stormed out, she tried to snatch the outfit from him, but Wei hid it behind his back so that she would have to embrace him for it and suddenly he pulled her to him, with one hand, holding the outfit behind his back in the other.

'You despicable . . .' Nuo couldn't continue because Wei kissed her. She resisted for a while, and then embraced him herself and kissed him back.

'You're despicable, and you'll crease it,' she said, purring softly, and started kissing his chest, 'and then they really won't let me in. But if you're coming like this,' she pushed herself away and lifted Wei's shirt, he had nothing on underneath, 'then they'll already shoot you down in the metro, as a satyr!'

She ran back into the bathroom to continue dressing. Wei liked this trait in her, this immoderation, this impulsiveness and spontaneity. And the fact that she tried to keep all this under control, trying to discipline herself. He had a feeling that if this had been a weekend, Nuo wouldn't have stopped at caressing his chest. It had happened before, that in a noble fight against desire, the *sense of duty* fell by the wayside and *love* triumphed. But not today, because today only *discipline* could triumph: this was a very special day on which *sense of duty* had no competitor.

'By the way, I noticed that you can hardly contain yourself since they changed your implant,' said Nuo with a smile, her impish eyes were reflected in the mirror, 'are you sure they gave you the right one?'

'Ha ha, very funny,' Wei mocked a pout and pulled on his dark trousers, drawn together with belts at the waist, and the white shirt. He put on a faux leather long coat on top and fastened it with a thick, red-dragon patterned belt around his waist. 'Mine isn't silk,' he said, looking at himself in the mirror, 'and it's not real leather. Who would have the money for that, nowadays? All the animals bred for leather are long since extinct.'

'Silkworm doesn't breed freely either, if you want to know.' Nuo flipped back and came hurrying out of the bathroom. 'Well, how do I look?'

Wei was lost for words. Nuo looked truly fabulous in this superbly effective gear. And this woman belonged to him. She was his wife. Even though many had queued up for her at one time.

'You're not saying anything?' she spread her hands open. 'I thought you would be pleased . . .'

'Come on now,' Wei snuggled up to her, 'you know very well that I live and die for you, and if I were the emperor, I would make you empress on the spot.'

They kissed for endless moments.

It was good to be newlyweds, Wei thought. He hadn't expected it to be such a rapturous experience. He used to think that once something was within reach and there was no more need to strive for it, the magic would be lost. But it hadn't turned out that way, thanks to the *Kami* of love.

'We have to go,' Nuo stroked his face, 'otherwise the Dragon Festival won't be complete!'

She picked up her handbag from the table, and Wei grabbed the handle of the suitcase on wheels. The door was already sliding open before them, when Nuo stepped back:

'The invitation letter!' she said, alarmed, running back to the living room, 'they wouldn't let us in without it, for sure!' She slapped Wei's nose with the letter and walked to the elevator.

'Hey, smarty-pants! We'll be settling accounts for that smack when we get home!' Wei said and hurried after her.

'You got that because your mind is on everything else, instead of reminding me about the most important thing.'

'Is it my job or yours?'

This flirting game took them to the elevator and ended up in another long kiss.

As the elevator door opened, a man stepped out, holding a package and headed in the direction of their apartment. Wei looked out of the elevator and quickly stopped the door from closing.

'Wait, we've got some kind of parcel,' he said to Nuo and ran back towards the apartment.

The man had been pressing the videophone button for a while, but only the computer answered. By the time Wei reached him, he was about to dictate a message to the machine.

'Good afternoon, are you looking for us?'

'Yes, sir, if you are Mr. Long Xu Wei , then I am indeed looking for you. I brought you a package, I need your digital impression here or you could signal through your biochip, whichever you prefer,' said the man and held out the electronic terminal in front of him. He wasn't

Chinese; his clothes appeared to be European. Perhaps he was North Asian. Wei couldn't detect any accent, he thought the chip would translate for him, so he turned the programme off, in order to find out what his original language was. To his surprise, the man spoke in a perfect Suzhou dialect, which startled Wei even more, since that was China's most elegant, most intellectual dialect. Foreigners usually spoke Mandarin or Cantonese, or perhaps Shanghai, but certainly not Suzhou. That meant that he was probably a local.

'And why the unexpected delivery? Where is the package from?' Wei asked, because the stark contrast between the man's appearance and his perfect pronunciation made him awfully curious.

'The package was sent to you from the Imperial Palace.'

Wei was astonished; he hadn't expected this answer.

'Thank you,' was all he could utter in his amazement, since he didn't have any connection with the New China Imperial Palace.

'Was it actually addressed to my wife, maybe . . .' he meant to ask but, by the time he turned around, the man was already in the elevator. Nuo was standing by the elevator with extended hands, indicating her incomprehension of what was happening.

'Just put it on the table! You can look at it when we get home!' she shouted from the end of the corridor. Wei did as he was told and placed the mysterious package on the dining room table.

Suzhou's hazy heat hit them as soon as they stepped out of the elevator. Nuo didn't want to go onto the moving walkway, she said she had calculated that it took exactly the same time to reach the metro on foot, and that way they could at least get a little exercise at the same time. She wanted to enjoy the pleasures of the cherry blossoms in the Japanese hanging garden during their walk.

'What do these little pink flowers mean to you?' she asked Wei, smiling, catching a petal in the air, licking it and pressing it onto his lapel.

'I don't know . . .' Wei pondered, seriously, 'should it mean something?'

'Yes, it should, it's an ancient symbol of your birthplace.'

Wei looked at the trees for a long time, as they spread a pink curtain before them, with their tiny petals, in the morning light. The wind swept them onto both sides of the promenade and beyond, down into the twenty-five-stories-deep chasm, or up, pressing on the windows of high-rises. They clung to the windows of floating taxis and buses, travelling freely along above the Imperial City.

'I feel that it must mean something, but I've been thinking about what the answer could be for a long time already,' said the young man softly, 'on my evening walks, I listen to what the *Kami* of the wind tells me about it, but so far I haven't found the answer.'

'You're a strange bird, someone who's definitely not from here,' Nuo laughed, 'I'm so happy that you became my husband.'

Wei pulled her closer. Now that they were walking on this pink carpet, he really felt that he never wanted to lose her. The *spirit* of the wind, however, whispered some foreboding into his ear, before they entered the air-train heading for the Forbidden City. This had the effect of keeping them from talking for the rest of the journey, and he kept an even tighter hold of his wife's hand.

Within half an hour, New China's Imperial Palace in Suzhou, the Forbidden City, made its appearance. It was an enormous island floating in the air, spread over an area of several hectares, in the Southern sky of Suzhou, far removed from Changsha Island, and above the sea. It reigned over the land beneath the clouds as the latest symbol of New China's omnipotence, proclaiming the magnitude of Emperor Jin Qin's Empire. The area was protected from all sides by the replica of the ancient Great Wall of China, built during the Qin dynasty, which was like China within China: it was the emperor's personal China.

The soon-to-be ruler tried to imitate his great predecessor, the earlier emperor who had unified the thousand-year-old China, in everything. As a consequence, he had taken the ancient name of Qin for his rule, signalling that he wanted to be a warring emperor. He was only one of the many warring warlords who had come into wealth, amongst those reigning in modern China. But he wanted more than that: he had once again adopted and prescribed the *Shi Huangdi* salutation, or the title of the first ruler, thereby announcing the arrival of a new age.

The investiture ceremony was organised for this week but related events, namely the Dragon Festival, had been taking place throughout the month. To mark the occasion, Jin Qin had decreed the organising of huge festivities in all twenty-two governorships, the governors of which had complied in full, without reservation. That month, the whole of New China would be an uninterrupted dragon's tail consisting of interconnected tables.

Jin Qin had sired nine children with his three wives, four of whom—a pair of twins and two boys—were still too young to participate in the investiture festivities. For this reason, the three empresses had contacted every nursery in Suzhou in order to select suitable nannies, who had the expertise and to whom they took a liking, to take care of their children during this particular week. The nursery where Nuo was employed was one of the most reputable and expensive institutions. Nuo had won the approbation of the youngest empress of similar age, thus being picked out of the four nurseries in the group. Security examinations of all kinds had taken place over the past few weeks. Even Wei had to go to a hearing, but of course they knew nothing about his origins, since there were no official adoption papers, so this was no obstacle to Nuo's hiring.

Nuo was immensely happy, she had been born in Dachang, near Beijing, and for her the ancient Forbidden City was a symbol: the secret of ancient China, guarded behind gates. So, of course, she accepted the assignment—which would permit her to enter the New Forbidden City—with great enthusiasm.

'Do you think that it'll be a fake, or have they salvaged something of our ancestral glory?' Nuo asked her husband, as the air-train let them off at the Changsha Island terminal. That inconceivably huge city floated above their heads, between the open sea and sky. Wei had to admit that, even though he wasn't overly enthusiastic about the warlord-turned-emperor and his expansionist politics, the structure was phenomenal in its own right.

'The impression it gives is anything but fake,' said Wei approvingly. He had never been so near the palace, having only seen it through a telescope or on TV recordings. The New Forbidden City had travelled on a slow journey that had lasted three weeks, from Beijing, in order to station itself here, in Suzhou, for the investiture ceremony. It was impossible to tell what Jin Qin's true intentions were: whether to irritate the Japanese Emperor with his proximity, or to approach him as a sign of peace. Whatever the truth, the 'Criminal Emperor' had no reason to fear any possible attack, because he and his city were protected by the most up-to-date energy shield and air defence systems.

They started to walk towards the meeting point, where, according to the arrangement, the car from the Imperial Court would meet them. The next time they would see each other again would be two days later, at the same place, when Nuo would be allowed to go home for the night. That would be two nights before the investiture ceremony. When she went back afterwards, she would only be allowed to return home a week later. But it was also possible that she would be hired as a permanent employee, and Wei would be allowed to move into the palace as well. Wei wasn't too keen about the idea, as he wouldn't be able to continue his work as an aircraft engineer, but he left it to luck and to *the spirit of future* to decide his fate for him. Whatever would be would be. What was important right now was Nuo's happiness.

The ocean waves spumed up high, a strong wind lashing them against the pier, where the long dragon-patterned limousine was waiting. It was yellow, with red twisting dragons, with the design of the first emperor's coronation attire. Nuo pressed a rather curt kiss on Wei's lips and walked to the imperial emissary, where she identified herself with her chip. The man checked her clothing, then opened the door of the limousine. Nuo blew her husband a quick kiss and then the darkened air-car began its steep ascent. Wei watched for a while, as it flew above the New China Great Wall, then started his way back towards the terminal.

All the way home, he kept questioning *the spirit of future* but the spirit remained silent.

He was preparing lunch in the apartment, when he took a closer look at the package on the table. The paper wrapping, which appeared to be old, held some soft object. There was no address or name on the outside, which meant that the man who had appeared to be a foreigner had brought it to him directly from the sender. He was no postal employee, that was for sure.

Well, let the mystery be revealed, he thought and tore off the tape.

The soft object was duly puzzling and, in its simplicity, was worthy of its wrapping: a thirty-centimetre-wide, white fabric, rolled up into a coil.

Wei pushed the rice and the soup aside, grabbed the end of the fabric, and unwound the coil onto the table's length. As it unrolled, red embroidery and characters became visible. The one-and-a-half-metre long, linen cloth was entirely covered with tiny stitches in little red circles. He didn't count them but estimated that there were about a thousand. He could only guess at its function: what it resembled most closely was a waist sash.

The fabric wasn't new; like the wrapping paper, it was rather aged, speckled with brownish spots everywhere. Some of them resembled spots of blood, on other parts it was clearly covered with mud stains or some earth-like substance.

In the corner, he saw two lines of characters, but in Chinese, they only signified fragments of words. He instructed his translation chip to connect to his optic nerves and to try to decipher its significance.

'The phrase is in Japanese, pronounced "bu-un-cho-kyu," signifying "eternal good luck in war,"' he heard the chip's translation programme in his head.

He was astounded by the realisation that this package hadn't been sent from the New China Palace, but by the Japanese emperor. The only Japanese he knew were Professor Yakizima and Miss Yuuna Joshida, but he was not in correspondence with the emperor; in fact, they had no contact whatsoever.

At least until now. One of these days he should perhaps call Futura, they might know something about this.

The object, this embroidered sash, mesmerised him no end; its presence here in their dining room was so unbelievable. Fascinating and interesting, but also a little disconcerting. So much so, that he refrained from touching it: he left it there, laid out on the table. He picked up his dinner instead and went to settle down before the TV-wall.

In the news, they had just announced that New China had closed the entire length of its borders with neighbouring countries and would remain quarantined until the Imperial Investiture Ceremonies and the related Dragon Festivities were over.

*

North American Union, Toronto, United Colony Bureau of Investigation Organized Crime and Gang Section

Richard Enderston successfully concluded the investigation into the Chu Jun case, and he was able to hand over the evidence, collected over the years, to the Prosecuting Office to prepare the accusation. Nevertheless, as he was leaving the Moon, he felt that he had stepped into a much bigger affair than the case of the Chinese mobster.

It was late afternoon when he braced himself to walk over to the neighbouring building to see Sam Kirkpatrick, his buddy from the Police Academy. Sam had always been a good sport and, although they hadn't been in touch for years, they had never severed their friendly ties. It was time for Richard to retighten that connection once again.

Sam was a deputy head in the United Colony Intelligence Service, therefore, precisely the man for the task of satisfying Richard's curiosity. The case of the Japanese 'Back into Society' organisation and their protégé, Noah Simpson, had continued to bother Richard. The organisation's Rio headquarters had ceased to exist in exactly the same week that he and his team had liquidated their Paris front office, the Moon Concession Corporation's headquarters. At the same time, Noah Simpson had returned in a rather sorry state from Mars, where an entire colony-wide epidemic had broken out. This had been confirmed officially, in the past few hours, when the quarantine of the red planet had been lifted. According to the latest news, the same epidemic had also ravaged India, where they had lifted quarantine procedures as well. That trail couldn't have had anything to do with Noah, but the photo shoots of the Russian vessel that had disappeared and the 'accidental' breakdown of the *For Asia* news organisation's satellite during their telecast of those same shots, made the already mysterious affair even more suspicious.

Yuuna Joshida, the nice lady from the 'Back to Society' organisation was the key to the matter. They had talked over Videocom, he could still remember her face. She was an attractive woman, not easy to forget. They had even screened her to make sure that she was in the clear. Only then had they accepted Noah's application, whose data and background had also been thoroughly scrutinised. Everything had appeared to be perfect, at the time, perhaps even too much so. Richard sensed, albeit too late, that something was amiss.

Sam received him as if it were only yesterday that they'd had a beer together. Richard was counting on the fact that his friend hadn't changed through the years. When he told Sam what he wanted to know, the latter immediately offered to be of help; as a matter of fact, his cop's instinct had been stirred up as well, whilst listening to the story.

Sam was sitting in front of the Intelligence Service's terminal. The terminal showed the entire map of the Mother Colony, with tiny dots by the billions. Each one marked the location of a biochip.

'I don't know, Richard, it stirred something up in me, too,' said Sam, signalling with an upturned forefinger, that he wasn't clear on something. 'What I find fishy in this whole affair is that the man you were working with had been on Mars before the Colony was placed under quarantine. Nearly everyone he had contact with, for example, Chu Jun and his gang, became infected with the disease.'

'Yes, it looks like collaborative evidence, but this part of the case isn't our speciality. Maybe the Epidemics Institute could shed more light on the matter.'

'Of course, but as a layman, I still say that it's glaringly obvious that the epidemic came to an end all at the same time within a hair's breadth, not only in one city, one region, but the whole world, the whole Solar System. That can't be a coincidence.'

Sam was deputy head of the Intelligence Service for a reason, he had put his finger unerringly on one of the most peculiar facts.

'Well then, let's look up this woman, this Miss Yuuna Joshida, if I recall correctly,' said Sam and turned to face the monitor. 'You must know that I'm only helping because I think this epidemic has the sort of suspicious elements that make us at the UC Intelligence Service sit up and pay attention. But while there's no official invitation, say by the Epidemics Institute for instance, or until the suspicion becomes stronger, I can only give you "friendly" assistance.'

'I'm only too well aware of the restrictions, Sam, and believe me, I'm not driven by self-interest in this case.'

'I know you and I'm sure of that,' said Sam reassuringly. He typed Miss Joshida's name into the system. Numbers scrolled down the monitor, until ninety-seven dots started flashing, the majority in Japan, although a few also appeared in other parts of the world.

'This is how many Yuuna Joshidas exist, not a bad average from the twenty-eight billion, and this only contains inhabitants of the Mother Colony,' said Sam and typed another text into the search engine. 'You said that she worked at the Japanese Health Ministry, right?'

'Exactly.'

'Then she's in Japan, in fact, she's in Kyoto at this very moment. Over there, it's already tomorrow morning; if you board a parabolic flight, you'll be there within an hour. You'd get there just in time for the start of the daily work routine,' smiled Sam.

'Not a single part of my body looks forward to it, but you're right, it's better to get to the bottom of this,' said Richard and looked at his watch. 'Could you check one more thing for me?'

'Of course, name it; I'm in this thing up to my ears anyway. But only if it's related to the same matter.'

'It is. Would you have a look to see if they're still holding Noah Simpson on the Moon Colony?'

'Unfortunately, my jurisdiction doesn't include the servers on the Moon Colony; I'd really need some kind of official authorisation for that,' Sam said, shaking his head. 'I could give you the usual rubbish again, that I don't want to take chances with my job, but as a matter of fact, that's really the way it is.'

'Alright, then please check if Noah returned to Earth,' Richard asked cautiously, perhaps this was still a feasible request.

'OK, wait a minute . . . No. He didn't come back to the Mother Colony. But I can verify if he had any calls on the Moon.'

'And how can you do that?'

'Well, because the Moon Colony is on the side facing the Earth, and they use Earth relays for communication, wherever they initiate a call to.'

'Of course! Have a look to see if he made any outgoing calls.'

Sam browsed around for a while, until three green rows and one red luminous row appeared on the screen.

'He had three outgoing calls, two of them to a Rio number...' said Sam.

'Well, well! Bingo!' smiled Richard. 'If it wasn't Miss Joshida's embracing arms that the little bird wanted to fly home to.'

'Right on! He was calling the "Back to Society" office, but the number was no longer in service. The other call went to New Cloud York, to a relative, or perhaps an acquaintance, since you mentioned that the young man was from there.'

'And the incoming call?'

'Unfortunately, I can't tell where that was from. As it doesn't show a number, I can only presume that the call didn't come from the Moon or from Earth.'

'Then it was from the Mars, or possibly the Europa Colony.'

'It could be Mars, someone he had visited. Didn't he ever tell your people what he was doing on Mars?' Sam wondered.

'We never got as far as an interrogation because the Epidemics Centre had put him into quarantine before we could start working on it. We only managed to get near Chu Jun, the Chinese godfather, in the last few hours.'

'Right, so you know what? Get on the first flight going to Kyoto; meanwhile, I'll get authorisation from the big boss to download this conversation-file and I'll forward it to you later,' suggested Sam. 'Once you get off in Japan, you'll have it on your communicator.'

'You're a real pal!' said Richard approvingly and gave Sam a high five. 'When I get back, we'll get together for a beer.'

'And also because the final dénouement of this case concerns me, as well.'

'So be it,' said Richard and said good-bye.

One hour later, he was already on the descending arc of the parabolic flight; they had just broken through the cloud blanket covering Japan when he heard the beeps on his communicator. The display showed Sam's name with the following message: 'Good luck, here's the conversation. It came from Mars, the number unfortunately is confidential.

The boss approved the stuff and is supportive in other matters, too. If you need us, just call!'

A great chum and a good specialist, thought Richard and linked up his biochip to the communicator in order to listen to the message via his inner ear.

'Noah?' he heard the voice of an unknown woman.

'Jess, Jessica, is that you?' this was Noah.

'Yes, thank heavens I could finally reach you. What's happening with you? How are you?'

'Oh, Jess, dear Jess, if you only knew . . . I'm fine now, I've just been released from quarantine, because apparently there was some kind of epidemic in your area . . . Are you OK?'

'Yes, of course, I'm OK. But we need to talk, it's very important that we talk in person. I'm just leaving for the Earth, I'll be in New Cloud York within two days,' said Jess.

'Right, then I'll go there, too, immediately. I've just called a friend to see if I could stay at his place . . .'

'OK, but we could rent a room together, if you think . . .' her voice faltered.

'Yes, I think.' He laughed softly. 'Oh, Jess, dear Jess. You'll have to help me . . .'

'I know. I'm going to the terminal. Take care of yourself, and take your medication regularly.'

She hung up, Noah's breathing could still be heard for a while, brooding on that last sentence, which Richard was pondering as well. Why would the woman remind him to take his medication regularly? He must consult the Moon Colony Epidemics Centre, to check whether the young man had been taking anything whilst staying there.

In any case, this was a new trail to follow.

Richard took a taxi at the terminal but, by some strange quirk, the chauffeur didn't have a translation programme in his biochip; in fact, the computer in his car couldn't cope with the language task either. It must have been some sort of older model. As he had to encounter innumerable foreigners in the course of his work, one would have thought that it would be an essential tool in the car. Consequently, Richard had to babble the address into the communicator and show the display to the chauffeur, who, in the midst of effusive bows, signalled that he understood everything, and so, off they went.

However, drive he could! In fact, he drove too fast. He had barely left the modern downtown and was already speeding along between two-floor, or one-level, villa-like buildings, leaving all behind on the expressway. Somehow, in the end, he still made it all in one piece to the given address.

'*Arigato*,' said Richard, he could only repeat the *thank you* word from the information that his own translator chip had sent to his inner ear. 'Is this the house? Miss Joshida?' he asked the cabbie, as there were no signs whatsoever on the houses, and the chauffer had stopped in the middle of the street, between two houses.

'*Joshida, hai*,' said the chauffeur smiling and bowing, which the biochip programme translated as 'yes, this is Joshida's house.'

The taxi sped off with the same insane velocity as when it had arrived, in the direction of the expressway. Now Richard was only hoping that he would find Miss Joshida at home. This was debatable, as the usual time to start work in the morning was approaching. She could already be at the Ministry, in which case he would have to call one of the lunatic taxi driver's colleagues.

There was a neat little garden in front of the house, enclosed by a wooden fence, a time-honoured flower garden. It had been a very long time since Richard had seen something like it, perhaps never in real life, rather in his childhood books or school textbooks. In Toronto and elsewhere in North America, people no longer lived at street level, unless they lived in the country, on farms. Here, however, there were entire districts in centuries-old condition.

Beyond the garden, an armoured door indicated that life, however, was no longer the same as it had been in olden times. Richard was just about to press the button on the videophone, but a voice was already greeting him:

'Good morning, how may I help you?' he heard in his inner ear, with the help of the translation programme.

'Good morning,' he replied in English, 'my name is Richard Enderston, I'm a friend of Miss Yoshida.

A moment of silence followed, the owner of the voice was probably speculating over what it had just heard, or else hadn't understood the language if it had no translator programme.

'I greet you, Mr. Enderston. I ran your name through the database, but couldn't find a person with that name on the list of friends. Are you sure you're at the right address?'

That's a pedantic computer, thought Richard, and immediately switched to English, as he'd heard the words through the speaker were pronounced in perfect, universal English, free of any accents.

'I'm absolutely sure. Couldn't you call someone for me? I'm a criminal investigator, and I need to see Miss Joshida on a very important matter.'

Another silence ensued, lasting for a few seconds.

'Your biochip is concealed, Mr. Enderston, I am unable to verify its authenticity. If you open it for me, I'll let you in.'

'Alright, here it is, the way to the scanner is clear,' said Richard and, thinking of the password, released the encryption on his chip.

Another set of agonising seconds followed.

'One moment, Investigator Enderston.'

One minute passed before the door opened. A short, older woman stood before him.

'*Ohayo Gozaimasu*,' the lady greeted him and waved her arm to invite the man into the house.

'Miss Joshida?' Richard asked, but knew he couldn't expect an answer. He stood facing an aged woman who wouldn't be using the feats of modern technology, a translator programme included.

'*Hai*,' she kept repeating and signalled him to enter the living room. In the simply furnished, spacious room, there were only a few pieces, a table with two chairs, and a kitchen robot in the corner. Other than these, there was nothing else but wide-open spaces.

'*Hai, Joshida*,' the elderly lady said, whom Richard finally identified as the housekeeper or servant. She pulled aside the room-divider folding screen, and behind the wood-panelled sliding door appeared a floating wheelchair, containing a young woman.

'Good day, Mr. Enderston,' she, or rather, the built-in sound generator in her wheelchair, said. '*Don't be surprised that I'm speaking to you through the chair with the help of my biochip. I hear that you are a criminal investigator and that we supposedly know each other from somewhere. What can I do for you?'*

'Miss Joshida . . .' Richard was terribly embarrassed, this whole thing wasn't adding up correctly. This was not the woman he'd spoken with before. 'Well, it's awfully difficult to explain what is happening here, but I presume I have indeed found the right Yuuna Joshida.'

'Why? Which one would you have been looking for?'

'The one that doesn't need to be sitting in a floating wheelchair, which in your case, I deeply regret and am sorry for.'

'There is no need to pity me, I live my life in relative happiness. Can you tell me more about this person?'

'She had been working earlier for the Japanese Health Ministry, and she is currently the head of the "Back to Society" rehabilitation organisation, which had a branch office in Rio, Brazil, not too long ago.'

'You've startled me, Mr. Enderston,' she said, her lips motionless, only the sudden quick flickering of her eyes denoting her nervousness, *'because I am that person, or rather was, before my accident five years ago. I have since dissolved this social organisation and have retired.'*

Richard looked as disconcerted as he felt.

'Miss Joshida, haven't you noticed that during these last five years, since you stopped working and became restricted to a floating wheelchair, someone has been making ill use of your identity?'

At this point, her eyes widened. Richard didn't know how deeply he should go into the explanations, but he was certain that he couldn't leave this lady without saying a word.

Although he would have preferred to be on his way to New Cloud York as soon as possible.

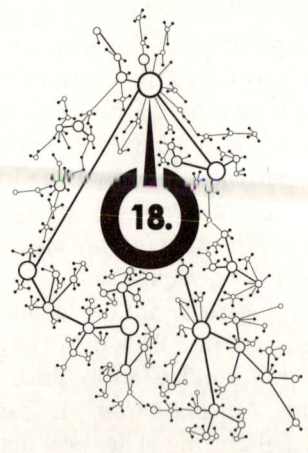

18.

New China, Sakha (Yakutsk) Province, north of Yakutsk

Anatoly Polovinkin brought the cross-country caterpillar to a stop. It was the only vehicle capable of battling its way through the mud in this vast Siberian wilderness. He followed the Lena River to Krest-Kytyl in an air-car. This was the next civilised spot north of Yakutsk. In former times, this had been just a tiny town. Now, it was Yakutsk's northern extension. Life hadn't changed in centuries. There were no tall buildings, as there were in Yakutsk, but the little islands carved out by the Lena had found their owners: they all had millionaires' holiday homes and villas built on them. Due to the climatic shift, the short, one-month summer now stretched to four months, making the weather conditions more enjoyable, even in the north.

He had rented the vehicle from a lumber yard. According to the coordinates that he had been given, he had to get to one of the alluvial islands. He was making his way through a clearing amongst the trees. Because of the rainy weather over the past few weeks, the caterpillar-tracks ploughed out enormous puddles along its route. According to the instruments, he still had another two kilometres to churn through to reach the meeting place.

A week ago, Anatoly had received notification from Futura, to report to the Ulan Bator headquarters in Mongolia. He had always known that this day would come; since childhood, all he had heard from his foster parents was that, one day, his homeland would ask for the return of all the good things it had given him. He had never known exactly how this would happen, but in his soul he tried to be prepared for it. Yet, when the day came, he vacillated, the enthusiasm slipping away, the fire of anticipation gone. He prayed before his home altar, to his spirit of courage for two days, to give him the strength to do what he had always been trained for. Sometimes strength grew in a person, like the waters of the Lena when it burst its banks, but sometimes it waned, as when the river retreated back to its ancient bed. In the same way it left the silt behind, so, too, the thoughts, the doubts, all remained behind to torture a person a little longer. At dawn on the second day, however, the *Kami* of courage came to hold his hand—at least he believed that this was the spirit guiding him—because it finally brought about his decision. *Shinto* had been determined for him, he was not allowed to deviate from it. The following day he left for Ulan Bator to have the implant changed.

Getting ready for the Dragon Festival was justification enough to leave the Yakutsk Province Palace's kitchen—he was working there as the chef's assistant—even though it was their busiest period. They prepared huge portions of traditional Yakutsk fish dishes, crucian carp soup and lamb meat specialities, daily because the Master of the Palace, Vasily Altyukov, entertained somebody practically every day. He had no problem in getting away, because he promised to visit the Mongol Provincial Centre's kitchen and bring back a couple of authentic Mongol recipes.

After his return, the wait had been nerve-racking. They had prepared him for the probable schedule years ago: they said that it would take two days, four at most, between the implanting and the start of the operation. And so it was; two days later, the message arrived, on schedule on his computer at home, simply announcing the coordinates for the exact place of the meeting. Earlier, they had also mentioned that, from that point on, he wouldn't have to take the pills he had received with the new implant.

Whatever has to be, so shall it be, as the Japanese emperor wills it.

He was thirteen when he had been in Japan for the first and last time—he was twenty-seven now. In those days, it had still been possible to travel freely between the two countries; later, as they had said, he would no longer have that opportunity, for security reasons. Although it was long ago, he still remembered the visit to one of his cousins. His parents and grandparents lived on Tsushima Island, near the Korean peninsula and, when New China had occupied the peninsula, this was the first place where the bombardments had begun. By the orders of the then-ruling Japanese emperor, His Highness Arai Shinobu, the Patriotic Alliance of Japanese Women, which had been founded sometime in the twentieth century and had been revived at the time of the first Asian conflict, rescued the surviving children and sent them to adoptive parents. That was how he ended up with his foster father, Maxim Polovinkin, an honest Yakutsk nationalist, who had supported the Yakutsk resistance against the New China troops to the very end. Later, he had abandoned his freedom-fighting efforts for the sake of his adopted son because he knew that, one day, his son would be the one to continue his interrupted war.

'This is my private war,' he remembered one of his father's favourite phrases.

But whose war is it, really? Considering that the warlords' coalition has conquered the whole of Asia. This is an entire continent's war. And this continent needs its heroes.

The flashing dot on the caterpillar's instrument panel, coupled with an audio signal, showed that it had arrived at the designated area. Perhaps there was some kind of cabin or ranger's lodge around. And sure enough, as the vehicle climbed up a small hill, a crumbling log cabin came into view beneath the trees. It had everything: a door, a window, a roof, but wasn't, however, a reassuring sight. Had it not been standing in a wind-free spot, a stronger gust of wind could have tipped it over.

He parked the caterpillar a little way off, about fifteen metres from the shack. He didn't know why he was being so cautious, perhaps it was because he didn't want the whole thing to collapse from the caterpillar's vibration. The mud was slowly left behind; summer had brought out a fragile turf, on which he trod up to the entrance. Though even the grass had imbibed some water, squelching under his feet as if he were walking through a swamp. He finally reached the dilapidated door and pushed aside the long plank serving as a crossbar.

He didn't know what to expect behind the door. A delegation, perhaps? Not the Japanese emperor himself, but say, his representative, one of his ministers or one of his generals. In the big war of the twentieth century it was the generals themselves who greeted those on their way to meet death.

But there was no one in the shack.

A brown paper package lay in the middle of the rickety table, tied up with red ribbons. They could leave it here quite safely, there was no prospect of someone else finding it. They had cleared the table nicely; everything else was covered with thick dust and wood shavings. There hadn't been anybody in this shed for years, perhaps for decades.

He opened the package slowly, circumspectly, and carefully rolled up the ribbons, placing them on the edge of the table. He peeled off the seemingly old brown paper, on which there was neither an address nor markings of any kind—it would obviously have been risky to provide any information. He folded up the paper neatly and placed it next to the ribbons.

Slowly, he unrolled the off-white, faded material. The linen, about a metre and a half long and thirty centimetres wide, was covered with tiny red circles, in the middle of which, were rows of red threaded stitches. He immediately recognised it: it was a *Senninbari*, a belt with a thousand stitches.

His foster parents had spoken a lot about this legendary piece of clothing: Japanese soldiers going to war were given these belts by their wives, mothers, or female relatives. The cross-stitches were sewn by all kinds of different women; the maker of the belt stood in front of busy stores and stations for days, asking female passersby to place a stitch, one by one, for the one leaving for the war. According to the legends, the thousand stitches were endowed with a magical spell: they offered protection from harm, wartime injury, and even from a bullet.

This belt he was now holding, however, didn't protect anyone from death, since the soldier who had worn it then had even left his bloodstains on it. Thus, others were inclined to think along the lines that, even though it wouldn't protect the wearer from a bullet, with it tied around the waist beneath the jacket, it would help the wearer to march boldly into the fight for his native country.

Even we are ready to sacrifice our lives for it.

Like this soldier—the original owner of the belt—had done, perhaps somewhere in the great war of the twentieth century. The diacritics seen in the left corner read as follows: 'bu-un chō-kyu,' signifying 'everlasting luck in the war.'
Luck lasting forever . . .
In the middle there was a *four-sen* coin, the agreed Japanese pronunciation being *shishen*, or *deadly war*, which is why it was placed in the middle of the belt.

Deadly war . . .

Deadly war . . . Eternal luck in the deadly war . . . he tasted the words on his tongue as he examined the faded war relic. What an irreconcilable contrast stretched between the word *deadly* and the word *luck*. Is there such a thing as everlasting luck in a deadly war?

Is there such a thing as someone who has been trained for war, who doesn't obey the call when the war finally catches up with him?

Time seemed to have stopped. He had no idea how much time he'd spent brooding in this shed, staring at the *Senninbari*. But he had to leave because here in the north, night fell quickly, even in summer.

He started to undress. It was no longer he who was controlling his hands but rather one of the Shinto spirits, *self-sacrifice*. It whispered to him that the only way to get to *Shinto's gate* was through *him*. It could even be lying, since there was no one else around except *him* and Anatoly, and there was no spirit that would defend Anatoly's interests. But perhaps there was no need. Anatoly had learned that self-sacrifice was one of the greatest virtues.

He stood naked from the waist up in the middle of the shack. Hands clasped together, he said a quick prayer to the *Kami* of self-sacrifice and asked all eight million deities to let him be one of the *Divine Winds*, one of the many that would storm and sweep through New China in the coming days and free Asia from the warlords.

Let me be one of the Kamikazes.

He tied the belt around his waist, got dressed, and with peace in his soul, made his way back to civilisation.

With the evening breeze, the *Divine Wind* was on its way toward the town of Yakutsk . . .

*

New China, Mongol Province, Ulan Bator

Professor Nujo Yakizima had sent Angelica home earlier, so he finished his work sooner himself. These past two days had been exhausting: they had finished exchanging all twenty-four implants, and all this had been packed into two days. He couldn't know what Angelica had surmised from the mad rush that accompanied the installation of the implants. Yakizima had no time to consider Angelica's thoughts, there was no time for hesitation: New China had closed its borders, and they could only hope that the provincial borders would be left open. Had they been closed before the implants could be exchanged, then they would have had to wait another fifty or hundred years for such a lucky stellar configuration. Not to mention that the United Colony Epidemics Institute wouldn't be satisfied with the fact that the root cause of the infection remained unresolved, which meant that it would go to great lengths, which might eventually lead to the Unmei Machines being discovered. And that would mean Japan's complete moral and political downfall.

The professor picked up the letter he had received yesterday from the Ulan Bator Provincial Governor's Secretary, from his desk. New China's vast coat of arms stretched across the top of the letterhead, with the imperial dragon embracing Asia, as well as the ancient Great Wall of yore. Underneath, it read:

'Esteemed Professor Yakizima, we invite you to the Mongol Provincial Governorship Palace, to the Dragon Festival organised on the occasion of the investiture of the First New China Emperor, His Highness Jin Qin. We would like to take this opportunity to thank you, as the Chairman and General Director of Futura Respondis, for the financial support towards the realisation of this festival. We are grateful that you have chosen our Governorship as your target for the inventive research project. Signature, provincial seal. Date of the event: the evening after tomorrow.'

So, his time had come as well.

He turned off the light in his study and walked over to the bedroom, where he switched on the bedside table lamp. He sat down on the edge of the bed and pulled the picture frame on the bedside table closer. It depicted his wife, prior to their wedding.

She was a beautiful, noble woman.

He unbuttoned his shirt and placed it meticulously on the hanger, leaving only his trousers on. He walked over to the closet and took out the garment wrapped in a loose cover. He laid it out on the bed and slowly, almost ritually, unfastened the clips with careful motions. He gently removed the cover and stepped back. It was his Air Force officer's uniform, the one that he had worn in the second Asian conflict.

If Major Joshida saw him now, she would probably berate him for such enormous insanity, bringing a military uniform into New China territory. The uniform of its former, as well as its current, enemy. It was indeed a huge audacity, thought the professor, but after all, their former lives, their former activities, and the entire Unmei Project, was a total audacity.

Madness and noble battle at the same time.

He examined his decorations on the breast of the coat. The *Hero's ribbon* earned after his twenty-two victorious aerial combats, the medal for his *Japanese Empire Military Service*, and finally, the most valuable, the *For a Free Asia* medal of merit. The third one had been given to him on the same day he had buried his wife, who had died during the bombardments in the last year of the war.

He unfastened the coat, taking care with every gilded clamp. He took it off the wooden hanger and laid it gently on the bed. Underneath the coat lay his *thousand-stitch* belt, which had been prepared by his wife before he left for the front the very first time. It was a stunningly beautiful piece, not from the usual white material with red stitches, such as the ones sent by Emperor Arai from his private collection in the last few days to the twenty-four Kamikazes. This one was on red pure silk, with white embroidery, and the stitches were in the usual white circles but formed the image of a leaping tiger. Because his wife, his beloved wife, wanted Nujo Yakizima to be like the most beautiful and the strongest tiger, who roams far away in the course of his tour but is capable of returning home, unharmed, from any distance.

This belt had been tied around his waist during the aerial combats as well. Nujo had often gone above the Korean peninsula to meet the bombers, but had nevertheless always unerringly brought his plane back home. Many times, he had been in parabolic orbit on the edge of space and the upper stratosphere, and had picked off the rockets aimed at Japan with his cannon or had shot up the New China military satellites. Yet, every time, after all two hundred and ten deployments, he had landed his aircraft safely on the Misawa base runway.

But now, if he donned the *Senninbari* again, he would no longer return. The *tiger* had gone too far, and he would be too old to find his way back from this tour of his.

He untied the thin straps of the belt from the slots in the hanger and spread it out before him on the bed. He checked the reverse of the fabric, to ensure that the stitches hadn't torn over the years, since they were the belt's source of strength. The French stitches were still in perfect condition everywhere, and the white silk thread held them together like an everlasting route, laid down for him by many girls' and women's hands—of all those whom his wife had asked to participate in its making, for him. A thousand destinies, a thousand lives, they all wanted the hero going into war to survive the battles with his eternal luck and to bring honour to Japan . . .

He took the belt and, holding it in his hands, walked to the home altar in the corner. He knelt down and spread the belt out on his thighs. He opened the shrine's door and prepared a piece of paper on which to write down his prayer request. The pen started resolutely on its way across the paper, the ball rolled steadily, imprinting the ink onto the handmade, special paper, but then it suddenly got stuck in the middle of the word . . .

Nujo exhaled forcefully. He looked to his right, at his wife's picture on the bedside table.

'I know you wouldn't want this,' he addressed his wife in his imagination, 'I know you wouldn't want the self-sacrifice missions, I know that you wouldn't want innocent lives . . . I know . . .'

He let out a big sigh and, nevertheless, finally wrote it down: *Unmei*—fate.

He asked his *Kami* of fate, his spirit of destiny, to help over the next few days.

He prayed for twenty minutes. He took account of all the spirits who could help him, in the *way of Shinto, the Spirits, the Gods* . . . When he had finished, he no longer harboured any doubts. The spirits already controlled his decision in every way.

Slowly, he rose to his feet and tied on the thousand-stitch belt, watching in the mirror. He had to check several times to make sure that the tiger design was centred and then, satisfied, he returned to his study.

He drew a small box from one of the drawers of his desk. It was black, like a starless night sky, with a black foam overlay inside. After lifting up the top layer of foam, he was able to hold the *Unmei Implant*, with its long implanting stem, in his hands.

He had never really thought it through, that one day this would happen. He hadn't thought he would have to stand in line, too. He had believed that, as a middle-aged man, he would be left as a reserve. But no, the emperor needed him as well.

He felt for his nape with his left hand and palpated the implant conduit. He found the match-head-sized cover for the entrance, hidden between hair roots. He carefully pushed it aside, opening up the path all the way to the hypothalamus. With his right hand, he then cautiously fitted the stem to the opening of the slit, pushing it in with his left, and then with a careful movement, introduced the implant. With the implant fitted into the spot, he sent a small signal into his inner ear. All he had to do then was to pull out the implanting stem and slide the cover back into place.

He took out the handheld terminal with which he usually carried out the programming of the implant. He went over the twenty-five-point checklist, which finally confirmed that the implant was properly linked to the lamella of the hypothalamus. All he had to do now was to initiate the program and configure the implant capsule's opening frequency. He set it to one day, instead of the previous two-day setting, since he had done the same with every volunteer. This way, the Unmei Machines would enter his bloodstream and lymph glands on a daily basis and then would slowly assume control over his body.

He looked at the vial containing the antidote for a long time. Perhaps he could still take one that evening, to have a final peaceful night spent in semi-slumber, without the onset of the side effects. But then he reckoned that none of the volunteers would be taking the antidote, as per their orders. So, he too would have to endure it silently.

In fact, the number one Kamikaze, Wei, had only been given a placebo, not the antidote; there was no way he could stop the side effects . . .

Courage and strife. This was the designated *Shinto* way for them all.

*

The border between New China and the Independent Russian Republic, a few hours before its closure

'No, all the more reason why I'm not getting off, may lightning strike you!' shouted Alex, looking at the electronic beam that had reached their air-car. The border closure had already begun. 'You have no right to pluck me off just like that!'

'They do have the right, Alex,' said Bianco quietly, 'set the car down, or they'll blow us out of the sky.'

Alex exhaled noisily, retracted the gas pedal, and started sinking in a slow spiral towards the border crossing.

'We came all the way up north just so we could still slip over here, if they closed the borders in the south. It boggles the mind. I didn't think that they'd nail us in Yekaterinburg,' Alexei fumed.

'And it's a good thing we didn't have any weapons with us,' said the bodyguard, pointing at the empty bags in the backseat.

Alex finally reached the large platform that they had raised to a height of three hundred metres above the New China side of Yekaterinburg. The city was cut in half by a two-thousand-metre-high electromagnetic wall, which brought all low-flying traffic to a halt. Since these cars couldn't fly any higher than that, they had no chance whatsoever of crossing the border with this model.

Yekaterinburg was one of the victims of the peace that ended the second Asian conflict. The New Chinese advance had been stopped short at the city's border, but it was only a matter of time before the never-ending influx of troops—and the mercenaries of various nationalities serving at their side, amongst whom there was also a great number of profit-seeking Russian criminals—would break through its established defences. At the time, the Russian army had evacuated the city's eastern side facing New China and had installed dirty bombs, abandoning its defensive positions. When the attackers, reinforced by mercenaries, marched in, these hidden bombs were activated and the territory became uninhabitable due to the nuclear fallout. It had been necessary to evacuate the entire city, of course, because the contamination didn't recognise manmade borders but, after a few years of decontamination work and buildings razed to the ground, the population was slowly sneaking back. The New China section, however, still remained a ghost town, to this very day. As Alex descended onto the platform, the nose of the air-car pointed towards a desolate, lustreless Yekaterinburg. His heart bled as he gazed over the ruins of this once-blooming city. Behind them, in the Russian section, the inner city had been rebuilt, its soaring buildings and reassuring lights poured out warmth.

'That damn war, and to think that's what I had been supporting with my weapons,' Alex muttered, whilst shutting off the driving mechanism and opening the butterfly door. There was fog outside or, more likely, there were low-flying clouds, but everything was covered in a white mass. The soldier stepping up to the side of the vehicle wore the New China frontier guard body armour, and his short-barrelled repeating-energy weapon left no doubt that he had serious intentions about inspecting the car.

'What's the problem then?' Alex asked, in lieu of a greeting, as he was furious. In reality, he still hoped to be able to enter the country before they closed off the borders.

'Sir, please have some respect, you are speaking with an official, uniformed officer of the New China Empire,' said the officer. The hostile tone made him take two steps back, and he drew his arm, which, up until then had been merely resting on the weapon, into a ready-to-fire position.

'OK, OK, I was just angry; excuse me, I'm in a hurry, that's why,' Alex explained, holding up his hands in surrender. He saw Bianco's venomous glance over the top of the car. He had to calm down; in the end, he could botch up the whole thing because of his hot-headedness.

'Alright, I understand, sir, but we're only doing our job,' the frontier guard said and signalled to his mate, who passed a hand-scanner over the vehicle. He was looking for easily disintegrating chemicals from firearms or explosives. As he walked slowly around the car, the scanner suddenly started to emit a signal. The man with the scanner pointed to the backseat. Alex looked at Bianco in panic, who just spread out his arms uncomprehendingly, to indicate that he had absolutely nothing.

'Sir, could you get me the bags from the backseat?' the armed man asked, this time wrapping his finger around the trigger. Alex slipped in and threw the two bags onto the concrete floor of the platform. Rain started to fall gently from the low-moving clouds. A few metres away, another pair of guards started to inspect another air-car.

'There, take a look, there's nothing in them,' said Alex.

The guard with the scanner said something in Chinese, but the translator program couldn't catch a single word of it.

'My mate says your satchel contains chemical substances derived from weapons. Do you have some kind of weapon on you, sir?' the guard asked, now decidedly taking up a firing position.

'No, I don't have a weapon on me.'

'Perhaps you had a weapon earlier? Do you usually carry one?'

Oh, if only the entire platform would collapse under you, Alex thought. He couldn't even understand why he had brought along the bag that he had carried all through Africa.

'I did. I'm an arms dealer. I usually wear a weapon; in fact, I have a license to possess them.'

'What is the purpose of your trip to New China?' asked the guard. Alex felt the guards were becoming increasingly suspicious of them. If this continued, they might even get arrested; in fact, they'd be lucky if they only got deported back. He was beginning to think, more and more, that he and Bianco would have to get out of there, one way or another.

'We're looking for one of our friends, we'd like to visit him,' replied Alex, but he was already watching the guards next to them and saw that, when they had finished with the inspection of the vehicle, they would open up the space above the electromagnetic network platform for a short while. At the moment, there were two other air-cars being inspected; they were slowly finishing with one of them. And the window of opportunity to escape was slowly opening.

'And where does your friend live?'

'Where is it again, Bianco?' he turned to the mercenary; meanwhile, through his chip, he gave the Italian a slight prod, who obviously felt the small electrical impulse because his eyes widened.

'Uh? Jun lives somewhere to the south, here it is on the map,' he said and leant in through the open door of the car.

The guards next to them opened up the passage, and the platform was covered by the thickest raincloud yet. Alex sensed that the moment had arrived. He bent forward and kicked the frontier guard in the stomach, making him reel backwards and disappear into the dense cloud. Bianco had already raised the car; Alex clambered aboard, just as energy beams broke through the grey clouds, but they only tracked haphazardly across the sky.

'Step on it, we're not stopping until Ulan Bator,' said Alex, looking back at the receding platform wrapped in clouds, which, within a few seconds, turned into a grey spot. This highly powered sports model had been the best choice for this trip. They wouldn't come after them now, and, if they hadn't recorded the information on their chips, they wouldn't know anything about them either.

'There's no point, they'll catch us,' said Bianco, when they had passed the dark, desolate mass that was Yekaterinburg, 'we left the bags on the platform. They'll find out who we are from those, in due course.'

Alexei grew stiff with the realisation. The vial containing the antidote was in his bag; the vial that had reached him by such a tortuous route whilst he had still been in Africa, and thanks to his friend sitting beside him, at that.

'That may well be, but first let's grab the Japanese professor and squeeze his balls,' he said and decided not to tell Bianco that he had also left the antidote on the platform. Surely the professor had a vial or two. That is, if they weren't caught by the Chinese in the meantime.

The air-car left the Ural Mountain region like a black arrow. Bianco kept it low enough, away from any motorways, so as not to be conspicuous. They streaked into the night line drawing its dark, arched shadow from the east along the Earth's surface, like a thunderbolt. Beneath them, only the larger cities' lights shone out and somewhere, on the horizon, loomed a mass of clouds, like quilted duvets.

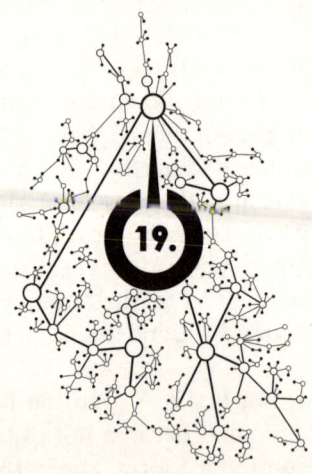

19.

New China, Suzhou Imperial City, the day before the emperor's investiture ceremony

Wei ascribed the fact that he had only slept for one or two hours over the past two days to loneliness. Since he had been married, he had never spent more than one day away from his wife. He missed the warmth of her skin and the way she rubbed and cuddled up against him like a kitten.

Alongside his insomnia, however, he felt strangely imbued with energy, as if he had slept the whole night through. At Futura, they had mentioned that he would experience these types of changes, but he hadn't thought that it would happen so suddenly.

On the other hand, he wasn't happy about having caught a nasty cold somewhere. It had either been outside, at the docks when he accompanied Nuo, or back at the Dragon Festival, that cold night, when they had gone down to the channels. He called up one of his doctor acquaintances who examined him superficially. According to him, it was just the usual end-of-summer flu, or some virus, nothing serious. He gave him some chewable pills, which he munched on after meals, but he hadn't felt any improvement. In the end, the illness subsided to a bearable level and he decided that, while it stayed that way, he wouldn't go to the Health Centre. It was a national holiday week throughout New China, everyone was on holiday and it wasn't easy to get hold of a doctor.

Right now, he was perspiring profusely. According to his biochip, his temperature was more than 38°C, but the strange thing about it was that all of this happened within just one minute. He was sweating so much that a little puddle accumulated beneath his palm, resting on top of the table. He couldn't decide whether the greenish colour came from the perspiration itself or whether it just appeared that way due to the colour of the imitation bamboo-leaf tabletop.

Or could this be the implant's side effect?

He was allergic to the pills he had to take every two days...

Could it be that something had gone wrong when the implant was installed? He even called Futura, but the switchboard asked for patience, all their lines were busy. He waited about twenty minutes, then gave up. Back in Mongolia, Miss Joshida had told him that everything had gone well with the implant. Why would she have lied? He had to believe her.

He was somewhat relieved to find that the sweating passed just as quickly as it had arrived, and his energy was back as well. He thought of Nuo and of how happy she must be looking after the emperor's twins on this historic day. Tomorrow, Jin Qin would be crowned, this time officially. And Nuo would be participating in this ceremony, albeit indirectly.

He decided that, before going out to the docks to pick up Nuo, he would run out to buy her a present. Nuo loved objects of nature—seashells, snail shells, semi-precious stones, and jewellery made from these materials. He wanted to surprise her with something of that sort. He had good taste in artistic matters and so would have no problem in selecting such a gift.

He walked through the Japanese garden once again, taking delight in the way the cherry blossoms coloured the sky. The pink mingled with the blue and turned into a lovely purple vanilla tint. There were many people picnicking under the cherry trees, adopting the famous Japanese tradition, the so-called *hanami*, flower blossom time, when people spent their lunch hours or had a cup of tea, under the trees.

Here, they could do it every day, at any time, since these genetically modified trees blossomed every month of the year. Meteorologists no longer had to announce on television, when blossoming would reach your neighbourhood, or when the heat wave would arrive to open up the flowers. Here, the flowers opened their petals constantly, without fail.

This was an incredible violation of nature. Could it possibly be that there wasn't a single cherry tree left in Japan that would blossom only in April, according to ancient, divine programming? People loved their comfort, they loved to feel nature at their feet . . .

They loved to play God . . .

'Wei, how are you? How is Nuo?' He hadn't even noticed that he had crossed the hanging garden and was already inside the shopping centre. It was Nuo's favourite jeweller, old Shui. The master had incredible hands that worked magic with the marvels found on the seashore, transforming them into beautiful jewellery.

'Ah, Master Shui, my apologies, I was lost in thought,' said Wei, while looking around the small store. 'Thank you, we're both fine. Nuo has been honoured with a great privilege! She has been chosen to work in the Imperial Palace looking after the children!'

'That's wonderful,' nodded the jeweller, 'but as you must know, I'm not a fan of the imperial rule, especially not this one that we're having now. But we've already discussed this a great deal. If it means a lot to Nuo, who adores ancient China and its history, then we should rejoice with her. But I don't have to explain my feelings, especially to you who are not a native of this country.'

Shui knew that Wei was of Japanese descent and that he wasn't overjoyed about the revival of imperial rule either.

'You know me as if I were your son,' Wei smiled, and he really thought of Shui as his second foster father, since he had moved into the area. It was as if he were meeting with a thousand-year-old sage every evening on his way home from work. That was the time when Shui would lock the store and would brew fresh tea, and they would talk for hours in the shade of the cherry trees. He was very fond of the old man.

'Shui, you have such fabulous new pieces in your shop, Nuo will be ecstatic! What is this made from?'

'That's a starfish skeleton, Wei, and it was in its infancy when it was destroyed, that's why it's so tiny. Sadly, because of the warming of the seawater, starfish have died off in almost all the oceans on Earth; only a couple of species remain on artificial barrier reefs established in the South Seas. Nuo will like it, but due to the lack of basic material, I can only produce medals with it.'

'That's incredible, Master Shui, my old friend,' Wei wanted to pay with his biochip but when the old man saw his remittance on the display, he held up his hand:

'No, Wei, just take it as a gift. I like Nuo, she is a very lovable creature, her happiness is mine, too,' said the old jeweller and shook Wei's hand firmly.

'You're perspiring,' he said.

'Yes, I must have caught a cold, excuse me, I don't want you to catch it.'

'Don't worry, I've gone through a lot of illnesses, this one is no different from the others.'

Wei shook his hand gratefully and said good-bye. On his way home, he stopped at a supermarket to buy Nuo's favourite crunchy vanilla-hazelnut pastry for that evening.

Going home on the air-train, Nuo chatted all the way. She couldn't stop talking; she was totally enchanted by the accumulated experiences of the last two days.

'The twins are darlings,' she smiled at her husband. 'I wish we could eventually have twins, too. It would be a fairy-tale gift from nature.'

'Or from doctors, if they're born via artificial methods,' said Wei laughing, but a coughing fit caught up with him. His handkerchief was full of ugly discharge.

'Where is the *spirit of health*? You forgot to ask him to look after you . . .' said Nuo, hugging him. 'Good Heavens, you're as damp as if you'd just been exercising.'

'It'll soon pass,' said Wei, shaking. 'It comes in waves. It started yesterday. One of my friends from University came to see me and said this was just a little cold.'

'OK, then. I'll put you under the shower at home, to get you back into shape.'

'My biochip says I still have a fever, but it should disappear within a minute.'

'Right, give me your hand,' said Nuo and slipped his hand into hers, to warm it up; perhaps the trembling would stop. That's when Wei dropped the starfish suspended on the chain that he'd been holding. There it was, hanging before Nuo's widening eyes.

'Wei, this is fantastic!' she said, smiling from ear to ear. 'Where did Master Shui get a starfish? I thought they had died out completely!'

Wei watched her contentedly, her joy, the fact that she could be set aflame to such a high degree by everything beautiful and every little moment. She enveloped his hand with the chain and kissed it repeatedly.

'Don't,' he said and tried to pull away; he didn't want her falling ill before the big day.

'Don't worry, nothing will happen,' she said, starry-eyed, embracing him.

Back home, Nuo did push him under the shower, she even slipped in beside him.

'I don't feel like it now, I really have no idea what's wrong with me,' he said, when she started stroking him in an unambiguous way.

'I told you, nothing bad will happen,' she said and started to kiss his chest. Not much later, he wasn't protesting anymore, he forgot about the sweating, the awful discharge, all he felt was her swaying against him.

The game continued in bed, twice more, and even more passionately than earlier in the shower. She had been starved for love and she showed it, too. That may have been their best night since they got married. But Wei wasn't feeling well. As if every time something left his body, something strange, not of this world. The spirits surrounding him weren't calm, either; they kept circling around the room, with ever-nastier expressions. Some kind of unusually powerful ambivalence, between ecstasy and death, resonated throughout the room. With the clamour of eight million *Kamis*, it was impossible to discern which power was winning.

New Cloud York, North American Union

Richard Enderston finally received support from Sam and his employer, the Intelligence Service. Both had seen something in these events that Richard had called to their attention, which at first sight appeared to be a haphazard game of chance but that were, nevertheless, a series of logical, related events. The theft of Miss Joshida's identity had finally tipped the scales and brought the vacillating voices down onto the side of crime.

The unmarked agency air-car was approaching the outskirts of the New Cloud York capital. In the suburbs, increasingly lower townhouses were lined up in rows, followed, before long, by the great ring-road and the expressway, beyond which only no-man's land stretched out into the distance. This was a restricted area that required a permit for flying because there wasn't any natural cover, arable land, undergrowth or asphalt here, just structures in unalloyed metal and reinforced concrete. Here, one could look down at the old town.

Some time ago, there had been a lookout tower somewhere around here, but so many ruined stockbrokers had used it to leap off to their deaths at the time of the Asian wars that it had to be closed down. Many suicide jumpers (and mad inventors) had a predilection for using this spot because this side of the Big Disk—as they called the giant ellipsoid holding up the cloud city—extended exactly over the former Washington Park, where the circular asphalt patch provided them with an excellent landing area.

The air-car flew over the outskirts of the city and started its spiral descent around the enormous supporting legs. The old city and Manhattan lay in the shade, the Great Disk depriving them of the sun. The supporting legs touched ground at the bottom of the ocean, in the centre of the triangle formed by Manhattan, Liberty Island, and Governors Island, surrounded by security systems. These installations were necessary, even for the protection of the North American Guardian because, when the New York stock market had suffered its meltdown causing the greatest shakeup in world history, unstoppable riots had swept across the old city. There were those who wanted the Great Disk destroyed and the torso that remained of the Statue of Liberty was a constant reminder of this devastation. Manhattan had come under fire from rockets for weeks on end. In this new world, it had been a long time since liberty had existed as in previous centuries, when the statue had been originally erected. Liberty existed in name only and its shackles rattled noisily.

'There was once a well-situated hotel on Eighth Avenue, not far from the submerged Lincoln Tunnel entrance. Today it ranks amongst one of the worst categories, but even so, it's the one that suffered the least amount of damage in the past few years,' said Richard to Eric, whom he had brought along for the operation. 'That's where Noah stayed. This is where they'll meet, if the lady gets here within the hour.'

'If indeed she ever gets as far as the hotel, in this neighbourhood,' said Eric, turning off from Lincoln Park onto Sixth Avenue. Down below, four-wheelers were threading their way along the street, wrapped in the semi-darkness of the Great Disk. Passersby looked up at the air-car whisking by since, apart from the two of them, no one else was using this technology here. Those who could afford it simply didn't come here in this type of vehicle unless they were law enforcement. Such as the two of them.

'She knows the way, I can assure you,' said Richard, pointing to the data sheet on the dashboard panel. 'Sarah-Jessica Thompson was born here, in former Manhattan, she was raised here until she finally succeeded in breaking out from this world, thanks to her university studies. She landed on Mars with a scholarship, where she got a job immediately and has been working up until now. Until exactly two days ago, when she handed in her notice, sold her flat, and moved back to Earth.'

'I see,' said Eric, 'so Noah went to visit her on Mars, when he asked me for time off.'

'That's right. They grew up together, theirs was a big childhood romance. He wanted to renew contact with her. Perhaps it was the commission from the deal that prompted him to try to break away from his former lifestyle, which kept pulling him back down, again and again, into this filth.'

'And we reduced his plans to dust...' said Eric, not completing the rest of the sentence. He still felt guilty for having recruited Noah.

'Eric, don't start moralising, this is our job. We needed a decoy, and fate gave him to us for this role.'

Eric preferred to concentrate on driving, he'd had enough of false guilt trips, he wanted to get rid of the feeling. This was his job, but he had taken a liking to Noah, which was one of the biggest errors in the cop business.

Meanwhile, they had reached the corner of North 34th Street and made a sharp turn to the left.

'Slow down, the hotel should be here soon. The room's windows look out in the opposite direction, towards the harbour, so they wouldn't be able to see out here. We have to be careful, you've seen what a conspicuous phenomenon we are,' Richard pointed downwards. Beneath them, passersby were pointing in their direction, whilst many raised their heads in surprise at the black shadow gliding by above their heads. 'There's a dilapidated skyscraper, two buildings past the hotel. The twenty upper floors are practically in ruins, we wouldn't disturb anyone. Park the car on the top there.'

Eric made a sharp right turn onto Broadway, then turned northwest again on 35th Street, until he reached the building that Richard had mentioned. He first raised the nose of the vehicle and then set the cop car down gently on the crumbling rooftop.

'There, south of us, on the same level, that's the hotel. I'll prepare the drone,' said Richard and opened the butterfly door. Eric got out as well. He was very curious, as he'd never seen such a device in action before. In the meantime, Richard took out a palm-sized spy droid from his case and switched it on, whereupon it started to hover at head height. He brought up the display on the directional console and checked the sound and the image transmitted by the drone.

'OK. Then I'll send it on its way,' said Richard, and the robot shot forward in the direction of the target two blocks away. It flew past the wall of one of the tall buildings then turned sharply into the next street. From then on, they couldn't see it with unaided eyes; they could only follow the image transmitted by the onboard camera. Richard didn't direct the spy droid, it navigated by means of its own guidance system towards the given location.

The solid mass of the hotel appeared on the monitor, with its four turret-like wings. The drone started ascending, up to the given level, and then attached itself to the wall between the two levels. From there, with the help of its suction arms, it wormed its way along to the wall of the room, where it virtually merged into the wall. If someone were to look out from a neighbouring window, the person would only have seen a chimney outlet or a pipe-like protrusion. The camouflage was perfect.

The drone became their eyes and their ears. It could see through the wall with its special cameras and hear with its sensitive microphones.

'There's Noah,' said Richard, pointing to the figure moving around in the room.

'What's he doing?'

'I don't know, he's putting things on the table, I haven't the faintest idea what they are, but they make a clattering, metallic sound. Perhaps he's setting the table. They're going to have supper in the room.'

'We'll soon find out. All we can do for now is wait.'

Half an hour passed in silent surveillance, when a call came through from reception. Noah became agitated, he ran to the mirror in the bathroom, probably to adjust his hair; it was obvious that he was getting ready for the meeting. Within one minute, there was a knock on the door.

Noah opened it and just stood there for a moment, until the girl flung herself around his neck from the corridor. 'No, don't!' said Noah, pulling back. 'Don't come any closer, I'll explain everything!'

'Noah, I know everything, but I'm immune,' said Jessica and embraced him and kissed him passionately.

The recorder had been taping already. Richard sent a meaningful look to Eric. Eric just nodded, that he understood perfectly the implications of what the woman had just said. Richard's suspicion concerning Noah's connection with the infection loosed on Mars appeared to be correct. With his forefinger raised, Richard indicated that this would probably only be the beginning.

The kiss was a lingering one; it must have been the fulfilment of a long-awaited moment.

'Jess, dear Jessica, I missed you so much, there are so many things I'd like to tell you.'

'You can start at the beginning,' she said and threw off her coat. He walked around the table, and the metallic noise was audible again, as he lifted something off it.

'Not until you get it out of me! I've had enough of this; I won't be a dealer of death on two legs!'

The two investigators' eyes flashed at each other again.

'What are you talking about? I've no idea what I have to get out of you! Start at the beginning, and then I'll tell you what we found on Mars as well.'

He just stood there for a few seconds, with head bowed, and then angrily threw the object back onto the table.

'Well, alright. I'll be brief, because I want to get it over with. I couldn't get off the merry-go-round and I needed the spin. There was this outfit, Futura Respondis . . .' Richard immediately logged on to the Secret Service network and looked up the company. Two dots appeared on the screen, one in Rio and the other in Ulan Bator. Richard drew his finger across from Rio to Ulan Bator, signalling to Eric that the firm had moved from there to here. *Futura Respondis = Back into Society*, said the small notepad in the corner of the screen.

' . . . And this company found me. I don't know how, but I'm beginning to understand why. I became a guinea pig, because they inserted this implant, which then established contact with my nervous system . . .'

'Good Lord,' said Jess.

' . . . and gave me continuous energy. I only had to take a pill every second day for the so-called side effects. I could work endlessly, I forgot about sleep and rest, they were suppressed by the implant, which, by the way, was designated as an anti-epilepsy chip.'

Eric kept looking at Richard, nodding repeatedly. This explained Noah's incredible stamina for work. In fact, that was the aspect he had liked most in him, but now it turned out to be an artificially produced attribute.

'They gave me work, which I happened to like. Everything was in tune and everything came together so well . . .' Noah stopped talking;

the silence between them was sombre for a few moments. They were shattered by the turn of events.

'But then I called you, Jess, and this entire merry-go-round became so insignificant. It really didn't interest me anymore; I just wanted that last profitable deal and then to get rid of the chip . . .'

'Did you know that this chip wasn't there only to supply you with energy?' she asked. 'Did you know that the people who designed this chip built tiny nanorobots into it that triggered off terrible infections on Mars and in India?'

He nodded quietly.

'The epidemics people on the Moon said that a deadly and uncontrollable epidemic had broken out there. From the symptoms, I recognised myself; I knew that only I could have been the originator of the epidemic.'

'Noah, these monstrosities are controllable, they can be switched on or off, they're like a death factory! They're letting them rest for now, but they can be reactivated at any time! Who knows how many guinea pigs are still walking around with this implant . . .'

Richard was becoming more and more restless as the seemingly incredible story unfolded before him.

'That's why you'll have to take it out of me right now!' said Noah nervously and picked up the metal object from the table again.

'Have you gone mad? These are veterinary pincers, what am I supposed to do with them?'

'I don't know, just tear it out, I don't want it inside me anymore!' Noah was already shouting at this point. 'There is an implant channel, all you have to do is pull it out, that's all! If you don't do it, I'll do it myself!'

'OK, alright, just show me where!' she said nervously and stepped over to him.

'We have to leave, right now!' said Richard and shut down the control console. 'We can't let them remove it because it may kill him in the process. We have no idea how this thing works. We need him alive, come on, let's go!'

They jumped into the air-car and proceeded immediately towards the hotel.

'I can see a little sliding metal lid in-between the roots of your hair, could that be it?' Jess's voice could be heard from the closed control box . . .

'Yes, that's it, exactly. Underneath there's a little implant tube, and you can reach in with that long pair of tweezers . . .'

'Oh, no, don't do it . . .' Richard squeezed the words out between gritted teeth and stepped on the gas even harder. They were now one corner away from the building.

'Don't you think this is a bad idea? These veterinary biopsy tweezers are designed to take samples from an animal's diseased internal organs . . . well, do you really think I can remove your implant with them?'

'Oh, no, tell her no . . .' Richard implored, as they slipped alongside the hotel, onto the thirty-second floor.

'Jess, if you love me, you'll do it, now, this minute!'

At that point, as the air-car came to stop at the side of the window, Richard switched on the flashing light bar concealed in its side, and Eric climbed out through the open door onto the windowsill.

'I'm Richard Enderston, an investigator with the United Colony Bureau of Investigation Organized Crime and Gang Section,' he announced into the speakerphone, while his partner pushed in the window, 'Please stand against the wall with your hands up. You are under arrest on well-founded suspicion of bioterrorism.'

Noah took Jess by the hand and began to run towards the door. The old flight instinct reflexes were still in him.

'Noah, stop!' Eric shouted after him, focussing the stun gun on them. Upon hearing the familiar voice, Noah stopped short and turned back.

'Eric?' Noah was totally confused. 'Are you a cop?'

'Sorry, my friend . . .' said Eric quietly. 'But you'd really be better off standing against the wall and raising your hands. This goes for you as well, Miss Thompson, if you don't mind.'

'You don't know what you're getting into; he is carrying and spreading a very dangerous infection, and there's little chance that you're immune against this infection,' said Jess, whilst they proceeded to stand up against the wall and put their hands behind their backs.

'Miss Thompson, you're probably not aware that we have been working together for almost a year, and if I'm not immune, I don't know who is.'

'You have no idea how this whole thing works. At the time when you two worked together, these artificial systems were being suppressed by some inhibitory substance, or else they were switched off. I've seen what they're capable of with my own eyes.'

'We still don't know how they function, but that's why we intervened, in order to find out. First and foremost, we're interested in who it is that brought them into existence and why. Richard?' he spoke into the communicator. 'You can call in the epidemics people; they can send the quarantine vehicle.'

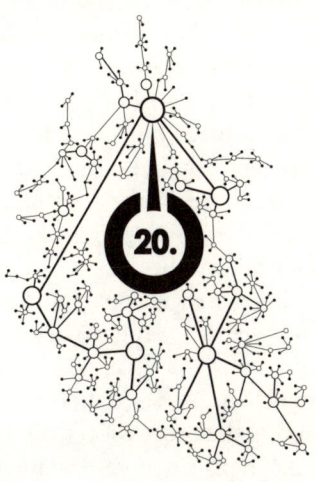

New China, Suzhou Imperial City, on the morning of Emperor Jin Qin's Investiture Ceremony

Chouko Ito had her medium-length black hair cut and dyed blond. It still felt strange to see her own reflection when passing by a glass wall. She wasn't against the reconversion because her intricate, gelled-down hair made her look younger. She'd been living as Yuuna Joshida for too long; it was time she took back her own identity.

Professor Yakizima had said good-bye to her the previous night: 'Chisa wa madowazu, yusha wa osorezu.' A wise man does not lose his way, a brave man does not fear—even if he loses it. She couldn't ignore the ambiguity of the message, since this path had already been determined years ago for all those who had participated in the Unmei Project. What could he have meant when he said that the brave are not afraid to lose their predetermined path? Was he perhaps capable of refusing the command of the Japanese emperor at the last minute? Or had he perhaps started to moralise at fate's door?

She got up at dawn so as to be ready in time and had already been waiting in the metro station for half an hour. She'd donned a short, split skirt, with thin leather pants underneath, and a gold-buckled, red jacket on top, with really high heels to match: she looked like a modern vamp. She blended into the surging crowd of New China's youth and looked exactly the opposite of her former, severely tailored self.

She had arrived yesterday from Ulan Bator and was staying at an elegant hotel. She switched off her phone even though her boss, Angelica Stockwell, had called, but she didn't want to be reached. Actually, Angelica was her employee, as Chouko was really the one pulling the strings behind the scenes, without the Englishwoman's knowledge. Being a major in the Japanese Secret Service, she played the part of the secretary brilliantly.

On Professor Yakizima's instructions, Futura Respondis had ceased to exist from that day onwards . . . it gave her an odd feeling, thinking about it.

It was nearly seven o'clock, Wei and Nuo should be arriving, if they didn't want to miss joining the procession from the docks to the palace. She had been watching them since yesterday; Wei was beginning to show the side effects of the Unmei Machines doing their job. The Project was, indeed, working perfectly. If, during the night, everything that one could expect from a young couple who hadn't seen each other for two days had happened, transmission of the infection would be guaranteed.

Nuo walked ahead with Wei merely trailing along, as they emerged onto the platform. The stuffing had been completely knocked out of him; the nanomachines had started to consume his system. Chouko tried to stay nearby, so that she could hear what they were saying. The train pulled into the platform from the right and then settled onto the pavement with a scarcely discernible thud. The doors opened, the couple got in and withdrew into a corner of the carriage, as there were no empty seats. Chouko arranged it so that she could be within hearing distance.

'Promise me that as soon as you get home you'll go straight to the hospital and you won't just rely on that charlatan friend of yours!' Nuo said, obviously worried.

'I promise, but you can't go back to the children like this, you'll contaminate everyone. For them, it's even more dangerous than for adults!' said Wei and let out a big sneeze. He grabbed the handhold with his sweaty hand. Chouko was sure that with that, the infection was on its way into the city as well. She was just worried that Wei would convince Nuo to report in sick. Although there was little chance of it because, in the early stages, the Fate Machines energised the infected person, making them feel fantastic. Nuo must be at this stage right now. She was contagious but feeling perfectly well.

'No, no, sweetheart, I'm bursting with energy,' came the expected reply from Nuo. 'Believe me, everything will go smoothly, but my mind will only be at ease if you go to the hospital. By the time I get home the day after tomorrow, I want you to be completely well.'

The train slowly left the inner city and emerged from the tunnel. The windows darkened automatically from the effect of the morning sun's rays. In the distance, the Imperial Palace was already visible, floating over the ocean, with the city below, all dressed up for the Dragon Festival. This would be a big day for the new emperor: it would be the first day of his reign, and hopefully the last. *Asia can no longer be ruled by a criminal, he has to be brought down,* thought Chouko.

'I'm shaking,' said Wei and set off towards a vacated seat. He pressed through the morning crowd, just behind Chouko. *How wonderful, and yet how limited the faculties of the human brain are!* thought Chouko. A little transformation, different clothes, a different hairdo, and she had immediately become unrecognisable. The familiar distinguishing marks had been lost, the Joshida that existed in memories had assumed a new shape.

Nuo followed him at once and sat down next to him when the seat became available.

'I'm beginning to get very worried about you, but I hope that you'll understand my decision, that I don't want to be left out of this big event.'

'OK, I understand,' said Wei who was already starting to breathe more laboriously. It looked like the tiny nanomachines had started to adhere to the mucous membranes as well. By evening, they would take full control over his body. 'But you'll have to understand, too, that if you love me, you won't leave me here in this condition.'

Chouko could feel the young woman's uncertainty. The palace was already looming up before them, only an arm's length away, and the success of their project would possibly hinge on this decision. Nuo was glancing back and forth, from the palace, decked out in festive splendour, visible through the window of the train, to her husband. Chouko deemed it to be the most opportune moment to intervene.

'Good day! My name is Chouko Ito, I'm a nurse from one of the hospitals in the city,' she addressed them, stopping by the seat. 'Can I be of assistance in any way?'

Nuo's eyes lit up; she looked as if she believed some angel had descended between them.

'Oh, Miss Ito, you must have been sent by one of my husband's *Kamis*; you know, he is also of Japanese descent, as you are, I mean, judging by your name,' she stammered, but it was obvious that she was almost jumping with joy, as now she would be able to calm down, knowing that she could leave her husband in good hands. Wei just looked up, he was in very bad shape, trying to sit up straight, with his head wobbling from side to side.

'Yes, it's quite possible; the world of the spirits is a power over which we have no control,' smiled Chouko. 'You just go on your way; I'll look after your husband and will help him get to hospital.'

'That's very kind of you; you don't know how happy you've made me!' But Chouko knew it only too well, and she also knew that the happiness was mutual.

'Of course, just leave him to me. I'll take care of him. We'll send a message from your husband's communicator and inform you about the situation. You don't have to worry.' She produced her loveliest smile. Meanwhile, Wei closed his eyes.

'It's better for him to rest now,' she added, glancing at the young man. Nuo nodded and started to prepare herself, pulling her bag over next to her. 'You can go now and just relax,' said Chouko, smiling.

'Oh, thank you!' said Nuo and flitted out onto the platform, as the train had meanwhile pulled into the docks. Her bliss and tranquillity were noticeable, since she would no longer have to tear herself apart trying to decide.

As the train pulled away from the platform, she waved once more before setting off towards the meeting point, from which she would hopefully be conveyed to the palace. The Fate Machines would be travelling on with her as well.

Chouko checked Wei's pulse: his heart was almost jumping out of his chest; he might possibly have a day and a half left. However, it would be bad if he got sick on the train, as he would have to be taken to the hospital sooner and, during the examination, the fact that his wife was looking after the emperor's children would come to light. That would almost certainly mean the end of the game.

She reached into her little handbag, which was a genuinely feminine piece; it couldn't contain very much at all, it was just for looks. Yet it could conceal a tiny vial. She took it out, broke it, and convinced Wei to swallow it.

It contained the antidote. That dose would help him to regain his faculties sufficiently by the evening, to enable him to go home after a long sleep in the metro, without being completely torn apart by the Fate Machines. She took out another vial and took it herself, since she and Professor Yakizima were the two members of the group whose genes didn't carry genetic immunity against the infection. The gene variation giving resistance against the machines wasn't typical of the southeastern Asian population, perhaps it only occurred in India, New Zealand, and Australia. That is why it was absolutely guaranteed that the Unmei Machines would turn against the emperor.

She put Wei's head on her shoulder. With the antidote, she could now keep him under control, as a primary carrier, until the very end of the operation.

*

New China, Sakha (Yakut) Province, Yakutsk, Provincial Government Palace. On the day of Emperor Jin Qin's Investiture Ceremony, at 12:23 p.m.

Anatoly Polovinkin, assistant chef, was already feeling the side effects of his implant. Frankly speaking, he couldn't distinguish the sweating caused by the steam rising in the four-hundred-square-metre kitchen from that being extruded by his lymph glands and sweat glands as a result of the implant's spreading infection. But the disgusting discharge accumulating up his nose signalled the start of the process.

He deliberately didn't wash his hands, conscious of his assignment for that night, as one of the Japanese emperor's faithful soldiers. He tasted every dish with the same spoon, making sure not to leave out a single one.

He kept his distance from his colleagues, avoiding them. He had taken a liking to all of them, despite understanding all too well exactly why, and for what, he had been trained since childhood. He was also aware of the fact that the infection wouldn't pick and choose, thus, his colleagues wouldn't be spared, in fact, none of those who would be eating from the food today, would escape. And so it would spread in ever-expanding, concentric circles.

But his target was Governor Vasily Altyukov. Every Kamikaze had been given a primary target: the men from the Provincial Government, the warlords and the gangsters, who had thrust Asia into its present condition. For that reason, he had to be sure that Altyukov would get his fair share of what was being served up. Once he shook hands with the chef and his assistant in order to thank them for the wonderful meal they had prepared, he would catch the pathogen without fail.

Perhaps the worst of it had been the preceding night, an impasse that he had only managed to overcome with great effort. He was young and strong; he had a good job, extensive connections, and a life that many could only dream of. These were precisely the reasons that made him forget that this life had actually been created for him by his native country, Japan. The Japanese Secret Service had provided his foster parents with the finance needed for his education, that's how he had become a skilled chef, in fact, a Master Chef, who had won prizes in high-ranking competitions in several countries around the world. When the governor's head cook had been looking for an assistant, the Secret Service had arranged for his application to be considered as the winner. The governor's staff loved money, and the head cook was no exception. All of that had been part of the long process, lasting for years, which had to end eventually.

For the past two hours, he had been discouraged several times. He retreated to his office and prayed for a few minutes in front of the altar concealed within the inner part of his locker. Questions reverberated in his head, questions that he should have perhaps been asking himself whilst still in his youth. Why had he been raised for this purpose? What could the State, the emperor, his country, ask of him? Would they want his life, the lives of others, every innocent human's life, in exchange for an intangible and invisible word, such as freedom?

Who would acquit the arbitrarily chosen and voluntarily trained martyrs from the unlawful acts they would perpetrate in the course of this path?

Who would give absolution for it?

He watched his colleagues. They appeared to be moving in slow motion before him, although today's mad tempo was several degrees higher than, and different from, the steady rhythm of the past few days. Their lives had also been put into his hands today, yet they were neither criminals nor warlords, nor gangsters, nor New China emperors . . .

They were merely simple people.

He found it interesting that this inner struggle appeared at its most violent precisely on this day. On the very day he had been preparing for all his life. Suddenly, he didn't know from where, the following sentence scurried into his mind: '*A wise man does not lose his way, a brave man does not fear, even if he loses his way.*' He had never heard this before, at least he had no recollection of ever having heard it. What did it mean? Was it some kind of divine inspiration? Could some spirit possibly be sending him a message by it?

'Chief . . .' it was as if the voice came from otherworldly depths, yet it was one of his pastry chefs, standing only half a metre away from him.

'Yes, Fedia? I'm sorry, I was lost in thought,' he said, self-consciously, trying to shake himself back to reality.

'We don't want to ruin the cream for the largest festive cake; come and taste it and add something to it, if necessary.'

Anatoly was once again the assistant chef, the task brought him back to his former life. He stepped over to the giant mixing bowl, reaching into the mass with his bare hand, as earlier, and tasted it, as so many times before.

'A bit more sugar, starch—otherwise it will fall apart—and vanilla,' he said with a smile and rapped the young apprentice cook on the head.

Shortly thereafter, he was again inundated by a wave of heat and sweat, and his face reflected his inner struggle. The chef had turned into a warrior again. The grip of the *Senninbari* around his waist reminded him which was his real homeland.

*

New China, Ulan Bator, on the day of Emperor Jin Qin's Investiture Ceremony, at 5:38 p.m.

Nujo Yakizima donned his best dark suit. He combed back his hair, fixing it with hairspray. He placed his wife's picture beside the mirror, as if he wanted to show her how smart and stylish he looked. Even the unmistakeable scar on his face was more attractive in this impeccable suit. *Moriko is smiling, too,* thought the professor, looking at his wife, with that same smile she used to give him when she was very proud of him.

Around noon, he sat down at his table to say good-bye to his immediate colleagues. He wrote a message to Chouko, he was sure she would understand this Japanese proverb, and when the time came, she would act in the appropriate manner. Then, half an hour later, he had a sudden inspiration and decided to send the message to the *Kamikazes* via the Unmei Machines.

That very morning, Angelica Stockwell had called him, asking when they would be starting back to work after the festival. He tried to be objective and less vague—although the Fate Machines had already started to control his consciousness—and told her that, after the past few difficult days, it would be better if they took a few days' rest. Angelica acquiesced and said good-bye. Yakizima thanked her for her work, mentioning how wonderful it had been to work with her. Because of her immunity, she would survive the worst period, the outbreak of the infection and the greatest devastation, so he wasn't worried about her. Even though he had grown very fond of her and would have gladly talked to her at greater length, he couldn't say anything else under the circumstances.

He would leave the flat exactly as it was at that moment. Even if they got as far as discovering the headquarters, they would be unlikely to find out by what method the would-be emperor warlord had been forced to his knees. If there were any such humans left at all, who would reach this apartment alive after the cleansing that the Fate Machines would propagate.

He activated the Unmei Island's control console on the desk in his study. The holographic menu opened up with a reduced model of the Fate Machine. On the left, the *Reproductive Process Acceleration* command appeared. By pressing the virtual button, the professor entered a new menu, where he could choose: he could either activate immediately or set a time for the command. He decided to set the command to be fulfilled at 8:00 p.m. local time, to coincide exactly with the start of the emperor's Investiture Ceremony.

The final step was now in place.

He exited the system and picked up his wife's portrait from the desk.

Moriko, my dear wife—he addressed the woman in his mind—*we'll soon be seeing each other.* He kissed the picture and placed it back on the desk.

He stepped over to the communicator and ordered an air-taxi. Half an hour later, he was in front of the Ulan Bator Government Palace, showing his invitation letter to the court servant.

Eternal luck in war, he summoned up the phrase on the *Senninbari* as he stepped under the giant archway, into the immense reception hall. Several hundred guests were waiting their turn, together with him and the Unmei Machines within his body.

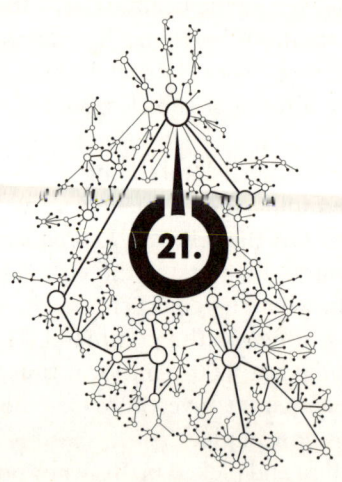

21.

New China, Ulan Bator, on the day of Emperor Jin Qin's investiture ceremony, at 6:45 p.m.

Alex thought he would suffocate; his head filled up with the familiar mass.

'Bianco, buddy, you'll have to stop in a city, in some sort of civilised place. You're going to have to buy some strong liquor so I can knock out these gizmos, otherwise they'll be the death of me . . . damned Futura!'

'Alexei, we'll be in Ulan Bator in another twenty minutes. Look, you can already see the outskirts down below.'

'Sorry, but I can't wait. You'll have to land the car and find the nearest place where they sell something strong, and you'll have to bring me a lot of it!' He ended up trying to shout, but his words culminated as choking coughs. 'I don't want any more discussion, got it? Or you'll be burying me before the finish line . . .'

'Alright, you're the boss. I'll look for a shop.'

'Good man,' said Alex and hunched over in his seat.

Bianco searched for a location on the dashboard panel.

'There's a recharging tower a few minutes to the south . . .'

'That'll be fine,' said Alex and took out a refresher towelette, wiped his face, and coughed into it. 'I hate it; do you understand, I hate it! This trial was the worst decision of my life.'

The big bodyguard began a slow descent. He had to keep his eyes open, as traffic was becoming heavier, with many turning off the north-south expressway to take a break at the recharging tower. This junction created the link to Ulan Bator's eastern ring-road, thus adding city traffic to what was already passing through.

Bianco turned onto one of the branches of the tree-like recharging station and cut the engine. An air cushion maintained the car aloft, while automatic connectors reached towards the car from the station's central column.

'Decline the recharge, we don't need it, otherwise they'll record the car's ID,' said Alex, rousing himself with an effort.

'Alright, hang on in there while I get the booze.'

Bianco stepped out onto the platform and rushed to the central building on the moving walkway. Alex thanked his good fortune that had brought this gorilla-like guy into his life. What's more, he was the only one who was able to remain healthy whilst travelling with him.

Science was a crazy business, a double-edged sword. It could liberate some and cripple others. It was just as treacherous as the weapons that he sold.

Would the Japanese Professor ever reveal what he was aiming for with this trial? Would Alex be able to worm it out of him by squeezing him a little?

Maybe he wasn't all that interested in the answer anymore...

I just want to see Angelica's eyes again.
One more time.

A patrol car glided silently into the charging connection next to him. The Mongolian government's golden winged-horse crest flashed on the side of the car, and on its roof sat the blue-red-yellow light bar. Alex panicked; he thought that they were following Bianco and him because of what had happened at the border crossing. Maybe they should have continued to avoid the populated areas, but he hadn't been able to bear it any longer: he had sensed that the implant was assuming control of his body. He had only taken the risk because it had occurred to him that if he didn't get the antidote, this would be his final crisis.

One of the cops got out of the car. Alex could see from behind the safety of the tinted glass that this was not a common traffic cop: he wore a type of full-body armour shell that could even stop energy-weapons. Alex knew this shield, it was one of the most sought-after items on the arms market. Only the cop's eyes were visible through the narrow peephole of his helmet, the rest of his body was covered with the unbroken body-armour shell. The extraordinary thing about it was that it combined maximum protection with maximum flexibility. He must have been a member of the elite team, probably ordered to be near the Provincial Centre because of the investiture ceremony that would be starting in a few hours. With a thickset, muscular body, his whole bearing radiated strength. *His very presence makes you feel guilty and worried*, thought Alex, trying to make himself smaller. He was absolutely petrified.

No sign of Bianco, and the cop is just standing there.

The patrol car wasn't recharging, so they hadn't stopped for that.

In this case, maybe they had just stopped to have a break.

At that point, the armoured cop began stretching his limbs—which meant that they really had stopped for a rest. *May they burn in hell, for choosing this particular point in time to pass by!* What should he do now? Call Bianco to hurry back? The window on the driver's side was rolled down . . . it would be pretty conspicuous if he were to raise it. It would be even more noticeable if he called the mercenary now.

Shit!

Then the other cop got out, too. He said something to his partner and pointed in Alex's direction. Hopefully, it was only the car he was admiring. The black sports car with silver stripes on the side, the tracing imitating twentieth century sports cars; it wasn't a common phenomenon. The problem was that was precisely what made it identifiable. If the two soldiers from the border patrol had been able to take a good look at him at Yekaterinburg despite the thundercloud, then his description must have been sent out everywhere.

The officer standing closer, who until then had been exercising his limbs, walked in a leisurely manner around the recharging unit. Alex used the moment while he was hidden to turn off all the lights inside the car and to wind up the window. Now he was in complete darkness.

The cop walked around to the front of the car, bent down a little, and looked at the emblem. He admired the silver insignia depicting a racing mustang, which Alex had copied from a museum piece, at the time when he had ordered this particular replica model. The cop spoke laughingly to his partner, pointing to the emblem. In the Mongol Province in New China, replicas must have been rare; everyone was buying the mass-produced models that the big factories were spewing out. The recharging tower was filled with them.

Thank God, it's just the car that they like! Alex thought and started to calm down. That's when the other cop stepped up beside his partner, holding a sizeable scanner. He's going to scan the car! Realisation shot through Alexei.

He slowly reached over to the driver's seat and pulled the steering wheel towards himself from the other side. He was careful not to rub against a switch or an instrument because if a light flickered inside, he would be discovered for sure. Meanwhile, the cop activated the scanner and started to pan slowly from side to side. Alex put his finger on the ignition button, while continuing to murmur to himself 'they won't notice me,' as if he could convince the cops to overlook him. He hoped that through some miracle he would be able to influence the scanner with his brainwaves, and started to send it endearing thoughts: *'Dear little scanner, please go bust, now...'*

Too late. The cop holding the device settled unequivocally on his side, more precisely directly on him. His gloved hand didn't move any further, merely holding the x-ray eye rigidly, and then he nodded.

This is it—the end! Alex would now have to press the ignition button and pull out of there, sweeping aside the two cops and leaving his bodyguard behind, without whom he would probably croak within a few hours anyway.

All this because of that damned Futura and the Japanese professor...

'Nazdrovje!' [Cheers!] could be heard in broken Russian, seemingly coming out of nowhere. It was Bianco. Because the two cops had

blocked out the arrival side of the upwardly arched moving walkway, even Alex hadn't noticed when Bianco arrived behind them, clutching two bottles of Vodka in his hands. Holding them high up in the air, he smiled at the two perplexed cops. He had probably got stuck activating the Mongolian language, or was incapable of pronouncing the words sent to his inner ear by the biochip, so he stayed with Russian, which he'd become accustomed to with Alex.

'Long live the emperor! Today we drink to him!' he continued in a loud voice and embraced the two patrolmen. The cops only reached the shoulders of the large South African and were so dumbfounded that they didn't even offer any resistance. The one with the scanner stopped panning, the other one shoved Bianco's hand away and raised his forefinger in a warning sign. Bianco jumped back a step and held out his hand in surrender.

'Hee hee, no problem! To Emperor Jin Qin and to His Excellency, the governor! Naturally, we'll be drinking to them tonight! But only once we have got home, of course!' said the bodyguard and started to walk around the vehicle. The two armoured officers continued to watch him steadily, but they only went as far as to place their hands on their pistols. Tension was mounting, so it was high time for Bianco to reach the door. Alex opened it for him, and the bodyguard slipped in quickly beside him.

'If they don't move from the front of the car, put it in reverse and shunt out of here as fast as you can,' he whispered to Alex, who had meanwhile pressed the ignition button. The motor started with a quiet buzz, and the rig that had been securing the air cushion until then, retracted back to its place.

The two cops hadn't moved an inch yet. Their thighs were practically grazing the Mustang emblem, as the floater rose gently upwards from the platform, supported by its own antigravitational motor.

'Don't wait any longer, they're staying on purpose now. They want us to shit our pants. Reverse out of here,' said Bianco, looking ready to take over the driving if Alex didn't do what he told him to. But Alexei finally set off backwards.

The cop, who had been holding the scanner earlier, suddenly swung his hand forwards and pointed it straight at Alex several times. As if trying to intimate that he had seen him behind the darkened glass.

'What the hell does he want?' asked Alex, although he had a feeling that this was some kind of power trip.

'Nothing, he just wanted to let you know that he'd seen you and if you screwed up in any way in his country, he would have your guts for garters. That's it,' said Bianco quite objectively. 'Alright, my Russian friend, push the wheel over and take a drag from the bottle, or your implant will finish you off before we reach our target.'

Alex gave it some gas, distancing himself from the recharging tower, then pushed the steering wheel over to the other side. The image from the rear camera confirmed that the two cops hadn't jumped into their car and started pursuing them. It was like Bianco had said: they only wanted to make the point that they didn't want to have any breach of the peace on this particular day.

Bianco took over the wheel and pointed to the instrument panel:

'Ulan Bator, Business district, 2242 East Gate Boulevard, somewhere between the 140th and the 145th floor, Angelica Stockwell is the woman's name, if I read every detail correctly.'

'Yes, oh, yesss,' said Alex and buckled down to the first bottle of Vodka. 'Try to bring me around, once we've arrived.'

*

North American Union, New Cloud York, Counterterrorist Centre on the day of the investiture ceremony of Emperor Jin Qin, at 6:52 p.m. (on the morning of that same day, at 5:52 a.m. Montreal time)

Richard and Eric took their seats on the inner side of the glass wall. Noah was sitting on the other side, looking very nervous, barely able to sit still. Earlier, he had stood up several times, gesticulating vehemently, explaining something to himself. Now, he only stared at the floor, his right foot moving rhythmically; his muscles were as taut as an overstretched guitar string that could break at any moment and dash against the glass separating the quarantine and the interrogation rooms.

'Noah, we'd both appreciate it, especially me, since we've formed a very good friendship over the years, if you would tell us everything now,' Eric started the interrogation. To a certain degree, he was attempting to play on the young man's feelings, straying somewhat from his usual professionalism, but there was also truth in what he was saying.

'You know very well, you of all people. You have been lying to me all along, what happened from the very start!' Noah's anger erupted and he whacked the tabletop. 'You're a cop; you must know who recommended me to your office.'

'That's exactly the problem, that we were also misled, Mr. Simpson,' said Richard, steering the interrogation along slightly more professional lines when he saw that Eric wouldn't be able to control the process. "We were victims too, just as much as you. Whoever the leader of Futura Respondis might be, he has vast experience in concealment and in the area of dissembling information. In this regard, he even surpassed us.'

'A Japanese scientist, I don't know his name, it never interested me. I've always had contact with an Englishwoman, at least she had an English accent, and her name was Angelica Stockwell.'

'OK, and why did you apply with us?' asked Eric. 'Were you aware that they wanted to use you for bioterrorism purposes?'

'What are you talking about, my friend? They simply found me and told me I could be a superman, for free, at no cost! What's this bioterrorism drivel you're giving me? Do you want to stitch me up with that as well, the way you took me for a ride with the Chinese Mafioso . . .'

'Noah, that was my job!'

'Drop it!' Richard motioned to Eric, 'Mr. Simpson. You are the only person who can untangle this convoluted matter for us. If you need more time to think, I would just like to inform you that you have precisely one minute to tell us everything about the motives of the group behind you. Otherwise, in the name of the law against terrorism, I will have you sent to a maximum-security prison. I warn you, I don't even need to request a court order for this, substantiated suspicion will suffice. It will be quite enough that, to all extents and purposes, you're responsible for the death of many thousands of people on Mars as well as on Earth.'

Noah's look at Richard was wide-eyed; he couldn't believe his ears.

'Hang on a second, are you threatening me? What do you think, that I haven't seen a prison or detention centre from the inside? Do you think I'm withholding something?'

'Yes, I do believe that you are, in fact, the key figure in a bioterrorist operation on a global scale, covering the entire Solar System, whose mission was to take the infection to Mars and then here to Earth, more specifically, to India.'

'I haven't been to India, and precisely when that epidemic broke out, I was squatting in the Moon Colony's quarantine section.'

'Indeed, it would appear impossible to have accomplished the operation all by yourself,' nodded Richard. 'However, not if you had a partner. Why don't you make it easier on yourself and your situation and reveal his name. What would you say to a plea bargain?'

'Have you gone mad? What plea bargain are you talking about? I know that there is another fellow who also had a similar chip implanted, but I wouldn't call him my partner, since we never met. They showed me a propaganda film in Rio that he had a part in, and he praised this cursed product to the skies. He was a businessman, rather well-off too. All I wanted was to be equally wealthy, just like him; that's why I accepted this whole thing.'

'So what you're saying is that you didn't know that this organisation was using you and another man to spread a lethal infection?' asked Richard, leaning forward, with an increasingly elevated tone in his voice.

'No, how the hell would I have known that?'

'Didn't you know that within your body, tiny nanomachines were disseminating death, causing tens of thousands, perhaps even a hundred thousand people to perish?!'

'No!'

'And that these machines can be controlled remotely and be switched on and off at any time?!' By then, Richard was so close to the dividing wall that his breath was visible on the glass, as he shouted the words at Noah.

'No! Stop it! I didn't know anything! I was given these rotten pills; I had to take them every other day for the side effects! That's how much I knew!' Noah yelled out and threw the vial against the glass. The wall let sounds through but not the broken parts of the vial. The bean-sized pill inside it rolled about under the desk. 'There's still a dose left for one more day! I'm going to look really horrible if you won't let me have the implant removed before then, after that I'll kick the bucket. And if you let that happen, that would be genuine, premeditated murder!'

Eric couldn't hide his wish for the investigator to stop torturing Noah, it was written all over his face. Richard hit the button on the wall, it turned dark, cut off its transparency, and instantly became soundproof.

'Nonsense, you know as well as I do that this whole thing is a big lie!' said Richard, gesturing violently, whilst pacing nervously up and down, and covering every possible route between the door and the chair. 'We're both clear with the fact that he's only pretending to be innocent! Can you imagine allowing such an implant to be put into you, which—according to Miss Thompson—takes over control of your entire body to such an extent that you have no idea of the small problem of exterminating every living being in the Solar System?'

'Richard, you don't know Noah as well as I do,' argued Eric. 'He's a sensitive and intelligent man, who'd come to us with a harsh past behind him, in order to tear himself out of that environment. He had also done drugs before, for him this was just another drug that would help him achieve a level of performance that no normal human being would be capable of reaching. What he is saying is not fabrication; it's a perfectly credible version. Moreover, there are countless different implants, just look it up on the Net, how many new upgrades and supplementary programmes you can download to the biochip. Plus, this had been registered as an epileptic chip, and that's a perfectly common implant, nobody gives it a second thought anymore . . .'

'In that case, they—however many there still are walking amongst us—were seeking some kind of drug and found it in this implant . . .' Richard was thinking aloud.

'Yes, this might explain why they chose someone for this mission who used to be a serious addict.'

'And what about the other implant user?'

'That one must be a workaholic, that's almost as dangerous as drugs.' Richard sat back into his seat and looked at Eric with folded arms.

'What do they know at the Epidemics Institute?'

'The Department only knows what Miss Thompson told them. These are nano-sized machines that can be switched on and off—they have been switched off and drained out from the infected people for the moment, but they could be restarted anywhere, any time. There are genetically protected people, like Miss Thompson, but there is a cop on Mars and another guy in India, a soldier, and there could be many hundreds, even thousands, more. The thing giving immunity is an unknown genetic mutation that, up to now, wasn't within the scientist's range of vision. And I'm one of them, the results came in not long ago,' said Eric. 'But the Epidemics Institute hasn't made any official report to the Council yet. It's unbelievable, the way they're procrastinating.'

'And what do we know?' asked Richard.

'That Futura Respondis has set up a head office in Ulan Bator and put out TV commercials over this past week in order to popularise their product.'

Enderston reflected, and then turned to face Eric suddenly, with a weird smile on his face.

'And tell me, my friend, where's this Ulan Bator?'

'In Mongolia . . . that is to say, New China, in the Mongolian Governorship . . .' Eric looked at him uncomprehendingly.

'Here, we are running twelve hours behind; in Mongolia, the sun has already set, and in an hour's time one of the greatest events in the era of colonisation will take place on the Asian continent . . .'

'That's it! Why the heck hadn't it occurred to me before! The investiture ceremony of Emperor Jin Qin!' Eric slapped his knee.

'Yes, they're getting ready for something, and with this little invention, this drug-implant, they can spread the infection within New China! And they were already inside, just in time, before the borders were closed . . .'

'If this is true, then this is a brilliant project,' said Eric.

'No. If this is true, then this is the most monstrous project I've ever heard of. We have to inform the president immediately, and he has to contact the United Colony Council,' said Richard and stepped to the door. 'You make the necessary arrangements to have the implant removed from him with the greatest possible care and to get the institute to start examining it immediately,' he said, still pointing at the darkened glass, in Noah's direction, before looking back from the door. 'When they have their hands on that beast, they should pick it to pieces! We've got to know everything possible about it!'

Eric smoothed his hair. He felt terribly weary. He was exhausted from the strenuous work of the past few days, and the worst of it was that, somehow, he felt that the the most difficult part was still to come.

He pushed the button on the wall. Behind the opalescent glass, Noah's expectant face appeared. He was facing Eric, rolling his last pill about on the table.

'I know you hate me and you're disappointed in me, but I can finally put an end to your agonies: I am going to have your implant removed,' said Eric, displaying a half-smile.

Noah looked up but didn't say anything, just gave the pill a last push, which sent it skipping onto the floor.

*

North American Union, Toronto, informal security meeting; 7:13 p.m. on the day of Emperor Jin Qin's investiture ceremony (6:13 a.m. local time)

'I hear you, Investigator Enderston,' said Jeremy G. Hausmann, president of the North American Union. In the darkened room, security experts, Secret Service agents, European heads of state and representatives of the colonies were sitting around the projected map, which was showing the entire realm of New China, covering the whole of Asia. Investigator Richard Enderston had to first call the head of the Secret Service, who then connected him to the room.

'Mr. President, I didn't think I would end up speaking to you in person.'

'No problem, Richard, go ahead and speak, I'm listening.'

'I have a very strong suspicion, in fact I have proof, that certain individuals are making an attempt to spread a deadly infection in New China. This infection is the same one that swept through Mars, as well as India, in the last few weeks.'

The president clasped his fingers in front of him; he had to think about how to respond. The high-ranking assembly sitting around the table already knew all about it, since they had received the reports of what had transpired in the last few hours in the New Cloud York interrogation room.

'Investigator Enderston, I very much appreciate your winding up this matter in such depth and with such levelheadedness. We know that this was just an offshoot of one of your other investigations. It's the mark of a shrewd investigator with a sharp nose.'

'Thank you, I'm honoured by your opinion, Mr. President.'

'In addition, I'm most grateful for all the work you have done, and I'd like you to hand the matter over to your superior, who shall be directing the investigation further.'

At the end of the line, there was a stunned and deafening silence, befitting the situation. After the praise, here came this request to transfer the investigative work, a request he hadn't expected and could not refuse. No one ever said 'no' to the president.

'I understand, Mr. President, I shall act accordingly,' said Enderston impassively.

'Thank you, I congratulate you for all your work up to now and for your promotion as well, in that I hereby appoint you as the Head of the Toronto District Police Station.

Another long, startled silence ensued; this was a turn of events that came as a complete surprise to the investigator.

'Mr. President, you know how to produce surprises. You honour me with the appointment.'

'I'm pleased that you feel this way. I wish you all the best in your new assignment, Chief of Police Enderston,' said the president and hung up.

In the room, all eyes were fixed on the president. Hausmann was looking at the expanding ruby red spot on Asia's map.

'Good, so we have cleared him out of the way. And from here on in, his boss will report directly to me,' he spoke up finally, gazing intently at all those sitting around the table. 'The Epidemics Institute have shut down all further investigations, until the UC Council gives immediate instructions for their continuation. However, the Council will wait until we here come to a decision about it, since Mr. Guys Van Huisen, the president of the Council, is also sitting in our circle.'

'Yes, Mr. President, the big question is, how long can we wait? How long can we allow this military operation to wipe out millions, in order to re-establish the same status quo in Asia as existed before the two Asian conflicts?' said President Van Huisen. 'The aim of the United Colony Council has always been to protect the safety of the colonised Solar System. This safety is compromised if we permit control of the military operation to get out of hand.'

'That's just the problem,' a voice interjected from the opposite side of the table, it belonged to one of the European security experts. 'We don't have control. Are we going to allow Japan, the Independent Russian Republic, and former Mongolia to act out this biological war, instead of us? What happens if this infection, this runaway horse, starts to gallop and can no longer be controlled?'

'Why, what could we do? In the past, we lost every war against the New China oligarchy, what chance would we have if we were to start marching again?' a high-ranking army officer shot back.

'According to the Secret Service reports, those earlier tests that the Japanese initiated in order to stop the infection were perfectly successful,' said the representative of the North American Union's Secret Service.

'We have been continuously overseeing everything and we have done this in such a way that neither Japan nor Russia could possibly have got to know that, in actual fact, we were assisting them in their operations.'

'Could we take over control of the nanomachines, if it became necessary?' asked President Hausmann.

'We could invade Unmei Island at any time. The only question remaining is whether, if we did so, would we activate some kind of security switch, a self-destruct process, which would also torpedo the operation launched to subvert the power of New China's emperor?'

'I don't think we should do it, let's let things play out and intervene only if the infection spreads into the civilian population,' said the representatives of one of the States seized by New China.

'It's a dangerous game, if we only find out at the last minute whether or not we are capable of putting a stop to the epidemic,' said Van Huisen, the UC Council President, again.

'New China is playing a dangerous game with the entire Solar System,' someone voiced in the background. 'The emperor-to-be announced that he would take over control of the Chinese district in the former Mars Colony. The old colony's independent administration doesn't even want to hear about the rising influence of the criminal gangs. Jin Qin's men have also obtained enormous tracts on the Moon and it is only a question of time before they show up on Europa Colony as well. Therefore, despite the fact that the infection reached Mars and claimed innocent lives, I still support the continuation of the operation.'

'Yes, there is no question about the *criminal emperor*—since he's already stuck with the name, I'll use it too—representing a huge security risk for the whole of humanity, but I still feel that this is the Mother Colony's problem,' said a female representative from the Europa Colony.

'Look, it doesn't bother us that you shuffle this responsibility off onto us,' said President Hausmann, 'but believe me, the load on our shoulders is big enough as it is, it doesn't have to be accentuated by the fact that you won't stand beside us. I'd be curious to see what you would do, if you were faced with some insoluble problem, which only the Earth could help you out with: what would you say then? Perhaps one should follow the example of the Mars New Home Colony; despite their losses, they fully support the operation to be used for the benefit of humanity. Isn't that so, Mr. Brademe?' he asked Claude Brademe, the Director of Special Events, from Mars. He nodded in agreement.

'Don't you think the reason for this is because Mars New Home is largely dependent on the North American Union and, therefore, indirectly on you too, Mr. President?' the female representative from Europa Colony asked again, with not insignificant emotion in her voice.

'I reject that!' Brademe thundered angrily. 'The infection resulted in a great number of victims on Mars, but we still continue to carry on. You can't accuse us of being prejudiced!'

'It's precisely because of the memory of the victims that you should say that you don't agree with this madness,' retorted the woman.

'Ladies and gentlemen! Please try to remain calm, this recrimination doesn't lead anywhere. No matter how difficult it is to assume responsibility for something that will ensue in the next two hours, we shall do so just the same, in the interests of the future of the world,' continued the President of the North American Union.

'Consequently, are we effectively supporting the use of biological weapons in an underhand manner, something which had been prohibited more than a hundred years ago on the colonies and throughout the entire Solar System? Or should I call this whole thing by its proper name? Should I say that this is bioterrorism?' asked President Van Huisen.

Total silence fell over the room; everyone understood perfectly what the president of the United Colony Council was saying.

'I don't think we should go as far as to call it that,' said a European expert. 'New China stopped at the Ural line at the end of the Second Asian Conflict but I don't think it could exercise self-restraint for too long. Europe, the Old Continent cannot remain calm, while provincial governors live off crime and a mafioso, who calls himself Emperor, reigns over Asia.

'The voice of Europa is also crucial in this question, precisely because it could be the point of impact in an ensuing conflict,' added President Hausmann. 'President Van Huisen, do you still have any objections on behalf of the Council, or could we prepare our next steps?'

The man being addressed deliberated with his head bowed. Everyone watched him closely to see what they could read on his face when he finally raised his head.

'Alright. We can continue with the preparations, but on one condition: if there is any sign that the infection breaks loose again, we shall intervene,' he said. His eyes reflected disappointment.

'Thank you, Mr. President. Please, Admiral, give the order for the mobilisation of the combined forces and the occupation of the positions laid down in the plans!' The man in uniform nodded and left the room.

'Ladies and Gentlemen, thank you for your support. I'd like to congratulate you for this courageous decision. Today is a grand day: if everything runs smoothly in the hours to come, the ground units of the

United Colonies' Army will encircle and launch an attack against the New China Empire.'

22.

New China, Suzhou Imperial City, on the day of Emperor Jin Qin's investiture ceremony, local time 8:37 p.m.

Nuo had gone to the bathroom twice already. She had terrible abdominal cramps, and she was feeling nauseous. She had been retching a lot in the children's room but there she could still hold it back. She was determined to be able to put up with it, no matter what, for the most extraordinary evening of her life. Whatever happened, she couldn't possibly pass it up.

It really looked as if she had caught the same miserable ailment that Wei had been grappling with yesterday. If that was the case, then she would soon look like Wei had that morning. And then she would be dropped from her duties and they would call in the substitute nanny.

She wanted to hang on at any cost because, according to the latest news, the emperor's children would be present at the investiture ceremony. Only in the background, of course, but accompanied by the nannies. This hadn't been in the plans earlier, since the tutors had been hired to allow the emperor's wives to be with the monarch, undisturbed by the children. But, in the end, the emperor had decided—most likely encouraged by his advisors—that it would look good for him if he had his children at the ceremony. A family-centred emperor always represented hope in the eyes of his people. In Chinese culture, the family always came first. If all was right in the family, then the State was making good progress.

This must be a revolting stomach infection, of the most insidious sort, which wrung and tortured you until you dried up completely. She couldn't go back to the children like this, in fact, she couldn't stand before the cameras either . . . what a misfortune this was for her, she was such an enthusiastic admirer of ancient traditions and she had been as happy as a lark when she had been given this honourable assignment.

What if, by some miracle, she could still tidy herself up? Her hopes were shattered at the sight of her reflected image, though: deeply sunken eyes in dark cavities, patches of skin eruption around her nose, and some sort of greenish mucus on her tongue . . . she felt like crying, but she controlled herself. However, one tear—with a similar emerald green sparkle—ran down her face.

If only I could believe, like Wei . . .

She could pray to some *Kami*, to the spirits of health and strength. But she didn't believe in these spirits and, if truth be told, she used to laugh at her husband, when he retreated into his meditation. Even the Buddhist doctrines she had heard from her great-grandparents didn't affect her. She had never yet reflected on why she was so drawn to the ancient Chinese symbols, why she was so passionate about history, when she rejected its spiritual background. Maybe she wasn't brave enough to cast aside her materialistic being and look into her own soul. Maybe that was why this day, abounding with ceremonial trappings, was so important to her.

She scrubbed her face with a freshening towel, took out lipstick and foundation from her purse, and tried to cover up the dark spots looming in her eye sockets like deep wells, and to magically transform her lips into a healthier colour. Then she set off down the corridor.

The palace conjured up an idealised image of the palatial complex of Beijing's Forbidden City, which had burnt down at the time of the second Asian conflict, but inside it was all modern luxury. The video walls of the connecting corridor leading from the tutors' lodgings to the children's quarters were projecting portraits of the children of great emperors, before the passersby. On her very first day, Nuo had examined these reproductions made from earlier woodcarvings. But now, as she passed by unsteadily, the pictures blurred and merged indistinctly into one another before her eyes, the faces became unrecognisable or leered down at her in the shape of frightening torsos. Nuo became confused at the sight; she flung her hands in front of her eyes, staggering, and leaned her back against the wall. She was on the verge of losing consciousness. Maybe it was time to give up; her momentary reason was shouting it out somewhere from the depths of her mind.

Then the double-winged door at the end of the corridor opened and a servant rushed through it, waving frantically from the distance.

'Nuo, come quickly, the emperor and his wives have just announced that we may participate in the ceremony!'

Nuo tried to regain her balance but had to lean up against the wall once again. Portraits of imperial offspring scrolled down beneath her hands, assailing her, like ghostly apparitions: each like an accusatory glance from the past. She felt as if they were saying, 'you mustn't do it, you can't do this, you'll bring disgrace down upon us!' But she turned away quickly and the hallucinations retreated into the background...

'What's the matter, little girl?' the elderly maid asked and reached under her armpit. 'You look terrible.'

'Nothing, it's just the excitement,' Nuo lied, still delaying her decision to give it up for good. Even though each step she took was like walking through a thick swamp. 'I was so looking forward to this day; my heart is practically jumping out of my chest.' She forced a pallid smile onto her face.

'Come, then, because the emperor is on his way here, and I don't want him to see that you're not with the children,' said the servant and grabbed her arm.

From the corridor, they entered a waiting room from where the imperial reception halls could be seen. Doors were opening and closing in quick succession, with uniformed staff scurrying around, carrying the necessary paraphernalia for the ceremony. As one of the doors opened, a silken fabric flashed into Nuo's eyes, it approached like a yellow blob, with white spots on its sides. *The emperor and his wives*—the realisation hit her, and she became so frightened that only the old servant's arm saved her from collapsing.

It's all over.

'Pull yourself together, girl, otherwise you can't stay in the Court of the Palace! The time is almost here!' the old woman said and put her arm deftly around Nuo.

Nuo just walked forward mechanically, wherever her feet took her, no longer seeing anything clearly. Only light and dark spots and the golden doorknob in front of her, as it slipped out of the palm of her hand covered in slippery, sweaty mucous...

She was able to turn and look back one last time. She saw the crimson dragons dancing amidst the blue embroidery on the yellow silk, as they swam in white clouds ever so swiftly in her direction. Then, the door closed: the maid had pulled it shut behind them...

Any second now and the Imperial Dragon himself would swoop down on her, and, from its beastly muzzle, would howl: *It's the end! You are unfit for the assignment, get out of my realm!*

Nuo took two more steps and fainted. The old maid couldn't hold her up and collapsed onto the floor with her. Behind them, the future emperor reached for the golden handle stained with green mucus...

*

New China, Ulan Bator, Business district, 2242 Eastern Gate Boulevard, 145th floor

Bianco parked the vehicle on the 145th level, the only free parking terrace. A vast number of taxis and air-cars circled around between the buildings; many would have liked to spend the Dragon Festival in the open air, but the drizzling rain falling from the ugly clouds arriving from the north drove them home. Above, up in the mountains, the anti-storm rockets could be heard—their rumbling roars were louder than the thunder itself—but the city-wide abomination wouldn't abate.

Alexei had fainted ten minutes ago. Bianco thought that was truly the end of him because, before falling into darkness, he had choked and made rattling noises in his throat for a long time. But luckily, the fact of falling unconscious had saved him. The bodyguard had reached across to the other seat and turned Alex over onto his side so that he wouldn't suffocate. He checked his pulse to see if he was still alive because anyone could easily have become poisoned from such a huge amount of alcohol. But the Russian was still alive, with the parasites planted inside his body. However, whether his liver or his heart would withstand further shock therapy, wasn't certain, not by a long shot.

He lifted Alex up onto his back and set off towards the staircase. The door wasn't locked, so he managed to get into the long corridor. The apartments opened up from an ever-widening atrium. A flora-filled island floated in the middle, with a holographic sparkling blue sky above it, with a globular object of some sort, presumably symbolising the Sun, emitting light at the same time.

He propped Alex up against the wall sideways, so as to free his airways. The Russian coughed twice; thank heavens, he was still alive.

The position scanner obtained through the Moscow connection couldn't give the exact location of the Englishwoman's apartment, so Bianco was forced to try and find it on his own. He stepped over to one of the doors and pressed the bell. Some fumbling could be heard from inside and then the upper third section of the door became transparent. A short man stood on the other side.

'Huh?' he wasn't very talkative; he just grunted and looked at the Italian inquiringly. Bianco fumbled in his chip's full language repertoire, but he couldn't find a single solitary expression in the Mongolian language, although it could well be that the man wasn't even Mongolian. He finally chose Cantonese.

'I'm looking for an English lady,' he heard the translation in his ear, while the chip sent the necessary phonation information to the speech centre of his brain.

The man made angry gestures that he did not want to be disturbed and the door turned opaque again. He had either chosen the wrong language and the guy loathed the Chinese invaders, as well as foreigners, or the man simply hated everyone in general. Sighing, Bianco stepped over to the next door. He was just about to ring, when the wall display lit up, showing a European woman's face.

'Greetings! I'm not available at the moment, please leave your number or leave a message and I'll call you back,' she said but didn't mention her name. Based on her accent, his biochip denoted England as her possible place of birth.

'Eh, Miss Stockwell, if that's you, please, wherever you are, I beg you, return home. An acquaintance of yours . . .' he glanced to his side to see if Alex had perhaps regained consciousness, but Alex was no longer up against the wall where he had left him!

'Where the hell . . . ?' he said, when he noticed that the door at the end of the corridor was being slammed about by the wind. He rushed to it and had barely stepped out onto the parking terrace, when Alex—probably in a state of unconsciousness—fell over the railings.

'Good Lord, Alex!' he yelled and, in his mind's eye, saw the Russian's body splattered all over a suspension bridge, or skewered on some protrusion. But as he leant over the railing, he couldn't see the man anywhere, yet he must have still been plummeting down into the depths or sliding down on the slanting glass walls. But he was nowhere to be seen. On the side of the building, there was a wide opening glowing with incandescent light; maybe he'd slipped down there.

'*Durak*!' That was the only word in Russian he remembered, because Alex had mentioned it repeatedly and, according to the dictionary, right now was an appropriate time to use it! He looked for the stairway and stormed down two floors. He guessed that was the place where Alex may have plunged into. Reaching the corridor, he found himself on a garage level. The Russian must have fallen into one of the garages.

'Alexei, my friend!' he shouted as he ran in the direction of the garage that he thought could be the one. Suddenly, a door burst open a few metres away.

'Come and help, here's your friend . . .' a blond woman stood before him in a long red gown. Perhaps she had just come back from the festivities, sent packing home by the storm. She didn't look like that other European woman on the videophone.

'. . . who is, by the way, one of our clients,' she added, pointing to Alex, who was lying on the windshield of an air-car, in a semi-unconscious state. 'I'm Angelica Stockwell. I know your friend very well,' she said, extending her hand.

'I know, he spoke a lot about you. My nickname is Bianco, bodyguard, mercenary, and now a medical attendant as well.'

'How long has he been like that?' Angelica pointed to Alex, as they were trying to pull him off the vehicle.

'He started an hour and a half ago.'

'Did you know he shouldn't be drinking?' asked Angelica, while they proceeded to the door of her apartment.

'That I didn't know but what I do know is that something is happening to him that he can only keep under control if he gets drunk.'

'And where are his pills?' asked Angelica, although she knew the answer very well. She, herself, was the one who had stopped shipping the additional pills, by Yakizima's orders. But she still lived in hope.

'He doesn't have them anymore.'

'But if he gets drunk, he'll die,' she said and ran into the bathroom. She brought out towels, trying to clean off the dried, green mucus from Alex's face. 'When he gets drunk, the side effect of the implant is suffocation.'

'Yes, I know. But the way I see it, you don't know much about anything, even though you work at that "damned Futura" and the "Jap Prof," as Alex used to refer to him, is your employer.'

Angelica stopped for a minute and looked at the Italian.

'Why, what should I know about? What I've been suspecting for a long time? That this whole thing isn't what it looks like?'

'Exactly. This man here in front of you is the angel of death. Anyone who got in contact with him, died shortly afterwards. Except for me. Somehow, the thing doesn't affect me.'

'It doesn't affect me either, I suppose. Perhaps that's why they chose me.'

Alex started to cough and vomit into the towel.

'The events of the past weeks prompted me to investigate as well. I tried to pretend that I didn't suspect anything and carry on with the work as if everything were in perfect order,' said Angelica and raised Alex's head. 'We let this man down, like we didn't even known him. This makes me feel awful. But I knew that this lunatic would come back to twist Yakizima's neck. He stressed this most emphatically in his last message on the recorder.'

'There was another one, too,' said Bianco, 'Another guinea pig. Because Alex wasn't ever on Mars, and, as we heard, there was a big screw-up there too. That was exactly at the same time as we were venturing through the jungles of East Africa; so, there is no way that it could have been Alex's doing.'

'Yes, there was,' acknowledged Angelica, 'not just one, but a lot more. And there are many others, who knows how many. This is a surprise for me too, believe me.'

'What's their purpose?'

Angelica looked at the man uncomprehendingly.

'Are you really that naive, or just pretending? You're the one who said it: your friend is a two-legged death dealer, and I'm an employee of the Japanese manufacturing firm of medical implants. Our company had introduced twenty-three implants over the past few days into New China, and today is the emperor's investiture ceremony...'

Bianco wasn't shaken by the news.

'In past years, I made a living off of the two Asian wars but, if what you're saying is really true, I won't be sad if I don't get any work after the fall of the empire.'

'Really? Surely you don't think that this biological weapon is going to stop within the borders, and will manage to do all that and spare the civilian population as well?'

'I don't know, I'm not an expert in these matters. I can't judge how it differs from my pulling the trigger.'

'It is different in that this trigger would then get jammed and you wouldn't be able to release it. It would slaughter everyone who came near you,' said Angelica.

Meanwhile, Alex had begun to regain consciousness. He wasn't coughing that much, his eyes opened to slits, and sometimes his hand started convulsing. Bianco finally held it down.

'I'll kill him...' Alex croaked; his pupils were wide, like some drug addict's.

'He's said it so many times, that at some point he is really going to do it. But then don't stand in his way,' Bianco tried to hold down the energies hyped up by the implant. 'What should we do with him?'

Angelica ran to a cabinet and brought out a small flask.

'This is a plain sedative. It won't stop the implant and its monsters, but it may calm him down until we go over to the Futura office, there's always some antidote there.'

'Alright, I'll carry him. We'll go in your car.'

Bianco put the Russian on his shoulder with such ease that Angelica had no doubt: the only reason this guardian angel didn't have any wings was because they couldn't have lifted up his enormous body.

But as she reversed out of the garage, she saw the tempest already swirling about above them. But the biggest problem on this particular night was the much bigger storm that was brewing.

*

New China, Sakha (Yakut) Province, Yakutsk, Provincial Government Palace.

Assistant chef Anatoly Polovinkin was nowhere to be found. Fedia was the one who had looked into every nook and cranny to find his friend. A few minutes later, Head Cook Borislav Kozerski came thundering in from the banquet hall with the news that there was something wrong with one of the dishes. The guests were complaining of stomach aches and nausea. Governor Altyukov was still hanging on, but he was furious, repeating that this was an assassination attempt, which had been timed to take place on exactly that day, and that heads would be rolling. That phrase, coming from such a man, was to be taken literally.

Fedia found Anatoly's office closed; he pressed his palm on the keypad in vain, repeating the password three times in a row: the door remained closed. Anatoly wasn't there and, if he was, then he had locked himself in from the inside and changed the code.

Now, Fedia would have to talk to the palace security and get them to look into the room, to see whether the motion-sensors registered anything. But he couldn't stand the mercenaries and loathed the idea of talking to them. Instead, he thought of looking through the neighbouring stockroom window to see if there was somebody in the office.

He fought his way through the stockpile of kitchen raw materials and pushed open the window.

The adrenalin rush caused by the sight left him practically breathless. Anatoly was sitting on one of the gargoyles, almost stark naked. The wind was so strong that each gust jostled his friend, who wasn't holding on; he was just sitting there, with palms together in front of him, as if meditating. All this at a height of twenty-five floors, balancing himself on the edge of a buttress.

'Anatoly, have you gone mad?' Fedia tried to shout over the wind. He was so nervous that he was gasping for breath. 'Why are you doing this? Come on in from there, you're going to fall!'

Anatoly's head moved only slightly in the direction of the voice. His eyes gleamed in the moonshine, but his gaze remained dead. Very slowly, he turned his head back in the direction of the city lights, apparently taking no notice of Fedia.

'Lord Almighty, don't do this to me, what's gotten into you? You could meditate in your room; you don't have to sit out there . . .' He actually had no idea what to say to him. But then, a shocking realisation suddenly dawned on him.

'Because of the complaints, right? You're afraid that everybody got sick because of you?' Fedia was glad he had found an apparently logical explanation for this surreal behaviour. 'But it wasn't because of you, believe me! We're a team. If anything was spoiled, we assume joint responsibility!'

Anatoly still didn't move. The evening wind became stronger. It blew from the north, from the pole, signalling that in a few months it would be cold enough to penetrate bones right through to the marrow. The gusts ruffled the man's hair, thrusting his body back and forth, tilting it every time, but somehow it always returned to equilibrium.

'Anatoly, please, don't do it! I take full responsibility for everything but please just come back from out there! I beg you on our friendship, come back in!' Fedia couldn't stand the strain any longer and burst into tears. 'Please! You're my only friend!'

At that point, Anatoly detached his palms and placed them on his knees. He didn't turn towards the window, just yelled the words straight out towards the city.

'If I'm your only friend, then give this message to the emperor: tell him, with all the strength and determination you're capable of, that I'm not his servant anymore!'

'What are you saying, Anatoly, please? Come inside!' cried Fedia.

'Tell him, I'm not his soldier, either!' Anatoly went on, but his words were choked into coughs. The wind flared up, as if it wanted to start a battle against his voice. He slowly reached to his waist and started to untie that white, belt-like thing, which resembled the traditional Mongol thick waist-sash.

'Tell him, I'm not going into his war!' The strips holding the belt were slowly loosening and fluttering in the wind behind him.

'Tell him, there is no *everlasting luck* in any war, that the whole thing is a lie!'

'No, please, don't do anything rash, Anatoly!' shouted Fedia.

'Tell him,' continued Anatoly, holding the white belt, on which countless tiny red spots were visible, even from that distance, high up in the air 'that I won't bring any disgrace on the original owner of this belt!'

The wind was blowing continuously; it was no longer trying to topple the man just with periodic gusts but now rushed at him with all its might.

'Tell him that I love my country...'

'Don't, please don't!' Fedia was virtually saying it to himself, he knew he was totally helpless in this situation.

'... but I'm not Japanese!' Anatoly said and sent the metre-long linen on its way. The fabric twisted this way and that just like the giant tail of some dragon snake. It flew up high, higher than the roof, and could only be seen for a few seconds.

By the time Fedia glanced at the tip of the buttress, Anatoly was no longer there.

He didn't stop sobbing until the palace guards came into the stockroom and led him out of there.

North American Union, Toronto, United Colony Bureau of Investigation Organized Crime and Gang Section

Investigator Richard Enderston was standing there speechless, holding the communicator. After what he had heard on it during the past few moments, he couldn't decide whether to throw the device to the ground or to smash it to smithereens by jumping up and down on it with both feet. But then he decided to put it back into his pocket instead and return to the interrogation room. Eric was still there, but they had taken Noah away in order to remove his implant.

'What did the president say?' asked Eric.

'The president said what you have to say when you stumble onto something huge, the kind of thing that—if, indeed, you have a sixth sense about it—you should have gotten out of a long time ago . . .'

'Did he thank you for your work?' squinted Eric smilingly at Richard.

'Exactly, my friend.'

'And he promoted you, too?'

'Yup,' said Richard mockingly, 'as is written in the big book "how we sweep the dirt under the rug".'

'Then we can watch, with folded arms, how the world falls into its moral grave?' said Eric sadly, shaking his head.

'Noooo . . .' said Richard suddenly and sat down in front of the terminal. He began to tap out something on the keyboard with one finger and then turned to Eric.

'No, Eric. We'll be naysayers and we'll prevent this madness.'

'Really? What's your plan?'

'For what I'm planning, I'll need you too. Because you're also immune to this infection.'

'Good,' nodded Eric slowly.

'You're well qualified to go to Ulan Bator, into the Futura headquarters, and if these nano-monsters can be controlled from there, then you will have to stop them somehow.'

Eric only took a moment to think.

'Right, and how will you manage to get me in there? The borders are closed, and even the fastest air-car won't take me there before the investiture ceremony.'

'You're not going by air-car but by parabolic, one of the Service's covert vehicles. I've just written out the order. They can't enforce the border closure for aircraft arriving from the upper stratosphere.'

'But their air-defence will blow me out of the sky before I reach cruising altitude.'

'Calm down! We've cracked the New Chinese transponder codes; they'll take you for a government plane.'

Eric rubbed his eyes and nodded.

'So I won't be sleeping well tonight, either?'

'If you were to stay here, you wouldn't sleep properly either, because tonight Asia is going to burst into flames, either way.'

Richard was right. Eric picked up his service pistol and proceeded to the plane waiting on the rooftop. Maybe he could still change the seemingly inevitable future.

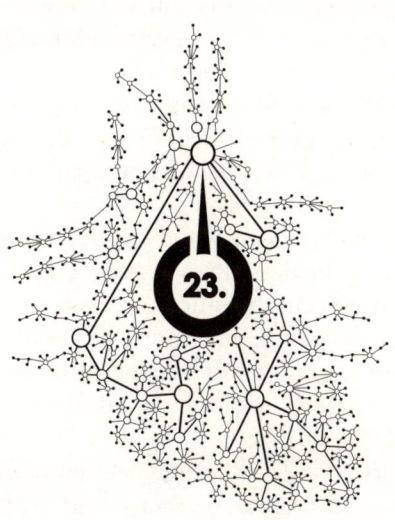

New China, Jiangsu Government-General, Suzhou Imperial City, Forbidden City Imperial Palace, local time 8:38 p.m.

'Your Imperial Majesty!'

Jin Qin's hand stopped in mid-air, hovering directly above the golden handle. He was perhaps a mere few millimetres away from it. His palm was just about to grasp it, to clutch the nanomachines' components enshrouded in mucus. Upon hearing the excited voice, however, he withdrew his hand and turned to his secretary.

'Please, forgive me for disturbing you, but we've just received these reports from the governorships. There is something afoot outside our borders,' he said and, bowing his head, handed over the message board. All of Jin Qin's Empire's Governorships, frontier lines and thickening little dots in the territories beyond the borders, appeared before him.

'The lunatics!' he said angrily and tossed the tablet far away, which skidded along the marble floor against the opposite wall, where it exploded into smithereens. His wives hopped aside with tiny screams. 'They think they can scare me with this, and that this would stop me from proclaiming myself emperor! What superior arrogance?!' He shouted to his secretary, who was still standing there with downcast eyes, having retreated a few metres away from Jin Qin.

'What does the defence minister say?'

'Sir, according to the defence minister, a significant concentration of troops took position in the Indian Ocean, the North Sea, the East-Siberian Sea, the Barents Sea, the Sea of Japan, in Australia, in New Zealand, and in Europe, as well.'

Jin Qin's face turned crimson with rage, he stormed at the door with his shoulder, twisting the door out of its frame, crash-landing onto the floor with a loud noise. On the other side of it, an elderly servant was washing the concrete floor, as the door fell onto her bucket. Terrified out of her wits, the servant fell to her knees and started to sponge up the water that had spilled everywhere, all the while beseeching the emperor's pardon.

'How many wars do they still want?' Jin Qin roared. 'Must I occupy Europe as well, in order to merit respect at last? When will they realise, that I am an unsurpassable force in Asia?'

'*Shi Huangdi*, Your Majesty is unsurpassable, the present situation proves it; nevertheless, perhaps we should postpone the ceremony, in order to prepare for a possible attack . . .'

'Shut up, cowardly worm!' The emperor roared at him. 'You're a useless cringer too, just like the others! The colonies' parade frightens you!'

The secretary would have liked to say something but changed his mind.

'Write this down! Message to all governorships: Everything to proceed according to schedule with the ceremonies. Reinforce the frontier defence units, put the army on alert and standby.'

The secretary noted it all down diligently.

'If they're so insane as to launch an attack, in an hour's time they will do so against New China's officially proclaimed emperor.'

At that moment, the door on the left slid open:

'Your Imperial Majesties! Oh . . . Your Imperial Majesties!' It was one of the nannies, arriving from the children's room. 'Please, come quickly! The twins and the boys! There's something terribly wrong!'

The emperor and his wives ran into the room. Inside, they were greeted by children crying; the three-month-old twins were in their governesses' arms, throwing themselves back and forth, perspiration streaming off them. The wives swiftly took them over and tried to calm them, but the little ones were being plagued by some kind of cramp. The two-year-old boy was lying on the knee of a nanny, choking with coughs, whilst the other boy, nine-month-old Jia, was crawling toward his father.

'We don't know what's happening with them, it started twenty minutes ago, almost at the same time,' said one of the older nannies, 'without anything setting it off. The symptoms are as if they had caught a really bad cold.'

In the meantime, Jia reached Jin Qin's leg, he fiddled with Jin Qin's shoes for a while, then raised his flushed face to his father. He may have been in a better state than the others because he even smiled, his cheeks showing little dimples. He then clutched the golden imperial attire and pulled himself up to a standing position.

'What's going on here?' The emperor looked around uncomprehendingly. 'Is everything turning against me today?' he asked, dazedly, then looked down at his smiling child and with an automatic and natural movement, pulled him up close and hugged him. The boy pressed his sweaty head to the thick collar but didn't touch his father's face.

'Where's Nuo?' his youngest wife asked, she was the one who had chosen Nuo for the job of nanny, and had only just noticed that she hadn't seen her in the room.

'Nuo wasn't feeling well, perhaps she has caught this disease as well, which is already infecting us, too,' said the nanny, coddling one of the twins. The sides of her nose were already red, as if she had a cold, and she was perspiring profusely.

'Find the girl!' the emperor gave the order, and one of the governesses rushed out to comply. Not even half a minute elapsed before she returned with the servant who had been washing the floor.

'Your Imperial Majesty,' said the servant in tears, 'unfortunately Miss Nuo is dead . . .'

Jin Qin felt as if the room was reeling around with him. He became nauseous and started to feel dizzy.

'This is the infection that made us close the borders! That slut brought it into the palace!' he said and held his child at arm's length.

'Take him away from me!' he shouted at one of his wives and wiped his hand on his imperial regalia.

'Everybody stays in the room! Complete lockdown of the entire palace area, nobody is allowed to leave! Secretary!' He bellowed at the frail man, who hastily scurried up to him. 'You'll have to burn these clothes; bring me another outfit for the ceremony!'

'But Your Majesty, this is the Chinese emperors' traditional outfit; it has been for centuries . . . we had it brought over from the museum.'

'I don't care, you idiot!' I don't want to die! Take it off of me here and burn it immediately, together with everybody else's clothes!'

The secretary reluctantly obeyed. He unfastened the waist-belt, peeled the golden garb off Jin Qin in such a way as not to touch the outer parts of the garment, and flung it down onto the floor.

'You, everybody! Give me your clothes, and everything that you've touched!' shouted the emperor. Tears dropped silently from the eyes of his wives as they, together with the nannies, obediently proceeded to strip, and then to remove their children's clothes. The naked, crying gathering drew back, as Jin Qin kicked off his shoes as well.

'Burn the girl's corpse in the back courtyard; no trace of it should be left! Organise a search for her relatives and anyone she could have had contact with in the last few days, execute them on the spot, and then burn their bodies!' he issued his commands. The women were already wailing more loudly, as were their children. 'Toss these things into the fire with them.'

'Secretary, the door!' The little man ran to push the door aside.

'Don't leave us, please don't leave us to die here!' The youngest wife ran towards him, clutching her son.

'Don't you dare!' Jin Qin raised his hand menacingly towards his wife. The woman held her child tightly and recoiled. Collapsing on the ground, she continued to weep as the emperor left the room.

'Conspiracy! Conspiracy!' His roars continued to be heard for a long time.

In the midst of all this, nano-sized death-dispensers were travelling through his lymph glands towards his nervous system.

*

New China, Ulan Bator Governorship, thirty-two minutes before the investiture of Emperor Jin Qin

With eyes like saucers, Nujo Yakizima looked at the beauty stopping by his table. The woman was the most exquisite creature he had ever seen. She stood before him in a long wedding gown, with a veil over her head, which she had folded secretively down at the front. Only her smile vas visible, but that was unmistakable.

'Moriko!' he said excitedly. He stood up and walked around the long table. The guests smiled as they followed him with their gaze. It was good to see this powerful human manifestation of passion towards a loved one.

'Darling, I thought you'd never get here!' said Nujo, and embraced her.

How fragrant she smelled! the professor shivered with rapture. A thousand spring flowers throbbed through his skin, wreathing him in an aura of sweet perfume. And he just laughed, giggling mischievously like a teenager, even though they were preparing for their wedding.

'The *Shinto priest* is already waiting for us . . .' Nujo said. He couldn't get enough of Moriko's smile. This was the best choice he had ever made. The everlasting choice.

The priest stood before them in front of the grand, open shrine. Nujo held his young bride's hand in the most tender way possible.

'I thank you for your offerings,' said the priest and bowed.

'Did you hear that? The *Kami* is thanking us for our sacrifices and our offerings!' Nujo was as enthusiastic as a child. Moriko looked at him with downcast eyes, with that little half-smile in the corner of her mouth that he had seen for the first time when they had met at the weekly market. They lived in the same village and their parents sent them to the neighbouring market; and so they had seen each other every week. For a long time, Nujo had only followed her from afar and then, on one occasion, he had waited for her, sitting on the hillside next to the road . . . *What a graceful gait she had, this adolescent elf!* After that, they had always walked together, always arranging their meeting place beforehand.

And this wonder was about to become his wife! He still had a hard time believing it . . .

'*San-san-kudo*,' said the priest.

'Oh, the *sake* ceremony!' Nujo took the decorated porcelain cup handed to him by the *Shinto* priest. As he looked around, he saw that all the guests were standing around them, waiting to drink to their becoming united in matrimony. According to ancient ritual, he should pass the drink to his wife, and then to the relatives, so that everyone would drink to their future from the same cup.

And so he drank from it and passed it to Moriko. Of course, she hesitated from drinking; she just laughed, as she had so many times before when she was teasing him.

'Listen!' said Moriko suddenly, but it was as if her face had changed: she became terrifyingly monstrous. As if thousands of spirits had invaded her all of a sudden, distorting, disfiguring her face. 'I have never told you that I support you and protect you! I've never been with you in any war and I have never been interested in victory! I'm only interested in destruction! If you contract an alliance with the world of the spirits, then you must accept the consequences!'

'But . . . the belt that you had sewn for me!' Nujo drew back, but he was no longer sure that he was talking to Moriko.

'I said, be quiet! I must finish, before it's too late and you leave this world!' she said, by which time she had become a total stranger, without a single one of her features resembling that of his beloved. The bridal gown turned into a scarlet dress. Her veil floated high behind her, coloured blood-red. 'I want you to finish what you have started but be aware that I'm not what you think I am. I'm not the one to whom the Shinto leads!'

'What are you? An evil spirit? Who are you!?' Nujo shouted, as she kept moving away, ever farther away, as if everything was shrinking and become narrower, as if he were looking through a pipe.

And then, darkness . . .

'I'm your escort, Mr. Yakizima . . .' said the young girl, at the very moment that the professor staggered backwards and sprawled unconscious onto the pavement. The call girl had already found the professor's behaviour strange when they had first met. He often spoke in Japanese but she just laughed at him, because he looked just like one of those eccentric scientists in those comedy films. He called her Moriko, and when he led her before Governor Ulanbataar so that the governor could thank him for his contributions towards the expenses for the ceremonies, he had even taken the drink from Ulanbataar's hand. He drank from it, and then wanted to offer it to her. She, of course, smiled self-consciously and timidly; she had never seen such an entertaining gentleman before, one who could banter so boldly with such a high-ranking official. Thank heavens the governor hadn't taken the matter seriously either, looking astonished at first, but then joining in the laughter.

However, this was no longer either a game or a joke: the elderly gentleman was writhing unconsciously, in convulsions, on the ballroom floor.

'Somebody, help!' The girl screamed, whilst more and more guests started surrounding them. 'A doctor, please, somebody call a doctor!'

'What's the matter, what happened?' the governor asked, looking towards the crowd.

'That funny little man, that scientist who was here standing before you, who even took your drink . . .' said his wife, 'he must have been taken ill.'

'Yes, more than likely, because he looked terrible. His hand was so clammy when he touched me,' said the governor, rubbing his palms together.

'Poor soul!'

'Don't worry,' he put his arms around her shoulder, 'we have excellent doctors, nothing will happen to him.'

By that time, Yakizima's soul was at peace once again. The tormenting demon had disappeared, and Moriko was running along a few metres in front of him, in the rainstorm of falling cherry blossoms. Her merry laughter led him forward, towards the light . . .

*

Japan, the Kokyo (Imperial Palace), twenty-three minutes before Emperor Jin Qin's investiture ceremony

'*Koutaishi-denka* Arai, your father, the emperor, Tennouheika Arai, is expecting you,' said the doctor, when the Imperial Crown Prince arrived at the hospital section adjoining the palace. His father had gone through two surgical interventions in the past few weeks but, unfortunately, even the second operation hadn't produced the desired improvement in the aging emperor's health condition.

The room was white, simple, and unadorned, with recessed opal-coloured border lighting and shades across the window. The bed faced the window so that the emperor could see the little lake in the eastern garden, lit with lanterns. Here and there, moonlight pierced through the cloud-scattered sky, spreading a bluish glimmer onto the sparkling white bed sheets.

When the prince stepped into the room, his father's eyes were closed, had stayed closed despite the hissing of the opening door. The emperor's hands were resting on the covers, lying stiff alongside his body, palms down. He appeared to be already dead. Only the slow rise and fall of his ribcage denoted that he was still alive.

Kazuki sat down on the chair beside the bed.

'Father . . .' Kazuki said softly. He felt that if he spoke a little louder, the fragile body lying before him would splinter into pieces. On the back of the emperor's hands, the meandering purplish veins ran upwards, the thin membrane of his skin stood out like a parchment-yellow patch on the dazzling sheet. The emperor's arms, thin as chopsticks, branched off into bony shoulders. His neck was wrinkled and withered; the skin of his face clung to his cheekbones. His eyes disappeared in their deep sockets, and a white cap covered his head where they'd operated on him. He didn't move, he didn't open his eyes, he didn't speak.

'Father, the world has found out about us,' the prince began, hoping that his father could hear him. 'It is as you predicted. They were watching all along, they knew what we were doing, the whole time, and they let us put our plan into action. In spite of all that, as we had hoped, the *Divine Wind* is sweeping through the New China Empire and is wiping out all those in power.

At that point, one of the emperor's fingers made a tiny movement. Perhaps this was a sign of consciousness, thought Kazuki. He carefully picked up and held the frail hand, shrunk to the bone, and caressed it.

'You have fought well, father . . . you have not been dishonoured, no one can say that you gave way and let down your country. Look, Japan is still free!'

Out there, the clouds had dispersed; the moon was now shining with its full disc, drawing a bluish halo around his father's head.

'And this time, you haven't fought just for Japan, but for the freedom of all Asia. We will show the world what we're capable of. We'll set an example of what self-sacrifice is . . .'

The emperor's hand moved again, his mouth also opened, albeit only to a slit, and his ribcage rose and fell more vigorously and more quickly. Kazuki sensed that his father heard what he was saying and that it excited him.

'I've done what you told me to do, I acted according to your wishes,' Kazuki went on. 'No one can take control of *Unmei* Island. No one can stop fate ahead of time, and no one can escape it; that is why I gave the order for it to be sunk. From now on, the emergency protocol and Plan B will come into effect.

Suddenly, an enormous sigh broke out of the emperor's mouth, and his gaunt body became taut. He held his son's hand with such a powerful grip that Kazuki winced. It was obvious that he was battling with something, perhaps with death, but wanted to say something beforehand. His lips moved, but no sound came. Kazuki sprang up, and held his ear right next to his father's face.

'Unmei . . .' his father groaned finally, at the cost of a great effort. Kazuki reached under his father's neck and raised his head, to help him get some air. Again, his father wheezed a few times, whilst the veins on his neck and his temples stood out.

'Stop . . .' and then his eyes sprung open. There was a deep darkness in them, which seemed to lead to another world, '. . . the red demon!' he said, whereupon his mouth closed and tightened, his eyes stuck open, and his neck strained backwards.

'Quick, come!' Kazuki shouted. Two nurses and a doctor came running in and examined the emperor. Moments later, the doctor stepped back and, bowing his head respectfully, announced that there was nothing more he could do. The three of them let their tears flow without interruption.

Kazuki stood silently for a few minutes at the foot of the bed, then took off his coat, unbuttoned his shirt, and placed them on the arm of the chair. On his bare upper body, only the *thousand-stitch* belt remained, the one that his father had worn in the Asian wars. Slowly, he untied the ribbons and unrolled the one-and-a-half-meter-long belt off his body. He smoothed it out neatly and arranged the stitches on its back. It was stained through with his father's blood, from one of his wartime wounds, leaving a shapeless, amoeba-like patch on the silk fabric.

'Blood to blood . . .' he said and laid the belt on his father's waist. He adjusted the ribbons neatly, smoothed out the blanket as well, then stopped at the edge of the bed and sprang to attention.

'Everlasting luck in war,' he said, and bowed his head.

On his way to the military aircraft waiting in the palace garden, he reflected upon whether he had understood his father's last message correctly. The red demon could be no other than Emperor Jin Qin, preparing for his investiture ceremony in the red dragon patterned attire. Kazuki was, indeed, proceeding on the right track in order to stop him.

*

New China, Mongolian Governorship, Ulan Bator, Professor Yakizima's residence, eleven minutes before Emperor Jin Qin's investiture ceremony

Alex brightened up fairly quickly. Perhaps too quickly, considering the previous events. He couldn't resist smiling, he was so happy. He couldn't take his eyes off Angelica. It would have been hard not to look at her, since his head was resting on her lap. He pretended to still be unconscious and just enjoyed her caressing touch, as she held his head in her hand. What a fantastic feeling it was! Love for her burst into flame within him, like some heavenly force. It was worth more than a thousand implants . . .

He looked at the silk dress clinging to her body, the glittering sparkles on the curves of her breasts, her neck, the tiny grooves in the corners of her lips . . . the way she worried, and the way she bit her lips. Thanks to Bianco's driving style, his head was rolling back and forth on her thighs; he felt her shape and her softness against the nape of his neck. The stimulating scent of her perspiration.

'If I die today, I won't have lived in vain,' he eventually said to her, when she finally looked down at him.

'I knew you were conscious,' she said, smiling, and stroking Alex's hair, 'that's exactly why I didn't let on, so that you would tell me that. But you won't die; I and your great friend are making sure of that.'

'Though now I'm ready for it,' he said. And he felt it, too. The rollercoaster of the last few years seemed to come to a halt at last at the bottom of the loop. 'Are we on the way to the cemetery?'

'Oh, no,' she laughed. 'No, we're going to the professor's place to stop this whole thing that you and I became innocently mixed up in. The Futura office has already been vacated; it seems I was the only one they forgot to tell about our closure . . .'

'Too bad, I would have kicked your professor's ass black and blue.'

'Don't try to be a hero, just relax, that's your task now.'

'I knew you were some kind of saviour . . .' said Alex, and he had a feeling that today, there was no possible evil that could wipe the smile off his face.

The air-car settled on the parking platform with a slight thud. Bianco jumped out, opened the back doors, and helped Alex get out. He was still too weak to walk, so he put his arm around Bianco's shoulder.

'I could be paying you for the rest of my life for this, for what you are doing for me now,' said Alex to the bodyguard.

'Alright, so be it, but we have to hurry because if we can't find an antidote for you, then I won't be able to enjoy that salary lasting several years,' said Bianco, supporting Alex until the door of the apartment.

'He's not at home,' said Angelica, 'but I didn't expect him to be. He left in a great hurry with Yuuna.'

'OK,' said Alex, 'so what's Plan B then?'

'I never make a Plan B,' said Bianco, and turned around in the direction of the terrace. 'Don't move!'

Angelica looked at Alex, puzzled.

'You must know him better, Alexei.'

'Oh, stop this. It's Alex,' he said, extending his hand.

'Pleased to meet you, I'm Angel.'

'I knew that you were an angel . . .' She had marvellous eyes, Alex was mesmerised.

At that point, an enormous vibration shook the building; they could barely maintain their balance. Within a few seconds, the door opened, with Bianco standing there. Dust and smoke rose from the flat, and the roar of the raging storm came from outside. In the background, the nose of Angelica's air-car could be seen, since it was parked halfway into the living room.

'This was my Plan A,' said Bianco, with a broad grin and stepped aside for the other two.

Complete chaos reigned in the living room, the furniture having been displaced by a good metre and a half. But in the corner sat the professor's desk with the activated navigation console lit up on it.

'*Unmei*,' Bianco read the text in Latin characters, 'it means fate in Japanese, doesn't it?'

'Yes, indeed, that's exactly what it means,' said Alex and collapsed onto the edge of the overturned sofa. 'That's what has brought us all here: fate.'

Meanwhile, Angelica searched the drawers, looking for the antidote. She pulled them out, one by one, pouring the contents onto the table. Medication vials rolled and scattered all over the place. She tore off the top of each of them, tossing them away angrily in the same motion.

'What's wrong?' asked Bianco.

'Placebos,' said Angelica furiously, smashing the boxes onto the floor, 'these aren't the right pills. It seems that many were given placebos instead of the antidote.'

'Of course,' said Alex, coughing. 'They had to raise up the angels of death somehow! This was the proper nourishment for them . . .'

'I can't believe that not a single dose was left!'

'But that's the way it is, my Angel . . .' said Alex, reaching his hand toward Angelica. 'It's a beautiful day to die. I want to die in your lap . . .'

'Nobody is going to die!' said Bianco. 'This is some kind of navigation console, and it's possible that it controls those monstrosities they implanted into Alex. How can you log on?'

'By knowing Japanese . . .' said Alex. He appeared to be losing strength again. 'And let's say you know the name of the professor's dog, or his first school, or his first love . . . so, you've got one of the possible passwords!'

Bianco thought that Alex was losing consciousness again and that the frenzied stupor was taking hold of him—it would explain why he was spouting all kinds of rubbish. But when he looked under his feet, he saw a picture frame. Behind the broken glass there was a picture of a woman dressed in a traditional Japanese kimono.

'Who's this?' Bianco asked.

'His wife, give it to me,' said Angelica and snatched the frame from his hand, carefully brushed off the glass fragments, and removed the picture from the frame.

'And do you know her name?'

'No, unfortunately not, I'm trying to find out. Here, it's on the back . . .' she said and turned over the picture. 'Oh, no—darn!'

'Well, what is it now?' asked Alex. 'Click on the menu item that says "password reminder question".'

'It's in *Kanji* writing, with Japanese characters—not even my chip can translate it. Mine is still of the old type, it's not linked to the optic nerve. The keyboard is European, with Latin fonts . . .'

'My chip is even older,' said Bianco.

'Oh, is that the only problem?' laughed Alex and pulled himself into a sitting position, with some difficulty. 'Give me that picture!'

He passed his hand very slowly over the characters.

'Mo-ri-ko . . .' he said, smiling, as he looked at the flabbergasted faces. 'I have the application for visually impaired writing and reading Braille, so I can use my fingers to get the picture included into the language program. Thanks to the old-fashioned ink, the writing is thick enough to stick out enough that I can feel it. Voila!'

Angelica stepped over to the keyboard and typed in the syllables. The password appeared to be successful, the image changed immediately. In the centre of the table, appeared the diagram of some kind of organic structure, beneath which minutes and seconds were rolling down backwards.

'The beast . . .' said Alex, pointing at the image, 'I carried these monsters around inside me, wherever I went. It looks pretty ugly.'

'I'm more concerned by what's underneath,' said Bianco. 'There are only about six minutes left before it reaches zero . . .'

'As I said, it's a beautiful day to die. You didn't believe me.' Alex laughed out loud, sardonically.

'We have to get out of this menu,' said Angelica in desperation and started to skip in-between the Japanese characters. 'We must find out how to stop it. Alex, you must read what's written there—'

'OK, then I'll palpate the hologram in the air, it will probably work,' he said and leaned back again on the sofa. He was already looking rather tormented. 'Let's leave it alone, come here, I want to see you for the last time. And just feel your hand . . .'

'What's written over here, what the hell is written over here?!' Angelica shouted heatedly.

'It says, back to the main menu.' The voice came from the door, a tall man stood in the opening, holding a gun, pointing directly at them.

'Great, somebody with a new translation chip. He came in at just the right time,' said Alex, in an increasingly faltering voice.

'Step back from that console and put your hands up. My name is Eric Kovasevic, I'm an investigator from the UC Bureau of Investigation. You are under arrest, charged with bioterrorism.'

Petrified, Bianco and Angelica stared at the stranger, who stepped over the tangled heap of furniture and started walking in their direction. On the retro-counter, only four minutes remained.

'Great entrance, applause . . .' said Alex and fainted once again.

*

New China, Jiangsu Government-General, Suzhou Imperial City, Imperial Palace of the Forbidden City, four minutes before the beginning of the emperor's investiture ceremony

Jin Qin raged, smashed, and pulverised everything around him for about half an hour. First, he threw the mirror against the wall, and then he continued with the smaller pieces of furniture in his dressing room. With nothing left in the room, he collapsed onto a clean spot on the floor.

The wrecking had started when he realized that he hadn't escaped the infection either. Greenish discharge dribbled from his nose, and his whole body kept breaking out in a sweat. He knew the symptoms only too well. At the time when India had become engulfed with the infection, he had been appropriately informed about everything.

He couldn't believe that he, the indestructible master of Asia, would be laid low by something that was much smaller in size than his body, he refused to accept it.

'Centre, put the courtyard image on the wall!' he instructed the palace's main computer to show the crowd waiting for his investiture. On both sides of the square, illustrious guests, ambassadors of allied countries and provinces, and high-ranking officials were taking their seats. Lighting was provided by two giant sources of illumination, imitating paper airships, and between them flitted crimson robot-dragons to the rhythm of a tune being played by the imperial orchestra. Automatic cameras belonging to various TV stations floated above the square. Background projectors showed the ebony-tree door through which they were expecting him to arrive.

'Can you become an emperor?' he asked himself, kneeling on the floor to look at his perspiring face in a piece of broken mirror. The whites of his eyes were swimming in a greenish film. 'Can you become the immortaliser and the heir to an ancient empire?' His hand started to tremble; his reflection in the mirror became fogged.

'Or just a dying torso!' he shouted and threw the mirror fragment at the wall. A white spark flashed through the image on the video-wall, as the sliver of mirror exploded into a million pieces.

He jumped up from the floor and set off towards the door. His secretary and the two dressing assistants tried to tidy his attire and fasten the long, dishevelled hair growing out of the top of his bald head.

'Leave me be, beat it! If I'm not good enough this way, then it's no other way!' He flung the door open and set off in the direction of the red exit looming at the end of the corridor. On both sides, the soldiers of the palace's guard of honour tried to keep up with him. His ministers, imperial delegates, and military commanders fell in line behind him. They all hurried along behind him, puffing and panting loudly.

'Defence Minister Guo, Army Commander Qiang, where are you?' Jin Qin yelled back, boiling with rage. The two officials quickened their steps to reach his side. 'After the investiture ceremony, open up the silos, the missiles must be armed and made ready, the defence network must be initiated, the assault satellites brought into position . . . we're not going to wait a single minute. The emperor will show that he's indestructible,' he said and stopped before the last door. This, at last, allowed the attendants to pin up his hair and straighten out his scarlet regalia.

'Let's go! For the empire!' he said and with his own hands pushed the giant doors, which opened and gave way to the thundering clamour outside: the rhythmic booming of the drums, the exploding fireworks, and the surging blast of thunderous applause.

Jin Qin gathered new strength, as soon as he saw the celebrating crowd and, encircled by the Palace Guard, moved in the direction of the throne.

The day had come, after all; the moment had arrived.

His day and his moment.

No conspiracy was capable of preventing it anymore . . .

*

New China, Jiangsu Government-General, Suzhou Imperial City, three minutes before the start of the emperor's investiture ceremony

'If you move, I'll shoot him!' said Wei to the policeman. The cop had just noticed that the gun that had disappeared from his holster was already in Wei's hand, pressed up against his partner's neck; he had been taken hostage. Wei, too, was surprised at how easy it had been to get hold of the pistol, but events were rolling relentlessly in that direction. As if *Shinto* had deviated from its path onto this junction. As if thousands and thousands of *spirits* were fighting inside him.

It was already evening when he had woken up at the air-train terminal. He had slept through the entire day, he had no idea how he had gotten there. He didn't even remember saying good-bye to Nuo. He only remembered a familiar-faced woman from somewhere, with short hair, who had embraced him at one point during the trip, like some mysterious escort. But when he woke up, she was nowhere to be seen.

His symptoms may have eased up somewhat, but he was still feeling terrible, he was nauseated and his head was full of this dreadful illness. With this sickness that appeared to burst out of him, to have originated in him . . . it was an inexplicable feeling, nothing compared to this sensation.

He felt like a parasite.

The spirits, however, led him all the way back to the door of his empty apartment. For about an hour, he looked at that peculiar belt-like fabric that he had left on the table earlier. There was an old coin sewn onto it, in the middle, between the cross-shaped stitches. It was a copper coin, tarnished green, with a hole in its centre, where the embroidery thread was looped through. He spent a long time counting the stitches; there were perhaps more than a thousand. Around the count of five hundred, he fainted again.

He woke up with his face on the table, but the stitched belt was no longer there. It took him several minutes to grasp that it wasn't there in front of him. He passed his hand repeatedly over the surface, but all it did was smear the greenish muck around on the tabletop. It had vanished. It was a dream. Just like all of this was a dream. Maybe he had even died, and *Shinto* continued on the other side.

In a state of near-unconsciousness, he descended in the lift to the Japanese hanging garden. Multitudes were jostling on the street, they were celebrating something, and he didn't have a clue what it was.

Concerning Nuo . . .
Nuo, the promise. The promise of happiness.
Where is Nuo?

They had never spent much time apart, the pain of her absence virtually pierced his bones. And that was a disquietingly different pain, more powerful than anything else. He wanted to ring her communicator, but he couldn't even find his own in his pocket.

She's in the palace, suffering . . .

He didn't know where this thought came from, but it seemed to find its way through the misty haze in his mind, onto the surface. Perhaps Nuo prodded his chip with her feelings, to let him know that she wasn't well. Wei wished this to be a dark thought, not the truth. He wanted to go to her, but he didn't think that he could get in there anyway, as they wouldn't take anyone inside those walls without an invitation.

Purple dragons were swimming through the cherry blossom clouds; at each turn, their open mouths would devour another fresh bouquet of petals. The silken pink petals would be converted into a stinking substance in their bodies, leaving their innards with putrid tendrils of gas, which burst into flames and disintegrated. At least that's how Wei saw the mad dance of the robot-dragons and the fireworks in his present condition.

There was a huge throng gathered at the bottom of the garden, where Master Shui had his shop. Could it be that Shui had created another marvel for this occasion, which everyone wanted to have? Wei set off, too, to visit his friend. A lot of people ran in the opposite direction, pushing and knocking against him, yelling for him to turn back, but he didn't.

When he got there, he saw his old friend's body convulsing on the ground, something he also knew very well. Petrified, he just looked at him, recognition and certainty dawning on him very slowly. The certitude that he was the one who had infected the old master.

'I'm telling you, if you move, I'll shoot your partner,' he said it again to the policeman whose pistol he had taken. He didn't know where the idea came from, but he felt that he should move closer to his friend, that was the only way he would succeed. The young cop hadn't been watching those standing behind him, which was how Wei had managed to pull the gun from his holster.

'OK, there's no need for that, calm down. This old man is just sick; he should be taken to the hospital.'

'I don't want you to be here,' said Wei to the uniformed man, but he couldn't distinguish the figures too well from the surroundings. Everything was floating in fog, a green-coloured fog. His tear ducts filled up with green-coloured drops. 'Put your gun and your radio down on the ground and kick them over to me,' he said and took the radio from the other cop's pocket, too. The cop did what he was told.

'And now, go and close down the bridge at the other end of the Japanese garden so that no one can come in here,' he said and pointed to the back of the garden with the gun. 'I represent great danger to everybody.'

The cop ran in the given direction, asked somebody for a communicator, and called for reinforcements, before directing everyone to the other side of the cherry blossom clouds.

'Get back in the corner,' he said to the other young cop, who obeyed with great relief. Wei climbed over to the old man and put his head on his lap. He pulled his shirt out from his trousers, to wipe his old friend's face. That's when he noticed that underneath his shirt he had another layer of clothing.

He saw the familiar red dots, with the countless hundreds, perhaps a thousand, cross-stitches: the white linen that had been laid out on the table was now tied to his waist.

"Everlasting luck in war," is what occurred to him, as he passed his hand over it.

*

New China, Mongolian Governorship, Ulan Bator, Professor Yakizima's residence, two minutes before Emperor Jin Qin's investiture ceremony

'Very well, if you understand the language, then do something,' said Bianco, still with hands raised, sitting at the edge of the sofa. Angelica was sitting next to him, trying to revive the unconscious Alex, without success.

'I would do it, but this is your monster. I've come here to arrest you and order you to stop the nanoviruses,' said Eric, pointing to the console with his gun.

'To do what?' asked Angelica. 'Believe me, I've worked here for a very long time, but I've never been informed about this thing. Until now, as far as I knew, our product was strictly for medical purposes.'

'Right, of course,' said Eric, 'for history's most fiendish purpose. So you can't stop it?'

'I don't even understand the language, never mind handling it . . .'

'You were working for a Japanese company and you didn't understand the language? Do you really think that I'll buy that? You didn't even purchase the language extension for your biochip?'

'We were a Japanese-owned international consortium, at least that's what they told me. Whether you believe it or not, I'd been receiving all the literature in universal English. They wrote anything that didn't concern me in Japanese.'

'Alright, you all stay where you are,' said Eric and set upon working the virtual keyboard. He studied the description for a few seconds and then clicked on one of the points in the menu.

'That's it,' he said, 'it says deactivation of the fate machines. Terminator Command.'

'Click on that, right now!' shouted Bianco. 'We barely have one minute before the counter reaches zero! If only we knew what comes after . . .'

'According to the description, the fate machines switch to full speed!'

'That can't be!' said Angelica and tried to pull Alex back to consciousness.

'Deactivate now!' snarled Bianco at Eric.

'Shut up and stay where you are!' Eric covered him with his pistol and pressed on the menu button. Another window appeared on the centre of the table.

'It's asking for a password!'

'Moriko!' said the ones held at bay, almost in unison.

Eric punched in the password. A long text appeared in a flashing red field.

'Lord Almighty, what's it saying?' asked Angelica.

'That overwriting the primary command is not possible and that sending the primary command will cause Unmei Island to be destroyed.'

Bianco and Angelica looked at Alex, who was still unconscious; in less than a minute, he wouldn't even have a chance to regain consciousness.

Angelica suddenly sprang up and started looking for something among the things on the table, at the most frantic pace, as the moment required.

*

New China, Jiangsu Government-General, Suzhou Imperial City, one-and-a-half minutes before the start of the emperor's investiture ceremony

Major Chouko arrived late. She had been careless. If this hadn't been her last day in service, they would have demoted her without mercy; she might have even been court-martialled. She had to acknowledge that she'd grown tired, and this exhaustion made her irresolute.

She thought that Wei wouldn't move from his apartment until his fate had overcome him. She had sneaked into the kitchen, carefully unbuttoned his shirt, and tied on the thousand-stitch belt. He had earned the right to die honourably, as a soldier. But then, he could miraculously still survive his mission. The belt might help him, since the magical phrase was stitched onto it: *Everlasting luck in war.*

But Wei had been unable to keep still. The apartment was already empty when Chouko returned, and she suspected that the tumult on the street was somehow connected with him. He may have fainted and collapsed out there.

An unarmed policeman tried to coax the crowd back but wouldn't allow anyone onto the bridge, although they all wanted to watch the telecast of the investiture ceremony—about to start at any moment—from underneath the cherry trees. The projector mounted on the airship was already showing the emperor, who was approaching his throne. *Hopefully, you will become emperor with our gifts in your body,* thought Chouko and walked over to the policeman.

'My friend is over there. Please let me in!' she said to the cop, who signalled an unequivocal no.

'I promise that your partner will be freed safely, let me go over there. He wants me, believe me.'

The cop glanced back to his partner, pondered for maybe a second, and nodded. Chouko took to her heels and shot across the garden. The wind in the wake of her feet swirled the petals behind her. A surreal feeling assailed her, as if she were stepping out of the world and were once again in her grandparents' garden. In her childhood, they used to have a lot of picnics under the big cherry tree. It was good to relive this sensation, even at this dire moment.

Wei watched the hazy figure approaching and slowly raised the pistol to aim at its position.

'Tell him to stop!' he said to the cop crouching in the corner.

'Wei!' shouted that someone, slowly taking shape. Whatever that was in front of him, a dream or a spirit, it now assumed the form of a woman. She stopped about ten metres from him. He was still aiming the pistol, but now he wasn't so sure anymore and lowered it a bit.

'I'm Yuuna!' said the apparition. It seemed unthinkable that this should be Yuuna, as she had been in Ulan Bator when he had last seen her. He liked her very much, he always thought of her as his mother, perhaps that was the reason why one of the spirits had taken her shape.

'Replace your hostage with me! I volunteer for the cop!' repeated the spirit, who called herself Yuuna. Wei looked at the cowering uniformed man in the corner, then nodded. *Whether this Kami is telling the truth or not, it's worth it, so I can see her face once more . . .*

'You may go,' Wei said to the cop. The young man got up and set off running in the direction of the distant crowd. Soon the pink cloud swallowed him up, as well.

'I'm coming over!' she said, but didn't wait for his permission and hurried in his direction. She crouched down next to him, took the gun from his hand with an expert movement, and placed it into her belt, then knelt down beside him.

'He died, Yuuna,' said Wei, pointing at his friend lying in his lap. 'I know that I was the one who killed him.'

'No, it wasn't you,' she said softly and laid the old man down onto the pavement. She embraced Wei and stroked his back. 'It wasn't you. It was Jin Qin,' and she pointed to the emperor's image filling up the projector screen.

Astounded, Wei looked at the live image on the airship floating above them.

'How could he have done that? He couldn't have known Shui, he had never met him. No,' he said in a very low, immensely sad voice. 'It's the evil within me that killed him . . .' said Wei and lowered his head.

Chouko's heart clinched and she hugged his head to her chest.

'There's no evil in you, you were always a good soul. An innocent, uncorrupted, wonderful man.'

On the other side of the bridge, an air-car slowed down and hovered gently, almost inaudibly, above the canopy of the trees. One of its doors slid open and the barrel of a gun protruded out of it.

'Is that him?' asked one of the agents.

'Yes. He is the husband of the nanny. He's known as Wei Xu Long. We have to terminate him, so that we can prevent further spread of the infection.'

'Who's that woman?'

'No idea, I have no data on her. Wait a minute . . .' said the man holding the binoculars. 'If my eyesight isn't deceiving me, I can see the handgrip of a pistol sticking out from her belt. She's armed. Get her, too.'

The gun's crosshairs showed the two sitting figures, and the sharpshooter's finger tightened slowly on the trigger . . .

*

New China, Mongolian Governorship, Ulan Bator, Professor Yakizima's residence, at the start of emperor Jin Qin's investiture ceremony.

The counter reached zero and the console disappeared from the table. The lights went off on the keyboard, the entire system ceased to exist. At exactly the same moment, the sofa started to shake as Alex's body thrashed about on it.

'Put that gun down and help!' Bianco shouted at Eric, who obeyed and tried to hold down Alex's body dancing the Saint Vitus Dance.

'He's incredibly strong!' he said, whilst holding down his legs.

'I know, I've seen this in Africa and, believe me, the end of it is the worst!' said Bianco, who was clutching Alex's upper body.

'I can't find it!' said Angelica, through her desperate weeping, having looked at everything on the table. 'There must be a tiny implanting stick somewhere! The professor had his own equipment, it must be here somewhere!' She could hardly see through her tears, she was crying so much. 'I don't want him to die, my God, please!'

'In that pulled-out drawer there's a black velvet case, look in there,' Eric said. Angelica quickly jumped over there, took out the case, and opened it up.

'That's it!' she exclaimed happily. 'Turn him over on his stomach, his head sideways, so he doesn't choke!'

'How safe is this?' asked Eric. He thought of the words of his boss, Richard, when he told him that removing an implant could entail the death of the carrier.

'At the moment, that doesn't really matter,' said Angelica and pushed aside the tiny cover on Alex's neck. 'Within one minute, his entire body will explode . . .'

Eric looked at her, stupefied.

'Hold him down better!' said Angelica and placed the needle-like tube into the implanting slit.

'Do you know what you're doing?' asked Eric.

'No, I don't, I've never done it before. Maybe it's just instinct, but I feel this is what I have to do.'

'Start already!' yelled Bianco, as he could barely keep Alex's body from falling off the sofa. Angelica plunged the needle deeper, until it bumped against something.

New China, Jiangsu Government-General, Suzhou Imperial City, Imperial Palace of the Forbidden City, at the beginning of Emperor Jin Qin's investiture ceremony

Jin Qin's head fell backwards, he was no longer the master of his body. He sensed that whatever had invaded him had taken control.

'Hold me!' he rattled, choking, to his secretary who was standing behind him. The frail and fragile man reluctantly reached to Jin Qin's neck and tried to hold his shaking skull.

'. . . so that New China may again be a great, powerful empire . . .' said the prime minister, who stood before the throne, holding his investiture speech. He fell silent momentarily when he saw the emperor's face becoming distorted. A murmur rippled through the crowd, '. . . so that this great man, Jin Qin *The First*, with his adopted name, Jin Qin *Huangdi*, may carry on the several-thousand-years' legacy . . .'

At that moment, the emperor's upper torso lunged forward. He was no longer able to hold back the growing tension in his body caused by the Unmei Machines. He spat green mucus onto the red carpet. A servant stepped over quickly and wiped off the foul stain. The crowd started murmuring again; panic-like screams could now be heard here and there. The servants, whose bodies were also in the grip of the fate machines, were also producing appalling symptoms. Many of them collapsed, others ran towards the adjoining buildings. The row of celebrating guests broke up, many left their places, heading towards the main gate. But the majority just stared, petrified, at the seemingly unbelievable events.

'Hold me!' Jin Qin groaned to his secretary. 'I shall become emperor . . . and I shall sweep them away!' That was the last phrase to leave his mouth, in a half-dead, zombie-like state.

*

Wei no longer saw what happened because the TV stations wiped the telecast, the projector had turned dark. They didn't want the world to witness the lifeless body of the emperor rolling down the staircase in front of the throne.

Wei's body arched in convulsive spasms. Chouko held his head in her lap, trying to alleviate his suffering with affectionate caresses. Her tears were dropping onto Wei's face.

'In the war...' he struggled to form the words, as a mucus bubble erupted in the corner of his mouth, 'in the war... there's no everlasting luck...' he said to Chouko, with dilated pupils.

'Shhh,' she soothed him, 'please, calm down. Don't think about the war now.'

She held his head in her lap as if she were rocking her baby. But that's what he was, after all, she had known him since he was tiny.

Since the time she donated her eggs to the woman who finally gave birth to Wei.

Chouko had no husband, but after donating her eggs, the instinct of maternal care had awakened in her. She wanted to find her child. When she found out that he was given up for adoption, she had looked for an opportunity to be near him. She accepted a job at the Secret Service and had found him through the wartime project. She joined the Unmei Project, because that was her fate. The path that had been marked out for them.

'This isn't *Shinto*...' said Wei in a faint voice.

'It's alright,' Chouko calmed him softly.

Suddenly, his eyes opened wide and he held onto his mother's arm.

'Stop it...' he moaned, 'stop the scarlet demon...'

At that point, above the canopy of the cherry trees, from out of the pink cloud stirred up by the air-car, two barely perceptible vortexes broke out. The charge of the energy-weapons penetrated the petals, ploughed above the crowd of people mourning the sudden death of their newly acclaimed emperor and, punching through the sides of the robot-dragons floating above the bridge, slammed down into the bodies of the two humans embracing each other.

Chouko leaned forwards, shielding her son Wei's body. On the *Senninbari* around Wei's waist, in the middle of the thousand-stitch belt, exactly by the side of the four-shen coin, tiny blood drops drew new circles in the stitches. It was his mother's blood that tinged the linen.

Wei could no longer see the scarlet demon, the war's loathsome demon. Nuo was running in front of him, in her bridal gown, in the forest of pink petals, calling him towards the distant light. Peace infused his tormented soul and he happily began to run after her.

– Epilogue –
(Prologue for the sequel)

'The coordinated attack was launched at 10:18 p.m. Central Asian time,' said the announcer of the breaking news broadcast. 'The United Colony troops capitalised on the evolving chaos in New China and landed on twenty-seven points of the empire. Special units occupied the Imperial City of Suzhou, including the palace floating above the gulf, whose defence systems had been switched off from the inside by the fugitives.'

'As you could see in our live programme, Emperor Jin Qin was taken ill during the investiture ceremony and died on the spot. He was stricken by the same mysterious disease as the one that had earlier raged on Mars and throughout India. The infection killed eighteen provincial governors and claimed countless victims among the imperial household and the invited guests. The intensity of the infection slackened significantly upon the death of the emperor and the governors and finally subsided altogether, according to tests and investigations. It ended in the same mysterious way as it had started, just as we saw in the case of the other two clusters. The allied troops occupying New China and its territories had received bio-protective clothing and masks for their safety, as you can see on the following images recorded on-site.'

The images showed troops pushing forward in formation, occupying a nuclear rocket base. The masked soldiers advanced inexorably, occupying the more important targets. The New China soldiers and the provinces' mercenaries only put up sporadic resistance, with minor struggles developing at some garrisons. In most of cases, they surrendered immediately; their fear of the infection outweighing anything else.

Alex switched off the channel, he'd had enough of the entire matter. He had been living off war for quite a while; he didn't want to see it any longer. It had controlled his life far too much, insinuating itself into his personality and changing him radically. It had almost extinguished all good in him. Almost . . . but what remained, that tiny seed, had sprouted and was putting up shoots.

'Good morning,' the incarnation of good, his own private angel, greeted him.

'Oh, Angel . . .' was all that he could say, he just enjoyed feeling the power of attraction emanating from her and he let himself drift, ever nearer.

'Oh, Alex,' Angelica playfully repeated it with his intonation.

'Are you happy?'

'If you call this happiness, then, yes, I am,' said Angelica and held his hand. 'I truly couldn't tell, as I've never been happy.'

'Funny . . . neither have I. But that's exactly why it feels so wonderful,' said Alex reflectively, pulling her closer to him.

Angelica was holding a tiny, few millimetre-sized object between her two fingers.

'Don't tell me: "Mr. Implant E4" in person,' smiled Alex, when he finally recognised it. 'After so many beautiful days together, eye to eye . . .'

'That's right, he finally surrendered.'

Alex stroked her hair.

'It was a brave thing you did,' he told her, 'thank you.'

Angelica slowly approached Alex's face, closed her eyes, and kissed him.

The first kiss lingered on for quite a while. Meanwhile, the Russian army transport plane began its final approach towards the Moscow metropolis. The flaming disc of the morning sun emerged over the Ural Mountains, shining into the hospital section of the plane.

It was a new day, the dawn of love for both of them.

**

'You have to forgive yourself and everyone else you're holding a grudge against because of what happened, that's the only way we can start a new life,' said Jess after a long silence.

Noah stood in front of the grave, tears streaming down his face. 'That day was his little girl's birthday; I remember, he had a cake in his hand...'

Jess stepped up behind him and put her arms around his shoulders.

'He seemed to be a cheerful, good-natured guy, but... then he met me.'

Jess stroked his back. 'Don't torture yourself. Put the flowers down and let's go. I can't stand in one place for long with them like this,' she said, running her hand over her belly. Her five-month-old twins fidgeted inside.

Slowly, the three towers of the cemetery receded behind them as the taxi swept towards the inner city of the Mars New Home Colony. Life was bustling again; no trace remained of the crisis that had raged there just a few short months ago. Perhaps just in people's heads. Particularly intensely in Noah's mind.

'We shouldn't have come back,' said Noah, turning to Jess. 'Over here, I'll always just be the Alpha-person to everybody.'

'No, sweetheart. You only feel that way... it's not true.'

'I was selfish, Jess. It was easy to use me, because that's what I wanted, too. I became an instrument for war, partly because of my addictions, but also by my own choice.

Jess clasped his hand tighter and wished that he would eventually find peace somehow, somewhere, at her side.

But until then, she would follow him. She would follow him wherever the pursuit of oblivion led him.

***

Thirty-one minutes after Emperor Jin Qin's investiture ceremony
Saturn's moon system
Enceladus Research Station (territory of the Japanese Empire)

Far from the human colonies, a ship glided along a trajectory parallel to the rings of Saturn. The energy strokes coming from the ship's thrusters—which were currently being used to brake—heated up the tiny dust and ice particles, producing a turbulent fireworks display in the orbital approach vector. On landing, it blew tiny ice slivers high up around the life support capsule, which stood on pillars. Even after the propulsion drive had been shut down, the cloud still wouldn't dissipate. A blindingly bright line materialized on the metallic body of the ship, widening out into a doorway. Four spacesuit-clad figures appeared on the exit ramp and stepped down onto the frozen ground of Enceladus.

One of them walked to the ice-crystal-covered console, wiped it clear, and turned on the switches. The massive airlock door moved, misty air gushed out, hissing from behind it, only to solidify into a frozen cloud on the spot. The crewmembers climbed up the ladder and disappeared inside the capsule.

Ryouta knew that they would come for her; they needed her. She had a mission once again, after so many idle years of unproductive existence. She was skilled in quantum communication and so had already known what was happening when the scientists had stepped into their ship on the space base circling around Saturn, to come and see her.

At the time when she had first met the humans, they hadn't known how to communicate with each other. The humans had fished her out of the ice-covered Ocean of Enceladus and had begun experimenting with her. They had extracted her body parts, injecting them into other living creatures and watched the resulting changes. Ryouta used these protein-based creatures for protection against other Enceladusian aquatic life forms.

Later, when the humans had discovered that she was capable of controlling these tiny creatures, they had built a control-console around Ryouta. They implanted electrodes into her nervous system and disabled her fins. In this manner, using the console, they were able to take the control and overwrite the commands that she gave via her ultrasonic speech organ. She had become an impotent puppet, a living dead.

Subsequently, they had captured a male, Shizuka: that was the name the humans had given him. They took him to another planet and built a console around him. Ryouta got into quantum contact with him several times, until they suspected that she was capable of doing it during the times that the humans left the console turned on. But then they had come and turned it off.

For years, they had left her with just her vegetative functions, together with her remote sensing ability. She had lived through everything that happened to Shizuka on that distant planet. She had felt all of the sufferings that Shizuka had gone through, over long and agonising years, when he had been forced to turn the creatures extracted from his body against other organisms, which he didn't consider as his enemies. Many times, the humans had demanded that he carry out destruction on an even larger scale, or they had ordered him to retract the attackers.

Shortly before the humans had left the base to come to her habitat, Shizuka fell silent. Ryouta had caught the last cry for help, and she knew right away that the humans would come to destroy her as well.

The human male who was the main negotiator in any communication between the two of them stepped over to the console and brought the machine back to life with the same familiar movement he'd used so many times before. Ryouta's nervous path was stimulated by the electrodes attached to her brain. She was astonished because she had expected that the humans were about to finish her off too, as they had done with Shizuka.

But that wasn't what happened, as they really did need her. The parasites that had been taken from Shizuka's body had ended up in the bodies of many living creatures on that distant place and she was supposed to stop that process.

That was more to her liking. The parasites were defence-weapons; they were only employed against the larger beasts of prey that lived in the deeper waters of Enceladus. Never for attack. Through the quantum-channels, she sensed that the creatures on that distant planet were suffering.

She gladly put them out of their misery. She split the parasites in her body up into their constituent parts, thus giving the quantum command to the distant ones to do the same.

She had felt some satisfaction at the time. She felt the same satisfaction flowing in the body of the human standing before her.

Now, she was in the human's hand. She had no idea what he was about to do with her. Perhaps Shizuka's fate would befall her, too.

But the human continued to communicate pleasure and happiness at the cellular level. He turned towards the buttons of the floodgate container. First, he disconnected the sensors and then disengaged the block on the skeletal muscles. It took her quite a while to start using her swimming mechanism again, having lost its ability to function after all the years of forced immobility. The human opened the top of the container and helped her with his own hand. It was good to feel his naked skin, his caressing touch. He could do it quite safely now, since Ryouta wouldn't want to infect him. She no longer regarded him as her enemy.

And then the human opened the bottom of the container, which led to her habitat. Ryouta had never dared hope that she would be able to return to it one day.

The human wasn't bad, after all. Perhaps he had also felt the many evils that Shizuka and Ryouta had felt, when the parasites had landed in other living creatures, and he wouldn't want to have that feeling anymore. He had realised that they couldn't be used for aggression.

Before she finally swam away, Ryouta turned back one last time. The human had just spread something over the transparent top of the container. Ryouta's eyes were sensitive enough to see the design on the material: it was a drawing of her finned body, in jagged outlines, on a bright fabric.

She didn't move, she just focussed on her image. She would have liked to tell the human that she could see, that she understood and was grateful for the message. But the human was already otherwise occupied. Not much later, darkness reigned in the cabin once again.

Ryouta turned towards the deep, preparing to return to her world after a very lengthy imprisonment. She had been used against her will for something evil but, in the end, it was Ryouta who had been able to redeem it all. Shizuka's sacrifice, therefore, hadn't been in vain, either.

Ryouta returned to the tank many times, afterwards. Then, one morning at dawn, an undersea volcanic eruption swept away her place of confinement. After a while, she even forgot the name that she had been given by the humans.

It was from that point on that she became totally free.

The universe of the novel

Most of these short stories are in the Human Colonisation Early and Middle Period of the Solar System.

The author's other novels, Cluster (also published in English) and The Seed (currently undergoing translation) lead you into the same rich, flourishing, and adventurous period of the Human Colonisation, which may be realised someday.

Special thanks:

My first and biggest thanks goes to my family. Thank all of you for the help you gave me in this big project to make a Hungarian SF novel known around the globe. Most of all: thanks for the patience and that you belived in this work.

I also very much appriciate the help of friends, Junko and Corrado. I got so much inspirations from you.

I would like to thank Paul and Margo for the outstanding help they gave me for my first two books in English.

Paige, I appreciate your effort to make the translation better and readable.

Lisa, thank you for your final reading and your comments.

And finally, above all:
I thank God that I was never forgotten, and for his promises that He kept without compromise; this is the reason I'm free.

Endnotes
Non-fiction material used

Lin Yutang - My country and my people, 1935, Benediction Classics; 1st edition (August 12, 2010) - Cluster p.285, ancient names of Chines people

Stephen Paul Thomas's new novel:
The Seed I.
There Are Other Worlds
coming soon in printed and e-book format (2015)
Articity SF

A few years after the events of Cluster, a delegation arrives at the Mars New Home Colony to celebrate the three-hundred-year anniversary of the Martian colonies. Many illustrious guests take part in the event. Among them is the hero of Mars—one of the founding fathers of the Martian colonies—Maximilian Kilbraun, returning to his beloved red planet after many long years of living on Earth. Frederic Bomont, the famous exobiologist, arrives on the same ship. He wants to conduct genetic research to find out why the astronauts of the famous Mission Twelve—like Max, who's celebrating his one hundred fiftieth birthday—can live such long and healthy lives without genetic modification. Julia Tot, the rowdy sculptor, joins his investigation as she embarks on her new ex-terra task; she's creating a sculpture on the main square for the tricentenary. Fred's genetic puzzle soon enlarges to a planet-wide quest when he finds the old video recording of the early private mission, the One Way to Mars. Meanwhile, Max's life becomes a nightmare; a strange madness begins to possess him. Everyone around him is haunted by a horrifying dream—an alien is seeking their lives.

Although The Seed begins with the last pages of Cluster, it is an independent, exciting, and captivating SF novel that keeps you on the edge until the last page . . . and saves some secrets for the next part too.

Watch the teaser by reading the QR code!

Stephen Paul Thomas's new short story collection:
Death in the Stars
in printed and e-book format (2015)
Articity SF

Death is taboo. Death is incomprehensible, inexplicable; and, yet, inevitable.

The most ancient desire of humankind is to conquer death; we humans don't see death as part of life. We want to play God, want to find a new direction in the eternal circle of life—or stop it altogether.

After publishing Cluster ("one of the best science fiction novels published from a Hungarian author" - Köki Terminal Bookshop), in Stephen Paul Thomas's new short story collection, we can look deeply into the problem that the whole of humankind wants to solve: How can we live longer? In eleven short stories, we follow the characters through different paths to prolong their own lives or the lives of others. For some of them, the soul is a separate entity (a thing that can live without the body); for others, this is impossible—they still live and die as before, in sickness and in old age, some in sacrifice for others. In the big race, in the fight for long life, we can see the picture of a big cataclysm; the collective death.

But at its deepest level, this book is not about death. The stories—set in the same Colonial Universe as Cluster—about Life; they are a quest for answers about incurable sickness, about how to replace the body in a world where the soul is immortal. Can humankind alone kill Death? Do we need to prolong life—sometimes even to a pointless, meaningless degree? Why would we do that, why would we want to live longer than the stars? Even they stop shining one day.

Watch the teaser by reading the QR code!